YA Lem
Lem, S u
The waterfall traveler.
Book 1

$24.95
ocn987857606
1st edition.

THE WATERFALL TRAVELER

Book 1

By S.J. Lem

CARPE NOCTEM PUBLISHING

CHICAGO, IL

Copyright © 2017 by **S.J. Lem**

All rights reserved. No part of this publication may be reproduced, distributed or transmitted in any form or by any means, without prior written permission.

Carpe Noctem Publishing
1440 W. Taylor Street
 # 450
Chicago, IL 60607

Publisher's Note: This is a work of fiction. Names, characters, places, and incidents are a product of the author's imagination. Any resemblance to actual people, living or dead, or to businesses, companies, events, institutions, or locales is completely coincidental.

Edited by Aaron S. Kaiserman

Cover illustration by Lindsay Nery

Cover design by Victor Sanchez

The Waterfall Traveler/ S.J. Lem. -- 1st ed.
ISBN 978-0-9986129-0-4

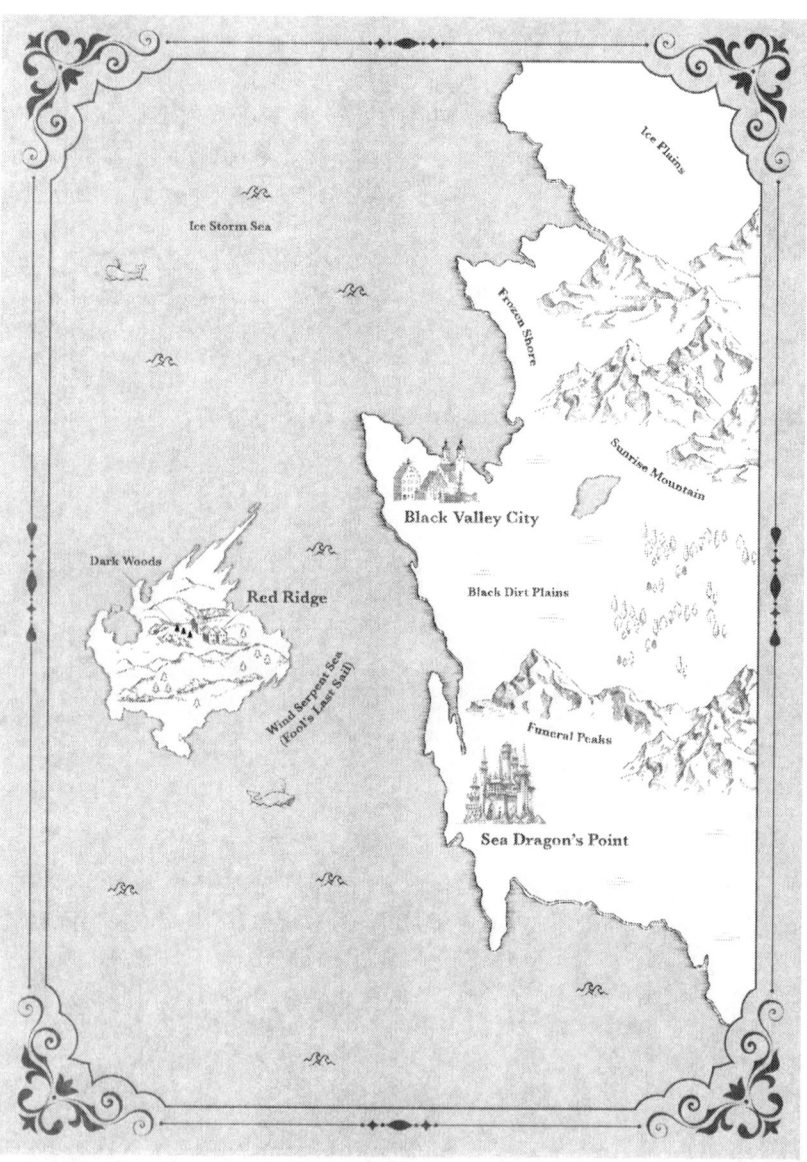

PROLOGUE

The goddess Eisanea knelt on the ground, exhausted from creating the mountains, forests, lakes, and rivers. She wiped the sweat from her forehead and let the moisture splatter to the ground. A fern sprouted from where the droplets fell.

She delicately brushed the leaves with her fingertips. "I am the beginning of all things. Without me, there is no life."

Her brother Death sat beside her and waved his hand over the plant. Its leaves immediately withered and crackled apart, enriching the dark dirt. "And I am the end of all things. But without me, there cannot be rebirth."

Eisanea pouted her lip, sifting through the soil.

Their sister Fate sauntered over to them. She held her hand parallel to the ground, extending a web half glistening and half dull. A spider poked its way through the pad of her fingertip and slid down the gossamer strands. "I am the happiness and misery of all things. Without me, there can only be chaos."

CHAPTER 1

No, no, no! How could I have slept so soundly while Samuel wandered out of our home? I swung my cottage's door open and bolted outside. The morning sun peeked over the mountains and cast soft light onto my cliff-top village. Everyone was still asleep. Samuel's tracks imprinted the dusty ground. They meandered through his garden, past neighboring thatch-roofed homes, and led into the forest.

Dammit! Of all places for him to roam. The forest was full of dangerous things: pumas searching for their next kill, rocks that protruded near neck-breaking slopes, and berries that could lull a man into permanent slumber.

But Samuel didn't know any better. He had the Sickness. Some folks called him a burden. Others prayed for the day he would leave. But I've set those fools straight on more than one occasion.

I dashed onward and followed his footprints, scattering a cluster of chickens along the way. What if he was injured? Or worse? I raced past the perimeter of the village and reached the forest's edge. Spruce trees rose into the sky, spreading their needled branches like raven feathers.

I threw a stone into the woodlands and it bounced off a tree. "Wake up!"

If anyone saw me shouting into the forest, they would have thought I had the Sickness too. I didn't, of course.

"Where are you?" I tossed another rock into the branches. This time, I got their attention.

Seven orbs, roughly the size of my fist, drifted from the treetops, radiating amber light. These orbs visited me—and only me—since childhood. When I was young, they comforted me during storms as Death lit up the sky in search of souls. When I reached the age to hunt, they showed me the best places to set my snares, and I always returned home with plenty. I didn't know what they were, but I named them the Fireflies.

They whooshed into the forest, zigzagging around trees like a ribbon of light, and I chased them down a familiar path. My hair whipped behind me, bound in a brown braid that hung to my waist. As I raced on, the canopy of pine needles sucked me back into the night. Owls, fooled by the darkness, still hooted threats at mice cowering in the brush. Scents of mud and bark wafted through the air. Brambles moist with morning dew slapped and stung my calves.

Before long, patches of light dabbed the forest floor. New grass poked through the black dirt until lush growth overtook the ground. We had reached a clearing. The Fireflies shot upward and disappeared.

I crouched behind a tree and scanned the area. A stream fed by a gentle waterfall carved the clearing in half. I breathed a sigh of relief when Samuel paced into view.

He looked older than his fifty-five years and hobbled with a hunch. Only a few tufts of white hair traced the lower regions of his scalp. He lost his left arm long ago, though he couldn't remember how. His sleeve knotted around the stub at his shoulder. Ricky, a gray mutt, pranced at his feet, intent on tripping him. But Samuel didn't seem to notice. He gestured wildly, mumbling his usual gibberish.

"Samuel," I called. With one last glance around the clearing, I rushed to his side.

He jerked his head in surprise. "Oh my, I didn't see you there, Ri." Smiling, he waved for me to join him.

He spoke in his native language, which I had learned by the age of seven. Our village called it the Crooked Tongue. Though Samuel raised me, we were not related. Fourteen years ago, a vicious beast killed my parents, so Samuel took me as ward when I was four years old. I remembered nothing of the incident or my family, but the beast had left a crescent-shaped scar on my back. I shivered whenever my fingers brushed against it.

"You promised that you wouldn't roam into the forest anymore." I disliked taking such a stern tone with him, but I meant it for his own good.

"Oh." He scratched his chin, disheveling his short beard. "I promised that?"

"It's all right, let's head back."

"Ah, but we don't want to miss this." His grin stretched across his face. "No, we definitely don't want to miss this."

As a youngster, I had listened to his storytelling long after the sun disappeared behind the mountains. His voice rallied with similar enthusiasm this morning, and I couldn't stop myself from asking, "Miss what?"

"I'll tell you, but don't go gabbing about this to anyone. Least not until we have the proof. This is quite extraordinary, and you know how the village is. No vision. Not like you and me."

"I won't go gabbing." I glanced at our surroundings, searching for what he might have seen.

"Well, this clearing hosts something unimaginable, an act of the goddess Eisanea, herself. I know it's Eisanea. There's no other explanation." He raised his arm toward the sky for emphasis. "It's not some figment of Crazy Samuel's imagination this time."

"You're not crazy."

I hated the nicknames the villagers called him. To them, we were outcasts and outsiders. My original village lay somewhere on the island's western lowlands, but I've never attempted to visit it. Samuel's village—which he called a city—was to the east across Wind Serpent Sea. Both were places I only knew through stories. Occasionally, he would recall details about his homeland, though the Sickness robbed him of most of his memories.

"What'd you see?" I asked.

A wrinkle deepened between his eyebrows. "Well, give an old man a minute. Just need to collect my thoughts. You know how they abandon me sometimes." He sat down on a log and stared at a river stone as if it would give him an answer.

I took a seat and rested my head on his shoulder. Our reflections wiggled on the stream's surface. Before Samuel's hair paled and fell out, it was wavy and black and touched the top of his shoulders. I used to admire it, along with his blue eyes. My reflection, lanky and lean, blended in with those of the cattails surrounding us.

"It's all right if you don't remember." I patted his knee.

"Ah, this must be it." His gaze landed on a patch of tall grass dotted with red blossoms. He struggled to his feet and plucked a flower out of the batch. With an ungraceful bow, he presented it to me. "This must be why I've come here, because what can be more spectacular than the first blooms of spring?"

I accepted the gift, twirling the stem between my fingertips. "Samuel," I began, "you can't enter the forest alone anymore. There're dangers."

"I'm not alone. Ricky is with me." His crow's feet fanned as his face widened in a smile.

I gave Ricky to Samuel because I thought he would make a good guard dog. Ricky lacked any qualities resembling bravery, but his antics entertained us. Samuel and I watched him paddle his oversized paws in a mud puddle. He sifted his nose through the water and, with a snort, snatched something up. His teeth clanked against the object.

"What'd he find?" I asked. "Ricky, get your gray butt over here."

His head drooped as he trotted over to me. He spat something hard into my hand before lying down and feigning indifference toward the treasure he sacrificed. I wiped the filth off with the cuff of my sleeve and examined the item.

"Glass," I said, astounded.

On my seventh birthday, Samuel gave me a compass with a glass face. A rare treasure, indeed! It came from his homeland, and no one in our village had ever owned one. The needle pointed west. How it worked, I didn't know. But sometimes, I suspected that Samuel came from a magical place where everyone owned such amazing contraptions. I carried the compass in my pocket, always.

"A glass jar." I showed it to Samuel.

"No," he said. "That's a glass vial."

His eyebrows sprung into round arches. "Yes, of course. I remember now. There's a handsome young man," he said, "and he appears out of nowhere. Bursts right through that waterfall over there." He pointed toward the cascade at the edge of the clearing.

"Samuel," I said, "handsome young men don't burst out of waterfalls."

"Yes, peculiar, isn't it? He has a knapsack. It's empty when he arrives and stuffed full when he departs."

"Is that all you saw?"

"Well, I think so." He smoothed his beard while scanning the clearing. "I wonder where that lad could've wandered off to."

I smiled. Fortunately, his mind only conjured up a harmless hallucination rather than the usual skeletal ghouls that hurl him into fits of panic. My village called his ailment mind sickness for a long time, and later just referred to it as the Sickness.

"Let's head back." I stood and helped Samuel to his feet. "I'll make us breakfast."

Samuel patted his belly before turning toward the waterfall and waving. "Until next time Waterfall Man," he hollered. Ricky added two barks, wagging his tail with enthusiasm.

The noise frightened some birds out of the branches. I glanced around and listened for other creatures. On the opposite side of the clearing, the Fireflies hovered over the brush. Their energy seeped into the space sheltered by my ribcage and tugged, urging me to follow them deeper into the forest. Instead, I hastened toward Samuel and caught his hand mid-wave, ending his farewell to the imaginary Waterfall Man.

The Fireflies had to wait until I led Samuel to safety. I hooked his arm around mine and we ambled home.

***

Overlaid with vines, a log archway served as the entrance to the village. A pair of sparrows greeted us as we slipped through, but not a single villager dawdled nearby. A few paces beyond the entry, an abandoned garment hung over the rim of a wash bucket.

We slipped past a couple homes and reached the courtyard. A dozen people huddled in a circle at its far end. They wore linen and leather that matched the dust underfoot. Someone in the center of the mob was bawling. Samuel paused, staring at the commotion.

"Who's that yelling over there?" He placed his hand over his brow to block the sun.

I tugged him along by the arm. "No one. It's only someone's goat bleating."

Of course, it wasn't a goat. But it was best to keep Samuel away from crowds to protect his feelings from their ridicule.

I nudged him onward. While the other homes nestled side by side, ours sat on its own plot at the westernmost edge of the village. We had a prime view. Our village had earned the name Red Ridge since it sprawled along the top of a red rock cliff, and Samuel and I could see the entire valley from our doorway. The vale was a bowl of evergreens and haze.

I led Samuel inside. He shuffled across the stone floor and eased himself onto a stool next to the hearth. While he caught his breath, I hurried past our bedrooms to a storage closet to fetch something to eat. The harsh winter had drained us of almost everything except for a half-dozen potatoes, a handful of beets, and two bottles of our homemade dandelion wine.

I grabbed a potato for Samuel. After cutting it into wedges and tossing it into a pot of water over the fire, I peeked out the window. The crowd had doubled.

I went to Samuel and braced his shoulders. "Can you watch that potato for me?"

"Of course, sweetie. I won't let that tater flee the kettle." He looked at the pot with unwavering attention, and I ran out the door, securing the outside latch with rope so he couldn't wander off again.

The mob didn't notice when I approached. The howling had quieted to a sob. I stood on my tiptoes to see over all the heads. Kaylan, a tall man of about fifty, knelt next to an old fellow who had a ten-inch gash below his knee. A satchel hung at Kaylan's hip, full of medical supplies. Blood covered his hands.

"You're a darn fool," Kaylan said to the man as he stitched the wound. "You should know better than to travel at night. You're lucky you made it back this morning."

The old fellow stared at him with teary, vacant eyes and nodded.

I sneezed.

A young man turned his head and locked a vindictive gaze on me. "Where's Crazy Samuel?" the oaf asked. He had thin lips and big teeth. With a chuckle, he placed his hand behind his back and started hobbling back and forth, mumbling nonsense. A couple of people in the crowd laughed.

I slapped him across the face.

"At least he's not an ignorant fool," I said.

The man raised his hand to me, but Kaylan broke out of the crowd and intervened. "Boy, the girl is right. I can stitch a gash and bring down a fever, but there's not a damn thing I can do for dumb."

The oaf gave me a look that hinted of future retribution before storming off. No one ever talked back to Kaylan since his skills tending injuries and illnesses were extraordinary.

Kaylan wiped his hands clean with a rag and then regarded the wounded man. "You'll be fine. Keep it bandaged and stay out of the woods."

He patted me on the shoulder and with a clever look in his gray eyes, he whispered, "Next time make a fist and aim for the nose."

Seemed like good advice to me. We walked away from the crowd and toward my home.

"What attacked that man?" I asked.

Kaylan cleared his throat. "He wouldn't say. He kept rambling about nightmares. I suppose the gash matched what a wild dog could do." We reached my door. "Ri, now you listen to me. Soon as the sky hints at dusk, you make sure you're back in this village from now on. Do you understand?"

I nodded and opened the door, following Kaylan inside. Samuel's eyes widened with glee when he realized he had a guest. Kaylan and his twin boys—who were roughly my age—were the only people who ever visited us.

"Would you mind staying with Samuel for a while?" I asked. "We're practically down to our last potato." Without waiting for his reply, I retrieved one of the bottles of dandelion wine and wrestled with the cork. Once removed, I poured the sweet drink into a mug.

"Well, how can I refuse now?" Kaylan grinned and grabbed the mug.

As he took a sip, I whispered in his ear, "Yesterday, Samuel talked about his homeland. Just random details as usual, but there was something different this time. A sort of clarity in his eyes."

Kaylan raised a hand to shush me. "Ri, I know what you're getting at. An illness of the mind can't be cured. We've been through this."

"Nonsense. One day I'll cure him."

He touched my arm and softened his tone. "One day you'll need to accept the truth."

"I better check on that potato." I huffed to the hearth and removed the pot. The people in Samuel's former village probably knew how to cure him. While I placed the potato on a plate and chopped it into wedges, Kaylan took a seat on the stool opposite Samuel. My mouth salivated as the aroma of food reached my nose.

"Ri, I didn't mean to upset you," Kaylan added. "But I would hate to see you get your hopes up."

Hope was all I had.

Samuel exchanged a baffled glance with each of us. I looked at my feet. How rude we were to talk about him as if he weren't even in the room.

Kaylan cleared his throat. "Why don't you go gather more food? I'll stay here."

I sighed, releasing my frustration, and handed Samuel his food. Then, I scooped up a small basket and my fishing pole before dashing outside. I raced through the courtyard, under the archway, and back to the clearing where I found Samuel earlier.

A patch of grass near the streambed invited me over. I cast my line and then secured the end of my fishing pole into the mud. While the hook waited for a nibble, I wandered over to a nearby blueberry bush. A few crushed berries lay scattered on the ground. I grumbled. Some animal had beaten me to the grub.

Regardless, I bent down and sifted through the leaves, rummaging for whatever remained. Not one berry left. I sat back on my heels and stared at the ground. Someone's footprint lay in the mud. Judging by the size, it belonged to a man. Odd horizontal ridges spanned across the footprint's length. Only one shoemaker lived in my village, and the soles he crafted were soft leather that made flat, smooth tracks.

So whom could this track belong to? I touched the unusual print, and moist dirt clung to my fingertips. It was fresh.

A tug on my line jolted me from my investigation.

I pulled in a small trout and tossed it into my basket. When I looked up, the Fireflies flew past my line of sight. They hovered at the opposite side of the clearing, waiting. With pole and basket in hand, I followed them, hoping they had found a blueberry bush that no one had foraged through yet.

The Fireflies wove around the trees, and I chased them down a deer trail until it disappeared into the brush. I trampled brambles underfoot, forcing my way through a forest that now seemed intent on stopping me. Above, the sun buried herself behind a heap of gray clouds. I stopped running and stumbled backward. I had accidentally entered the section of the forest known as the Dark Woods. Here, the nocturnal hunters never slept, for it was always night.

Despite the dangers, the Fireflies dove into the wretched place, pausing to float above a cream-colored object poking through the dirt. It lay roughly twenty steps ahead.

"No, absolutely not." I wagged a finger at them. "This is a bad idea." I stepped away, but they whizzed toward me, circled my waist once, and then returned to the object. They had never done that before.

"What's gotten into you?" I asked.

They swarmed over the object like bees buzzing around a hive. The item they discovered must have been something of value.

"All right, but only for a moment. This is madness."

I stepped forward. No light trickled through the ceiling of tangled branches and cobwebs. Ivory mushrooms clung to trees that twisted their roots into a rug of endless black dirt.

When I approached, the Fireflies zoomed farther into the Dark Woods. As small as they were, they sure were brave, or at least reckless. They led me to the glistening object, half buried in the dirt. I bent down and touched the thing and it coated my fingertip with clear ooze that reeked like a carcass in the summer. Cringing, I dug it free. The gooey film covered the entire object, so removing the filth required a few wipes. After cleaning one side, I identified it: a human jawbone. I hurled the grotesque thing to the ground, and it showed me a grin full of missing teeth.

A crow squawked. The vile birds lined the branches, screeching and cocking their ugly heads, but the Fireflies lured me onward. And they had never led me wrong.

Though my knees trembled, I followed my glowing companions farther into the Dark Woods. I held my breath and grasped the handle of my basket so tight that it cut into my palm. Then, without warning, the Fireflies flitted off like a school of startled minnows. I staggered backward. Something moved, roughly twenty feet ahead. A man.

I leapt to the cover of a nearby tree and pressed my back against its trunk. Bark dug into my shoulder blades, but I stayed still. His footsteps neared. I peeked around the tree.

Only fifteen strides separated me from the stranger. He fussed with a canteen attached to his belt. Sweat stains soiled his shirt, which draped in tatters over the waist of his hole-ridden pants. Two sheathed weapons hung from his belt: a dagger and a sword with an ornate handle. Though I had never seen a sword, Samuel taught me about them. A knot coiled in my stomach.

He brought the canteen to his lips. His bristle-covered throat pulsed with each gulp. He took two more steps in my direction, kicking the jawbone along the way with a whoop. A man who showed such disrespect for the dead was dangerous. I ducked back behind the tree. What was I thinking entering the Dark Woods?

His footsteps continued to approach, snapping twigs. I should have run. Instead I froze, heart pounding. He made his way to my side of the tree, inches from where I stood. He sneered, crinkling his blood-spattered face.

"Well, well," he said, speaking in Samuel's native language. "A little bird flew too far from her nest."

CHAPTER 2

I pressed against the tree, cornered by the stranger. He leaned in close, and the stench of dirt and blood filled my nose. My heart hammered against my ribs.

"Pretty little bird flew into trouble." His chapped lips parted into a sneer that revealed surprisingly straight and healthy teeth for a man dressed like a filthy vagabond.

He looked about thirty-five years old. The bridge of his nose zigzagged, suggesting it had been broken. A scar stretched from the side of his nostril to his jaw, while another sliced through his brow. Sweat dripped from his forehead. He wiped it away, dragging his hand through short-cropped blond hair. I had never met an outsider who spoke the Crooked Tongue. No one, other than Kaylan and myself, chose to learn the language from Samuel.

"Why you out here all alone, girl? You the village fool or something?" He chuckled to himself.

The perimeter of the Dark Woods—safety from this madman—taunted me from over fifty feet away. My leg muscles filled with energy, fueled by the fear coursing through my system. I bolted to the side, but he pivoted and blocked my path.

"Not so fast. Let's see what you brought me." He reached for the trout I caught earlier, but I flinched and dropped the basket. It landed on its side, and the lifeless fish flopped over the brim.

Shaking, I dug into my pocket and rubbed the smooth face of my compass. I had adopted this practice years ago as a method to calm myself. "You need to let me pass," I said in the Crooked Tongue. "My … um … friends will be here shortly."

"Then they're as foolish as you." He glanced at my pocket. His smirk deepened the scar on his cheek. "What're you hiding?" He rammed two fingers into my pocket and pulled out my compass. I cringed from his touch.

"Well, well." He raised my compass toward the sky, tilting it back and forth with amusement. "How'd a simple girl like you get something like this?"

His preoccupation presented an opportunity to flee, but I couldn't leave my most treasured possession behind. It begged for rescue. I swatted at his hand, but he raised the compass out of my reach.

"There's an inscription on the back." He brought the compass to his nose and mouthed a couple of words. Then his jaw hung slack. His pupils zipped left to right, reading the inscription a second time. He looked back at me. "Well, I'll be damned. Where'd you get this?"

The hair on my nape stood. I looked around, scanning the trees for the Fireflies, yearning for their help.

"Girl? I asked you where you got this." His eyes were dark as the midnight sky reflected on a pond.

"Next to that jawbone." With a trembling hand, I pointed to the bone, and it didn't refute my lie.

He lifted an eyebrow and juggled the compass in a single hand. The glass face gleamed each time it caught a hint of light. "It looks too well cared for to have been rotting alongside a body."

"W-Well, I-I …"

"Relax, girl. I don't need your compass to figure out where I need to go." He tossed it back to me, and I fumbled to catch it. I inspected the brass casing and wiped off his grungy fingerprints.

"However," he continued, "I will take that fish off your hands." He went for the basket, but I grabbed it first and swung it behind my back.

"I need this fish," I said.

The stranger cracked his knuckles in a threatening manner.

"But I'll make a deal with you." I squared my shoulders. "I'll give you half if you tell me what the inscription says."

Samuel wasn't able to teach me how to read, though I longed to know the meaning of the inscription. On the day he gave me the compass, he told me that the engraving said:

If a duck doesn't dunk her head in the water, she misses dinner.

That same day, he read it again, reciting a new phrase. Over the years, this practice became habit. He never repeated the same expression twice, which led me to believe that none were true.

"Bold little bird to suggest a deal with me," he said.

Perhaps. But the scribble on the back of my compass was a clue to Samuel's past. And a clue to his past might lead to his cure. I had to take my chances. "You've nothing to lose, do you?"

"All right, I'll play your game." His tone reeked of wicked amusement. "But I'm taking the whole fish."

I brought the basket in front of me, slow, like a mama rabbit nudging her kit out of the burrow for the first time. The man drooled as the fish reappeared. "This meal was meant for someone special to me."

"Samuel?" he asked.

I gaped at him, unable to breathe.

"Looks like I hit it on the nose." He considered me for a moment. "You didn't find the compass next to that jawbone. It means something to you, as does Samuel."

There was no point denying it. He could see through my lies.

"All right," I said meekly. "Whole fish." I showed the back of the compass to him, but he waved his palm.

"I don't need to see it again." A disgusting slurp gurgled in his throat as he turned his head and spat a chunk of phlegm on the ground. "It says:

Samuel:

I salute your loyalty, just advisement, and unwavering commitment.

May Eisanea always shelter you in her light.

- Robert Renselar"

He grimaced when he said the name, Robert Renselar. While I absorbed his words, he swiped the fish out of my basket and dug into its silver flesh. Raw juices, blood, and scales covered his hands. My stomach turned. After devouring a few strips and muttering approval, he sat down on a boulder to finish eating.

"Who's Robert Renselar?" I asked, looking at the cluster of letters that may have represented the mysterious name.

"Said I'd read it, not discuss it." He went on, tearing off meat and shoving it into his mouth before swallowing the previous piece. Fish guts ran down his chin. "You can go now."

I stepped away, testing him. He remained planted on the rock. He seemed to have no interest in harming Samuel or me. Perhaps I could draw more information from him with some friendly conversation.

"My name is Ri."

He snorted.

"After the Riseas flower," I added, defending the name that Samuel chose for me.

"It's a fine enough name, I suppose." He stuck his fingers into his mouth and dug out a fish bone. "My name doesn't sit so well on the tongue. Mallory means ill fated, it does. It scares folks. If I didn't speak my name, no one would. It'd be swept off the world's edge without a soul to remember it. Now what kind of man gives his newborn a name like that?"

I parted my lips to speak, but he cut me off.

"A madman, that's who. But I've never introduced myself with an inferior name even though the goddess Fate has thrown every nightmarish thing you could imagine at me. That wicked hag is no match for Mallory."

I had never heard someone speak against Fate in my entire life. In my village, we believed that Fate weaved an equal amount of happiness and misery into our life-threads—but our experiences were the results of our own choices. "You shouldn't insult Fate. She may add an extra dose of misery into your life-thread."

He laughed. "Let my words travel to her pathetic kingdom in Oblivion. And to Death's kingdom at the Violet Star, and to Eisanea, wherever she lurks amongst us. I don't fear the gods, little girl."

Overhead, a couple of crows squawked as they deserted the branches for the sky. An eerie silence sprawled over the forest. Mallory watched the last bird retreat and then glanced at the trees.

"There's something in these woods," he said without concern and then continued eating. He picked around the gills, scouring for any remaining meat.

Goose bumps prickled on my arms. Though it was late morning, nocturnal things sung in the branches. An unfamiliar sound clicked in the distance. Then, somewhere within the cluster of spruce, a puma snarled.

"We need to run." I staggered toward him.

Mallory flung the decimated fish carcass on the ground and stood, placing his hand on the ornate handle of his sword. The weapon's golden hilt was adorned with red jewels and filigree, contrasting with the rough look of its owner.

"That puma's no threat. It's dealing with its own problems, girl." His grin pressed his eyes nearly shut.

Not more than fifty paces away, the top of a flimsy pine swayed. The unusual clicking sound pulsed rapid and loud. I couldn't see anything through the forest's thick growth. Mallory, on the other hand, seemed pleased by whatever was happening.

He sauntered toward me until I was craning my neck to look up at him. "That puma doesn't stand a chance."

"What would attack a puma?" I asked.

Mallory's grin widened.

The clamor of yelps, snarls, clicks, and snapping branches pierced through the woods. Then in one climactic feline yowl, the racket ceased. The clicking sound dulled to a contented purr. Eisanea made the puma her guardian because it was the strongest beast in the woods. What could defeat it?

"Time for you to go home, girl." Mallory headed in the direction that the fight had taken place.

"Wait." I chased after him. "I need to know who Robert Renselar is. He may be able to help someone very close to me."

He turned toward me. "What makes you think I know who he is?"

"You looked disgusted when you said his name."

He smirked. "You may be perceptive, but you lack good judgment. You'd rather converse with a cursed man in a cursed forest than scurry home to safety."

"There's nothing wrong with my judgment." I pointed at the inscription on my compass. "Who is this man?"

Mallory hooted. "Tell you what. Not only will I tell you who he is, but I'll tell you exactly where you can find him."

"You will?" That seemed easy.

"Sure will." He pulled his dagger out of its sheath and offered it to me.

"I don't understand." I backed away.

"My terms," he said. "Once your curiosity has been quenched and Mr. Renselar is of no more use to you, you take this dagger and you drive it into his heart."

"You're crazy," I said. "I'm not going to murder him."

He returned the dagger to its sheath. "If you're not willing to kill him, then you're not ready to meet him. Go home. You've nothing to offer me."

"That's not true," I said, but he walked off. "If you want Robert Renselar dead so badly, then why don't you kill him yourself?"

"I've got more vicious snakes to toast over the fire first." Without glancing at me, he waved his hand in the air, shooing me off.

I dashed after him. "Please, I need to know how to find this man."

He yanked me close by my collar. "Dammit. Didn't your pop ever teach you not to chitchat with questionable men in evil forests?"

"Please," I said. "I need to know."

The clicking sound grew faint as whatever it belonged to wandered off. Mallory cursed under his breath.

"Now you listen real close," he said. "You tell everyone in your village to barricade their doors and windows and to sleep alongside their weapons. Dark things are coming for them."

I squirmed out of his grip as a cool breeze slithered through the Dark Woods. It brought with it the sound of chanting. The words, indecipherable, came in short, sharp whispers, like dozens of snakes hissing at once.

"Now you got their attention," he said.

"Whose attention?" I looked around, but saw no one.

"Go home." He grabbed my compass and hurled it out of the Dark Woods. It landed in a patch of brambles.

"That was uncalled for," I snapped.

The chanting thickened as more voices joined in. Things moved in the brush. I went rigid with dread. As much as I wanted answers, it was time to flee. With basket and fishing pole in hand, I raced to where my compass had landed. Trembling, I rummaged through the prickly brambles until I found it next to a rock sprinkled with shattered glass. I covered my mouth, holding back a cry.

"You broke it!" I shouted at Mallory, but he ignored me and trekked farther into the Dark Woods. How could he do such a terrible thing and then saunter off without an apology? My ears burned hot, but there was no time to have words with him. The eerie melody closed in.

A ripple of cool air whizzed past my nose, followed by a thud. An arrowhead-sized thing pierced a nearby tree. I tensed. Another whooshed through the air and grazed my chin with a scorching sting. Wincing, I shoved my compass into my pocket, grabbed my pole, and left my basket behind.

I cut through the forest, heaving with panicked breath. The chanting faded in the distance. Halfway back to the clearing, my legs grew unusually heavy. The scrape on my chin throbbed. I fell to my knees, but got back up, pushing forward. The forest spun around me. My energy slipped away. The surrounding trees blurred into streaks of brown and gray. Something was wrong with me. I needed to get home. Fast.

By the time I reached the stream near the waterfall, my run had morphed into a drunken stagger. One more step. Just one more step. I crashed onto a mat of spongy moss and remained there, too exhausted to rise. Flowers dabbed the riverbed. Their orange petals reminded me of the vibrant sunset that blazed the sky on my seventh birthday.

Samuel had presented me with a small box, and my eager child hands tore it open. The most glorious gift glistened inside.

"That's called a compass," Samuel had explained. "It belonged to me for a long time and now it's yours. As long as you carry it, you'll always find what you're looking for."

"Did you find what you were looking for?" I asked.

"Well, I found you, didn't I?" Chuckling, he tickled my side and I giggled. I flipped the compass over and noticed the engraving.

"That's a secret message," he said. "I'll tell you what it says."

I closed my eyes.

***

I awoke to the sound of approaching footsteps. A young man roughly my age was hurrying toward me from the opposite side of the stream. I grabbed the closest thing next to me for defense—my fishing pole—and leapt to my feet.

"Don't cross this stream." I aimed the pole at him.

He stopped at the stream's edge and raised his hands in surrender. My heart was racing from a nightmare that I couldn't remember. I scanned the tree line, searching. Crickets chirped, worshipping the oncoming dusk. What had happened? I knew better than to fall asleep in the forest.

"I didn't mean to startle you," the newcomer said in the Crooked Tongue. I had never met an outsider who could speak Samuel's language. No, there was someone once, but I couldn't recall his name. Slumber left my mind foggy. Even my limbs failed to work properly. I wobbled, struggling to hold my fishing pole straight. A cold sweat lingered on my brow.

"Such drastic measures aren't necessary." The corner of his mouth curved upward as he looked at my flimsy, makeshift weapon. He wore a slate cloak, and forest debris clung to his disheveled black hair. Dirt smudged his hands. "Can I talk you into lowering your ... um ... weapon so I can help you?"

"Help me?" I squinted at him, blinking blurriness from my eyes.

He touched his chin and I in turn did the same. Dry blood flaked onto my fingertips, but more alarmingly, the entire area from my chin to my neck was numb. I repeatedly pressed my fingers against my throat.

"In my village, I'm a healer." He contemplated the combined barrier of pole and stream for a moment and stepped closer.

Two other villages neighbored mine, and their healers were old men. How could he—young and attractive—be a healer? Silly as it was, I thrust my pole at him. I needed a moment to think. "Stay put."

He brushed my fishing pole to the side, and his brows knitted together as if he was trying to solve a puzzle. "All right, I can see you're disoriented. What if I keep my hands up and cross the stream slowly? I mean you no harm, Miss. I'm here to help."

It took four steps to cross the stream. Each time his foot sank into the water, I missed an opportunity to do something—but do what, I didn't know. He steadied his gaze on me. At the halfway point, he gave me a charming grin and I faltered. That was it. He stood on dry ground, close enough that I could count the light freckles sprinkled on his nose.

"This is better, don't you think? My name's Bryce." His eyes glinted with flecks of gold. A strap stretched across his shoulder, burdened by the weight of a heavy knapsack. He lowered his head to meet my eyes. "And your name is?"

"Ri." I clenched the fishing pole, still measuring him up.

"All right, Ri. I'm going to take a look at your cut." He waited for my nod before he placed his fingers on my chin and tilted my head up. Though my injury left me numb, his touch sent a shiver through me.

"Where did you come from?" I asked.

He smiled. "You wouldn't believe me if I told you." He brushed his hair off his forehead and shot me a worried look. "How'd this happen? It's festering with puss."

"I can't remember. An insect. I think."

"I don't think an insect did this." He swung the knapsack off his back and opened its flap. Leafy herbs and root vegetables stuffed the inside. He pulled out a wooden box and unclasped it. Metal tools, dainty like Kaylan might use to stitch a gash or pull a bad tooth, lay on one side of the box. A row of glass vials lined the opposite half.

Knapsack. Vials. Samuel and I had a discussion earlier about those things, but I couldn't recall the details.

"A bit of clove oil will ward off inflammation." He removed the cork from a vial glistening with pale liquid. He dabbed some on a cloth and patted my chin with it. With parted lips, he breathed slowly, concentrating on my wound. He smelled like the forest.

My cheeks warmed. "Thank you. Sorry, I acted so spooked. I was having this dream."

He finished and put the cloth away. "No need to thank me, Ri. I'm glad to help." Kneeling on the ground, he packed the wooden box into his knapsack and then looked at my fishing pole. "You didn't catch anything today?"

"No, I did." The fine fish I caught would delight Samuel. I glanced at the patch of moss where I had slept. "What'd I do with my basket?"

An image of a man hit the front of my mind. He spoke the Crooked Tongue. The entrails of a silver-colored fish dripped down his lips. My heart thumped as memories of Mallory pieced together. Bryce slung the knapsack over his shoulder. Finding one man who spoke Samuel's language was unusual enough, let alone two. They must have come together. I swatted Bryce in the arm with my pole, and he jerked in surprise.

"Your friend broke my compass," I said.

"What are you talking about?" He raised his hand to block another assault from my pole. "I'm here alone."

I swiveled around, searching. Another memory surfaced in my mind—horrid voices that whispered like storm winds through field grass. I touched the cut on my chin as I recalled Mallory's warning of the dark things to come.

"We need to get somewhere safe," I said. "My village isn't far."

"You attack me and now you want to take me home? You're a very irrational girl."

"You may be friends with a rude man, but there're spirits—or something—out here." I grabbed his hand. "I can't leave you."

He made a confused sound as I tugged him along.

A whistle shrieked through the air. Something struck my shoulder. I tried to brush it away, but I smacked my neck instead. My legs buckled. I fell onto my back. The puncture in my shoulder pulsed, pumping fire into my body. The inferno flickered across my skin. I couldn't move. My breath came fast and shallow.

Bryce quickly crouched next to me. He pulled the insect—or whatever it was—out of my shoulder. Stars speckled my vision. The object he held resembled a large, black thorn.

Another sailed past and buried its tip into the dirt. Bryce ducked, protecting my body with his. He whispered, "Something's attacking us."

"I can't run." My words sounded like whimpering nonsense. The chanting returned. Bryce glanced in all directions with wide eyes. He seemed clueless regarding the identity of our assailants. Perhaps he hadn't arrived with Mallory. That blood-spattered man clearly encountered these things before.

Bryce lifted me and raced toward the waterfall. My body, cradled in his grasp, trembled. Numbness spread up my arm and over my chest. I was going to die, and Samuel would be left alone with no one to care for him.

"You're going the wrong way." Once again, my words slurred together. How would he ever understand me? "We need to get to my village healer." My eyelids fluttered, growing heavy.

"Ri, keep talking," he pleaded. "Don't fall asleep. Stay with me." His feet splashed into the stream. The Fireflies appeared and sped after us.

Another bite nipped my thigh like a spark from a fire. Bryce yanked it out. My panicked gasps slowed. Water droplets gathered on my cheeks, extinguishing the heat crawling over my skin. Bryce tucked my head close to his chest as we plunged into the waterfall and entered a cave.

"No," I mumbled, straining to look behind us. The Fireflies remained on the opposite side of the cascade. Unable to follow, they bounced against the water like fish poking their noses against a net.

The light died away until everything went black.

CHAPTER 3

The sun drenched the late afternoon sky in hues of gold and red. Beyond the perimeter of my village, a maple tree snaked her roots down a bank and into a pond. I seated myself on a grassy patch under the mottled shade of the tree and dipped my feet into the water. A refreshing chill scurried up my calves and spread through my body. I closed my eyes and burrowed my toes into the pond floor until mounds of sand rose up to my ankles. Ah, peace.

A twig snapped a few feet away. I flinched, shaken from my tranquil state.

I opened one eye, squinting from the sunlight. A slender woman draped in a white linen dress stood at the opposite side of the pond. She had a young, sculpted face with high eyebrows and cheekbones. I jerked my head in surprise, for I'd never seen anyone so graceful. With an elegant hand, she brushed an auburn curl off her shoulder and scooped some water into her palm.

"Water is Eisanea's gift." Her voice was serene as a babbling brook.

"Who are you?" I gaped at her.

She tipped her hand and contemplated the water drizzling out of her palm as if it was a stream of precious beads. "I am the mother."

"Whose mother?" I scanned the area for a wandering child.

"Ri? Can you hear me?" asked a male voice.

"Who's there?" Startled, I looked around, but saw no one.

"Pure goddess Eisanea," the man continued, "daughter of the sun and moon."

The hairs on my arms stood. I leapt to my feet and swiveled around, searching for the speaker. "Stop fooling around and show yourself."

The woman stepped into the pond. She mumbled gibberish as she drifted deeper into the water.

"Share the water from your sacred well," the man said.

The woman's attention snapped to me as if I had made the request. Submerged up to her lower lip, she stood in the center of the pond and bared her teeth like a dog about to bite. The frightful expression sent chills crawling over my flesh.

"The sacred well is filled with dust and bones," she spat out the words.

I backed up a few steps. A cool sweat formed on my brow. With a gasp, the woman took a final step and vanished underwater. A couple of bubbles wiggled to the pond's surface. I waited a moment, expecting the tendrils of auburn hair to reappear. Two butterflies passed over the pond in leisurely flight, but the woman still hadn't come up for breath.

"Are you crazy?" I called. Despite her menacing behavior, I couldn't let her drown. I clomped toward the center of the pond. Algae soft as unspun wool greeted my feet. "Where are you?"

She didn't answer, so I gulped down a breath and dunked my head underwater. Squinting, I looked in all directions, struggling to see through a cloud of disturbed sand. My eyes burned, but I swam farther, searching until my lungs quivered for air.

"Ri, wake up," the man shouted.

I splashed to the water's surface, smacking my wet bangs out of my eyes. "Where are you? Stop playing games."

Something grabbed my ankles and I yelped. The woman stared at me from the bottom of the pond with her hands clasped around each of my legs. I froze like a panicked kitten in a thunderstorm.

"The sacred well is filled with dust and bones," she chanted. Her mouth expelled a cluster of bubbles as she spoke, but her words resonated clearly. "Dust and bones and dead men's screams and moans."

"Let go!" I bolted upright.

Cold. Dark. Dry. I patted my clothes to be sure. My shirt's fabric scratched my palms. I glanced at the thick threads in the weave, frayed and broken in random patches. The garment layered over my light linen clothing wasn't mine. Neither was the tattered blanket pooled around my waist. I had been sleeping on an unfamiliar straw mat. My heartbeat sped.

"What's going on?" I said to myself.

"It's all right. You're safe." A young man wearing a gray cloak sat by my side. With palms facing down, he waved his hands in a calming motion.

I blinked, adjusting my eyes to the dim room. Rock floor, rock ceiling, rock walls, and dank smell. I was in a cave. On the opposite side of me, a nook carved into the stone served as a fireplace. Flames dwindled on a single log, sending a thread of smoke climbing through a vent hole. The firelight formed shadows that lurked about the crevices.

"That must have been quite a dream." His warm hazel eyes reflected the fire. He picked up a nearby bowl filled with green goop and dabbed some of the mixture onto his finger. "You've been burning up, but I prayed continuously for your recovery. I was beginning to lose hope when you finally started to stir. You're very fortunate."

I was hardly fortunate. I was freezing in a cave with a stranger and a splitting headache.

"Who are you and where am I?" I pulled my knees to my chest and circled my arms around my legs. Even though he seemed good-natured, I eyed him, measuring him up.

He frowned. "You don't remember? Perhaps your fever is higher than I thought." He wiped his finger clean on the brim of the bowl and touched my forehead. His fingers were cool against my skin.

He hurried to a small table flanked by two chairs made from tree stumps. Not far from the table stood two tall barrels with clothes and personal items stacked on each. Aside from those things, no other furnishings occupied the space. He retrieved a mortar and pestle from the table, a kettle from the hearth, and a mug from atop the barrels. Then he returned to my side and arranged the objects in front of him.

When he caught me staring at him, he smiled and dimples formed on his cheeks. My heart stopped for a second.

"I think a second introduction is in order since you greeted me with a fair amount of hostility during our first." The corner of his mouth lifted. "I'm Bryce and this is my home. I know you must have a hundred questions, and I'll answer them all, but first we must take care of your fever."

I touched my head. A warm film of sweat coated my skin. "That's a good idea. My head is buzzing." The sooner he remedied me, the sooner I might remember how I wound up in the cave with him.

He worked vigorously, crushing the herbs inside the mortar into a powder. The scent of rosemary and yarrow mingled with the earthy scent surrounding us. He poured hot water into the mug and stirred in the herbal mixture. "This is an old recipe of mine. It never fails to break a fever."

I relaxed when he handed the mug to me. Clearly, he had kind intentions. The steam swirled up and greeted my nose with a pleasant aroma, but the mixture inside the mug curdled. I scrunched my nose. "This looks disgusting."

"Most remedies do, but I promise it'll work." Once again, he scooped up some of the green goop onto his finger and plopped it onto my chin before I could jerk away. "And that will heal your cut."

"My cut?" I raised my hand to my chin, but he grabbed my wrist gently, stopping me.

"Don't wipe it off. It'll prevent scarring." He glanced at the mug I hadn't yet sipped from and raised his eyebrows. "It really doesn't taste that bad."

"I was merely letting it cool." I brought the mug to my lips and choked down the grainy mixture. It left a grassy aftertaste on my tongue.

He watched me with amusement. "It's a shame you don't remember anything. I had rescued you so heroically."

I set the mug down. "Rescued?"

Something furry brushed against my arm and I flinched. A gray cat raced past me and jumped onto Bryce's lap.

"This is Miss Meow," he explained.

With one eye missing, a gnawed off ear, and a bald spot on her rear leg, Miss Meow looked far more ragged than her dainty name implied. Poor thing. I reached to pat her head, but she warned me with a low growl. I tucked my hand back under the safety of the blanket.

"Sorry, she's not used to visitors," Bryce said. "We don't get many."

The cat nudged her head against Bryce's chin, and he happily returned the affection by scratching her behind the ear. She burst out in purr.

"Have you been keeping the tunnels free of rats, Miss Meow?" he asked the cat in a playful tone.

"Rats?" I looked around, mistaking shadows for vermin.

"Oh, yes. They used to squeak all night until Miss Meow came along. It wasn't easy getting a restful sleep with rodents crawling about," he said through a chuckle.

I closed my mouth after realizing it had been hanging open. "I don't understand. Why do you live in a cave?"

He stopped petting Miss Meow. "It's what I must do for now."

The cat glowered at me with her single yellow eye and lashed her tail back and forth. Perhaps my judgmental question warranted her attitude. Throwing the wrong words into a conversation was like tossing a rotten tomato into a stew pot, as Samuel would say. Samuel.

Oh no! Memories hit me like clashes of thunder. Mallory. The puma-eating beast. Chanting. Bryce.

"I'm sorry, but I have to go. Now." I threw the blanket off me.

"Did I say something wrong? Was it the rats?" He pushed Miss Meow off his lap. She flopped on the floor and rolled onto her back. "They're more afraid of you than you are of them."

"Doubtful." I staggered to my feet, searching for an exit.

A white canvas sheet, each corner hooked to a peg, gleamed against the rock wall. Wind pressed against its backside, rippling the fabric. Another sheet hung on the opposite wall, bucking. Both covered tunnels.

"Which tunnel leads outside?" I asked.

He stood and braced my shoulders. "Ri, I think you should sit down."

"No, no, I'm fine. Really." I alternated glances between the two canvas sheets. "I need to get back to my village right away."

"You're worried about the older gentleman." He maneuvered into my line of sight, blocking my view of the potential exit. "I saw you leading him out of the forest the day we met."

I nodded. "Yes, he's rather intrigued by you. He thinks you appear out of nowhere. Like magic."

"Uh ..." His eyes widened. "He does?"

"Yes, I know it sounds ridiculous. Wait. Did you say, *the day* we met? We met today."

"No, Ri. You've been here for three days."

"Three days? I've been lying there for three days?" I pointed at the blanket as if it stole this precious time from me. Samuel could not care for himself one day, let alone three. What if he wandered into the forest again? "I'm sorry, you've been very kind, and I don't mean to run out of here after you helped me, but I really have to go."

I hurried toward the canvas sheet to my right, and he trailed me close on my heels. Could I act anymore ungrateful? I paused and faced him. "Why don't you come to my village? A cave is no place to live. Besides, it's dangerous to stay here with whatever is out there in the forest."

"Yes, about that ... we don't need to worry about the things in the forest finding us here. Please Ri, have a seat." He guided me toward the chair. A black dart-sized object rested atop the table on a piece of cloth.

I grabbed the thing and rotated it between my fingers, examining it. "This is what struck me in the clearing."

The object's weight, texture, and size reminded me of a chicken leg bone. One end of the cylinder-shaped object was blunt, while the other tapered to a point. A shiver scurried up my spine like a centipede.

"Please be careful." Bryce eased the thing out of my hand using the cloth. "It's poisonous."

"Who would want to poison us?"

"I don't know. I was hoping that you could answer that." He set the strange thing back on the table. His forehead wrinkled with worry. "Ri, you're not going to like this, but ... I can't take you back to your village."

A hard weight formed in my stomach. Perhaps he was afraid to enter the forest again after being attacked.

"We can make it together if we move fast." I hurried toward the canvas sheet on my right. The corner of the covering flopped over as I unfastened the tie from the first peg.

"No." Bryce wedged himself between the tunnel and me. "You must never go down this tunnel. Never."

"Fine," I said, raising my voice to get the urgency across. "I'll take the other tunnel."

I spun around and rushed toward the tunnel to my left. The fire had diminished to a faint wisp, barely lighting the cavern, and I accidentally knocked over a pile of books sitting on the ground. I gasped, counting at least a dozen. I had only seen one book in my lifetime—a leather-bound collection of wilted pages that Samuel owned. He had called the book an evil thing and tossed it into the valley shortly after taking me as his ward. I always wondered if someone else had found it.

I kicked Bryce's books out of my way and headed toward the tunnel. He had quite an assortment of the wicked things. Perhaps he wasn't as noble as I first thought. I quickened my pace toward the tunnel, but he grabbed my arm.

"Let go," I said. "I want to go home."

"Ri, please calm down and listen to me. This is going to sound crazy, but … we're no longer on your island, and we can't return until the next dark moon."

I stopped struggling. The effects of panic paired with my fever. Dizzy, I braced the rock wall. "We're no longer on my island?"

He nodded. "I know it's not ideal. But I *will* take you home."

"But not until the dark moon?" I plunged my hand into my pocket and rubbed my thumb against the glass face of my compass. I struggled to calm my breaths. Inhale. Exhale. Calm. Ouch. The broken glass pricked me.

"It's not so bad," Bryce said through a nervous laugh. "The dark moon comes every month. It's rather predictable that way."

"But the dark moon just passed. You want me here for a month?"

"Well, no. Of course, I don't want you here for a month." His jaw dropped, and he chopped his hands back and forth. "I'm so sorry, I didn't mean it like that. I'm sure you'd make pleasant enough company. There's plenty we could do together. I mean …"

I glanced at the books. What if the evil things had affected Bryce's mind? After all, his story made no sense.

"Come with me." I cupped his shoulder. "There's a very good healer in my village who can help … um … manage your condition."

He jerked his head. "Great, you think I've lost my mind." He raised his arms and then let them flop to his side in defeat. "Well, prepare yourself, because there's more. I walk through an underground waterfall in this cave and emerge from the one near your village. It's exactly as the older gentleman explained it to you. Magic."

"Please, Bryce, I really need to go home." Samuel was probably so scared not having me around.

"Let me show you something." He picked up a green book near the bottom of the pile. "This book has maps. I'll show you where we are."

The cover flopped open and he flipped through the pages. I stepped back.

"Oh, here it is. Look at this." He pointed to a spot in the middle of a drawing that consisted of a twist of wavy lines littered with dots and symbols. I smacked the foul book from his hands, sending it flying through the air. It landed closed—thank Eisanea—with a hard thud.

Bryce yelped. "Whoa! And you think I'm the crazy one?" His wide eyes stared at the book five feet away.

A thread of light sprawled across the book's cover and ran across the floor. It fell from a tunnel, absent of covering, nearly hidden in the rocky shadows. If there was light, there was a way out. I hurried into the circular, three-foot-diameter tunnel like a bunny zipping into a burrow. I crawled upward at a diagonal angle toward a small round door at the top of the channel.

"Stop, someone might see you out there." Bryce grabbed my heel, but I wrestled away from his grip by sliding my foot out of my moccasin. The tunnel's walls snagged my shoulders as I struggled toward the door. I reached for the latch as Bryce seized my pant leg.

"Please, come out of there." His voice echoed. "You don't understand. There're dangerous people above ground."

"No, I'm going home." With a quick jerk, I forced my knee up. My pants slid out of his grasp.

A slit of light seeped through a gap between the door and the curvature of the cavern. The eerie wind howled outside. With all my strength, I pushed the frost-coated door latch, but it wouldn't budge. Odd how cold it felt.

"Please don't go out there." Bryce crept into the tunnel and clutched my ankles, pulling me.

"Get off." I held onto to a small outcrop, ready to sink my fingernails into the stone in order to hold on. No longer able to push with him yanking at me, I rammed my palm repeatedly against the latch. "Come on. Open."

The latch released. Wind invaded the tunnel. Bryce let go of me as a gust of snowy mist burst through the door. I forced my way outside and placed my forearm over my eyes to shield them from icy droplets.

A moist chill trickled into my shoe, but the unlucky foot that lost the moccasin numbed as the cold bit into my flesh. I lowered my arm, squinting. A puff of steam rose from my mouth when I exhaled, caressing my cheeks with a fleeting moment of warmth.

Ahead, a white sheet of snow stretched all the way to the horizon, merging with gray clouds that swirled in an equally colorless sky. It was nearing dusk. The wind sang a ghostly chant across the treeless terrain. I closed my eyes for a moment and then, with lashes sticky with frost, I opened them. Where was I? My legs went weak, and I collapsed to my knees.

"Please come back inside," Bryce said.

This had to be a nightmare. Wake up. Wake up. Wake up. I scooped some snow into my palm, and all of the individual fragments of ice glistened. My dreams were never so vivid. How could this be happening? I felt like I might throw up. Samuel and I had never been separated before. How would he survive without me?

"Please, Ri." Bryce extended his hand. "Come back inside and I'll explain everything."

Too overwhelmed to speak, I nodded and followed him into the cave.

CHAPTER 4

Bryce tossed another log onto the fire. The blaze flickered back to life, licking the bottom of a kettle hanging in the hearth. I sat at the table with the tattered blanket draped over my shoulders. Bryce had given me some tea, but instead of drinking it, I mindlessly tilted the mug back and forth, and watched the liquid inside distort my reflection.

After setting a small bowl of blueberries in front of me, Bryce sat on the opposite stump and went about chopping a handful of potatoes. Miss Meow slept near his feet.

It had been three days since I had last eaten, and hunger left a maddening, hollow ache in my stomach. Despite this, I stared at the berries. How could I eat not knowing whether Samuel had a solid meal? Was Kaylan keeping him safe at home? Adding exactly two spoons of honey to his tea? Making sure he didn't kick off his blankets while he slept?

Of course, Kaylan was doing all of those things. He was an excellent caregiver. But if other responsibilities called him away, he would have no choice but to leave Samuel with his twin sons. Would they care for him with the same level of dedication as Kaylan? Probably not. And if Samuel wandered into the forest again, any number of things could hurt him.

Trembling, I folded my arms over my stomach. "What am I going to do?"

"I'm sorry," Bryce said through a sigh. "I didn't mean to complicate your life like this. But I had to get you somewhere safe." He nudged the blueberry bowl closer to me. "Please eat something."

To ease his worry, I shoveled some berries into my mouth. Their pleasant tart flavor burst on my tongue. I swallowed them quickly. I refused to enjoy anything until I returned to my village and found Samuel unharmed.

"I can't stay here for four weeks." I took a deep breath to calm myself. "All right. I can handle this. Explain how you ... um ... travel through waterfalls again." Understanding his ability seemed like a good place to start in figuring out this mess.

"Of course." He set the potato aside and leaned forward, resting his elbows on the table. "It's like walking through a door that leads to another part of the world. One moment I'm in one place, but once I step through a waterfall, I'm somewhere else. The problem is, I have no control as to where I end up. That's determined by the moon cycle."

"And the waterfall delivers you to my island when the moon is dark?" How ridiculous those words sounded, but I couldn't deny this painful reality.

He nodded. "And the day after the dark moon, I'm able to return here. If I were to step into the waterfall today, I'd wind up near an abandoned city, and tomorrow, a place plagued by dust storms. It's taken me years to log most of the destinations into a journal. Your island and this place are the most bearable."

I glanced around the cave. How could he call this cold, dreary place bearable?

"Wouldn't you prefer to live on the island?" I asked.

"Yes, very much so." He contemplated the fire for a moment. "But I have responsibilities here. I'll explain all that later. First, if it brings you any comfort, we're not that far from your home."

I perked up, straightening my posture. "We're not?" My tone reached a higher pitch, lightened by hope.

"Let me show you." He sliced a peel, nearly the width and length of a potato, and placed it flat on the table. Then he cut another peel, no larger than a potato's eye, and positioned it about an inch away from the first. "The small peel is your island and the larger one is where we are, the mainland. Of course, the space in between is the sea. But that's all that separates us. Right now, we're directly parallel to your island, on the mainland's west coast."

"But how can we be so close to my island when it's so cold here?" I asked.

"I don't know." He pursed his lips. "It wasn't always this cold. But at least we still have a few months of harvest."

"Harvest?" I turned toward the tunnel that he forbade me to enter earlier. "Are there more people through that tunnel?"

"Yes, but many of them are bad people. If you stay here, you'll be safe. But out there—"

"Out there I might find a faster way home. Perhaps I could build a raft and sail across the sea. I'd return to my village in a couple of days instead of four weeks."

He raised his eyebrows and blinked at me, mouth gaping. "Or you wouldn't return at all. That sea is aptly named Fool's Last Sail for a reason. You'd wind up at the Violet Star with Death."

"We call it Wind Serpent Sea in my village." I nodded at the pile of chopped potatoes. "As soon as I eat and regain some strength, I want to have a look down that tunnel."

He got up from his seat with the chopped potatoes in hand. "I hope as soon as you regain some strength, you'll start to think rationally."

My jaw dropped. "I *am* thinking rationally. Why can't you understand how important this is?"

"I do understand, Ri." He tossed the potatoes into the kettle. The boiling water hissed and released a billow of steam, before quieting to a gurgle. "I know you're worried about the older gentleman, but—"

"Yes, I'm worried! There're chanting things in the forest attacking people, and a questionable man wandering in the Dark Woods." Mallory's ugly sneer surfaced in my mind. If I ever saw him again, I'd slap him across his scarred face for breaking my compass.

Bryce sat back down at the table and looked me squarely in the eye. "When we return to your island, I'm going to find out who attacked us and make sure they never harm you again. The same goes for the stranger you met. But for now, I need you to stay here. Please, trust me."

Trust him? I hardly knew him, but he had saved my life. No one other than Samuel and Kaylan had ever worried for my wellbeing. But I wasn't a child who needed looking after. I was quite capable of taking care of myself. Once he dozed off, I would make my escape.

"All right, I'll stay here," I lied, shifting in my seat.

He let out a breath and smiled. "Thank you, Ri. I know this is hard for you, but I'm grateful that you've given me your trust. I won't let you down."

I averted my gaze. What would he think when he woke the next morning and found me missing? No doubt, he'd feel hurt and betrayed. Tightness formed in the back of my throat. Lying came easy for some folks, but never me.

He stood and grabbed a spoon from atop one of the barrels. "What's your favorite potato recipe? Mashed or wedges?"

"Wedges, please." I gnawed on my lip, keeping my gaze locked on my tea mug.

"Perfect. That's my favorite too." He stirred the pot's contents and the sound of boiling water filled my ears.

I scanned the room for items I might need for my journey. An unlit lantern sat in the corner. Hopefully, oil filled its container. I cringed. Bryce owned so little, and here I was plotting to steal from him. I had never stolen anything in my life, but I had to do this for Samuel's sake.

A loud clunk came from the forbidden tunnel. Bryce and I both jolted. Miss Meow hissed, puffed her tail, and hid behind a barrel.

"What was that?" I asked as Bryce pulled me to standing and guided me to the far side of the room.

"Someone's coming." He grabbed his potato-chopping knife.

Approaching footsteps echoed within the tunnel. My breath quickened. Bryce held his knife and waited alongside the canvas sheet. Did he plan to kill the intruder? Did we need to? How dangerous were the people through that tunnel? I glanced around for anything that might make a suitable weapon. Only clothes and clay plates rested atop the nearby barrels.

The canvas covering bulged as someone on the opposite side pushed against it. I grabbed one of the plates and raised it, preparing to throw it at whoever entered. A lump moved up the sheet until a hand poked out through the space where the top of the canvas met the wall. Let the intruder come. I had a good aim.

"I know you're in there," said a smooth male voice. Its owner groped the rocky surface, repeatedly missing the peg to detach the sheet. "Bryce? A little help?"

Bryce sighed and his posture relaxed. "It's all right," he told me. "Our guest is completely harmless." He tossed the knife on the table and yanked the covering free. "But I should warn you—"

The covering fell to the ground, and a man, roughly mid-twenties, barged into our space. Bryce stumbled out of the way, off balance. I went to help him, but the stranger blocked my path, grinning.

"Well hello," he said in a tone dripping with practiced charm. His clover-green eyes fixated on me as he brushed off his crisp, white shirt. Puffs of dust vanished into the air.

"Hello?" I gaped at him. After Bryce's warning of bad people, I hardly expected a well-groomed, decent-smelling man to appear out of the tunnel. His trousers didn't bunch with extra fabric at the belt like Bryce's did. They appeared tailored to his size. A vest adorned with gold buttons molded his chest and waist into a flattering V shape.

The stranger looked me up and down. "It's a shame you've been stuck down here. It's no place for a lady. This cave is absolutely filthy."

He sniffed his sleeve. "Whew! Cave stench. This stink will never come out."

"You should know not to wear your best clothes down here." Bryce refastened the canvas sheet.

"These aren't my best clothes." The stranger glanced down at his garments and gasped at the sight of a muddy splotch on his pants. He curled his lip in disgust. "Dammit, this blasted cave."

What a prissy man! I'd never met someone so troubled by a little muck. The tension in my shoulders disappeared, and I set the plate down on the table.

"Do you live through that tunnel?" I asked the stranger.

He scraped the smudge off his pants, ignoring my question. All of the grime clumped under his flawless fingernails. Cursing under his breath, he jabbed his pinky nail beneath all the others, lifting away the crud.

"Didn't you hear me?" I asked, watching him preen himself.

"Ri, this is Carter." Bryce gestured at our guest. "Carter, this is Ri. But I suppose you know that already."

I scratched my head. "How would he know my name?"

"Yes," Carter snapped back into the conversation. "I live above ground like a normal person."

"Oh? I've been told it's dangerous out there." I narrowed an eye at Bryce. "And I've been forbidden from entering that tunnel."

"Ri, it's complicated," Bryce said firmly, folding his arms.

I wished he would stop acting overprotective.

"Complicated?" Carter broke in, mouth twitching with a smile. He looked around and shuddered. "Well, I'd choose to live a complicated life above ground than suffer in this dismal place any day. This whole cave could certainly use a lady's touch. And so could its occupant."

Bryce's cheeks reddened. "Don't say stuff like that. It's inappropriate."

Carter chuckled at Bryce's embarrassment and then regarded me. "He lacks any sense of humor. But do not fret my dear, more enjoyable company has arrived." He kissed my hand, grinning arrogantly, as if he thought the sun rose each morning for the sole purpose of shining upon him.

When he released my hand, I discreetly wiped it clean on my pant leg. Samuel once told me that a genuine smile crinkled the eyes, and Carter's expression did no such thing.

"You're here early." Bryce returned to the hearth and resumed stirring the potatoes.

"Well, I couldn't allow the beautiful lady to endure another day without the necessities, so I've brought you both gifts." Carter flicked an auburn curl away from his eye and then swung a knapsack off his back.

Gifts? How kind, but unexpected from a stranger.

Bryce's jaw tensed. "We don't need your gifts. Keep them."

"Are you going to let him speak for you like that?" Carter opened his mouth round as an apple, as if Bryce had deeply insulted me.

"I speak for myself." I gave a terse nod. The items inside that knapsack might provide clues to the nature of the world beyond the tunnel.

"Good. Then let's get acquainted." Carter impolitely brushed Bryce's potato-peel map off the table and let it fall to the floor.

"Where're your manners?" I said.

"This is a cave, not an estate, Honey," he answered.

"Well, I don't know what an estate is, but this is still a home." I placed my hands on my hips.

"Don't bother reprimanding him, he never listens." Bryce scooped the peels off the ground and tossed them into the fire. I bent down to help him clean the mess, but Carter bowed, leveling his eyes with mine. "Don't worry about that. I'm sure Bryce's rats will gobble up those scraps."

I stood upright, angling my body away from Carter's. "You've got a lot of nerve."

"Testy, aren't we Buttercup?" Carter smirked and set the knapsack on the table. "But you won't always be. One day I'll steal your heart."

"A haughty man like you would never steal my heart," I said through a mocking laugh.

Bryce joined us at the table, positioning himself between the two of us. I touched his arm to set him at ease. I could handle a silly man like Carter.

"We'll see." Carter flipped the knapsack's flap open, revealing an assortment of packages wrapped in brown cloth. One by one, he announced each item as he removed them from the bag and placed them on the table. "Cheese. Bread. Crackers. Some fruit. Oh, and sausage. I bet you love sausage. At least, I hope you do." For some reason, he wiggled his eyebrows at me, which spurred a scowl from Bryce. "And lastly, some fresh clothes. Well, they're older things of mine, but better than anything he's got." He pointed a thumb at Bryce.

The items on the table, from the cheese to the well-crafted garments, suggested that productive people resided through that tunnel. While this didn't mean that no danger existed, it certainly raised my doubts.

Bryce picked up the package of cheese and glared at it as if he might hurl it into the fire. "Which one of your lady friends gave you all of this stuff?"

"Oh, I don't know," Carter said. "It's so hard to keep track."

"You're inexcusable." Bryce pounded the cheese back onto the table, grabbed the plate, and then hurried to the kettle to check on our food.

"I don't see why he's so upset," Carter whispered to me. "I can't help that women enjoy giving me things. Look at me. I'm handsome, charming, intelligent, and witty."

"And incredibly humble," I said sarcastically. Weakness from lack of food crept up on me, and I gripped the table for balance.

"And yet I've swept you off your feet." Carter grasped my arm and guided me to sit on the stump. Then he opened the package of bread and offered it to me.

I broke off a small piece. Unlike the hard, grainy bread from my village, this loaf was soft as a down-filled pillow.

Bryce pointed at the bread. "What will this cost me?"

Carter raised his palms. "Nothing. Why do you always assume there's a price?" The pitch of his voice rose with exasperation.

"Because there always is," Bryce said.

I put the bread down in case Bryce spoke the truth. I would be indebted to no one.

Carter gave Bryce a smug sideways glance. "Oh, please. I do kind things for you all the time. I've even brought you more tea."

Frowning, Bryce shook his head as he scooped the potatoes out of the kettle and onto the plate. Something wasn't right between these two.

"Well, anyway." Carter looked back at me. "I have a few more things."

The knapsack deflated as he pulled out a plush blanket. He unraveled it with a shake and draped it over my shoulders. Though the thick fabric warded off the cave's damp chill, I tensed as he leaned close.

"Luxury is nice, don't you agree?" He caressed the edge of the blanket near my neck. "But it's much nicer when shared with someone. Perhaps you and I should spend some time under the blanket together?"

"I don't think so!" I gripped the fabric around me, forming a cocoon that he couldn't burrow into.

"That's enough." Bryce banged the spoon against the pot and glowered in Carter's direction. The kettle swung back and forth, spilling juices from the rim. He jumped backward, wiping the splatter off his shirt.

"Are the potatoes fighting back?" Carter asked. "Are they tired of you transforming them into an assortment of tasteless meals?"

Bryce stormed toward us and slammed the plate of potatoes on the table. "You need to stop. Right now. I know what you're up to and you're wasting your time."

Worse than that, Carter's ridiculous advances were wasting *my* time. How could I sneak away with both him and Bryce in the cave?

Carter placed his hand over his chest. "I'm not up to anything. Can't you see that I'm merely trying to bring a new friend comfort while she's away from all that's familiar to her?" He slipped his hand into his pocket, pulled out a folded piece of paper, and handed it to me. "This is my final gift. It's something very special."

I unfolded the paper and stared at the two lines of writing penned on the center of the sheet. "I don't understand."

Bryce snatched the paper from my hand, tearing it nearly in half. He scanned it for a brief moment and then threw it on the table. It glided off and drifted to the floor. "It's an address. Who does it belong to?"

I picked the paper off the ground and smoothed the wrinkles out of it.

"That's the name of a man who'll fix her compass," Carter said.

"What?" My heart lifted at his words. I looked at Bryce. "When did you tell him about my compass?"

"I didn't."

Carter knelt in front of me and enveloped my hands in his. "It will shine as perfectly as the day it was first given to you. I promise. I know how painful it is to look upon something you cherish and not be able to fix it. I'd be more than happy to escort you above ground."

"Above ground?" This was my chance to get out of Bryce's cave. "Yes, I'd love to go."

"No, absolutely not," Bryce said. "Don't listen to him. He knows exactly what you want to hear." He wagged his finger at Carter as if lecturing a child. "The way you abuse the gift Eisanea has blessed you with is disgraceful."

"Which gift do you speak of? Eisanea has blessed me with so many." Carter smiled, showing all of his straight, white teeth.

"You know exactly what I speak of." Bryce directed his attention toward me. "It's how he knew you were here. It's how he knew about your broken compass. He sees things before they happen. An incredible gift, but he uses it to manipulate people—usually women—to get what he wants."

Carter shrugged as if bored. "Honey, four weeks will be quite dull with him, but I could make things much more fun."

"Wait," I said, needing a moment to absorb Bryce's words. "You're saying Carter can see the future?"

"Yes, and he should be ashamed." Bryce glared at Carter.

Carter dismissed the comment with a wave. "Ashamed of what? I live life fully with no regrets." His gaze slid back toward me. "A night above ground, under the stars with me, and you'll have no regrets either, Honey."

"Ew." I leaned away from him.

Bryce huffed. "Ri, give me the compass and note. I'll get it repaired for you." He beckoned for my treasured possession.

"No, I want to see what's through that tunnel," I said.

"Please, Ri. This isn't the time to be stubborn."

"But she is stubborn," Carter interrupted. "And a bit reckless if you ask me." He rubbed his finger against his lips. "Yes, I see it. She's going to wander up that tunnel while we're making our delivery tonight. You'll never find her again."

Bryce looked hurt. "Ri, you promised you'd stay here."

"Um ... well, I ..." Why was I explaining myself? I hadn't done anything wrong. I crossed my arms and glared at Carter. "You don't know what I'll do."

"I know exactly what you'll do." Carter sat down on the opposite stump and impatiently drummed his fingers on the table. "Neither of you need to be concerned. If she goes with us, she'll be fine. When am I ever wrong?"

"You're never wrong," Bryce said, irritated. "But you often lie."

"Oh please! I've never led anyone toward harm. Besides, you can't leave her here with that ugly thing." He pointed at Miss Meow, who had returned from hiding and lay sprawled on the ground.

"There's nothing wrong with Miss Meow." They watched the cat as she rolled onto her back and licked her paw.

"Why are we making the delivery tonight?" Bryce asked. "It's four days early."

"There's been a slight schedule change." Carter slapped his palms flat on the table. "Show some spontaneity."

I had no idea what the delivery they spoke of was, but venturing into that tunnel would be my first step in returning to Samuel.

"I'm going with you." I stood so I could face Bryce eye to eye. "That's final."

"Three packs are better than two, are they not?" Carter lifted the empty knapsack off the ground and held it up as if offering a treat to a well-behaved puppy.

"I swear," Bryce said, "if anything happens …"

"Do exactly as I tell you and you'll both be safe."

"Fine. Give me the knapsack." Bryce extended one hand while rubbing tension out of his forehead with the other.

Carter tossed him the knapsack and then flashed his green eyes at me. "I'm excited to show you the world, Buttercup."

"I don't need to see the world. All I want to see is my home."

"I'll get you home, Ri. I promise." Bryce went to one of the barrels and threw its lid onto the floor. He reached inside and grabbed a packet of plants, bound in twine, and stuffed them into the knapsack. Miss Meow weaved around his ankles as he continued to pack.

"That's what Bryce harvests during his journeys to your island," Carter explained. "He tells me that over there, it's impossible to look at the ground and not find some sort of healing plant sprouting about. But here, they're very rare and very expensive." He smiled, and this time his eyes crinkled.

Bryce handed a packet of the plants to me. I pried one of the dark-green leaves free from the twine wrapping. Samuel complained about this plant often, ripping it from his garden as the summer sun reddened his scalp.

"This one's a weed," I said.

"Boiled down, it soothes the stomach," Bryce said.

"That's merely one of many types Bryce collects. And tonight," Carter lowered his voice to a whisper, "we deliver two packs to the sick and one to our enemies."

CHAPTER 5

Carter leaned against the wall, turning his nose up at the boiled potatoes Bryce had prepared. "A meal without flavor is like a night sky without stars."

"Tastes fine to me." Grub stuffed my cheeks. Bryce and I sat at the table, sharing the plate of potato wedges. Perhaps the food lacked zest, but I gobbled it up. I needed the energy if I wanted to make it home.

Next to the forbidden tunnel sat the three knapsacks we were to deliver. Though I didn't like the idea of meeting dangerous people, I had to venture out of the cave for Samuel's sake.

"Ri, I only ask two things of you tonight." Bryce wiped his mouth and gestured for me to take the last scrap of food on the plate. "First, please stay close. If we get separated—"

"Perhaps I should hold her hand," Carter broke in, smirking.

"Stop making jokes." Bryce angled his body away from Carter and leaned closer to me. "I'm serious, I don't want anything bad to happen."

"I understand," I said. "I'll stay near you at all times. What's the second request?"

"If we run into anyone, let me do the talking."

No one spoke for me, so if I needed to have a word with someone, I would do so. But for now, I nodded. Anxious to leave, I got up and layered on the extra shirt Carter had brought me. Then, still chewing the last potato, I retrieved one of the knapsacks. With food filling my stomach, I felt revitalized.

Carter joined me, swinging a knapsack onto his back. Meanwhile, Bryce unhooked the canvas covering from the tunnel. The fabric fell to the ground, revealing the passage's five-foot-tall oval opening. Firelight from the hearth slipped into the corridor, illuminating the jagged interior. The craggy rock walls glistened with moisture, making the tunnel look like the innards of a living thing.

An unexpected thrill of panic shot through me. I hated tight places, especially tight, dark places with creepy things crawling in them. With sweaty palms, I adjusted the knapsack's straps.

"How long is this tunnel?" I eyed the dark passage.

"Not terribly long." Bryce picked up the last knapsack. "But we'll be moving slowly and carefully. It'll take an hour to clear it."

An hour? Clearly our definition of *long* differed. But I could handle an hour in a cramped place, even if my thrashing heart disagreed.

Bryce ducked his head and entered the tunnel. After a few steps inside of the passage, his silhouette waved me to join him. His knapsack scraped against the rock walls.

I shoved my hand into my pocket and rubbed the back of my compass to soothe the jitters. With a deep breath, I composed myself and followed him. The immediate drop in temperature sent a shiver scurrying over my arms.

Behind me, Carter's footsteps approached. He refastened the canvas covering, cutting off the light supplied by the hearth. Uninterrupted darkness embraced us. I took another calming breath, but yelped when something crawled over my feet. Carter laughed.

"It's just Miss Meow," Bryce said. "She usually follows us for a little while."

Carter continued to snicker.

"She surprised me," I said. "I wasn't scared."

"It's all right." Bryce's tone lifted with a hint of amusement. "I was uneasy when I first started crawling through caves too."

"Oh please!" Carter tapped my elbow. "The truth is, as a youngster, Bryce plowed into the first cave he discovered as if there was treasure inside."

"I was trying to make her feel better," Bryce said.

"I'm fine." I brushed back my hair, collecting my wits. "But what do you two have against lanterns?"

"I don't need one. It's a waste of oil." Bryce's voice echoed against our rocky surroundings. He grasped my hand and guided it to what felt like a cord fastened to the wall.

"I've connected this rope to pegs hammered into the rock every few dozen paces," he explained. "As long as we follow it, we'll never veer off path."

He patted my hand, closing my fingers around the rope. Once I had a firm grip, he trekked onward. I opted to keep my other hand on his knapsack so I wouldn't lose him. One wrong move and I might have cracked my head on a low hanging rock, or twisted an ankle on the uneven ground. But Bryce warned me of oncoming bends, twists, and low ceilings. I was completely dependent on his guidance. Though I hated this loss of control, a warm feeling flourished in my chest: the first sparks of trust, I thought.

Carter whistled a cheerful melody as we maneuvered through the corridor. The tune mingled with the repetitive splatter of moisture dripping off rocks. It reminded me of something ... a forgotten childhood song, perhaps. For a brief moment, my thoughts lingered on pleasant memories of home, rather than the cramped tunnel.

Bryce slowed to a stop. "We've reached the half-way point. It's going to start getting tight. Carry your knapsack and walk sideways."

I did as he asked and then patted around searching for him. My palm landed on his shoulder, so I clutched a clump of his cloak. Miss

Meow scampered over my feet again, this time heading in the opposite direction toward Bryce's home.

Bryce shuffled forward and I followed. A rock jabbed me in the back, and the pain warned of a bruise to come. Then another scraped against my front side. I tightened my grip on Bryce's shoulder.

"Sorry." He placed his hand on my waist and pulled me closer. "I'll try to guide you better."

Though the gesture was meant to reassure me, my breath quickened. Protruding stone snagged my shirt. I was wedged between walls and people. Trapped. My pulse throbbed in my ears. Carter resumed whistling a melody, a rapid string of notes that rivaled the pace of my heart.

"Carter, have you always been able to see the future?" I asked in hopes of distracting myself.

"I don't see it, I hear a man's voice," Carter said. "I call him my Whisperer, and he's been with me since my fifteenth birthday."

Rock caught on the front and back of my clothes. The walls shrank around us. I squeezed past the jaws of an enormous snake and entered its throat. Pressure built in my head, and I felt the urge to kick and push.

"Whisperer?" I asked. My fingers stiffened around Bryce's shoulder. The scent of wet earth nearly suffocated me.

"That's right," Carter said. "You see, I've always found Fate's threads to be particularly harsh, and I prefer something woven at a finer grade. I was meant to be clad in premium fabrics, not the awful, coarse stuff that vagabonds like Bryce wear. My Whisperer leads me to all the things that I deserve."

"There's nothing wrong with my clothes," Bryce broke in. Then, whispering to me, he asked, "You're breathing heavy. Are you all right?"

"Of course," I answered as if his question was the most ridiculous thing I had ever been asked. "I must still be recovering from the fever."

"Have you ever felt silk?" Carter touched my arm. "Honey, you would look ravishing in a silk dress. The fabric is as soft as rose petals."

"It sounds too delicate for my tastes," I said through my ragged breaths. Spots fluttered in my vision. I wanted out. I breathed deeper, attempting to banish my silly fears. How foolish I would look in front of my new companions if I collapsed in panic. "So, this Whisperer is like ... strong intuition?"

"I think it's more than that," he said. "But who cares? It gets me what I want."

"I would be concerned as to who the voice belonged to," I said.

"Almost there." Bryce's hand pressed harder against my waist, comforting me with a fleeting wave of security.

We took one more step and the walls disappeared. Though still draped in darkness, I inhaled a relieved breath, glad to be free of the vice-like tunnel. An awful odor assaulted me, so I quickly covered my nose, gagging.

"Sorry, I should have warned you," Bryce said. "The tunnel deposits us into the city's crypts, but in a few moments we'll be outside."

My eyes watered from the stench of rotting flesh. I coughed into my palm as Bryce led me onward. The space widened and we easily walked side by side. The echo of our footsteps bounced off walls that seemed far away.

After a few steps, Bryce stopped walking and I heard him fiddling with something. There was a clank followed by the sound of metal grating against metal. Then a slice of moonlight fanned before me as he opened a door. Twirls of snowy mist rushed in with a blast of wind. I gasped, welcoming the fresh air and stepped outside. The moon, a narrow slash of gold, cast muted light onto our surroundings.

Ahead, dozens of headstones poked through the snow. Unlike the simple grave markers used by my village, these were imposing blocks of granite, capped with frost.

"This is where we first met nearly two years ago." Carter wrapped his arm around Bryce. "You should've seen how surprised he was when he crept out of that door and found me waiting for him. Do you remember that, good friend?"

Bryce shoved Carter away. "You handed me an empty knapsack and ordered me to fill it."

"Well, I gave you a purpose and that was what you needed."

Bryce angrily shook his head and then turned to me, softening his expression. "I want to run ahead to have a quick look around."

"You don't need to worry, but do as you must," Carter said.

"I have good reason to take extra precautions tonight." Bryce glanced at me, acting overprotective once again. "Wait until I give the signal." He dashed to the nearest headstone, hid behind it, looked around, and then raced off to the next. He did this until he reached an iron fence about fifty feet away. He crouched and waited.

Beyond the fence sat clusters of squat, brick dwellings. Each was roughly twenty-feet wide by forty-feet long, had two doors, five windows, and tiled roofs concaving from the weight of snow. Some had lost the battle, leaving gaping holes open to the sky. Row after row, the grid of dwellings loomed ahead until they vanished into the distance. Even though it was late, I would have expected to see some sign of life coming out of these buildings—perhaps smoke from a chimney—instead there was only eerie loneliness. The homes must have been abandoned.

"Finally!" Carter clapped his hands together. "We have some time alone." He leaned against the doorframe, grinning at me. "I bet you've been looking forward to this moment all day. I know I have."

"You don't give up, do you?" I folded my arms over my chest and looked back toward the village, watching for hints of danger.

"The bear might get stung a few times when swatting at the hive, but he eventually gets the honey, Honey."

"You're not getting any honey." I gave him a sideways glance. "And I can't believe that you compared my personality to a swarm of bees."

"What's so hard to believe? It's a perfect comparison." An auburn curl fell over his eye as he cocked his head. "Bees protect what they hold dear with unwavering courage and their sense of responsibility never falters. It's not unlike yourself."

"And now you're complimenting me." I shook my head. How many angles did he plan to try?

He cleared his throat and looked at the ground. "Unfortunately, bees are so fixated on their tasks that they often fail to enjoy the sweetness that surrounds them. Also, not unlike yourself."

"This is silly. I'm going to join Bryce." I marched two steps before he grabbed my arm.

"Wait, I'm sorry if we got off on the wrong foot." He dug the toe of his shoe into the snow, burrowing toward the black earth. Then he picked something up and placed it into my palm.

"Why are you giving me a rock from a graveyard?" I stared at the strawberry-sized stone he had handed to me.

His mouth tilted into a lopsided smile. Faint creases formed at the outer corners of eyes. "I grew up in a farming village far east of here. It's long gone now—abandoned when the rain stopped coming—but I like to keep its traditions alive. When a newcomer arrived, my people would offer them a piece of the earth in order to welcome them." He closed my hand around the stone. "That said, I'd like to be the first to welcome you to Black Valley. It's hardly as beautiful or forgiving as your homeland, but while you're here, what is mine is yours."

"That's very ... um ... unexpected." The stone pressed against my palm. Only Kaylan had welcomed Samuel and me to Red Ridge, but I always wished that others had too. "You hardly know me. Why would you offer me this?"

"Because," he embraced my hands, "I know how hard this experience must be for you. And I would like to help this little bee," he tapped my nose, "return to her hive."

"I don't know what to say." How could this thoughtful man be the same person who had crudely flirted with me while insulting Bryce and his home? Perhaps I had misjudged him. After all that had happened to me, I had been more on edge than usual. I placed the stone in the pocket opposite the one that held my compass. "Thank you."

His smile spread. "If you do exactly as I tell you, you'll return to Samuel's awaiting embrace soon."

"I never told you or Bryce his name," I said.

He pointed to his temple. "I know all, Buttercup. You need to trust me." He swung the knapsack off his shoulder and pulled Bryce's potato-chopping knife from the outer flap. "First, you'll need to deliver this for me tonight."

"Deliver it? It's not even yours to give away," I said louder than intended. Bryce gestured for us to keep quiet, so I lowered my voice to a whisper. "I'm not going to steal Bryce's knife and give it to someone else."

"It's all right. I'll bring him a finer blade by tomorrow morning." He held up the knife, squinting at it. "Yes, this is poor quality. I'm doing him a favor by getting rid of it."

"Not only are you haughty and self-absorbed, but you're also a thief." How could I have let my guard down? Clearly, he had told me what I wanted to hear so I'd help him with this dishonest task.

"My, you're difficult." He rolled his eyes, sighing. "Let's do this. Take the knife with you. If you meet this man and do not think he deserves this blade, then you may place it back on Bryce's table when the two of you return later. Deal?" He tucked the knife under my belt before I could agree.

"It's going back on the table," I said.

"We'll see." He fiddled with the hem of my shirt, concealing the knife beneath it.

From the corner of my eye, I noticed Bryce waving for us to join him.

"Looks like we're being summoned." Carter hooked his arm around mine. "Shall we?"

I scanned our surroundings once more and, seeing no sign of danger, I stepped out into the open with Carter. We walked about fifteen feet before two men appeared from behind a building. Bryce stood and faced them as they approached.

"Who are they?" I asked.

"Red Bands. Members of Black Valley's City Guard." Carter spoke low into my ear. "As long as we bribe these two each month, they keep hush regarding Bryce's whereabouts and give us passage into the city."

"I don't understand," I said. "Why would Bryce's location need to be kept secret?"

"It's a long story. Ask Bryce to tell you sometime." He quickened his pace, avoiding eye contact with me. "Right now, I have business to attend to."

Tightness formed in my chest. Whatever forced Bryce into hiding couldn't be good.

The men were no farther than five steps away from the graveyard's fence. One, a portly man in his forties, carried a lantern. Each time he stepped forward, the flame's glow whisked across his prominent nose and angled brows. The other man, tall and thin, slunk behind him, looking nervously over his shoulder. Each man wore a knee-length black coat with brass buttons. A red band adorned their sleeves. Swords—less ornate than Mallory's—hung from their belted waists. When they reached Bryce, the portly man spoke. I strained to hear their conversation.

"Half a pack," Bryce said to the guards. "That's always been our arrangement."

The guards glared at Carter and me when we joined them. If the exchange went badly, I could outrun the heavy one. The other, with his long legs, might keep up with me.

"Good evening, gentlemen." Carter strode forward, extending both arms as if presenting himself to an audience. The guards exhaled with impatience.

Bryce frowned at Carter. "I'm being told that we owe an entire pack. Is there something you forgot to tell me?"

Carter shrugged nonchalantly. "I needed some extra things this month, and our fine friends were able to retrieve them for me." He patted the portly guard on the shoulder affectionately. "In return, I promised them a full pack for their excellent work."

Bryce clutched Carter by the vest and pulled him close. "Do you know how many people in the Slag those medicinal plants can help? What was so important that you had to have? " Bryce shoved him away without waiting for an answer and turned to the two guards. "We're not doubling your cut. That's final."

The thin guard leapt over the fence and lunged toward Bryce. The two scowled at each other, their faces mere inches apart.

I placed my fingers on the knife. I would fight alongside Bryce. He saved my life, and I owed him for that. Not to mention, I might never return to Samuel if something happened to him. Of course, I had never assaulted anyone before with a knife.

"What will you do?" Bryce said to the guard. "Kill me? Cut off your supply permanently? I think not."

"I'm tired of this month-to-month game with you, healer." The guard's mouth twisted into a threating sneer as he placed his hand on his weapon's handle. "I think it's time you reveal your source." Then, glancing at his companion, he added, "How long are we supposed to act like dogs begging for scraps?"

Carter glimpsed at my hand, which now gripped the knife's handle. He mouthed the word "no," to me and then wedged himself between Bryce and the guard.

"There's no need for violence." Carter brushed off the guard's coat. "I honestly had no idea that you felt like you weren't being fairly compensated. Next month, we'll bring you two full packs. I doubt you'll be able to move more than that without drawing attention to yourselves." In a singsong voice, he added, "One often makes mistakes when their judgment is clouded by greed."

The thin guard grabbed Carter by the neck. "You, of all people, are calling me greedy?"

In unison, Bryce and I dove to help Carter, pulling at the guard's arms. The portly one shouted at us while struggling to climb over the fence. Once he landed on our side with a thump, he barged into our scuffle, pushing us apart.

"Knock it off," he said. "Carter's right. We'll need the help of his blasted visions especially now that the silver-haired prick has returned to Black Valley. That man would behead us on the spot if he caught us doing business with the likes of him." He glowered at Bryce, who glared back in challenge.

Goose bumps tingled on my arms. I'd never heard of an act as violent as beheading. For a moment, I rubbed my neck, praying we wouldn't encounter the silver-haired man.

"Well, it's best we stop wasting time then." Carter tugged at my knapsack, but I jerked away and glanced at Bryce.

"It's all right." Bryce slouched in defeat. "Give him the knapsack."

I nudged Carter away and offered the knapsack to the portly guard. He rummaged through the contents before grunting with satisfaction. Then he emptied the contents into his own knapsack and handed me back ours.

The thin guard stared at me, sliding his tongue across his lower lip. "They won't bring us two knapsacks next month. That is, unless we hold onto some collateral."

My heart stopped.

Bryce moved in front of me. "You'll do no such thing."

"Agreed," the other guard said. "They'll keep their word. I know what Carter holds dear in this city." He looked directly at Carter, who in turn swallowed so hard that his Adam's apple bobbed.

"Then I suppose we have everything squared away." Carter pulled at his collar. His neck was still red from where the guard had grabbed him. "Morning will be on us in a few hours. I'm sure the two of you must be off to protect our fine city from the Culling and so on."

"The Culling?" Both guards laughed, and then the portly one nudged his foul companion in the arm. "Come on, we got what we came for."

His companion glowered at us. "Good idea. These three stink like graveyard dirt. I can barely stomach it." He spat on the ground near our feet and then the two left together.

I relaxed, relieved to have them gone.

"I can't believe you sometimes," Bryce said to Carter once the guards were out of earshot. "How am I supposed to harvest two full packs for them and have enough for the ill?"

After seeing how the thin guard threatened Bryce, I feared what might happen if he didn't deliver two packs next month. "Bryce, I'll help you. That is, providing I make it home."

"Problem solved." Carter grinned, straightening Bryce's cloak. "An island native will be there to help you from now on. So quit worrying."

Bryce swatted Carter away. "Give me the map."

Carter dug into his pocket, pulled out a folded sheet of paper, and handed it to Bryce. "Take this route and you'll avoid patrol. Waste no time." Then, he regarded me. "Darling," the word roused his familiar smile, "I'm afraid I must depart and leave you with less enjoyable company. Just for now."

"Where're you going?" I asked.

"Don't fret, Sunshine. You'll do exactly as you're meant to." He then gave a solemn nod to Bryce before hopping the fence and dashing into the village.

"He forgot to leave us his knapsack," I said. "Don't we need to deliver it to the ill?"

"Carter's pack will make it to them eventually. For a high price, of course. He sells his share exactly like those guards do." He rubbed his neck, sighing. "I have to bring him one full knapsack every month in order to pay for his help. Carter does for Carter, Ri. He'll never change. Don't let him fool you."

"Oh," was all I could muster. I placed my hand in my pocket and rolled the stone he had given me between my fingers. His gift seemed so sincere, but there was a lot I didn't know about Carter's intentions.

"There's not much time." Bryce glanced at the map. "The man who can repair your compass is on the way. We'll stop there first." He hurried ahead and I followed him into the village.

CHAPTER 6

The stench of feces assaulted me as I raced after Bryce into the cover of a moonlit alley. Dilapidated brick homes blackened by crud flanked us on either side. Their doors and shutters rattled in the bone-chilling wind. Every few yards, small lanterns dangled from iron poles, casting patches of light on the snow-covered ground. Apparently, these homes weren't abandoned like I thought.

Without slowing his pace, Bryce studied Carter's map. A red line zigzagged across the sheet of paper. "Carter provides me a map each month so I can avoid patrol."

"I don't understand. Why do the guards want to hurt you?" I leapt over a mound of snow to keep up. Slush soaked my shoes, numbing my toes.

He tucked the map back into his pocket. "I'll explain later. Promise."

Our alley intersected with another, and he turned right, speeding up. We raced farther into the maze of pathways, and the gale plowed into us. Waves of snowy mist cascaded off tiled roofs. I covered my face to shield myself from the flurry of ice droplets.

My heart had just started to pound from the run when Bryce stopped near a squat, brick building. Hunching, he grasped his ribs with one hand and leaned against the building with the other. A faint sheen of sweat glistened on his forehead. His breath came fast and shallow, flaring his nostrils.

"Are you all right?" I asked.

Grimacing, he nodded quickly and consulted the map once more. "Block thirty-eight. The man who can fix your compass lives here." He covered his mouth to muffle a cough.

"Are you sure you're all right?" I placed my hand on his back.

At my touch, he immediately straightened his posture and inhaled deeply. A raspy sound came with his breath. "I'm a little winded, that's all."

A little winded? Unlikely! His face had turned pallid. "You look like you're about to pass out."

"You don't need to worry." His lips pinched into a pained smile as he turned away and knocked on the building's door. "I'm fine. Honest."

"Clearly he wasn't.

The door swung open and I flinched. An old man poked his head out the door and looked in both directions.

"You must be Parkin?" Bryce asked.

Without answering, the man tugged us inside and closed the door, sealing us in a mixed stench of boiled food and waste. Gagging, I pulled my collar over my nose to block the odor. Though the home's exterior didn't promise much, I had hoped that an exciting workshop filled with mysterious contraptions awaited inside. But instead of walls stocked with tools or shiny brass things like my compass, a drab, dark hallway stretched before us.

Parkin raised his lantern—the only source of light in the room—and scrutinized us. Shadows pooled under his eyes, and the corners of his mouth drooped to his jawline. He had a face like a withered apple, lined with creases that suggested years of mean-spiritedness.

Bryce offered his hand and a well-mannered smile. "I'm Bryce, and this is Ri." Though his breathing had returned to normal, his words came hoarse.

"I know." Parkin narrowed one eye. "Carter said you'd be pestering me tonight. The two of you have no respect, waking an old man up at this hour." An accent roughened his words, making the Crooked Tongue sound much less refined.

"Oh." Bryce's smile faded. "I'm sorry. Carter didn't tell us that our visit would inconvenience you."

The old man shook his head and spit on the dirt floor. "That's Carter's way, isn't it? Only tellin' people the half of things." He waved us forward. "Let's get on with it. Follow me."

The glowing orb of Parkin's lantern swayed as he limped ahead. Never had I entered a home with no main room or hearth. Even Bryce's cave had that much. This place, cold as its owner, seemed like nothing more than an endless corridor. Shelter perhaps, but not a home.

Every half dozen steps or so, the lantern's light landed on hole-ridden, floor-to-ceiling curtains covering the entrances of other rooms. Curious, I peeked behind one. A small room awaited on the opposite side. On the floor, two sleeping children were huddled together on a patch of straw. Next to them, a weak fire flickered in an earthenware pot. The light fell onto the children's ashen faces, filling the hollows of their cheeks with shadows. Had they not been shivering, I would have mistaken them for corpses.

"This is horrible." I scanned the room in search of a blanket. "Why are they all alone in this cold room? Where are their parents?"

Bryce joined me while Parkin continued on without us.

"This area is known as the Slag, Black Valley's poorest quarter. These are merely two of the countless orphans that reside here." Hints of moisture glistened in his eyes as he removed his cloak. "I do what I can to help, but it's hardly enough."

Parkin cleared his throat loudly. He stood at the end of the hall with one hand on his hip while the other held the lantern in front of his face. Disapproval shone in his hooded eyes. "Would you two lovebirds hurry up?"

Bryce nudged me onward. "Go ahead, I'll catch up."

After walking a few steps, I looked over my shoulder. Bryce had slipped into the room. When he emerged he was no longer holding his cloak.

"You covered them with your cloak?" I placed my hand over my heart, staring at the goose bumps forming on his neck.

He shrugged one shoulder. "They need it more than I do."

The worn-down fabric of his shirt looked like it might disintegrate in a strong wind. Since I was layered up with the extra clothing Carter had brought me, I started to remove a shirt to offer him. He grasped my hand to stop me.

"That's not necessary." He tugged the hem of my shirt back down to my waist. "The cold will help me stay alert tonight."

I gaped at him, stunned by his generosity. Even in the dim hallway, honey-tone glints sparkled in his kind eyes. I couldn't break my gaze from them.

"Ri," he whispered, "Parkin's waiting."

I jolted. "Oh, of course, Parkin." What had come over me? Quickly, I turned around and hastened down the hall.

Parkin disappeared behind a curtain, taking the lantern light with him. Bryce and I followed him into a room that was identical in size to the one the children occupied. Moonlight fell through a single glass-paned window. Flames crackled on a pile of wood in a small fireplace. Baskets cluttered the floor, leaving sparse patches in which to stand. The baskets overflowed with chipped plates and mugs, random fragments of wood furnishings, and unrecognizable metal items. Every movement we made stirred dust motes, giving the room a hazy feel.

Bryce knelt and sifted through a basket filled to the brim with fancy buttons. "You've salvaged all this?"

Parkin affirmed with a grunt. "I'll sell any of it for a fair price."

Bryce stepped away from the basket, waving his hands from side to side. "Oh, I have no money."

"Then keep your paws off," Parkin barked. "Carter said you had a broken compass."

I pulled the compass from my pocket and offered it to him. While he examined the damage by the firelight, scraps of wood in the corner of the room caught my attention. Though splintered and smashed, the curved panels resembled the bow of a small rowboat.

"I have a glass face that will fit this nicely." Parkin opened a small chest and dug through its contents.

I pointed at the shards of wood. "What happened to that boat?"

He raised his chin and offered a satisfied smile that showed his yellowed teeth. "My boys and I chopped it up. That's what happened to it. It's better used for kindling than boating. There's no place left in the world worth sailing to."

I exhaled an irritated breath. My homeland was worth sailing to.

Bryce rubbed is jaw. "No boats have been allowed in or out of Black Valley for over a decade. Where did you find it?"

"Carter gave me a tip two nights prior." Parkin's laugh grated against my ears. "He said there'd be a treasure waiting for me where the docks used to be, and wouldn't you know it, he was right."

My heart sank. How would I ever find another boat to take me home? "I can't believe you destroyed it."

Parkin nodded, still chuckling. "Don't look so broken up over it. Carter gave me that tip as means of payment for repairing your compass." He went back to rummaging through the chest.

Keeping an eye on the old man, I turned to Bryce and lowered my voice. "Carter would have known I needed that boat."

So much for the self-absorbed liar helping the little bee return to her hive.

"I understand how badly you want to return home," Bryce whispered. "But if you took to the sea, you'd get yourself killed. For once, Carter did the right thing."

Parkin banged a wrench against a metal chest three times. Bryce and I flinched at the racket. "Quit murmuring sweet nothings over there," the old man said. "Finish your delivery. I'll have this compass fixed by the time you return."

"No offense, but I don't know you." I swiped my compass out of his hand. "I'm not going to leave it here."

Parkin's frown deepened the wrinkles around his mouth. "Foolish girl. Do you think I'd cross Carter and keep your blasted compass?"

"I have no idea if you'd cross Carter." I turned to leave.

Bryce blocked my path. "Ri, wait. He may be a grouch, but I believe he'll do as promised."

"I'm not so sure …" I looked down at my compass. The frail needle bobbed beneath the fractured glass. If I refused Parkin's help, my most treasured possession would never see repair.

Bryce gently prodded me. "We have to hurry."

I nodded. "Well, I suppose if a duck doesn't dunk her head in the water, she misses dinner."

"Uh …" Bryce smiled. "That's a way of putting it."

I handed the compass to Parkin. Then, I placed my hands on my hips, puffing my chest. "Crossing me will be far worse than crossing Carter."

He looked me up and down, smirking. "Oh, I doubt that."

Bryce tugged my sleeve. I stepped around the baskets and followed him toward the frayed curtain that covered the door. I paused at the threshold and glanced at Parkin one last time. He had found a glass face and was comparing its size against my compass's casing. With a deep breath, I exited the room.

Together, Bryce and I patted the walls of the dark corridor, finding our way to the building's exit. After a few dozen steps, he pushed the door open. A gust of fresh air greeted me, saving me from the putrid stench that festered inside.

Bryce referred to his map once more and then we were off, racing through Black Valley's grid of pathways. Before long, the sound of rushing water rose in the distance.

"Is that the ocean?" I asked. It sounded no more than fifty feet away.

"It is." Panting, he stopped running and bent over, placing his hands on his knees. His ribs expanded and collapsed with rapid breaths.

"You look like you're near collapse." I hovered near him. "Why don't we rest?"

He stood upright, inhaling through his nose and exhaling through his mouth. "No, we must keep moving. Are you all right to continue?"

At my nod, we ran a few more bounds before he paused once more, slouched over, and coughed.

"You need to catch your breath," I said.

"No, I'm good," he coughed out the words.

Damn his pride. I took his hand, guiding him toward the roar of the waves. Pausing to view the sea provided an opportunity for him to recover. "I want you to show me the ocean. I've never seen it before."

Clutching his ribs, he considered my demand. His skin had paled to a sickly color. "There's no time—"

"It won't take long. Just a glimpse." I tugged him with more force.

He gnawed on his lip. "All right. A glimpse."

After a short walk down the alley, we emerged from Black Valley's maze of identical homes. Torrents of wind whipped my clothes as we strode toward the edge of a cliff. Roughly twenty feet below, at the base of the bluff, a mass of black water began, stretching all the way to the horizon. Waves rose in massive peaks before crashing down into frills of froth.

I shivered at the sight. Even if I had a boat, the ocean's wrath would smash it as soon as I cast off from shore. I imagined myself clinging to the splintered boards of my destroyed vessel, floating helplessly. My shoulders sank. Four weeks. I was truly going to be trapped in Black Valley until the next dark moon.

Bryce wrapped his arm around me, sheltering me from the wind. Grassy scents lingered in the fabric of his shirt. He must have worn it while foraging on my island. I leaned into him, comforted by the smells of home. The heat of tears formed behind my eyelids.

"Ri," he said softly. "What's wrong?"

"Nothing." I looked down at my feet buried in the snow. "It's just ... you were right. The sea's too dangerous to sail across."

He jerked his head, raising his eyebrows. "Oh. That's why you wanted to see the ocean so badly." Grasping my elbows, he positioned himself in front of me. "Ri, if I could get you home sooner, I would. But reaching your island by boat is impossible. Everyone that has ever tried drowned. Your island earned the nickname Warning Rock because it's believed to mark the cursed edge of the world."

"That's silly." I shook my head. "It's not impossible to reach. I'm proof that it's been done before. Haven't you wondered how I know your language? I learned it from someone who hailed from this side of the sea."

"Um ..." He averted his gaze. "We should get moving. We've wasted a lot of time."

"You're changing the subject." I pivoted in front of him, regaining eye contact. "You have wondered how I know your language, haven't you?"

He spun around and hurried back toward the alley, still breathing heavy. "Please, Ri. We must hurry."

What was he hiding? Once we delivered the medicinal plants, I expected answers. We raced down half a dozen pathways, and the sound of the sea and its tangy scent faded. The alley eventually led to the entrance of a large courtyard. Bryce paused and scanned the expansive area.

The only structure occupying the space was a wall made of a single slab of black stone. It stood alone in the center of the courtyard next to a pair of lanterns atop tall poles. Their light reflected on the stone's polished surface.

"We're almost there," Bryce said, panting.

We raced into the courtyard and took cover behind the wall. Pressing our backs against the slab, we peeked around the corner. Fortunately, no one—guards or otherwise—strolled the courtyard. We exchanged a glance and then snuck toward the far end of the wall. Halfway, I noticed something move across the slab—perhaps a flicker of light from the nearby lanterns. My gaze darted to the spot.

"Oh my." I gasped.

Dozens of lifelike portraits were etched into one half of the wall. A column of writing scrolled down the opposite half.

"What is this?" I stepped backward, taking it in.

"It's called the Stained Wall." Bryce gestured at the column of writing. "Those are the ordinances. Breaking any of those rules is punishable by death. And on that side," he pointed to the portraits, "are the wanted. They live as fugitives now, hiding from Black Valley's unforgiving Red Bands." He sighed. "Third column, fourth one down. That's me."

Though the engraved portrait resembled Bryce, the brows were thick, the eyes dark slits, and the mouth a twisted sneer.

"It's a rather menacing depiction of me, of course," he added.

After seeing Bryce give his only cloak to the two shivering children in the Slag, I couldn't imagine him committing an act so heinous that it warranted his death. "That's absurd. It can't be you."

He opened and closed his mouth as if trying to find the right words. Just then, one of the engravings disappeared.

I pointed at the vacant spot. "Did you see that?"

He pulled me close, placing his index finger over his lips. "Shhh. Please, not so loud. Let's find cover, then I'll explain."

"Of course," I whispered, bobbing my head. Moving carefully, I avoided contact with the creepy wall and followed him. But the portraits continued to lure my attention. A haggard old woman with short-cropped hair. A man with thick eyebrows pressed together in a fierce scowl. Another man whose lips pulled back, baring large teeth as he snarled. And an old man, bald, save a few tufts of hair tracing the lower regions of his scalp.

"Stop!" I yanked Bryce's arm and leaned toward the wall, squinting at the etching. "That's Samuel."

"What?" He tilted his head and gave me a blank look.

"That's Samuel." I jabbed my finger at the drawing. "Don't you recognize him from the forest?"

"The forest?" His mouth fell open as he looked back and forth between the portrait and me. "No, Ri." He shook his head. "That can't be the man I saw you with."

"Yes, it is! Why's he on this awful wall?" I scraped some ice off the portrait, hoping that my mind was playing tricks on me. The subject's eyes glared with sternness, but the creases in the forehead, the slight bump on the bridge of the nose, and the ears that stuck out ever so slightly, matched Samuel's likeness perfectly.

Bryce pulled me away from the wall. "We can't stay here. Come on."

I stumbled after him, looking over my shoulder at the eerie engravings. Not once had I considered that Samuel hailed from dismal Black Valley. In his stories, the people of his city valued art, invention, and fairness. He never spoke of starving children, greedy guards, or merciless beheadings.

Bryce tugged me out of our hiding place and we bolted toward an alley on the opposite side of the courtyard. Once we reached cover, we slowed our pace to a brisk walk.

"The tyrant who rules this city used dark magic to create that wall." Bryce kept his voice low while his gaze darted around our surroundings. "When one of the wanted dies, their etching disappears.

Likewise, as the offender ages, so does their portrait. Are you sure you recognized that engraving? It's rather dark out."

"I've never been so sure of anything." Chills raced over my flesh. Voice wavering, I asked, "What crime is he accused of?"

Bryce placed his hand on my back, urging me to quicken my pace. I felt his muscles go tense. "Inciting a massacre."

"What!" I stopped walking. The warmth of blood drained from my face. "Samuel's the kindest person I know. He took me as a ward when I had no one else to care for me. A killer would never do something like that."

Bryce faced me, bracing my shoulders. "Ri, when we met and I heard you speak this language, I suspected you had a connection with one of Black Valley's fugitives. I never brought it up because I didn't want to offend you."

He glanced toward the courtyard, listening for a moment. "A couple decades ago, a silly rumor popped up among the city's wanted that they could seek refuge on Warning Rock. It was said that Eisanea would bless the innocent and grant them safe passage across the sea so they could start a new, peaceful life." He looked down at our feet, shuffling snow around. "Dozens of people made secret journeys in poorly crafted boats and rafts—some with entire families aboard. It was said that every vessel sunk shortly after casting off. The sea took all. Innocent and guilty alike."

I covered my mouth. "That's terrible ... those poor people ... but if Samuel survived the journey, does that mean—"

"Eisanea granted him safe passage?" Bryce shook his head. "Unlikely. It was just a silly rumor."

"Samuel's success is not a fluke." I searched his eyes. "Eisanea protects the innocent."

"Let's finish the delivery and we'll discuss this later when we're somewhere safe." He rubbed his hands together for warmth. His flimsy shirt flapped in the wind, and his nose had turned red-raw from the cold.

"All right." I wanted answers, but Bryce needed shelter from the brutal winds since he no longer wore his cloak.

When we reached the end of the alley, he crouched near a home and wiggled a loose brick out of its foundation. "This is where I drop off my delivery each month."

He shoved his hand into the gap he had made and patted around inside. "I had a couple of apprentices before I moved underground. It's too risky to meet them in person now that I'm wanted, but they'll pick up this delivery by sunrise and use the herbs to treat the sick."

I knelt next to him. "So why are you on the wall?"

A grin tugged at his mouth. "I punched a Red Band. It was foolish, but it felt good at the time. Sometimes I have a hard time holding my tongue around them." He pulled a small cloth bag out of the hole and sighed. "I always ask them not to do this."

"What is it?"

He opened the bag. "My apprentices left some turnips and carrots for us. Normally I wouldn't take food from them, but I have barely enough at home stored for myself, let alone you."

I shrugged. "I'll be fine. I'm used to skipping meals."

"Don't be silly. I brought you here, the least I can do is make sure that you don't starve to death." He removed his knapsack and flipped it open. Our hands collided as we both reached for the herbs at the same time. My stomach fluttered at our accidental touch.

"You first," he said with a smile.

I grabbed a few packets and placed them carefully through the slot in the wall. As we unloaded the pack, my mind swirled with the horrid story he told me. Gentle Samuel would have never started a massacre. It had to be a mistake.

We had almost emptied the knapsack when someone coughed in the courtyard.

Heart in my throat, I leapt to my feet and raced to the end of the alley to investigate. A guard was heading in our direction. In about ten paces he'd reach the mouth of the alley. I looked at Bryce, who was hurriedly dumping the knapsack's contents into the hole. I dashed back to him as he shoved the brick into place.

"It's a guard." My heartbeat ramped up.

"I'm going to lead him off. I don't want you to get caught with me." He pulled a necklace cord out from under his shirt. At its end dangled a charm that caught the moonlight, glistening like a shard of ice.

"This amulet is what allows me to travel through waterfalls. Hold on to it and hide here. If I don't make it back, one of my apprentices will arrive in a few hours. They'll look after you. Do you remember what I told you about moon cycles?"

He stared at me with wide eyes, clutching his ribs.

"Um ..." I imagined the guard pursuing him like a dog on a hare. How long would it take before Bryce buckled over, wheezing? In his condition, even an unfit guard could capture him. "I ... uh ..."

"Ri, listen. Wait until the dark moon and then ask my apprentice to take you to the crypts. Follow the rope. Get to the waterfall. Understand?"

At some point I had stopped breathing. Was he seriously rambling about a backup plan in case a guard captured—or killed—him? Every part of me was shaking. "No." I shoved him and the amulet away.

He stumbled backward, reaching for me as I raced off. "What the—"

"I'm faster. Meet me at Parkin's." I hurried away before he had any hope of catching up.

"Are you crazy? Come back!" His words trailed off as I burst into the open courtyard.

CHAPTER 7

I was alone in the open courtyard when reality hit me hard as the fierce wind. I hardly knew Bryce, yet I was risking my life in order to save his. Had I gone mad?

The guard cursed as I cut across his path. Immediately, he took pursuit. Pulse pounding, I quickened my pace. My breath rose in visible puffs to join the night sky. The crystalline crunch of snow accompanied the sound of my footfalls. I darted past the Stained Wall and rushed into an alley, wrecking its silence as my shoe smashed through a frozen puddle.

"Stop, Slag-trash!" the guard shouted.

I rounded the corner into the next alley, tripping as I charged into a heap of calf-deep snow. Hastily, I rose back to standing. A few seconds lost, a few strides gained by my pursuer. Unlike the other alleys, this pathway rose and dipped in white dunes, promising to slow me down further. My island rarely saw more than a foot of powder, so my legs fumbled, unfamiliar with the challenge. By the time I reached the next alley—a packed down, trodden path, thank Eisanea—the guard's voice echoed no more than twenty feet behind me.

Anxiety skittered through my veins. I glanced over my shoulder. The guard pumped his arms, leaping over snow, gaining on me.

Clouds of steam puffed out of his mouth. Without slowing his pace, he scooped something off the ground and hurled it at me.

The object, a thick scrap of wood, whacked my ankle, sending a sharp pain up my leg. I pitched forward, landing full-length on the ground. The impact knocked the air out of my lungs. I went cold with panic. The sound of the guard's footsteps rushed toward me. My heart hammered. I rolled over as he pounced.

He landed on my hips, his weight clamping me firmly in place against the snow. I clawed at his face, flailing like a fish in a bear's mouth. Homes surrounded us. I screamed. No one came to help.

"You're past curfew, Slag-girl." Pockmarks covered his cheeks and the tip of his wide nose. When he sneered, the crevices in his lumpy skin deepened, and the texture of his flesh resembled a head of cauliflower.

I swung at him with all the force I had, but he snatched my arms and pinned them over my head. Pinpricks tingled in my fingers as the blood stopped flowing into my hands.

"What's the matter Slag-girl?" he yelled, heaving booze-heavy breath. During the struggle, a flask had fallen out of his coat's side pocket. "Do you think I bite?" He bared his chipped teeth and chomped the air in front of my face.

My thoughts scattered like startled sparrows. I shoved my feet into the snow and tried to push free, but my soles slipped. "Letting me go will be the smartest choice you make tonight," I said, voice shaking.

"You think someone's coming for you?" He chuckled to himself. His eyes glinted with malice as he looked around. "They know better."

Chatter murmured from within the hovels, but no rescue came. I was on my own. Swallowing hard, I shoved down my fear. I arched my head back and glanced at his chapped hands around my wrists. He'd need to let go of one wrist to do anything further to me. The flat of Bryce's potato-chopping knife pressed against my hip.

"Just my luck to get captured by the ugliest guard in the lot," I said.

Laughing, he gripped the collar of my shirt in his teeth and yanked the fabric. Three buttons popped off my garment. His hot breath hit my skin. I wanted to disappear. I wanted to wake up safe in my bed, in my own village.

I jerked my head, but he rammed his mouth, flakey and rough as sawdust, against mine. His tongue pushed against my lips, prying them apart.

That was his mistake.

I sank my teeth into his lower lip. The tender skin broke, gushing. He reeled back and let out a scream that drove into my skull. I spat blood and a slug-like piece of his lip out of my mouth. The acrid taste remained on my tongue.

He backhanded me. Heat and pain raced across my cheek. My head lolled to the side. Stars flooded my vision like sparks snapping out of a fire. The taste of blood swelled in my mouth. I shook the dazed feeling away.

Cursing, the guard patted his mouth, exploring his new deformity. I went for my knife. It slid out of my belt as if it had been waiting for the opportunity all night. I aimed at his thigh. The blade ripped his pants and skidded along his flesh, but the impact knocked the weapon from my frozen fingers. My captor's leg jerked, giving me enough space to slide out from under him. I staggered to my feet and ran off into the night, leaving the knife behind.

He soon followed. Though my ankle throbbed painfully, I gritted my teeth, forcing myself onward. Then, a single Firefly appeared from behind a shack. Where were the others? My glowing companion led me toward an iron fence at the end of the alley. The posts, twice as tall as a man, resembled spears aiming toward the heavens.

"I like it when they run," the guard shouted, roughly thirty paces behind me. His words slurred together.

Using the posts for balance, I limped along the fence chasing the Firefly. My ankle was about to give. Between my soaked shoes and clothes, I was numbed to my bones. I tried to hold my shirt closed. I felt nauseous. I wanted to be home and listening to one of Samuel's stories by the warmth of our hearth. I hated Black Valley. I hated that guard. The Firefly circled a loose post in the fence and then disappeared.

"Slag-girl," the guard called. "I can chase you all night."

I pushed the loose post forward, making a gap large enough that I could squeeze through. I hurried toward a cluster of abandoned, dilapidated hovels that lacked doors and shutters.

"An eye for an eye, Slag-girl," the guard shouted. "But I'll cut off more than your lips."

I looked over my shoulder. He had slipped through the fence and was sprinting in my direction. Clenching my teeth, I hobbled quickly as I could, but the sound of his heavy stomps grew louder behind me.

There was a tug on my braid and then my sleeve. I stumbled. His hand smacked the back of my head. I whipped around and punched him in the lip. He slammed me against a wall, holding me in place by the neck. I swung at his face, but he dodged me. He pressed his hand harder against my throat, cutting off my air. I scratched at his wrist, while my legs went weak.

"Step away from the girl." A man emerged from a hovel that marked the end of the alley and the beginning of a courtyard. He had a muscular build and posture that was unusually straight and rigid, as if a spear carved of hard oak supported his spine. A sword hung at his hip and an odd cross-shaped bow clung to his back. He strode toward us with an air of superiority.

The guard released me. I gasped for air. My knees buckled and I would have fallen into the snow if the newcomer hadn't grasped my arm. He wore black leather gloves and a City Guard coat. I froze. I couldn't fight off two Red Bands. Outrunning them was out of the question considering my injury. My breath came in short, panicked breaths. I was going to die.

"Go find your own." The scoundrel glared at the newcomer with a crooked eye. He wiped the ever-flowing blood off his chin with his sleeve.

The man from the hovel made a guttural sound of disapproval. He had a well-built jaw. His shaggy hair matched the color of sleet—and it moved like sleet, blowing sharply in the wind. Earlier, the portly guard had mentioned a silver-haired man bent on beheading people. I glanced at his sword once more. The hilt was plain, with a leather-wrapped grip. The sheathed, straight blade stretched nearly four feet long. It was the perfect weapon for hacking off heads. My lips quivered as I touched my neck.

"You're beyond your reach, Slag-guard," the silver-haired man said. Though it was too dark to see his features or expression, his tone resonated with authority.

The scoundrel placed his hand on his sword and spat a glob of blood near Silver's boots. "This isn't your concern. Go back to your hovel."

Silver stepped closer and some moonlight caught his shoulder. Unlike the scoundrel, he had a symbol on his sleeve consisting of angled stripes. The scoundrel's eyes bulged at the sight of it. He staggered a few steps backward.

"Oh, sir. That's not what I meant." The scoundrel laughed nervously, waving his palms back and forth. "I mean, you don't need to concern yourself with such trivial matters. I'm handling this. You see, this Slag-girl's on the Stained Wall and I'm arresting her."

"That's not true," I blurted.

"Quiet," Silver ordered. He placed two fingers on my chin, gently turned my head, and looked at my cheek. It still burned from the Slag-guard's backhand. The moonlight shone on my face, and I was sure that both men noticed my lip trembling. Silver's expression still remained hidden in shadow.

"I know all of the faces on the wall. She's not one of them." The glint in Silver's eyes shifted downward, toward my torn shirt. "And this doesn't look like an arrest to me."

"Well, sir ..." The guard rubbed the back of his neck. "I assure you, all is in order."

Silver turned his head and looked down his nose at the guard. At that angle, the moonlight illuminated his features. I guessed him to be in his late twenties as only few lines creased his forehead. The sandy grit of facial hair lined his jaw. He had clever gray eyes deep set under low eyebrows. His lips curved downward, and I doubted he smiled often.

The guard scrunched his face, studying Silver as well. Then, as if someone splashed him with cold water, he opened his eyes wide and his body jolted. "Oh bollocks, it's you. I mean, you're back. I mean ..." He patted Silver on the shoulder, grinning. His eyes twitched nervously. "Welcome home, sir. I didn't realize it was you. Uh ..." He glanced at me as if I might help him string together his sentence. I folded my arms. He looked back at Silver. "Forgive these old eyes of mine, sir. I'm sorry, I should've recognized you."

Silver lifted his hand to hush the guard. "Return to the Slag."

"Yes, sir." The guard walked backward, bobbing his head. "Thank you, sir."

"You can't let him leave," I said to Silver. Perhaps it was foolish to take such a demanding tone with an intimidating stranger, but letting that filth run off was hardly justice. "That man planned to kill me."

Silver watched the guard slip through the fence and disappear into the Slag. He gave me a sideways glance. "You're not from the Slag."

"I most certainly am." I stepped to the side to wedge some space between us, but he raised his arm, blocking my path. His sleeve ended at the wrist, perfectly fitted. The fabric was black as a raven's feather. None of the other Red Bands I had encountered that night donned such crisp, new garments.

"Not so fast." He drew his eyebrows together, scowling. The look would have made anyone nervous. Perhaps this was no rescue at all. Perhaps this was one dog claiming another's bone.

"The way you enunciate your words is too refined," he continued. "No one speaks like that in the Slag. However," he drew out the word, rubbing the stubble on his chin, "you're not from the Rose Quarter either."

I craned my neck, trying to level my eyes with his. An impossible task since he towered at least a foot taller than me. I spoke to the underside of his chin. "Please, I just want to go home." A lump formed in my throat. I had never meant those words more in my life.

He reached over my head and I flinched. "For the swelling." He knocked a couple of icicles off the roof's eave and placed them on my cheek.

I accepted the icicles and pressed them flat against the corner of my mouth. My cheek throbbed underneath the chill.

"A young lady should know better than to wander Black Valley at night." He gestured toward his hovel. "Come with me. I'll have someone escort you home—wherever that may be."

I dropped one of the icicles, and it speared the snow at my feet. My stomach fell to join it. I nearly died leading one guard away from Bryce. I couldn't return to the Slag with another. "I don't need to be escorted home."

"Yes, you do."

"No." I hobbled a few steps over a mound of snow, heading toward the fence. Wincing, I reacquainted myself with the pain of placing pressure on my ankle. "I can find my way."

"All you'll find is more trouble," he said. "You can't walk, let alone run."

From behind, I heard him huffing toward me, each step heavy and determined. He caught up and grabbed me by the waist. I smacked his arm once in protest before he scooped me up and hoisted me over his shoulder like a sack of turnips.

"Put me down right now!" I pummeled his back with my fists, but he didn't seem to care.

"Quiet. This is an inconvenience for me as well." He carried me into the one-room shack.

A window let in a smudge of moonlight. It traced the edges of worn-down furniture: a two-person table, a chair with broken legs, and a wardrobe closet. He set me down in the corner of the room farthest from the door.

"I don't need someone to take me home," I said.

He had the nerve to walk away from me and head to the wardrobe closet. The lopsided cabinet blew a cloud of dust in his face when he opened the door. He swatted the air, scattering the motes, and then he reached inside the cabinet and pulled out a blanket. "You're in luck."

"You have an odd definition of luck." I stared at the door. With my injury, I'd never make it past the threshold without him stopping me.

He tossed me the blanket, and I caught it out of reflex—not because I wanted it. The sticky cotton of spider webs clung to my palms.

"How long has this been in there? I think it's filled with spiders." I dropped the blanket on the ground.

"Any spiders in there are long frozen." He strode to the window and leaned against its frame. He whistled twice, as if to call a dog. "I have five men investigating the square with me tonight. One will be here shortly to take you home."

I joined him and looked out the window at the courtyard. A fountain with a statue in its center dominated its far end. Other than that, the area was lifeless. Only the snow-shredding wind explored the surrounding buildings.

"Do you live here?" I asked.

"No." He looked at me for a second. "I live where duty calls me."

"Oh." I fidgeted with my sleeve. "But what duty calls you to abandoned buildings?"

"If I answer that question, you'll be too afraid to close your eyes tonight." He swept the blanket off the floor and shook it. I heard what sounded like the drizzle of pebbles tapping the floor. I shuddered, imagining hard, frozen spider bodies. After three shakes, he beat the cobwebs out of the fabric and swung the blanket around me, netting me like a fish. At first, the cool fabric sent goose bumps racing over my skin, but it soon collected enough of my body heat to reflect back to me.

I looked out the window again. "You may think I scare easily because I'm a girl, but I assure you I don't."

He looked at me with his unfriendly, hard-as-hail eyes and drew his dagger. I jerked back. He grabbed the edge of the blanket and sliced a long strip of fabric from it. Then he bent down and proceeded to wrap my ankle.

"Oh," I said. "Um ... thank you."

He secured the dressing in a tight knot and stood.

"Sir?" A young guard entered the door. He had a solid build and stood a couple inches shorter than Silver. Baby fat plumped his cheeks and his eyes were round, alert pools of blue. I guessed him to be a year or two younger than I was. His belt hitched a sword and dagger, though the weapons were hardly as impressive as Silver's.

"Take this young lady home," Silver said. "She claims to live in the Slag."

"Yes sir." The boy bobbed his head and gestured for me to follow him. "Miss?"

Ignoring the young guard, I shoved myself in front of Silver. "I told you that I don't want anyone to escort me home."

He looked me in the eye and smirked. "Her ankle is injured. Carry her if you must."

"Understood, sir." The young guard picked me up, cradling me.

Swaddled in the blanket, I wiggled like a worm. "Tell him to put me down. Right now!"

Silver raised his hand, shooing us off with a bored expression on his face. We were out the door before I could say another word.

The young guard ran with long strides, jumbling me around as he went. I grasped his coat, afraid I might bounce out of his arms. He looked at me with an innocent smile.

"Sorry, to jostle you," he said. "I don't want to be gone too long. What's your block number?"

Though this young guard seemed good-natured, I needed to separate from him before returning to Bryce. He would treat an alleged criminal with much less kindness than an injured girl. "You can set me down at the fence ahead. I don't want to be any more trouble to you."

"Absolutely not." He smiled. His cheeks flushed from the run. "This is no trouble at all. Besides, an order's an order."

"This is silly," I said. "Your leader is being overbearing."

The young man laughed. "Well, that's his nature. You'll have to forgive him for that. After all, he's been hunting the Culling alone for the past six years. He may not be polite, but the man's a legend! Under his command, Black Valley will rise victorious against the Culling."

The guards that Bryce had bribed earlier laughed the Culling off, but I had yet to learn what it was.

"Um ... is that why you're out here tonight?" I asked, hoping that my question didn't reveal my unfamiliarity with Black Valley.

"Now, Miss, you know I can't talk about my mission. But I assure you that you have nothing to fear. Black Valley's strongest and most daring protect the city tonight." He winked.

"But only five of you?" I asked.

A male scream rang through the alley. The young guard stopped, startled. His breath quickened, forming a cloud of steam around his face. Chanting—the same that I had heard in the Dark Woods—laced the wind.

The guard rushed me into an abandoned hovel and set me down. "Stay here and don't come out until I return for you."

"No." I grabbed his sleeve. My hands trembled. "I've encountered these things before. One killed a puma."

"A what-a?" He cocked a brow. "I've no idea what you're talking about, but it's my calling to protect Black Valley."

He pried my hand off his sleeve and charged out the door. The chanting intensified. Making myself small, I scooted into the corner of the room, crouching. Each time a man screamed, I jolted as if stabbed. A thwack and a whimper came from outside the window. My blood raced through my veins. Panic seized my mind. I closed my eyes and took three deep breaths. I needed a weapon.

A split table leg lay to my right. It was the only thing in the room so I grabbed it. The soaked wood broke apart in my hand. I threw it back on the ground. Defense? What a silly idea. The Culling—whatever it was—could probably tear me apart with little effort. My only hope was to retreat to the Slag while the guards kept the predators busy. Judging by the men's horrific cries, the battle would end quickly—and not in Black Valley's favor. I crawled toward the door as footsteps hurried toward the hovel.

The young guard staggered through the door, hunched over and gripping his stomach. He collapsed. I hastened over to him. Blood soaked his clothes. A mess of intestines spilled out of him like a heap of purple rope. It smelled rancid. I couldn't fix this wound. No one could. He looked down at the mess that used to be his torso and cried. I eased him against the wall. His flesh felt clammy as a stone pulled out of a river.

My throat was too tight too speak. So much blood poured out of him. The sound of his raspy breath filled the hovel. Tears pricked behind my eyelids, building each time he whimpered.

Keeping one hand on his wound, he patted around until his other landed upon mine. He squeezed my fingers, coating them in scarlet, as if holding onto me was a means to hold onto life itself. "Stay. Don't leave me alone. Please don't leave me alone."

Goose bumps tingled on my skin at the touch of his cold palm. Helpless to do anything to ease his pain, I layered my other hand over his. "All right, I'm not going anywhere." Of course, deep down,

I wanted to flee. My gaze alternated between him and the door. But instead of racing off, I clasped his hand tighter.

"What's out there?" I asked, shaking.

"Monsters ... the destroyers of mankind." No longer was he the prideful protector. His eyes had seen true horror. His lips trembled, paling to a troubling shade. "The captain ... everyone thought he was crazy, but ... he's right. The Harbingers of the Culling ... travel through water ... through the fountain."

"Did you say through water?" The ability sounded exactly like Bryce's power.

"Through water ..." His last puff of breath rolled into the night air, fading away. Dilated pupils fixed on me in a vacant stare. For a moment, I watched him, as if expecting him to say something else. But the hovel went eerily quiet, and his hand, still grasped in my own, lost any hint of warmth.

There was no more screaming outside, but the chanting continued, roaring as if boosted by victory. I pulled the young man's dagger out of its sheath and huddled in the corner of the room, terrified.

CHAPTER 8

The hovel shuddered in the wind. Crouched in the corner, I gripped my newly acquired dagger as the chanting outside grated against my ears. I remained still as a rock, except for my trembling hands.

Across the room, the dead guard leaned against the wall. His gaping mouth made him look as though he froze while singing a haunting song to the heavens. If only he had listened to me. We could have escaped together. But he was gone. Soon, whatever was out there would find me too. It would rip me apart and leave me to suffer the same fate. Doing my best to stay quiet, I gulped down panicked breaths. Each time the night air brushed against my skin, I swore it was Death's icy fingertips on my neck.

Long minutes passed. Then, in a single gust of wind, the voices vanished. I dared not move. It had to be a trick. Some awful thing planned to pounce on me as soon as I emerged from the hovel. I waited. The wind ceased. Dead silence. I strained, listening. Nothing.

What if the Culling had moved into the Slag in search of more victims? What if Bryce was wandering the alleys, unaware of the danger? What if he heard a sound and mistook it for me. The blood froze in my veins. I imagined the Culling flowing through Black Valley like an expanding shroud: chanting beasts equipped with deadly fangs spilling out of the darkness.

My gaze slid toward the guard again, despite the dread the sight inspired in me. His hand still clutched the purple tangle of intestines blossoming from his center. I covered my mouth as nausea set in.

"Please Bryce," I whispered. "Go to Parkin's and wait for me."

Nerves jangling, I crept to the door. Evidence of a brutal fight scored the moonlit snow. A mash of prints chopped up the powder. Smudges of blood settled into slushy mounds. Boot tracks mottled with crimson trailed toward Silver's hovel and ended in a dark lump outside the door. My breath hitched. I was sure it was the captain lying dead in the snow.

Pulling on the doorframe for balance, I stood, easing weight onto my injured ankle. Spikes of pain shot up my leg, but I gritted my teeth and concentrated on my surroundings. No Fireflies to lead me. A fifty-foot expanse of open space separated me from the fence that marked the edge of the Slag. I placed more weight on my ankle, testing its strength. Tears formed in the corners of my eyes as the agony intensified.

"On the count of three." I prepared myself, inching over the threshold. "One, two …"

I looked at the dark lump again. Perhaps Silver was still alive, but injured. No. He was dead. All of the guards in the Abandoned Quarter were dead. I turned back toward the fence. Its finials knifed into the night sky. I needed to return to the Slag and ultimately to the safety of Bryce's cave.

I took a deep breath. "One." Silver rescued me. "Two." The Slag-guard would have killed me if not for him. "Three." Samuel and Bryce were my priority. Not Silver.

I bolted out of the hovel, racing in the opposite direction of the fence, locking my gaze on the body ahead. Dammit, what was I doing? Did I lack all regard for self-preservation? I hardly knew Silver. I didn't even know his real name! Anxious energy rippled through my veins. I tightened my grip on my dagger. As I neared, the body took shape in the darkness. Limbs sprawled in all directions.

"Silver," I called, but he didn't budge.

I reached the body. The throat was torn from jaw to collarbone. Blood and chunks of viscera clotted around the gash. I collapsed, dizzy from the sight of the gore. How excruciating his final moments must have been. Through tear-blurred vision, I continued to stare at the body. A full head of black hair curled into the snow. It wasn't Silver.

The wind picked up and became a cruel prankster. It clinked against roof tiles and wiggled things that liked to creak. Something howled. With a jolt, I stopped breathing to listen. Surely the sound was a trick of the mind. I fumbled to standing as a man's voice called from the courtyard.

"Is someone there?" The words came strained and desperate. Another guard, no doubt. Not Silver. His authoritative voice could never transform into such a vulnerable, high-pitched tone. "Please don't leave me here."

I snuck along the hovel's wall toward the entry of the courtyard. I peeked around the corner and saw a man lying near the fountain, raising his arm as if begging the heavens for salvation.

I ducked back behind the hovel. If the Culling returned, the last place I would want to be was in an open courtyard with no cover. I remembered how the young guard had warned that the Harbingers of the Culling arrived through the fountain. If some dark creature leapt from its basin, it'd pounce on me instantly. I needed to get back to the Slag, not venture into a deathtrap.

Backing away, I swallowed my sobs. How cowardly I was. But I had no choice if I wanted to survive. Guilt sat in my stomach like a rock.

"Please!" His cries weakened, clearly losing hope. How terrified he must have been, alone and hurt. Samuel raised me better than this.

"Dammit," I whispered to myself. My inner voice of reason faded into the back of my mind. I tightened the bandage around my ankle and hastened into the courtyard. The man turned his head in my direction. Using one arm, he dragged himself toward me. A trail of blood marred the snow behind him.

"Please help me." He struggled to lift his head as I knelt beside him. His smooth skin, probably never roughened by stubble, hinted that he was close in age to me. A stream of crimson slid down his forehead and dripped off the bridge of his upturned nose. His blue eyes, wide with fear and disbelief, glanced over my features before scanning the courtyard behind me. "You're alone?"

I nodded.

"Of all my blasted luck." Wincing, his head collapsed back into the snow. He grasped his stomach with blood-covered hands. The corners of his mouth pulled back as he inhaled rapidly through clenched teeth. At least a half-dozen darts like the one that had struck me near the stream clung to his pants. I went cold, staring at the undeniable proof that the things that attacked Bryce and me in the forest were the same that mauled Black Valley's guards tonight. If Samuel encountered these creatures he'd be incapable of defending himself.

I couldn't stop gawking at all the blood. It was everywhere, an ever-expanding splotch of scarlet crawling over the snow. "Where's your captain?" I asked, unable to steady my voice.

"Fountain." Wheezing, he curled into a fetal position.

Though no movement or sound came from the fountain, I sprang to my feet to search for Silver. If he still lived, he would know if anything could be done to save his subordinate—unless he suffered the same fate. With desperate hope, I rounded the basin. No one lay on the opposite side, but footprints dappled the snow. In one area, a skid mark stretched toward the basin, as if someone had been dragged into it. But only shattered sheets of ice bobbed in the shallow water.

I shuddered at a horrid thought. The Culling—whatever it was—took Silver.

As if expecting answers, I looked up at the stone statue of a woman towering over the fountain's center. The artist carved her generously with full lips and luxurious hair that cascaded down her back in soft waves. Her gown flowed over the curve of her hips down to the arch of her dainty foot. Pink-tinged snow gathered in the folds of her dress. This portrait of feminine beauty, immortalized in a chunk of rock, glared down her nose at the carnage with a triumphant smile that sent chills through me.

"It's only a statue," I told myself. "Stop being silly." I rushed back to the injured guard, eager to escape her unsettling expression.

"I'm going to find help." I grasped his shoulder, but he didn't respond. His vacant eyes stared up at the stars. Dead. He was dead, but the splotch of blood continued to bloom, melting the snow into poppy-colored slush. I choked out a breath, unsure as to how long I had been holding it. Then, from the corner of my eye, I noticed someone emerge from the alley. I drew my dagger. The figure hunched, grasping his side as he raced toward me.

"Ri!" The voice sent my heart leaping.

"Bryce!" I tucked the dagger under my belt and hurried toward him, ignoring the jabs of pain from my ankle.

He sped his pace, but quivered with a cough every few steps. His breath puffed into clouds of mist. I fell into his embrace, repeatedly thanking the gods for his safety.

Clearly exhausted, he leaned most of his weight onto me. Sweat dampened his clothes, and his breath came in short gasps that stirred loose strands of hair poking out of my braid. Once the rise and fall of his chest slowed, he leaned back and looked me over. His gaze bounced from my swollen cheek to my wrapped ankle, and of course to the dead guard curled up in the snow.

"What happened?" His eyes locked on my torn shirt. Loose threads swayed in the breeze, searching for the buttons they once fastened. "I heard you calling for me."

I had never called for him. It must've been a trick of the wind.

I grabbed his arm, tugging him in the direction of the Slag. "We have to get out of here."

"Understood." Pulling me close, he scanned the courtyard as we made our way.

"It was the Culling," I said, trembling. "It was here."

"The Culling?" His brow furrowed as he shook his head. "The Culling's nothing more than a nightmarish tale dreamed up by Black Valley's tyrant to cow people. It's not real. I've been to many cities—dead cities—and it was man, not beast that destroyed them."

How dare he dismiss my story? I stopped walking and looked him in the eye. "No, it's true! Monsters killed that guard. They chanted like the things that attacked us near my village."

He rubbed my arm consolingly. "Ri, monsters don't exist. I believe it was people that ambushed us on your island, and tonight's attack was likely a pack of wild dogs in search of food. It's not uncommon—"

"It wasn't a pack of dogs!" I backed away from him. "They came from the fountain. They travel through water. Like you do."

He tilted his head. "Like I do? I don't travel through water. I travel through water*falls*." He glared at the creepy statue. "Wait here." He jogged toward the fountain, picking up a three-foot-long stick along the way.

"Are you crazy?" I limped after him. "What are you doing?"

"Investigating." He dunked the stick into the water and pushed it toward the bottom of the fountain. It sank into the water, deeper and deeper until its end disappeared in a glow of blue light.

"Uh oh." His jaw hung slack. Only a small portion of the stick remained. "I can feel the current on the other side."

I joined him near the dark pool. "Come on. We need to get out of here."

He bobbed his head in agreement just as a black-gloved hand exploded from the water and latched onto the stick. Bryce yelped, jumping backward. He released the branch, and both it and the hand plunged back into the water, vanishing.

I shook Bryce's arm. "That was Silver. Quick, help him!"

"Silver?" Bryce's eyes rounded to the size of walnuts.

"He's the captain. Quick, pull him out!"

"Captain? Oh no! You ran into a captain?" He raked his hand through his hair, pacing and glaring at the fountain before huffing back to it. "Dammit, let's hope he doesn't chop our heads off." He shoved his hand into the water and like the stick, a blue glow radiated around his arm as it slipped into the unknown. A second later, leather-clad fingers wrapped around his wrist.

Bryce leaned toward the pool, weighed down by Silver's bulk. He anchored his legs against the basin for balance. I jumped into the struggle, grasping Bryce by the waist. My shoes slipped in the snow, making it impossible to secure footing. Silver's head broke through the water.

We tugged the captain and he crawled out of the basin, falling on hands and knees next to me. Panting, he slapped his soaked hair back, plastering it to the top of his head. Cuts and scrapes marred his pale face. A dart pierced his neck. I reached to pull it free, but Bryce grabbed my arm and yanked me to standing, keeping me far from Silver.

"We all have to get out of here," I said. "The Harbingers of the Culling might return."

"They won't return tonight." Silver's voice was a ragged whisper. He plucked the offending dart from his neck and discarded it into the snow. "It was only a small pack and they've been dealt with."

A small pack? They killed three armed guards in seconds!

Silver remained slouched to catch his breath. Earlier, I had no hope of breaking free from his strong grasp, but at that moment he swayed with weakness. A child could have knocked him over with a careless snowball. Either the poison was rendering his limbs useless or …

"Are you hurt?" I took a step toward him, but Bryce pulled me back once again, positioning himself in front of me.

Silver looked up and fixed a hard stare on my friend. "I know you. You're on the Stained Wall," he said, slurring his words like a drunkard.

"What will you do? Behead me?" Bryce asked. "You hardly look in condition to lift your weapon."

"What are you doing?" I whispered harshly in Bryce's ear. "Goading him hardly seems like a good idea."

Silver smirked, lumbering to standing on unsteady legs. He patted around his waist until his hand found the hilt of his sword. Unbelievable! After Bryce and I had rescued him, he planned to repay us with execution. Good thing he could hardly stand.

Bryce widened his stance and slipped my dagger out from under my belt. Then, tilting his head toward my ear, he whispered, "Stand back."

"No! Are you mad?" Then regarding Silver, I added, "You can't be serious. We just helped you."

Silver mumbled incoherently. His eyebrows knotted together as he repeated the same gibberish. He tried a few more times, but not a single intelligible word escaped his mouth. The hand that had rested on his sword moved to his forehead. He groaned as if suffering from an intense headache. Then his eyes rolled back into his skull and he fainted, landing face down in the snow.

Bryce gawked at him. "Uh ..."

I knelt next to Silver and felt his neck for a pulse. A faint throb beat against my fingertips.

Bryce questioned me with arched eyebrows.

"Well, we can't leave him here in the snow." I struggled, trying to roll Silver onto his back.

With a sigh, Bryce joined me. Together, we flopped Silver over.

"More guards will come soon." Bryce scanned the far corners of the courtyard. "I'm sure they heard the screaming earlier. It's best to leave him here for his own to deal with."

"But what if the Culling comes back?" I placed Silver's head on my lap to protect it from the cold snow. "Surely you believe me now that it was here?"

"I do, Ri. Unbelievable as it is, I do." He gripped my shoulder. "But this man is a captain. If he wakes, he will kill me for my crime and you for being associated with me. Understand?"

"I know, but he helped me. I'm still finding it hard to believe that he would harm us."

Bryce shook me slightly. "Didn't you see him readying to pull his weapon?"

"Well, yes."

Clearly, Silver wanted to carry out the punishment that the Stained Wall demanded. But the thought of abandoning him in the freezing night triggered a sick feeling in my gut. I pulled his collar up around his neck, hoping it'd lend some warmth.

A rip in the fabric caught my eye. Silver's pale skin peeked through, smudged in crimson.

"He's hurt!" I pulled at the coat, exposing Silver's bare stomach. A five-inch gash stretched across his waist. The deep cut in his flesh breathed with him, oozing blood with each exhalation.

Bryce placed his hands over the wound while I unraveled the tattered strip of blanket from my ankle and looped it around Silver's waist. A dab of red swelled over the cloth, dyeing the dirty rag.

"He's going to bleed to death." I applied pressure to the wound. "We can't leave him. Who knows how long it will take for more guards arrive."

Bryce stared at my hands, which were coated in Silver's blood. The muscle in his jaw flexed repeatedly.

"Did you hear me?" I said. "If we leave, this man's death is on us."

He nodded reluctantly and looked beneath the makeshift bandage. "The laceration doesn't go through the muscle. I think I can help him, but I need supplies." He took a deep breath. "We won't be able to haul him as far as Parkin's. And we can't bring him to his own people. If they got a look at me …"

He looked toward the east side of the courtyard. "The Rose Quarter's nearby. We'll bring him to Carter's house."

"Carter? That man can't be trusted. Shouldn't he have predicted all of this?" I waved my hand, gesturing at the bloodstained courtyard.

Bryce shook his head. "I can't explain it, but he'd never put us in a dangerous situation on purpose. That much I know."

My stomach tensed, but I had no alternate ideas. "All right, let's get this over with."

After removing the extra bulk of Silver's weapons, we each draped one of his arms over our shoulders and lifted him. The shock of his weight sent a stabbing pain from my ankle to my knee. My shoulders ached as the burden sunk over them. I inhaled to steady myself. Silver smelled of sweat, leather, and blood.

"I think I can carry him on my own." Bryce's cheeks flushed red.

"No, I can do this." I set my jaw and stepped forward.

My injury showed me new depths of pain, but if I gave up and lowered Silver back into the snow, he would likely join his subordinates at the Violet Star. Blood dripped off him, leaving a trail of diluted red spatter at our feet. His shaggy hair hung over his lowered head. He came to when we reached the cover of an alley. Slumped over, he still relied on Bryce and me for support, but at least he was now dragging his feet, freeing us from some of his weight.

As his legs fumbled clumsily, he gazed at me from the corner of his eye as if he badly wanted to tell me something. He muttered some incoherent words and passed out again. My knees buckled at the return of his full weight.

"Not much farther," Bryce promised.

A few moments later, we slipped through a fence and emerged onto a road cleared of snow. The bumps of cobbles pressed against the soles of my feet. Ahead, a dozen silhouettes of gabled homes flanked each side of the road. Their chimneys sent the comforting aroma of wood smoke into the night air, and I yearned for the warmth inside. I glanced at windows as we passed, but the decorative, amber-colored glass shielded the occupants from my curious gaze.

"It's hard to believe that the Slag exists in the same village as this quarter," I said, my voice strained from the effort of lugging Silver.

"Black Valley's wealthiest live here," Bryce explained, panting.

In my village, everyone worked hard, and the rewards from our labor were shared equally. But in Black Valley, they allowed children to starve in the Slag while others lived in luxury. It made no sense.

I glanced at the captain. His mouth hung open, releasing faint puffs of breath, each weaker than the last. Meanwhile, Bryce coughed every other step. His body shuddered, heaving air in and out of his lungs. I stood straighter, doing my best to bear more of Silver's weight.

If Silver passed away, I could console myself, knowing that I had done all that I could to save him. But Bryce … I couldn't lose him. He was my friend. By the time he stopped in front of one of the homes, his legs wobbled. He raised his fist to knock on the door, but it flew open before his knuckles struck the wood.

Carter gripped each side of the doorframe, glaring at Bryce. "I told you never to come here."

CHAPTER 9

"The two of you are going to ruin everything for me." Carter wrinkled his nose at the unconscious captain we had dragged to his front step.

He was swaddled in a housecoat thick as bear fur, while Bryce and I shivered in the night wind. Inside, a fireplace crackled, teasing us with its warmth. But Carter—who had promised to give me all that I needed a few hours ago—left us waiting in the cold.

"Take him somewhere else." Carter moved to close the door, but Bryce placed his foot in the way, wedging himself between the door and the frame. Carter glared at us through the crack.

"There's nowhere else to go." Bryce glowered. "Are you seriously going to turn us away?"

"Yes! Now let me close this door." He kicked at Bryce's leg with his slipper-clad foot.

"You're such a coward," I said. "If you don't let us inside, Death will claim this man tonight."

"Good." The tendons stood out in Carter's neck. "The dead don't make trouble for us."

"How can you be so cold?" I yanked the black stone he had given me out of my pocket and hurled it at him. "You're a piece of work."

He deftly dodged the stone. "A little dramatic, Sunshine, don't you think?"

"I'll show you dramatic." I swatted at him, but he flinched out of my reach.

"Think about this." Carter wildly pointed his index finger at us as he spoke. "If you leave this man in an alley, he'll never bother us again. But the second you bring him through this door, everything changes. I'm trying to protect you both."

Bryce pressed his lips together in a slight grimace and looked at me. He pulled in a deep breath and released it slowly. "We know the risks."

There were more risks than I cared to count. Possible beheading scared me the most. No, Samuel living the rest of his days alone and without my care terrified me more. Still, I couldn't sink to Carter's level and let a man die.

"We'll take our chances," I said.

"Carter?" A woman called from inside the house. Her voice was melodic as chiming bells. "You let them through this instant."

Bryce and I raised our eyebrows questioningly at Carter. He had flirted with me relentlessly earlier, yet he already had someone waiting for him at home. What a pathetic womanizer.

"I'm handling this," Carter said over his shoulder. His mouth formed a tight smile. "Go back to sleep, dear sister."

Sister? All right, perhaps I judged too soon.

"Sending them off is no way to handle anything." His sister's voice reached a higher pitch. "You're better than this."

"Katie." Carter's tone adopted a firm, parental note. "Go back to bed. You need your rest."

"Nonsense," she fired back. "Hello, out there? Can you hear me? I have everything ready. Medicine, blankets, towels."

Bryce and I exchanged a glance and a nod. Then, together, we plowed through the door, dragging Silver like a battering ram. Carter stumbled out of the way, tangling himself in his plush robe. He cursed under his breath as he smoothed his clothing.

A girl roughly my age stood behind him in the hallway. Wisps of straw-blond hair fell out of her bun, framing her narrow face. She wore a nightgown with a frilly hem that brushed against the floor. The fabric hung loose over her frail body, and her sleeves repeatedly slipped off her shoulders. Her eyes widened at the sight of Silver, and she covered her gasping mouth.

"Oh my ..." She stared for a moment before clearing her throat. "This way, please." She gestured toward a lofty chamber to the right.

The wood-paneled walls and mahogany furnishings lent rich, earthy hues to the interior, while the purple drapes, embellished with embroidery, boosted the room's regal air. Fresh bread and wine scented the room. An unfinished landscape painting sat on an easel, while finished ones framed in gold perked up the walls. For the first time since arriving at Black Valley, I found the temperature pleasant.

I gaped at the grandiose room. "I've never seen a home quite like this."

Katie led us toward a marble fireplace carved with ornate motifs of birds. A blanket sprawled on the floor, warmed by the glow of flames. Next to the blanket awaited a bucket of water, a pile of towels, and a small metal box.

A floral-patterned rug, fringed with tassels, dared us to drag the bloody Silver across it. We accepted the challenge.

"How about a little help?" I snapped at Carter, wheezing.

"Oh, no, no, no." He flapped his palms, gesturing at his housecoat. "This happens to be made of the finest angora wool. I'm not getting that man's filth all over it."

"Carter William Buxton." Katie stomped her foot before I had a chance to call her brother a materialistic snot. Her exertion triggered a bout of coughing and Carter hurried to her side.

"You shouldn't be up this late," he whispered consolingly and wrapped his arm around her.

While Carter fussed over his sister, Bryce and I carried Silver across the room, passing a claw-footed table along the way. Two mugs, a teakettle, and a mortar filled with an herb paste sat on top of it. We reached the blanket and gently lay Silver down. My shoulders and injured ankle rejoiced at being free of his weight.

Bryce brushed his black, sweaty bangs off his forehead and unbuttoned Silver's coat. The garment fell open, revealing the blood-drenched shirt underneath. Bryce tore it open, while I tugged Silver's belt free. The dagger—the only weapon we hadn't discarded in the courtyard—came with it. Tossing it behind me, I reminded myself to keep the blade out of the captain's reach in case he woke. But his ashen face and weak breaths made me doubt that he would.

"What can I do next?" I asked Bryce.

In the background, Carter and Katie bickered in hushed voices. There was no time to subdue their argument. Silver's open wound oozed blood. My stomach twisted with nausea at the wretched sight.

Bryce patted a cloth over Silver's muscular stomach, soaking up the crimson. He nodded toward the metal box. "We need to stitch the wound. Can you look for a needle and thread?"

I shuffled through cloth bandages, bottles, and various instruments inside of the box until I found what he needed. Hands shaking, I threaded the needle and handed it to him.

I tensed as he punctured Silver's flesh and pulled the needle through. Blood spurted from the wound, coating his fingers in red. Silver moaned and his cheek twitched, but Bryce continued binding the flaps of skin together with unwavering focus. A pack of wild boars could have barged into the room and he wouldn't have faltered. I held my breath and waited, transfixed by his steady hands until he knotted the last stitch.

He stared at his handiwork for a moment. An even zigzag of black embroidery stretched across Silver's pale flesh. With a deep breath, he dunked his hands into the bucket of water and closed his eyes. "We did the right thing."

"Let's hope the captain agrees," I said.

Katie swooped down next to us, mortar in hand. "I have something that will help him."

At her words, Carter huffed out of the room, shaking his head.

The firelight illuminated Katie's features. Her hands trembled, as if the mortar weighed fifty stone, and her concaved cheeks barely plumped when she smiled. Purple circles hung under her eyes. She muffled a cough. Judging by her frail frame, I suspected she had been sickly for many years. Sadness touched my heart at this thought.

Bryce accepted the mortar, sniffed the herb paste inside of it twice, and then handed it back to Katie. "Lavender and mint? Thank you, but these plants won't help."

"Perhaps you'll humor a girl so she'll feel useful." She pushed the bowl back toward Bryce. She had clover-green eyes like Carter did, but unlike his, hers glowed with genuine kindness. "Trust me, I know what I'm doing."

Bryce raised an eyebrow at the mixture. "Perhaps after I clean the area with some clove oil."

Carter returned, hovering around Katie with a blanket. "It's time for bed." He helped her to her feet and wrapped her in the plush quilt, which she didn't refuse.

"Place the mixture over his stitches," Katie instructed. "The plants know what to do."

Both Bryce and I tilted our heads. Though my knowledge of healing plants was limited, I knew lavender and mint would not aid Silver's wound.

"Oh, and dab some under his nose," she added. "It will keep him at rest. We don't want him waking any time soon." She shuddered, staring at Silver's hard expression. "Red Bands are intimidating even when they sleep."

At least a dozen pale scars crisscrossed Silver's chest, proving he had survived numerous battles. An image of his defeated opponents, dead at his feet, flitted through my mind. I wiped my clammy hands on my pants.

"We saved his life. He's not going to hurt us when he wakes," I said to reassure myself, more than the others.

Everyone stared at the floor silently. If only someone would have agreed, if only to eliminate my doubt.

Finally, Carter exhaled a loud breath. Then, turning to Katie he said, "Don't you fret about a thing. I'm going to take care of this. Have I ever let you down?"

She shook her head, smiling. "Never."

"Then that settles it." He tightened the blanket around her and straightened his posture confidently. His worry lines vanished as his mouth spread into a grin, but the expression didn't crinkle his eyes. It was a fake smile if I ever saw one. "You go get some rest, and by morning I'll have a plan." He tapped her on the nose and I remembered how he had done the same to me.

Still smiling, she kissed him on the cheek. "All right." She took two steps toward the room's exit and then looked at me. "Oh, forgive me. In all the excitement, I almost forgot. Carter said that you'd arrive with an injured ankle."

I flexed my foot. Now that the rush of activity had settled, my attention returned to the throbbing pain. "It's fine. I fell, that's all."

Carter cleared his throat and looked away. Perhaps he knew that I had been attacked—although after all that had happened tonight, I questioned his Whisperer's accuracy. Nothing went *fine* as he told me it would.

"I've prepared some medicine for you too." She took my hand. Her fingers, thin as twigs, chilled my skin. "And I have clean clothes for you. You can change in my room."

I glanced at my shirt. Splotches of Silver's blood stained my sleeves. "I really do want to clean up, but …" I glanced at Bryce.

"Go ahead, Ri." He slathered the herb paste onto Silver's wound, giving in to Katie's unusual remedy. "I doubt he'll wake before morning."

"All right," I said to Katie. "I need a few minutes to talk to your brother."

"Of course." She left the room.

Once the sound of her footsteps disappeared down the hall, I smacked my palms against Carter's chest. "Things did not go fine tonight. Did you know this would happen?"

"Whoa!" Bryce leapt to his feet, spilling the mortar.

Carter leaned forward, his narrowed eyes inches from mine. "Are you crazy, Honey? If I knew you'd show up here with a Red Band," he gestured at Silver, "I would've told you both to stay in that vile cave tonight."

Bryce wedged his palms between us, easing us apart. "Calm down. Both of you. We're going to figure this out."

"Figure this out?" Carter's cheeks burned red. "I've got a damn captain on my floor and a criminal that I'm now harboring in my home. Do you think we'll gather for friendly conversation over tea when he wakes?"

I doubted Silver was the type of man to enjoy chatter over tea. Carter backed away, pacing. The scarlet hue slowly left his face.

Bryce took a deep breath. "Everyone, relax. We need to think this through." He regarded Carter. "First off, is there something wrong with your ability that we need to be aware of? Why didn't you know about the guard at the drop-off point?"

Carter curled his lip as if Bryce had deeply insulted him. "There's nothing wrong with me." He waved his finger at both of us. "You two had to go gazing at the ocean. It threw all the timing off. If you followed my map and went straight to the drop-off point, none of this would've happened."

Bryce grasped his forehead. "He's right. We did waste a lot of time near the ocean."

"But we were only there for a few minutes," I said.

"Well, that's all it took," Carter replied sharply. He flopped down on a cushioned armchair near the table, as if exhausted from a day's worth of hard labor. "I was enjoying a hot bath and a splendid glass of wine with the most divine floral notes ..." He closed his eyes, apparently lingering on the memory. "Then—bam—my Whisperer told me of your troubles. Thank you for ruining my whole evening."

He buried his face into his palms.

I touched Bryce's arm. "I'm so sorry. Between hesitating at Parkin's and stalling near the ocean ... this is all my fault."

Bryce placed a comforting hand on my shoulder. "It's going to be all right. Why don't you go get cleaned up?"

"Sure," I said weakly. I needed some time to process all that had happened. I entered the dark hallway. About ten paces ahead, firelight escaped out of a door. The din of Bryce and Carter's conversation faded as I made my way down the corridor. I reached the room. Inside, Katie placed a towel next to a bucket of water.

A small fireplace lit up the chamber, illuminating items that I had only heard about in Samuel's stories. A lacey canopy bed occupied the center of the room. Five overstuffed pillows crowded the headboard. What an excessive arrangement for sleeping! Night tables flanked each side of the bed, both topped with a vase of flowers. Where in the world did she find fresh tulips in frozen Black Valley? A mirror hung on the wall to my right, reflecting my horrendous appearance. A bruise stretched from below my eye to my jaw, and my disheveled hair badly required a brushing. I picked a twig out of my braid.

"Don't fret over the bruising," Katie said. "I'll prepare a remedy for it and you'll be back to normal by morning."

A bruise like mine would take over a week to fade, but I didn't want to squelch her optimism. "Sounds wonderful."

She gestured to the bucket. "I'm sorry we didn't have enough time to prepare a bath, but there's a clean nightgown folded on the bed." She looked around, as if searching for something else to offer me. "It was Carter's idea to have these things waiting for you. He said you had a difficult night."

I lowered my head. I didn't want to relive the night's events by talking about them. Fortunately, Katie understood.

"I'll check on you shortly." She left, closing the door behind her. The room fell quiet.

I undressed and sat next to the wash bucket. The soapy bubbles smelled like the spring flowers in Samuel's garden. I closed my eyes and imagined home for a moment. I might only see my village—and Samuel—in memories now. I opened my eyes and returned to the strange room in a strange city. A sponge floated around in the bucket, pleading with me to pick it up. Instead I broke down and sobbed. What awful things were out there, slashing up guards? Only Silver and that madman Mallory knew the answer.

My eyes were burning from sobs when knuckles rapped on the door.

"Ri?" Katie called from the opposite side.

My attention snapped to her. I was supposed to be washing, but instead I was huddling naked next to a bucket, watching my tears fall into the water.

"I need a few more minutes," I answered.

I wiped the moisture from my eyes and took a deep breath. Hurrying, I washed my hair and then whisked the lukewarm sponge over my shoulders, chest, and lower back—I paused at the dip of my spine where my awful scar started. The crescent-shaped bump of smoothed skin was the size of a large potato, and I always dreaded touching it.

I dried off and slipped into the nightgown. The softest fabric I had ever felt flowed down my body, caressing my skin. Despite the luxuriant feel, the fine cloth failed to bolster my mood. A knock came at the door again.

"Come in," I said.

Katie entered, carrying a bowl in one hand and a bandage in the other. She smiled at the gown. "Isn't silk marvelous? I never dreamed I'd own anything so lavish when Carter and I lived in the Slag."

"You lived in the Slag?"

"Yes. Many years ago. It was absolutely horrid." She guided me to a chair and I sat down. She knelt near my feet, unraveling the cloth bandage. "If I didn't have Carter, well, I never would have survived it."

I recalled the two orphans Bryce and I had encountered. Had Carter and Katie once shivered together, hoping to survive the night in a dilapidated shack? "I'm sorry. No one should have to live like that."

She turned her head to cough. Poor girl.

"I'm all right," I said. "Why don't you get some rest and we'll handle my injury later. I'm sure Bryce can help."

"No, Ri." Her boney fingers tightened around the bandage, wrinkling the fabric. "I'm fine, really. Carter fusses over me day and night. Please, treat me like a normal person. I can handle this small task."

I understood how she felt. Samuel longed to be treated like a normal person too. I moved my ankle toward her.

She scooped an herb paste out of the mortar. It smelled like the same concoction she had prepared for Silver. Other than offering a pleasant aroma, it wouldn't do much good. But I allowed her to slather it on my ankle anyway.

"I know you think lowly of my brother," she said.

"So you both have a Whisperer?"

With a smile, she set the mortar down and started to wrap my ankle. "No, no. My gift is healing others. But it's clear you dislike him by the way you look at him."

I raised my eyebrow. "I think he's a liar and a womanizer."

She half-shrugged. "He's also a con-artist and a thief. But the Slag made him that way. It's not his fault. He's a good person, deep down."

"He wanted us to leave the captain in an alley to die," I said, louder than intended. I lowered my voice. "No good person would do that."

She yanked the bandage tight, pinching my skin. "I love my brother, Ri, despite all the questionable things he does. He'll come around one day. I know he will."

How naïve! But I dared not say it. If she wrapped my ankle any tighter, I might have lost the foot.

"Carter will have a plan tomorrow," she continued. "And we'll have to do whatever he says if we want to survive."

We would see about that. Carter probably only cared to protect himself and Katie. Where would Bryce and I fall into his plans?

She secured the bandage and then dabbed my cheek with the herb mixture before I could jerk away. "It will help."

"It's cold." The goop tingled on my cheek, but I let her finish.

Carter entered the room without knocking. His gaze traveled over my nightgown-clad body, and I prepared myself for one of his crude remarks.

Instead, he sat on the bed and stared blankly at the frilly rug at his feet. "I have a plan."

"That's wonderful." Katie sat next to him, wiping her hands clean.

He clasped her hand. His eyes looked near tears. A hard feeling formed in my gut. Something was wrong.

He turned to me. "I need to speak with Katie. Privately. Bryce will explain everything to you."

"Um … of course," I said. I left the room as Carter murmured something indecipherable to his sister.

"No, we can't do that!" she shouted. I shut the door to the sound of her sobs.

CHAPTER 10

I hurried down the hall and burst into the main room. "Why's Carter's plan making Katie cry?"

Bryce was kneeling on the floor, binding the unconscious Silver's wrists with rope. He had borrowed clean clothes from Carter. A linen shirt fit him snug in the chest and shoulders, making the top two buttons impossible to fasten. As he completed the knot, faint ripples of his lean, muscular build moved beneath the fabric. The fireplace lent a warm glow to his complexion, defining his features with flattering shadows. I stared at him, breathless.

He looked up and gawked at me. The nightgown's thin fabric showed the curves of my hips and breasts.

"Oh, wow, um ..." His ears turned a faint shade of red. He immediately picked up another short length of rope and concentrated on tying it around Silver's ankles. "I'm sorry. I didn't mean to ... stare at you."

I averted my gaze toward the window, rubbing my neck. To save us both from embarrassment, I touched my cheek where Katie had plastered the herb mixture. "Oh, this? It's Katie's remedy. I know it won't heal my bruise, but I figured I should play along." I feigned a light chuckle. "I must look like I crawled out of a bog. Sorry to startle you."

With a slight smile, he grabbed one of the cloths near the bucket of water and offered it to me. "I'm not startled. In fact, I would strike up conversation with a girl who looked like she crawled out of a bog any day."

"You would?" My cheek ached from my smirk.

"Of course, I'm an herbalist after all. And there's no better place than a swamp to find sweet flag and bog bean. I'd ask her where she came from."

A laugh snuck out of both of us. He watched me with amusement as I finished wiping the paste away. My chest lightened, freeing some of the anxiety that had been festering there since I arrived at Black Valley.

Bryce glanced at my injured ankle, and his brow wrinkled with concern. "How are you feeling?"

"I'll be all right." I glanced at Silver's bound limbs. Judging by the rope's complex twists, the captain would never break free from Bryce's knots. That was fine by me until we knew what his intentions were. "But I have to admit, I'm scared."

Bryce offered an understanding nod as he pulled out one of the ornate mahogany chairs from the table. I took a seat, sinking into the chair's plush cushion.

He sat in the opposite chair and let out a sigh. "So, the plan ..."

I grasped my seat, preparing myself.

"Carter believes that he and Katie have been compromised." He rested his elbows on the table, slouching. "So, prior to dawn tomorrow, he wants us all to go back to the cave and—"

"Go back to the cave?" I flinched. "That's crazy! Anyone will be able to follow our tracks."

"True, but they won't be able to follow us the whole way."

It took a moment for his meaning to sink in. "You can't be suggesting that we travel through the waterfall."

"Carter believes it's the only way we'll survive—aside from killing Silver. I know neither of us wants that. But if we stay here, we'll have plenty of problems once he wakes. And if we hide in my cave—well, you said it—they'll follow our tracks. But if we travel through the waterfall, we can live off the land for a month until the dark moon."

"And then return to my village?"

He nodded.

Folding my arms, I leaned back in my chair and stared at the hearth. Flames wavered on the pile of logs, creating sharp contrasts of light and shadow throughout the room. That morning, Bryce had explained that the waterfall led to dangerous places, so Carter's plan hardly seemed safe. Not to mention that the waterfall would likely transport me farther from Samuel. Any hope of reaching my island before the dark moon would vanish the moment we stepped through the cascade.

"Ri," Bryce said in a soft voice. He extended his arms across the table and clasped both my hands in his.

Though I was sure he meant to comfort me with the gesture, I couldn't help but think of a butterfly enclosed between someone's palms. Trapped.

"We need to think this plan through," I said. "Do you even trust Carter?"

"Trust?" He raised an eyebrow. "Not in the least. But I know him. He's always been out for himself, so the last thing he would do is give up his luxurious life."

Carter had everything in Black Valley. Live off the land? A prissy man like him? I laughed to myself at the thought.

"I suppose you have a point."

"He's also willing to go to your island," Bryce continued. "Everyone—even he—believes it to be a cursed place. I've never been able to persuade him to go with me once. But now he's convinced that a life there is safer than remaining here. That's why I believe the threat is very real if we stay."

I glared at Silver, asleep near a pile of bloody rags and his shredded shirt. Our brief encounter promised the possibility of something—at the very least a truce to not kill each other. "I still have a hard time believing this man would behead us after we saved his life."

Bryce's hands tightened around mine. "Carter says we have to leave. I've survived the lands beyond Black Valley before. It's dangerous, but I won't let anything bad happen to you."

"What about the Culling? Chances are we haven't seen the last of it." I pulled out of his grip, stood, and paced the room. My ankle ached, but I needed space to breathe. "It's worth staying to question Silver about it when he wakes. I'd like to know what we're up against."

He stood and braced my shoulders, stopping my pacing. Once again, I was trapped, arms pressed against my body. His wide hazel eyes searched mine. "Believe me, no one wants to know what the Culling is more than me, but we'll be risking our lives if we stay to question him."

He ran his hand through his hair and sat back down. "If this ... Culling ... has the same power that I do ... well, I don't know what that means, but it's my responsibility to find out." He pulled his amulet out from under his shirt and contemplated its smooth surface.

In all the night's activity, I hadn't considered the uneasiness he must have felt since learning this evil force could travel through water like him. I joined him at the table.

The glimmers that raced along the amulet's curves mesmerized me. Beneath the transparent shell, swirls of liquid rushed and crashed, as if a miniature ocean existed within. A straight, jagged edge interrupted the otherwise circular shape, hinting that a piece had broken off.

I pulled my chair closer to his. "Your amulet looks like it's broken in half. Do you know what happened to the missing piece?"

He shrugged. "I always thought my parents kept it."

"Your parents?" Since Bryce lived alone in a cave, I had assumed his family members were deceased. "Where's your family now?"

"I don't know." Looking out the window, he tucked the amulet back under his shirt. "I was placed in an orphanage far from here when I was a baby, with nothing more than the blanket I was wrapped in and the amulet."

"Oh," I said quietly. When my parents died, the irresponsibility of childhood flittered away like autumn leaves before a cruel winter. Perhaps he had a similar experience growing up in an orphanage. I touched his arm. "I'm sorry. I know how hard it is growing up without your parents."

We sat in silence for a moment, listening to the fire spark and clack. After a breath, I scooted my chair closer. Scents of the spruce forest still clung to his hair and skin.

"It was hard when I was young, but that was a long time ago." His gaze lingered on the sliver of space between us. "Besides, I'm sure they had a good reason to leave me at the orphanage. I meant something to them, otherwise they wouldn't have tucked the amulet in my blanket. But I wish they had left me a note or something. What if I'm not using the amulet the way they intended me to?"

"How can you ask yourself that? You're using it to gather medicinal plants for the ill. Your parents would be proud."

He shook his head. "But what if they knew about the Culling? What if the amulet was meant to stop it? I figured out how to travel through waterfalls by accident, so perhaps the amulet has other powers that I'm unaware of." His gaze sharpened with determination. "I want answers."

I understood his need for answers, as any fellow orphan would. Although, I had simpler questions: Did my mother love daisies and springtime like I did? Was my father stubborn like me? Which one did I owe my impulsiveness to? But if my parents had left me with a mysterious amulet like Bryce's, I would also question whether I had a larger responsibility.

He placed his hand atop mine. "I suppose I should take one step at a time. Let's first concentrate on getting back to your village. Are you comfortable with the plan?"

My clammy hand stuck to his cool, dry skin. "I'm not sure I would use the word comfortable." I glanced at Silver's bound hands. My imagination conjured a frightening vision of his rough fingers wrapped around the hilt of his sword. The blade swung toward my neck and I flinched, jolting myself from the daydream.

"I'm scared too," Bryce said. "But after tonight, I know that we can face anything together." His eyebrows knotted in a pained expression. "I never want you to do something as dangerous as you did tonight. When you ran off, I swear my heart stopped. Red Bands are bad people, Ri. Do you have any idea what would've happened if that guard had caught you?"

I had plenty of ideas. Each one made my skin crawl. "I know. I was lucky."

"Yes, you were," he said, squeezing my hand on the last word. "You were very lucky."

"You would get along well with the healer in my village," I said. "He lectures me all the time too."

My poor attempt at a joke didn't spur a smile from him.

"I'm sorry, I didn't mean to lecture. But I was worried about you." He rubbed my hand, and for a brief moment his touch was all I could think about.

"Though I have to admit, what you did was extremely brave. No one has ever risked their life for me."

Staring at our joined hands, I shrugged one shoulder. "Well, I knew I could outrun that guard. It was nothing."

He nudged closer. The flames from the fireplace reflected off the faint gold hues in his eyes. "Ri, let me look after you next time. Have faith in me. I'll protect you and get you home. Everything is going to be all right."

Having someone else take the responsibility of looking after me seemed to lower my capacity for doing so myself. I didn't like this loss of control. Despite this, I nodded because his eyes begged me to agree. It was probably the only way I could set his mind at ease for the night.

Perhaps he saw through my small fib, because he continued to search my face. Then, he closed his eyes and parted his mouth, leaning closer. My heartbeat started racing. What was he doing? The faintest tickle of his breath brushed against my lips. Time was moving too fast. We couldn't kiss! I leapt up, accidently knocked over my chair, and stumbled over Silver as I fled a few feet away from the table. Bryce made a confused sound. Grasping my forehead, I struggled to have a clear thought.

"I'm sorry." He raised his hands in a calming motion, as if I might scurry away. "I didn't mean to … I just thought … I felt something, you know …"

I gaped at him, touching my mouth. Had I wanted that kiss? I didn't know. I hardly knew him.

"No, I'm sorry, I … um …" Sweat gathered on my brow. The fireplace was scorching the room. How many logs was Carter burning? "I'm a little overwhelmed, that's all."

Overwhelmed? What a lousy excuse. I wanted to be Bryce's friend. But love? He had no idea what he was getting into. After all, I was the village outcast. How could I offer him a normal life? If, by some miracle, we survived all this, he deserved a quality life with a girl who wasn't ridiculed by her village. As for me, I had pushed away the hope for love long ago. Samuel was my highest priority. I accepted that. I couldn't complicate things.

Bryce cleared his throat and picked up my chair. Despite my erratic behavior, he offered a kind smile as if nothing happened. "For the sake of the furniture, I promise I won't try that again."

I stared at the chair. How foolish he must have thought me. My cheeks burned hot.

"I have some good news." He reached into his pocket and pulled out my compass. "I stopped at Parkin's while I was searching for you."

"You did?" I swiped my most treasured possession out of his hand. "I can't believe it! It's like new!" The glass face captured my reflection, stretching my smile from the west marker to the east marker. I sat back down and further inspected it, turning it over.

A muscle in Bryce's jaw tensed as his gaze fell on the inscription. He cleared his throat. "I triple-checked it to make sure Parkin didn't do shoddy work. It all looks good, except," he scratched his chin, "the needle seems to be pointing west."

I waved off his concern. "Oh, it's always done that."

"Hmm. Interesting." He pursed his lips and shifted in his seat. Though he looked like he wanted to say something else, he got up and retrieved a blanket from atop a chest. "It's getting late. Why don't you catch a few hours of rest? When Carter wakes, we'll discuss the plan further." He wrapped the blanket around me.

"One of us should stay up to guard Silver," I said.

"I can do that." He covered a yawn with his hand. Away from the firelight, his skin appeared pallid. His hair, which seemed handsomely disheveled when I first entered the room, was actually a ragged mess. He probably hadn't slept at all in the past three days while he was tending me.

"Nonsense," I said. "You sleep and I'll wake you if Silver stirs. I've had three solid days of rest and I'm not tired."

He stretched his neck from side to side. "You don't need to do that for me. I'm fine."

I removed the blanket and offered it to him. "This is non-negotiable."

The corner of his mouth curved up as he considered the blanket in my hand. "Well, knowing how stubborn you are, I think I'll end up losing this battle. Sleep it is." He accepted the quilt and whirled it around his shoulders. "But the second you feel your eyelids growing heavy, wake me."

"Of course."

He found a spot in the corner of the room, and within seconds of laying his head down, his breath turned to soft snores. When Samuel snored, I'd wake in fright thinking a boar snuck into our cottage. Bryce sounded like a kitten purring. The melody could have lulled me to sleep if I didn't need to make a life-altering decision in a few hours. That thought alone kept me awake.

Two choices, both dangerous: leave Black Valley and face treacherous lands, or stay and risk the sharp edge of Silver's unforgiving blade.

CHAPTER 11

Morning came not with sunlight slanting through the windows, but with the sound of slipper-padded footfalls from the hallway. Wrapped in his housecoat, Carter entered the room carrying folded clothing, a stack of letters, and two knapsacks. He set the knapsacks on the floor and placed the garments on top of them.

I still sat in the cushy chair at the table, resting my chin in my palm. My eyelids, though heavy from exhaustion, widened once the questionable man entered the room.

"You packed?" I asked.

"Yes, I expect us to leave on time." He spoke with an air of impatience, devoid of the flirtatious lilt that saturated his words when we first met. Even his eyes lacked their usual mischievous sparkle.

"Well, we need to discuss your plan." I glanced at Bryce and Silver to make sure I hadn't woken them. Bryce slept with a relaxed expression, lips slightly parted. Occasionally his lashes fluttered in a dream state. Silver, on the other hand, clenched his facial muscles. His eyebrows drew together, forming a vertical line between them. Whatever he fought while awake must have been fighting back in his dreams.

"Bryce and I haven't decided whether we plan to leave Black Valley." I folded my arms and narrowed my eyes at Carter. How could he pack without even hearing my opinion? "You shouldn't just assume—"

"I never assume." He stepped over Silver as if he were a disgusting puddle of mud and added another log onto the fire. The flames rose up and reflected in his glassy, bloodshot eyes. "Hopefully some extra kindling will help me survive the cold bite of your mood this morning. It's chilling the room."

"You're calling me cold? You wanted to leave Silver in the alley to die last night!"

He passed me a sideways glance as he tossed the stack of letters on the table and headed toward a mahogany cabinet on the opposite side of the room. "Did you stay awake all night?"

"Yes, I stayed up so Bryce could sleep. Now as I was saying—"

"That's a shame." He scoured the cabinet and pulled out two packages wrapped in brown cloth.

"What's a shame?" I huffed.

He plopped down in the chair opposite me and set the two packages next to the letters. "If I knew you were going to stay up all night, I would've joined you. We could've done things that would've put you in a much more blissful state this morning." The corner of his mouth curved up.

"Oh, please." I shook my head. "Keep dreaming."

"My dreams usually come true." He tapped his temple.

I rolled my eyes. "Give it up."

His lips pressed into a strained smile. "Perhaps we should start over. Again. And I see no better way to do that than with some honest conversation over good food." He unwrapped the packages. Inside was nestled a small slab of cheese and a loaf of grainy bread, bursting with the scents of spice.

I leaned back in my chair, doing my best to ignore the tempting aroma. "I think Silver is going to be grateful that we saved his life."

"No, Honey. You're not thinking. You're hoping. And let me tell you, hope should never be trusted." He pushed the cheese toward me. "Please eat something."

"I'm not hungry." My stomach growled, disagreeing.

"Your loss. This cheese has been aged to peak ripeness. You'll never have the chance to taste anything crafted so perfectly again." He slid a knife through the soft cheese and waved the slice in front my nose.

My stomach rumbled loudly, so I glanced over my shoulder again to make sure the racket didn't wake Bryce or Silver. They continued to sleep.

"Fine, I suppose I should eat something." Minimally, the nourishment would give me the energy to stay attentive around Carter—whether that meant warding off his advances or avoiding his tricks.

I whisked the slice of cheese out of his hand and shoved it into my mouth. Its creamy texture melted on my tongue as it offered flavors that started nutty and ended earthy. After I swallowed it, my mouth watered for another piece.

"I knew you'd give in." He smiled, mocking me. "Did you enjoy it?"

"I've had better."

"Clearly you have poor taste." As he cut the bread, his elbow accidently bumped into the stack of letters, knocking them over.

"What are those?" I asked, distracting myself from the spicy bread.

He sighed, gingerly arranging the letters into an organized pile. "Those are letters addressed to my stars. I couldn't abandon them without leaving word."

"Your stars? What are you talking about?"

"My lady friends," he explained.

I scanned the pile, counting. "There's eleven letters in that stack! How do you even have the energy to court eleven ladies?"

"Ten ladies." He leaned his elbow on the table and rested his face in his palm, bunching up his cheek. "One letter is for Parkin."

"Parkin didn't strike me as your type."

No smile came to his lips. "I wrote to Parkin asking him to close some unfinished business for me. And to deliver my correspondence, of course."

"That's a lot of walking for an old man."

He gathered the pile and flipped through the collection. A dab of wax sealed each letter. He studied the name elegantly penned on each one before looking at the next. "Beatrice. She's stunning. Poised and stylish. Intelligent too. Her husband doesn't appreciate her, so I show her what it feels like to be loved."

While he stared at the letters, reminiscing, I grabbed another slice of cheese and quickly hid it in my mouth.

He smiled, contemplating the next letter. "And Agnes. She has a wicked snaggletooth, but when she smiles, her nose scrunches up in the most adorable way. It forms a little crinkle, right here," he touched the bridge of his nose, "and that's the beauty that every man overlooks except for me."

"I don't want to hear about all the women you seduced." This conversation was a waste of time. I glanced at Bryce, planning to wake him.

Carter cleared his throat before I could do so. "I realized as soon as you brought him here," he glowered at Silver, "my life in Black Valley was over. However, it wasn't until I started writing the letters that it felt over. I'll never see my stars again. Nor will I sleep in silk sheets or taste fine wine."

"I'm sure you'll make do." I looked out the window webbed with crystalline frost.

"You're so cold, Honey." He set the stack of letters down. "It took me all night to find the right words to write to them ... my darling stars. They will dream of me for years to come."

"Years? You're so full of yourself," I scoffed. "You're lucky they never found out about each other. That many vexed women would be a greater threat to you than the captain."

"No one would be vexed. I loved them all and they knew it." With a sad sigh, he tore a piece of bread off the loaf and plopped it in his mouth. "My relationships with them were uncomplicated and fun, two concepts clearly foreign to you."

What right did this womanizing liar have to comment on my personality? "Are you calling me complicated and dull?"

"Complicated? Yes." He chewed the bread, taking his time. "But I wouldn't call you dull. Dull doesn't arrive to my door after midnight lugging an unconscious captain. I can't stress enough how bad this situation is for us."

"But your plan's too dangerous. We have no idea what we'll face if we leave Black Valley. Not to mention, Katie and I are hardly in condition to make such a journey." I looked under the table at my injured ankle, flexing my foot. No pain shot up my calf. "That's odd."

I stood, placing full weight on my ankle. Again, not a hint of pain. "Very odd. I think I'm healed." I hopped lightly from foot to foot. A laugh snuck past my lips. "Katie's healing power is real? I can't believe it."

"Yes, it's very real," Carter said flatly. "She can ask plants to conjure nature's power to heal others. I saw her mend a broken leg once by sprinkling weeds on it." He looked down at the table with sad eyes, fiddling with the cheese knife.

I absorbed his words for a moment. "Well, a girl that can talk to plants doesn't seem so farfetched after all I've seen the past few days." I sat back down and began removing the bandage from my ankle. "It's an incredible gift, but why doesn't she use it to cure herself?"

Carter set the knife down. "That's what breaks my heart. Her ability is limited to minor ailments. She can heal a broken bone or remedy the flu overnight, but for fatal illnesses, her gift only stalls the inevitable."

"Oh." I stopped fussing with the bandage so I could look him in the eye. "But surely Katie can be cured?"

"I tell her that she can be cured." He looked away from me as he wiped some moisture from his eyes. "On her worst days, I feed her that lie as I feed her soup in bed, holding her head up because she's too weak to do it on her own." He took a bite of cheese, chewing it, but not savoring it. Judging by his lackluster expression, he might as well have been eating straw.

"I tell her, 'Katie, you're full of promise. Keep honing your gift and one day you'll breathe without coughing. One day you'll go outside and feel the sun blushing your nose. One day you'll run barefoot on spring grass. One day you'll know marriage and true love,' and she says back to me, 'Carter, I already know true love.'" He choked out a sob. "One day she'll know that these were the worst lies I've ever told, and her life will go out like a flame on a spent wick."

"Oh, Carter." I placed my hand over my heart. His situation sounded familiar. Some mornings, Samuel was so weak that it was all I could do to get him to take a few sips of water. Every day, I promised him a cure. Many times I doubted myself, but his trusting eyes always spoke his faith in me.

"There has to be something we can do for her," I added.

"I would do anything to cure her. Anything." His lower lip trembled, but he flexed his jaw, pulling himself together. He pointed at the surrounding artwork of lakes, mountains, and forests that looked so real I could almost feel the sunlight filtering through the branches. "I paint those for her so she can see the world's beauty. I want her to have that before—"

"Carter, if your sister is this ill," I interrupted, "how can she possibly make the journey through the waterfall?" I hoped Bryce would wake with a refreshed mind and reconsider the idea as well.

"Honey, I don't want to put her through this, believe me. I wish I could give you a peek inside my head so you can see how dire our predicament is. If we stay, her situation—and ours—will be far worse."

He reached across the table and layered his hands on top of mine. His palms were soft with no callouses to suggest he knew hard work.

"I know you don't trust me," he continued. "But if we don't leave, I'll have to watch Black Valley's guards execute little Katie in a few hours. I know you're hesitant, but please see that this is our only option."

Silver had attempted to draw his weapon when he recognized Bryce the night before. Perhaps I did need to trust in Carter, rather than the man who enforced the ordinances etched into that horrendous Stained Wall.

"What about the Culling?" I asked.

"My Whisperer will keep us one step ahead of it." Somehow, he managed to interlock our hands, squeezing each of my fingers. "And no matter what happens, I'll get you back to Samuel. I won't break this promise to you."

I stared at him for a long moment and he didn't break eye contact. "You know how important Samuel is to me."

"We may have different pursuits in life, but ultimately you and I are more alike than you realize. I need you to go out on a limb and trust me."

Carter would have to be more than selfish to make such a promise and not intend to keep it. He would have to be downright heartless. I didn't believe he was.

"If you break your promise, I swear you'll regret it."

"I wouldn't dare tempt your wrath." He smirked, patting my hand.

I nodded, slowly. "All right. I'll go."

"Thank you for believing in me. I know that isn't easy for you to do, but you won't regret it." He heaved a heavy breath as if he had pushed a cart full of rocks uphill. "We must hurry. I'll get dressed and wake Katie." He got up and offered me the clothes he had set on the knapsack. "I've brought you fresh garments. They're mine, of course. I knew you wouldn't be comfortable in one of my sister's dresses." Then with a slight smile, he glanced at my nightgown-draped body. "This is the only time in my life that I'll ask you to put more clothes on."

I swiped the clothing out of his hand. "Go get ready."

After Carter left the room, I made sure my companions were still asleep before slipping out of the nightgown. The new garments smelled like Carter: a mixture of spice and spring meadow rain. Once dressed, I knelt next to Bryce.

The first time I nudged him in the shoulder, he mumbled and smacked my hand away. The second time I prodded him, he bolted upright, scanning the room in panic until his gaze landed on Silver.

"He slept through the night." I touched his arm, calming him. Then, after a deep breath, I added, "I spoke to Carter, and I'd never thought I'd say this, but I believe him. We have to leave Black Valley."

Bryce offered an understanding nod and rubbed my arm. Strange how his touch could soothe my nerves. "Don't worry, we'll get through this."

I looked down, brushing some of the remaining herbs off my ankle. Shreds of dried leaves fell from my skin, light as snowflakes. The scent of mint and lavender mingled in the air.

"Ri!" Bryce scrambled to the metal box and pulled out a bandage. "Your ankle still needs to be wrapped."

"No, Katie fixed it," I protested as he unraveled the cloth. "She can make plants heal people."

Bryce rested my heel in his palm and pushed my pant leg up. My ankle looked delicate next to his hands and arms.

"There's no swelling," he said. With one hand still cupping my heel and the other supporting the underside of my calf, he tenderly tilted my foot upward. "No pain?"

I shook my head.

"This is impossible."

I cocked an eyebrow. "You travel through waterfalls and you call Katie's power impossible?"

"You're right, I guess I should be more open minded." He smiled and his gaze met mine. For just waking up, his hazel irises gleamed with inner light. "Between me, Carter, and Katie, you must think everyone in Black Valley has a gift."

I shrugged a shoulder. "It is peculiar." Perhaps I should've told him about the Fireflies then, but given no one else could see them, I opted not to. The last thing I wanted was for him to think I saw hallucinations like Samuel. He'd think me crazy, not gifted.

Still holding my ankle, he asked, "Can you put full weight on it?"

I stood, demonstrating. "It's like new."

Bryce opened his mouth to say something else when the sound of Carter and Katie's footsteps came clomping toward us.

"We're ready to go," Carter said.

Both he and Katie donned navy blue cloaks, but Katie wore layers of clothes underneath, making her look like an overstuffed doll. Carter went to a chest in the corner of the room and withdrew a thick shawl from it. He wrapped it over the crown of his sister's head and then over the bottom half of her face, until the only part of her showing was her eyes.

"There you are," he said to her. "Nice and cozy."

She responded with a muffled sound. Poor girl.

Bryce and I glanced at each other. This was it. We were leaving. My stomach fluttered.

"What about Silver?" I asked. "Will anyone find him here?"

Grinning, Carter held up a sheet of paper with red writing on it. "I'll put this on my door. It's sure to draw attention."

"What does it say?" I looked at Bryce, who was smirking.

"A very derogatory comment about Red Bands that I'm not about to repeat in front of you and Katie," Bryce explained. "I'm sure one of Silver's own will bust through this door by daybreak."

Carter tossed Bryce and me a cloak and a scarf. "Our first destination will be the most taxing. After that it will be smooth sailing. Promise."

CHAPTER 12

The four of us made our way outside and onto the quiet cobbled street. The sky had paled to a soft blue. When Bryce and I arrived the prior night, the Rose Quarter was a cluster of shapes in the darkness. But in the early morning light, the gabled, half-timbered homes boasted their charm, each painted in shades of yellow, orange, or red. Their wood beams crisscrossed between rows of artfully placed brick, and motifs capped their doors and windows.

At the end of the road opposite from the Abandoned Quarter loomed an imposing fieldstone building. Two corner towers topped with cone-shaped roofs flanked either side of its trio of gables. A red double door served as the entrance, though I doubted it often welcomed guests. Its iron accents and handles lent it an intimidating air.

"Who lives there?" I asked Bryce.

He glared at the building and frowned. "The tyrant of Black Valley."

"He's a madman, and a cruel one at that," Carter jumped in. "No one dares to challenge him."

"Oh." Goose bumps skittered over my skin. I craned my neck, scanning the rows of arched windows of the north tower. I imagined a broad-shouldered man with hands clasped behind his back, looking down his nose at us through the top window, his dark eyes hinting of cold, calculated intentions. I shook away the frightful thought. There was no point in worrying about a man I would never meet.

Bryce tugged my arm. "Come on. We need to get moving."

Carter hoisted Katie onto his back to protect her feet from the damp snow. His cheeks reddened from the burden of her weight, but he managed a strained smile to ease her concern for him. Bryce and I carried the knapsacks. A dagger hung from each of our belts. My blade belonged to the noble young guard. Bryce had claimed Silver's dagger.

Together, we trudged toward the Abandoned Quarter. Though the cloak Carter loaned me offered a barrier from Black Valley's brutal cold, with each step I had to kick away the ridiculous tassels that decorated its hemline. Its red fabric fluttered in the wind, offering no camouflage whatsoever.

By the time the Rose Quarter's attractive homes grew small behind us, Carter was panting for breath. He marched onward, despite Katie's worried protest.

"I don't need to rest," he said, wheezing a cloud of breath into the cold air. "The sooner we're out of Black Valley, the better. I don't want to leave anything to chance."

We reached the hovels of the Abandoned Quarter and weaved through the narrow alleys. I went rigid as we neared the square. Horrific memories raced through my mind, but the area was quiet, disturbed only by the sound of our breath and the crunching snow underfoot. Even so, I placed my hand atop my weapon's handle for extra measure.

We strode quickly into the square. Apparently, Black Valley's guards hadn't yet arrived, because everything remained exactly as Bryce and I had left it. Roughly fifty feet away from us, near the base of the fountain, Silver's sword and bow poked out of the snow. Not far from those lay the deceased guard that I failed to save. Sprawled on his back and furred with frost, he stared toward the sky.

Katie peeked over her brother's shoulder. "Oh my! Is that man dead?"

Perhaps Carter's Whisperer had explained the gruesome and unfair nature of the man's death, because he didn't bother to turn his head to look. He trekked forward, determined gaze fixed ahead. "That horror isn't for your eyes, sweet sister. Please look away."

She did as he asked, but I couldn't look away. Even when I closed my eyes, the vision remained before me, fresh in my mind. The Culling would likely return to Black Valley, and more men would join those who died. But I couldn't worry about that. I had to return to my village and protect my own.

"We could use those weapons," Bryce said. "Keep going. I'll catch up." He dashed off toward Silver's collection of abandoned things.

"Dammit, no!" Carter stumbled in his tracks. "You're wasting time. And you'll lop off your leg trying to swing that broadsword."

He chased after Bryce. Not wanting to be left standing alone, I followed.

Bryce turned around, running backward. "Give me some credit." A dab of annoyance flavored his tone. "I can handle a crossbow. If you want to eat, we'll need something better than daggers to hunt with."

"I packed snares. That's all we'll need." Carter jumped over a mound of snow, cursing under his breath. "Every minute we spend on this nonsense puts us at risk of getting caught."

"Carter," Katie whined. "Please slow down. I feel nauseous." As Carter ran, Katie bounced, clinging to his shoulders.

"One moment," he said in a consoling voice. "I'll have you somewhere safe and warm before you know it."

We joined Bryce near the fountain. Swirls of snowy mist danced around its basin, as if entertaining the statue poised in its center. Once again, I shuddered at the sight of the stone woman's unsettling smile. She lorded over this space, head held high and arms outstretched over the bloodied ice at her feet.

Bryce slipped the dagger from the stiffened corpse's belt first and then offered the blade to Carter.

He wrinkled his nose at the weapon. "Stealing from the dead won't earn us any favors from the gods." Shaking his head, he tucked the weapon away. "Can we please go now?"

"Once I find the arrows." Bryce collected the crossbow and then swiveled around, scanning the area.

"I said leave it!" Carter tilted his head back and rolled his eyes. "This is taking too long. I swear you'll be the death of us."

Part of me wanted to yank Bryce onward and flee that dangerous place. But he had a valid point. We required weapons for both protection and hunting. So instead of siding with Carter, I scoured the area until I discovered the quiver of arrows jutting out of the fountain's icy basin.

"It's about time." Carter spun around, stomping toward the Slag as I pulled the soggy quiver from the fountain and handed it to Bryce. While doing so, I happened to glance at the statue's vacant eyes. "That woman spooks me," I whispered to Bryce as we trailed Carter.

"Spooks you?" Bryce asked. "That's an unusual reaction."

"Well, I think she has a creepy smile."

He nodded. "Her name was Sera, and the people of Black Valley once loved her. Including the tyrant. He made her his wife."

"It's a terribly sad story," Katie piped up. "She was murdered while carrying child right in this very square. The tyrant was so distraught that he ordered seven artists to build that fountain in her memory. They gave up sleep and chiseled away for a straight week because they feared him so."

"You're straining yourself," Carter said to his sister. "You should be using this time to rest."

She looked at me, round eyes watery from the cold. Keeping her voice low, she leaned toward me. "I understand, Ri. That statue spooks me too. The crazy tyrant believed that the artists failed to capture the love his wife always carried in her expression, so he had her heart removed from her corpse and placed into that memorial."

I glimpsed over my shoulder as we exited the square. The stone woman gazed downward, contemplating the frost coating her crumbling pedestal. "This tyrant you speak of sounds beyond disturbed."

"Yes, he is," Bryce interrupted. "How about we change the subject."

"I agree." Carter shifted, securing a better grip on Katie and quickening his pace.

As we left the courtyard, Bryce gave the statue a last lingering glance, as if listening to something only he could hear.

By the time we arrived to the graveyard, the sun was edging over the mountains, striating the horizon with pink and gold. The headstones, covered with frost, sparkled in the morning light. We weaved around them, heading toward the entrance of the underground burial chamber.

Bryce pushed the door open, revealing the crypt's uninterrupted blackness. Inside, all was quiet except for the repetitive drip of water droplets. The pungent stench of rotting flesh wafted past the threshold. I covered my nose.

"Oh my." Katie peeked over Carter's shoulder, gaping. "Are you sure it's safe in there?"

Poor girl. She was brave to face a journey that would prove burdensome for a healthy person, let alone someone with a fatal illness like her.

"Perfectly." Bryce gave a reassuring smile and gestured for us to enter. Once we were all inside the chamber, he closed the door, sealing us in the stink. I couldn't see a thing in the darkness. Nearby, Katie gagged uncontrollably, spurring a rush of consoling words from Carter.

Someone grabbed my hand, and I jumped with a yelp.

"Sorry," Bryce said, "I didn't mean to startle you. Hold onto me and I'll lead the way." He guided me across the chamber. After a short walk, I heard his body scrape against the rock walls of the tunnel that led to his home. I took a breath to prepare myself.

"It's merely a tunnel," I said under my breath. An extremely narrow tunnel. Brushing my anxiety aside, I slipped into the tight space, followed by Carter and Katie.

A few steps in, my heartbeat quickened. I choked on the suffocating scent of earth. Already panic had set in. A cold sweat chilled the back of my neck. How foolish I was acting. One, two, three … I counted sideway steps, concentrating on moving forward, rather than on the unpleasant sensations coursing through my body.

The walls narrowed, pressing against my back and chest like a vice. I couldn't breathe. Four, five … I heard Carter and Katie behind me, clogging the path if I needed to turn around and flee. Trapped. I lost count of my steps. My breath came ragged.

"We're almost there." Bryce squeezed my hand. For a fleeting second, I forgot about our dreadful surroundings.

About a half dozen steps later, the tunnel widened. I patted the walls, stretching my arms to either side. My joints cracked as if I had popped the anxiety right out of them. My breath and heartbeat slowed to a normal pace.

We walked a bit farther before Bryce stopped. I heard him fiddling with the canvas sheet that covered the entrance into his home. Familiar scents of smoke, timber, and starchy potatoes lingered in the air. The fire had gone out, so we had no relief from the darkness. Bryce led me out of the tunnel and then let go of my hand, leaving me waving around, searching. Purring erupted in the darkness, so I opted to remain where I stood until Bryce returned for me. The last thing I wanted was to trip over Miss Meow. The cat already despised me.

A thud echoed near the barrels.

"Don't waste time packing!" Carter emerged from the tunnel, bumping into me.

"This will only take a moment." Bryce clicked on a lantern light, and a startled Miss Meow darted under the table. One of the barrel lids lay on the floor. Bryce set the lantern on the table and slid Carter's knapsack off his back. "Ri, do you have room in your pack?"

I nodded. Since my pack was already heavy from holding the canteens, Carter hadn't filled it to the top.

"Great." Bryce handed me his wooden box of medicines and some dried packets of herbs to stuff into my knapsack. "Save room for Miss Meow," he instructed.

"What?" I flinched. "That cat won't stay on my back! If you hadn't noticed, she hates me."

"Nonsense." Bryce placed the wrapped food Carter brought yesterday into his knapsack. "She's growing fond of you."

"We don't have time for this," Carter said, shaking his head. He helped his sister to one of the seats near the table and then pulled Bryce and me to the side.

"You two are killing me. Have you forgotten what happened last night when you wasted time?" He jabbed Bryce in the chest with two fingers. "I need you both to do exactly as I say," he spoke through his teeth, forcing restraint, "or this whole plan will fail, understood?"

Carter's fears were valid. A clever guard might have noticed our tracks leading into the crypts and considered them suspicious. Still, we had spent less than five minutes packing so far, and who could argue against the need for extra supplies?

"I know what I'm doing." Bryce swung the knapsack onto his back and then coaxed Miss Meow to come out from under the table.

"Are you serious?" Carter asked. "You're bringing a mangy flea-ridden cat with a bad temper?"

"I'm not leaving my cat." He scooped Miss Meow into his arms and she mewed a greeting. Then he tucked her inside my knapsack, instructing her to stay. I felt her settle in, growling. Clearly, neither of us enjoyed this experience.

"One last thing." Bryce scoured his collection of books until he found one with a worn, blue cover. "My journal," he explained, stuffing it into his pocket.

Carter threw his hands up, exasperated. "Can we go now, please?" Without waiting for an answer, he ripped the canvas covering off the tunnel that led to the waterfall and then grabbed the lantern.

He went to his sister and helped her to a standing position. Since entering the underground labyrinth, her flesh had paled, and sweat beaded above her upper lip. Still, she set her jaw and shadowed Carter into the tunnel. Bryce and I followed.

Ahead, the lantern flickered, illuminating the slick rock walls. Rather than narrowing, the passage widened, and before long the sound of rushing water echoed through the corridor. The temperature dropped and mist moistened my cheeks. The air smelled fresh as snowfall. We emerged from the tunnel, arriving at a chamber that rose at least twelve feet high. Though the lantern light was too weak to reach the perimeter of the room, it glinted off an underground river that meandered past us like spilled ink. Not far off, a waterfall slid down the rock, smooth as a veil of silk.

Katie coughed. Her legs were shaking. The poor girl looked ready to pass out.

"Carter," Bryce said firmly. "She needs to rest for a moment."

"I'm fine." Katie waved off Bryce's concern, but then slumped to the ground. Her weight wasn't enough to pull Carter down, but they both eased to the floor together. Kneeling, they clasped each other's elbows as if one might fall if not supported by the other.

"No, no, no," Carter pleaded, his face worn and tired. "We can't stop now. Come on, I can carry you."

She nodded, working her grasp up to his shoulders. Then, without warning, she swung her head away from him and vomited. Carter's eyes went wide, but then he snapped out of his shock and proceeded to rub Katie's back as she choked up phlegm. He whispered to her with quivering lips.

"I have something that might help." Bryce reached into my knapsack. Miss Meow purred as he rummaged around. He withdrew his wooden box of tools and vials.

"No, we have to go now," Carter said. "Katie, please, you know I wouldn't ask you to do this if it wasn't absolutely necessary." Cradling her in his arms, he picked her up and headed toward the waterfall. Bryce and I chased after him.

Katie gagged again, soiling the front of her cloak. She clutched her stomach, wincing. "It's all the movement. Can't we stop for a moment, the room is spinning."

"Dammit." Carter set her down, rubbing his forehead as if to smooth the worry lines from it. "This was supposed to happen after we passed through the falls."

"I'm sorry, Carter." Moisture welled in Katie's eyes. "I'm doing my best. I wish I wasn't such a burden."

My heart ached for her.

"No, no, sweet sister. I didn't mean to sound upset." Carter sat next to her and brushed her sweaty bangs off her forehead. "You don't need to apologize. I know you're trying so very hard. And I'm asking so much of you, but I need you to try a little harder."

"Carter!" Bryce scolded him. "Let her collect herself before we go through the waterfall." While he hurried to Katie with the medicine, I slid the dagger out of my belt and sawed at the bottom of my cloak to make a cloth. I didn't have all the knowledge that Bryce did when it came to healing others, but at least I could help her clean up while she waited for the queasiness to pass.

Miss Meow stirred, growling. I looked over my shoulder as she poked her head out of the knapsack. To my surprise, she wasn't directing her anger at me. Her single yellow eye glared at the tunnel that led back to Bryce's home. I stopped cutting the cloak for a moment and glanced at the passage. Nothing.

"Crazy cat. Aren't you used to this cave by now?" I asked.

Her whiskers arched forward and her nose twitched, sniffing. With a mew, she ducked her head back under the flap of the knapsack. I shredded through the rest of the cloak, producing a washcloth-sized rag. After dipping it in the stream, I joined the others and patted Katie's face and garments with the damp cloth.

"Enough," Carter said. "We need to keep moving." He lifted Katie, and the four of us followed the stream to the waterfall.

Bryce shoved his arm into the cascade. "The current on the opposite side isn't strong, but if I remember correctly from my last visit, it slopes at a slight angle for about thirty feet. Soon as you can, anchor your feet on something and make your way to land. Understood?"

The three of us nodded. There was no turning back. I wiped my sweaty palms off on my pants.

"I never traveled with this many people before," Bryce continued. "Carter you go in first so you can help the girls on the other side. I'll go in last to make sure everyone makes it through safely."

Carter set the lantern down and took Katie's hand. Katie then took mine and I took Bryce's. He smiled as our fingers interlocked.

"We're going to be all right," he said to me in a soothing tone. "The anticipation right before the jump is the hardest part, but I'll be by your side the entire time. I promise."

All my tension released at his words. He had honed a new skill over the past twenty-four hours: the ability to subdue my worry with only a gentle touch. It seemed this power was growing stronger the more I got to know him.

I returned his smile and with a deep breath, I said, "All right, I'm ready."

Carter stepped through the waterfall without hesitation. He must have started to slide immediately, because Katie and I jolted forward, tugged by his weight. She disappeared into the cascade next. I slid halfway into the water.

From behind, footfalls approached.

"Dammit!" Bryce yelled. "Go, go, go!"

Bryce shoved me into the water and followed close behind. Just as the ice-cold water chilled the crown of my head, his body jerked backward and his hand slid out of mine. The last thing I heard was him screaming, "Get off me."

CHAPTER 13

The ground disappeared beneath my feet, and I slid down in a rush of water. My stomach climbed into my throat. Katie's bony hand slid out of mine. I squinted against the blinding sunlight, catching a glimpse of the ocean before I plunged right into it. Cold bored into me. I kicked and paddled, fighting to reach the shore, but the torrents tossed me in all directions.

Miss Meow scrambled out of my knapsack, nicking my neck with her splayed claws. Hissing, she launched off my shoulders and into the water. I lost sight of her as waves towered over my head and crashed into explosions of foam. Foul tasting water burned my throat and found its way to my stomach, nauseating me. If only I knew how to swim! The current pulled me under, filling my ears with a hollow sound that muted the chaotic rumble above. I flailed about in the murk as my lungs begged for air.

I slammed into something rough and unmoving. Pain shot through my side. My cloak billowed around me, tangling my limbs in endless fabric. I grasped the object I had struck and secured a palm-cutting grip on its jagged outcrops. With a gasp, I broke through the water's surface, clinging to a boulder, struggling to keep my chin above the waves. I panted, ribs aching, exhausted. It took all the strength I had to hold on and not be swept back out to sea.

Someone called to me. I blinked, adjusting to the sun's brightness. Waves swirled and splashed around my head, burying me in froth. I sputtered and shouted back. My raw throat only croaked with an indecipherable sound. The voice bellowed again, louder, closer.

A few seconds later, Carter's head bobbed up next to mine. Soaked, his auburn hair looked almost black, yet it was already coiling back into irrepressible curls. He latched onto the boulder, catching his breath.

Still keeping a firm grip on the rock with one hand, I grasped Carter's arm with the other. I never thought I would be so glad to have his company.

He frantically scanned the surrounding waters. "What happened? Where's Bryce?"

"Someone else was in the cave and grabbed him." I imagined a group of Black Valley's guards hauling Bryce away and slashing his throat. "We have to go back! We have to go back!"

"We can't without the amulet," Carter said, looking toward the shore. Red faced, he cursed repeatedly, smacking his palm against the rock. "I knew we wasted too much time." He exhaled a sharp breath to cool off. "Can you swim?"

I shook my head.

"All right." He moved closer, maintaining a firm grasp on the rock. "Grab ahold. I'll get you to shore."

I stared at him. "You know how to swim?"

"Like a fish." He pointed a thumb at his back. "Hop on."

Trembling, I wrapped my arms around his neck and shoulders, hugging my body close to his. Before I could change my mind, he pushed his feet against the boulder and propelled us toward shore. I yelped, clinging to him, craning my head above the waves. He cut through whitecaps with each stroke, swaying with the tide, gliding skillfully as a swallow on the gale. Ahead, the waves broke into ripples of foam onto a rocky bank. We stumbled onto the gravel beach and collapsed, completely spent.

Aching from the ocean's unmerciful power, I remained on hands and knees, vomiting seawater while Carter limped upslope to join his sister. Immediately, he fussed over her, wringing the water out of her clothes and hair. Miss Meow sat on a rock next to them, soaked skinny.

A dozen strides away, the waterfall slid down the bank at a slight angle. Its smooth, straight chute proved that men, rather than nature, designed the cascade. At its pinnacle perched a stone building with a wooden wheel attached to it. As the waterfall flowed past the building, its current sent the wheel spinning. Samuel described a structure like this in a story once. It was a tide mill.

I clutched the front of my cloak in my fists, willing Bryce to appear. "Come on, where are you?" A rock formed in my gut, churning, building mass. What if a guard had already beheaded him on the spot for his crime?

"Pull it together," I ordered myself as I took a calming breath. I couldn't lose my wits. I staggered upslope to join Carter and Katie.

"Please tell me that your Whisperer has told you something," I said to Carter.

He stared at me, slack-jawed. "I ... I can't, Buttercup. I'm so tired. We wasted too much time in Black Valley and now everything is ... awry. I can hardly think." He held his sister, rocking her back and forth. Though she was awake, her eyes went vacant. He pulled her closer, and her head lolled to the side. "Please hold on, Katie. Please don't leave me."

Instead of holding on, Katie passed out.

"This wasn't supposed to happen!" Carter pulled at his hair screaming. "No, no, no! Dammit!"

The siblings huddled together. Carter was falling apart. Katie might have been dying. My legs shook from the panic racing through my veins. Despite this, I stiffened my lower lip and surveyed our surroundings. With the exception of the tide mill, nothing but rock occupied the bank. Someone had to live nearby in order to keep the mill running.

"We're going to need warm shelter for her." I raced upslope to get a look at the landscape over the bank. Hopefully, either a friendly village or a forest resided at the top so I could build Katie a warm fire. Once she woke, I'd search for Bryce. I wasn't giving up on him.

I was a dozen feet from the top of the bank when a splash erupted from the crest of the waterfall. Two figures burst out of the cascade in a tangle of limbs. Wrestling and shouting, they tumbled down the channel and plunged into the ocean below.

"Bryce!" I screamed, racing to the base of the waterfall.

Searching the waves, I repeatedly called Bryce's name. But the ocean, hateful thing that it was, roared over my words. I mistook driftwood for his arms and reached out in hope. Then in one swift movement, his head shot above the water. He fought the current, swimming toward me. With one hand grasping mine and the other gripping the bank, he lurched out of the sea, heaving for breath and clutching his side.

I hugged him. "I was so worried." Breaking down, I spilled tears of relief.

The other figure emerged from the water. I pulled out of the embrace, gawking at our visitor. My body went cold.

Silver.

He stood on the opposite side of the narrow cascade donning his coat and sword. During his and Bryce's scuffle, he reclaimed his crossbow and quiver. Both Bryce and I scrambled to our feet. Bryce nudged me behind him, widening his stance and hunching slightly. He continued to wince with each breath. Ignoring his protective gesture, I shoved forward to stand alongside him.

"Let me handle this," Bryce whispered.

"No. You don't have to do this on your own," I answered. "We're in this together."

Silver paid no attention to our quibbling. He swiveled around, eyebrows raised, scanning our new environment. "I'll be damned. You travel through water exactly like the Harbingers of the Culling do." He turned to face us. His wet bangs clung to his forehead, burying his eyes in shadow. "How do you do it?"

"I'm not sharing my secret with Red Band filth." The pitch of Bryce's voice lowered with contempt.

Once again, he gently pushed me behind him, narrowing his eyes at Silver. The veins in his hands bulged as he balled them into fists. I touched Bryce's shoulder, attempting to set him at ease. Since Silver carried deadly weapons, we needed to solve this with words and smarts, not violence.

Silver's gaze brushed over Bryce's defensive stance, but his posture remained relaxed. "I didn't come here to arrest you, Fugitive."

Bryce's jaw tensed. "So you plan to skip the arrest and go straight to execution? Typical of Red Bands."

My jaw dropped. In all the encounters with guards I'd witnessed, Bryce always spat out an insult. His words nearly provoked a fight with the guards he bribed, and he had taunted Silver near the fountain, doubting that he could raise his weapon. Sometimes he had no tact.

"Why did you follow us?" I piped up, stepping alongside Bryce. Once again, he positioned himself in front of me, so I poked my head around his shoulder.

"I need your help," Silver said.

"Our help?" I asked. "So you don't want to kill us?"

Silver stared at me as if I had sprouted another head. "No, of course not." He turned back to Bryce. "Show me how to travel through water so I can hunt down the Culling and destroy it. In exchange, I'll see that your portrait is removed from the Stained Wall."

Bryce jerked his head. "You want me to help you find the source of the Culling?"

"Ideally, yes. This is your chance for redemption, Fugitive. Together, we can save our city."

Bryce straightened his posture and relaxed his hands. "I want to see the Culling stopped as much as you do. But I don't think I can help," he said, tone softening. "When I jump through a waterfall, I have no control as to where I end up. It all depends on the moon phase. I can't return you to Black Valley until the first day of the waxing crescent."

"Don't play games with me." Silver's mouth arched into a frown, and his brow sunk low over his eyes. "That's nearly four weeks from now."

"He's not playing games," I said. "If he could return you, he would. Waterfall travel is a one-way journey."

Silver glared at us for a moment. I couldn't read anything behind his hard gray eyes.

"This is unacceptable. My city won't survive four weeks without me." Silver stared at the sun rising in the east. "How far are we from Black Valley?"

Bryce shrugged. "I don't know exactly. But given the time of day and the temperature, I'd guess we're to the south."

Without another word, Silver turned and headed up the bank.

"Where are you going?" I shouted at his back, but he didn't respond.

"Let him go," Bryce said. "He probably needs a moment to digest all of this."

"Bryce," Carter yelled from up the bank, hugging Katie to his chest. "Please come quickly."

Bryce gaped at Katie, who hung limp in Carter's arms.

We raced upslope to join the siblings. From the corner of my eye, I noticed Silver at the top of the bank, surveying the landscape. Against the warming sky, his silhouette resembled a dark badge embroidered in vibrant cloth.

"She won't wake up," Carter said as we approached. He tenderly brushed the damp hair off Katie's face. "Please, do something. Save her."

Bryce knelt next to the girl and placed his hand on her forehead. "She's burning up. We need to get her somewhere warm and dry." He glanced at the tide mill, eyeing the gaping hole in its west-facing wall.

Carter's gaze followed his line of sight. "Good idea. We'll take shelter in the tide mill."

"Are you mad?" I asked. "That place looks ready to fall over."

"I know what I'm doing, Honey." Carter wedged his arms under Katie and lifted her. As he straightened to standing, he grimaced, cursing between his gritted teeth. He fell back to the ground. I recalled how he limped moments before when we arrived to shore. He looked at Bryce. "I need you to carry her."

One injured. One sick. The odds were stacking up against us.

The sound of footsteps crunching against gravel neared. Silver joined us, cocking an eyebrow at Katie. "What's wrong with her?"

"She's ill," I said.

Without warning, Silver tore Katie from Carter's arms and heaved her over his shoulder. "Follow me." He rushed up the bank.

Carter hobbled after him, clenching his fists. "Give me back my sister, you damn Red Band!"

Bryce held him back. "Carter, we need better shelter than that tide mill. He won't harm her."

"You don't know that!" Carter struggled against Bryce's grip.

I scooped up Miss Meow and dashed after Silver while the two of them argued. The cat swatted me once in the chin with her sheathed paw, but then settled into my arms, growling. She'd put up with this, but she clearly didn't approve.

I grappled my way up the stony bank. When I reached the top, I froze. A barren desert sprawled before me, stretching to a horizon capped with purple mountains. Their jagged peaks stabbed toward the pale-yellow sky. At their base, a city spiked with coned turrets rose out of the sandy haze. Silver trekked over the dunes, carrying Katie directly toward it.

Collecting my bearings, I continued the pursuit. Silver was already at least two-dozen feet ahead of me. The ocean breeze vanished. After a few steps, thirst overtook me. Hot, dry air sucked the moisture off my skin, leaving a gritty film of sand and salt on my cheeks.

"You can't keep tossing people over your shoulder and carrying them off," I shouted at Silver's back.

Poor Katie. At least she was unconscious for this indignity.

He gave me an over-the-shoulder glance with a deadpan expression. "Yet it appears I'm doing just that. Does it bring back fond memories?"

"Fond memories?" A vein pulsed in my neck as I recalled the overbearing manner with which he lugged me into the shack despite my protest. "Do you think you're being funny?"

He kept walking.

Between the scorching sun and my anger, I was burning up. "You have absolutely no manners. Bryce and I saved your life. A normal person would show some gratitude."

He sped his pace.

I hurried after him. My feet sank into sand fine as flour. "Silver," I yelled. "Slow down."

"Silver?" He turned his head toward me. One eye narrowed with a hint of amusement, though his lips remained in a straight line.

"You never told me your name, so I had to call you something."

He made a thoughtful grunt. "It's kinder than the name I gave you."

"What are you talking about? What name did you give me?"

"Pain in the neck."

"You've got some nerve! You better call me nothing but my name: Ri." I looked over my shoulder, glad to see my two companions racing to join us. "That's Bryce. Carter is the one lagging behind. The poor girl you have your boorish hands on is Katie. And we don't report to you, so you might as well stop ordering us around. We're not your men."

"You're right. We'd be there already if you were." He trained his eyes on the city, now no more than two hundred feet away. There was an arched entry with shards of wood clinging to huge iron hinges: the remains of a door long destroyed.

"We can't march into that city in plain view without knowing who lives there." I fell into the sand, but immediately got back up. "Are you listening to me? Silver!"

"My name is Baxter. Baxter Renselar."

I stopped as if someone punched me in the gut. "Did you say Renselar?"

"I did," he said without slowing his stride.

Bryce caught up to me. "Renselar?" he asked under his breath. "This is bad. Very bad."

"No, it's good." While Baxter marched onward, I pulled my compass out of my pocket and flipped it over, showing the inscription to Bryce. "A man named Robert Renselar gave this compass to Samuel."

"I know. I saw the inscription last night." Bryce pivoted in front of me and guided my hand—including the compass—back into my pocket. "Listen to me," he whispered. "You must never show your compass to that man. Never."

"But they have the same surname. He might know who Robert Renselar is, and Robert Renselar might know how to cure Samuel."

He clutched my elbows, stilling me. "Please Ri. I promise to explain everything, but for now, please keep that compass hidden."

"Wait a minute." I wriggled out of his grip. "You saw the inscription last night? Does that mean you know who Robert is, but didn't tell me?"

He pursed his lips and switched his gaze from me to Carter, who finally joined us. Bryce grabbed his arm, stopping him mid-run, and pulled him close. "Did your Whisperer tell you that captain is a Renselar?"

"What?" Carter's eyes widened as he turned to look toward Baxter, who was heading back in our direction. He had shifted Katie from his shoulder and now cradled her in his arms. Her face was nested inside of his coat, safe from the strands of dust swirling in the breeze.

"We need to move. Now." Baxter nodded toward the eastern sky. A brown fog rose from the desert's horizon line, billowing into clouds that climbed higher and higher. It was a giant wall of dust, barreling toward us like a fire fueled by all the trees in a forest.

CHAPTER 14

Dust. So much dust. Clouds rose into the heavens, blotting out the sun and sky with yellow-brown haze. Tumbleweed bounced across the land as if attempting to flee, and withered plants bobbed about as their roots clung to the dry, cracked earth. Nothing escaped the storm's wrath as it rumbled across the desert, bloating its massive plumes. Trembling, I pulled my scarf over my nose and mouth.

Bryce took Miss Meow from me and tucked her into my knapsack. Then, he swiftly linked his arms around Carter's and mine. Meanwhile, Baxter grabbed my opposite arm, securing a strong grip on my wrist. He had already protectively tied Katie's shawl around her face and hoisted her unconscious body back over his shoulder. With Baxter leading, we fled toward the city, scrabbling over the powder-soft sand.

At first, gentle ribbons of dust swirled through the air, brushing against my body like the swish of a river. But as the billows neared, the winds raised in roaring intensity. Sprays of grit acquired the sharpness of thorns and the sting of fire sparks.

Baxter tugged me onward with such force that it felt like my arm might dislocate. Sand stuck to his damp hair and clothes, camouflaging him against the dunes. With Bryce and Carter lagging, I couldn't speed up. I glanced behind me. Bryce repeatedly shuddered with coughs while Carter winced, hobbling on his injured leg. Blood gushed from a wound at the edge of his hairline. He squinted through the stream of scarlet as it trailed into his eyes.

A heavy weight formed in my chest. Outrunning this storm would be a challenge for a healthy, uninjured person, let alone my two ailing companions. We weren't going to make it. I imagined the five of us staggering our final steps, suffocating as the murky clouds covered us.

"Go with Baxter," Bryce shouted, unhooking his arm from mine. "Get to safety."

"No." I snatched his sleeve before any distance grew between us. If we separated, I'd never see him or Carter again. "We stay together. That's final."

We passed through the city's arched entry as the clouds rolled over the easternmost quarters, boiling over the turrets. Nearby, crumbling foundations lined the cobbled streets. My heart sank at the sight. There was no way these pathetic ruins could offer us the shelter we needed.

Despite this, Baxter kept a quick pace. He led us through the lanes as if he was familiar with this place and headed west where the distant silhouette of a temple's peaked roof promised safe haven. But a dangerous brew of flying debris threatened us every step along the way. Anything not secured to the ground took flight. A board whizzed toward us, spinning wildly, but Baxter pivoted to protect me, taking the hit on his upper arm. With a grunt, he shifted Katie off his shoulder and hugged her close to his body.

"Keep ahold of me," he shouted. Scratches covered his unshielded face.

I latched onto his coat and we charged forward. The dust thickened until I could no longer see anything—not even my own hands in front of me. I closed my eyes tightly to protect them from the constant assault. Grit spattered against the stone ruins, making a sound like frying eggs. Fine powder snuck under my makeshift mask, coating my lips and nostrils. I hunched over, coughing fiercely. I couldn't breathe. Lightheadedness overtook me. I tripped, banging my knees against the cobblestone road. Baxter's coat slipped out of my grasp. He must have failed to notice because he didn't turn back. Bryce helped me to standing.

"I lost Baxter and Katie!" The wind swept my words away. I waved my hand, searching through the blur of sand as I stumbled along with Bryce. "Baxter!"

The captain called back to me. Or perhaps it was a trick of the wind. I tugged Bryce and Carter toward the voice as an object crashed next to my feet with a bang. Shards struck my calves. I gasped, sucking down a gulp of sand.

"This way," Bryce shouted, pulling me in a different direction as I gagged on the unbreathable air.

After a few steps, the wind ceased to pummel my front side. I patted around, and my palm landed upon a stone wall before me. Carefully, I opened one eye to a slit. The dust continued to pour down from above, but the wall blocked the storm just enough that I could see Bryce and Carter next to me. Baxter and Katie were nowhere in sight. Carter slumped against the wall with head inclined. His eyelids fluttered, as if he were struggling to stay awake.

"He's lost a lot of blood," Bryce said. "We need to get him to the temple—it's straight ahead—I think I can feel my way toward it."

"What about Baxter and Katie?" I asked.

"I think Baxter was heading toward the temple." His dark bangs whipped in the wind. "I'm hoping we'll find them both there waiting for us."

Carter's eyes closed, and he leaned off balance to the side. Bryce caught him before he collapsed to the ground and then shook him frantically, stirring him from the brink of unconsciousness.

"Either way," Bryce continued, "Carter needs immediate attention, and I can't see a thing out here."

We draped Carter's arms over our shoulders and emerged from cover.

"Katie," Carter murmured, dragging his feet.

"She'll be all right," I assured him, though my voice wavered with uncertainty. "Baxter will protect her."

Together, we trekked against a gale that plowed into us with the power of white-water rapids. Random things smacked into me. I tucked my head closer to Carter's so I could protect both of our faces with my forearm.

"I found it!" Bryce said after we staggered a few hundred feet. I heard a loud thump as he yanked Carter and me to the right.

Within an instant, the intensity of the wind dropped to a single strong gust at my back. I squinted through my grime-coated eyelashes at the imposing room we had entered. An aisle flanked by rows of benches stretched ahead, ending at an altar encircled by 30-foot-tall alabaster effigies of Eisanea's eight priestesses. Faint light fell through stained-glass windows, tracing heaps of rubble and broken furniture. Carter collapsed to his knees, coughing.

Behind me, Bryce fought against the wind to close a wooden door twice his height. I swiveled around, searching. Only the three of us occupied the room. Katie and Baxter were still outside in the havoc. My stomach fell to the room's slate floor.

Bryce slammed the door closed, cutting off the stream of wind. All the things that had been swirling in the air dropped to the ground. Miss Meow scrambled out of my knapsack, wailing, and fled to the rear of the room.

"Ri, I need my supplies and water," Bryce said, removing his knapsack.

"Right." I removed my pack and rummaged inside until I located the small wooden chest and a canteen. I handed both to Bryce and in exchange he offered me a tinderbox, flint, and steel from his sack.

We both got to work. While I collected a metal cauldron and scraps of wood from the rubble, Bryce knelt next to Carter and gave him a vial of amber-colored medicine. "It's for the pain," he explained as Carter continued to mumble gibberish.

Once I gathered a good amount of kindling, I began striking the steel against the flint. Samuel taught me how to do this long ago, using supplies he brought with him from his homeland. I caught a spark on the shriveled charcoal cloth inside the tinderbox and blew the ember into a flame. In a quick motion, I transferred the flame to my assortment of firewood, giving us better lighting.

"My sister needs her medicine," Carter said weakly. His cheeks had paled to a sickly color and his eyelids drooped. At least Bryce had managed to clean most of the dirt away from his gash.

"Don't worry, I'm going to go back out there and find her." Bryce concentrated on threading a needle.

"No, we're wasting too much time." Carter crawled toward the door, swaying on hands and knees. The flow of crimson slid down his face, dampening the dust on his cheeks. "She needs her medicine now or she'll die. That damn Red Band. I'll kill him." He collapsed, clutching his forehead. "Dammit, everything's spinning."

"Stay still." Bryce hovered over him, pinching the bloody gash closed. He poked the needle through the flesh. Carter screamed in agony.

Unable to do much else, I clutched Carter's shoulders, keeping him still. "Hold on, only a few more stitches left."

"I need to find my sister," he mumbled and then passed out cold.

"We'll find her," I whispered. "I promise."

After seeing Katie faint on the beach earlier, I believed Carter when he said she didn't have time to spare. Even if Baxter found her shelter, the storm could rage on for hours. And we had all the supplies. Without fresh water and her blessed plants, Death stalked toward Katie by the second. I pictured the god—a dark shadow with a wicked smile—circling her, anticipating her final breath.

While Bryce completed the stitch, I searched the knapsacks until I found two jars of Katie's herbal concoction. I placed one in my pocket and then stood, securing my scarf back over my nose.

"No, Ri." Bryce rose to his feet. With his index finger, he slipped my mask back down. "One of us has to stay here."

"Stay here? Have you gone mad? I'm not letting you go out there alone." I yanked my mask back into place. "We stick together."

He clasped my face gently between his palms, bringing my gaze up to meet his. "I need you to watch over Carter. Who knows what foolish thing he'll do if he wakes to find us both missing."

"But ..." I clutched his wrist with strength I never realized I had. I couldn't let go. "What if something hits you? What if something knocks you out?" I rambled without pausing for breath. "We have to look out for each other."

"We are, Ri." His palms moved to my shoulders. Outside, the storm thrashed against the building. "Right now, this is where I need your help."

I glanced down at Carter. Katie meant everything to him. If anything happened to her, he'd fall into a hysterical mess.

"I should go," I said. "I have less trouble breathing and I'm quick."

"I can't let you do that. I'm guessing you've never been in a sandstorm before, but I have." He locked his gaze with mine. "I know what I'm doing. Have faith in me. I'll make it back to you." He pulled his scarf over his nose. His hazel eyes crinkled, suggesting that his kind smile existed underneath his makeshift mask.

My insides twisted. Every minute we debated decreased our chances of finding the others. Reluctantly, I released his arm. Doing so inspired a fear in me that I never experienced before.

"Everything's going to be all right." He pulled me close and kissed my forehead through his mask. I clutched his cloak, drawing him nearer until I heard the quick beat of his heart. The scent of the forest no longer clung to his clothes and hair. Instead, a mixture of sweat and dirt filled my nose. Regardless, I lingered in that moment for a few seconds longer. Then I let go, even though I wasn't ready to, and handed him the jar of medicine from my pocket.

"With any luck, I'll return quickly." He opened the door to a crack and peeked outside. "The storm has thinned somewhat. When I find them, we're going to take shelter in the first place we find, so I may not see you until the storm passes."

How excruciating every minute would be until his return!

He looked about ready to venture outside when he paused and glanced over his shoulder at me. His forehead creased with worry lines. "One last thing." He closed the door and tucked his hand underneath the collar of his shirt. "Hold onto this for me." He removed his amulet. Dust coated the smooth surface.

I jerked away from the pendant, raising my palms. "No, you're coming back. I don't want it."

He placed it around my neck. "Please, take it. Just in case."

Then, he turned and left, clothes flapping wildly as he pulled the door shut behind him.

For a moment, I stared at the exit as if he might return. His absence created an unsettling quiet in the temple. I clutched the amulet to my chest, gripping it so tightly that its rough ridges pressed painfully against my palm.

"He's going to make it back," I told myself and took a deep breath.

A clap of thunder boomed overhead, and all the windows went black from the thickening dust.

CHAPTER 15

Carter still needed tending to, and I needed a distraction from my worries. I retrieved the second jar of Katie's herbal remedy and dabbed the mixture onto his wound. Then I smeared the herbal concoction onto his bruised knee and bandaged it.

Now I just had to wait for the havoc outside to end. Grit clattered against the building's exterior while large objects struck the shuddering windows. Fortunately, the stained-glass depictions of forests, oceans, and crop-yielding fields withstood the vicious blows. After two hours had passed, my sleeves were a wrinkled mess from wringing them as I paced the temple's aisles. Surely Bryce had found safe shelter with Baxter and Katie, and was waiting for the storm to end … unless they were buried, or injured, or … dead.

"No. Bryce knows what he's doing," I rambled to myself, twisting a sand-coated strand of hair around my finger. "They're going to make it back. Safe. All of them."

A loud clunk echoed through the chamber as an object hit the roof. I jumped, hugging my arms around me. Staring up at the domed ceiling, I listened to debris assault the building.

"They're going to make it back," I said more forcefully, as if challenging the storm itself.

I glanced at Carter, who lay unconscious on the floor. Sitting at his side, I shook his shoulder, attempting to wake him. Not even a groggy mumble escaped his lips. I sat back on my heels, defeated.

Miss Meow emerged from under a bench and joined me, bumping her head against my leg. She mewed, flicking her tail back and forth. I poured some water into the base of a broken clay pot and then gave her a small piece of dried meat that Carter had packed.

While she enjoyed the offerings, I swept dust off one of the benches and sat down. Skipping a night's rest, nearly drowning in the ocean, and fighting my way through a sandstorm left me exhausted. If not for my jangling nerves, I would have dozed off hours ago.

As I rested my head on the back of the bench, I imagined this temple once full of life, bustling with chatter and hymns honoring Eisanea. Crescendos would have echoed against the forty-foot walls, while candle smoke mingled with the aroma of incense and bouquets of herbs. At the right hour, sunlight probably set the stained-glass windows aglow, warming the interior's textures of mahogany, iron, and slate. It was quite a contrast from the dim, musty ruins that surrounded me at that moment. Only the lonely effigies, representing the eight priestesses of Eisanea, were here to offer company.

The priestess Honesty stood in a patch of honeysuckle, hand over her heart and speaking toward the heavens. Bravery's dress fluttered in flames as she raised her sword to the sky. Empathy simply bowed her head, accommodating all with open arms. Love clasped the stem of a thorny rose, accepting the pain and beauty of the emotion. Loyalty held a candle in one hand while petting her wolf with the other. Justice stared blindly ahead with an owl perched on her shoulder, evaluating two men who stated their case before her: the criminal and the officer. Generosity held a blanket in her outstretched arms, sheltering two children that knelt at her feet. Tolerance placed a hand behind her ear, willing to listen to all.

According to folklore, every newborn child received a blessing from one priestess and would live a life dedicated to the trait she represented. I liked to believe the tale because it meant everyone, even the wicked, might have a little good in their souls.

The sound of pebbles trickling down Justice's arm brought my attention back to the owl upon her shoulder. The bird no longer stared at the two stone men below. Instead, it blinked its vacant, round eyes at me.

I jolted. "What the?"

Clearly, I had lost my wits. A stone bird couldn't move.

Just then, the bird spread its wings and swooped down, aiming its talon-tipped claws at me. Closing my eyes, I swatted at the flurry of feathers smacking my face, cursing the awful bird.

"Honey, wake up!"

I opened my eyes. Carter crouched near my bench and shook me. I glanced at Justice. Her stone owl resided in its rightful place, exactly as a lifeless hunk of carved stone should.

"Dammit! How long was I asleep?" I asked.

"I'm not sure. I just woke up myself." He crossed his lips with his index finger to shush me. "Keep it down. We're not alone."

He pointed toward a bolted chamber door on the opposite side of the altar. For a moment I stared at it, holding my breath. Then a loud thump came from the other side.

"I think someone's trapped in there!" I hastened toward the door, but Carter grabbed my wrist.

"Wait." His eyes rounded, full of panic. "That's not someone you want to help."

I wiggled out of his grip. "What? Why not?"

He looked around the room and then whispered, "I had a dream about this city. Everything was afire. And the hordes ... so much violence. Their hunger was maddening."

I shivered. "It was merely a nightmare, I'm sure."

He shook his head. "I think my Whisperer was trying to show me something." His pupils shrunk in his green irises, as if in some sort of trance. It reminded me of the distant, terrified look Samuel would get in his eyes when a hallucination tormented him.

"Those who survived the chaos, sought immortality," he said. "They sought to cheat Death, but Death wouldn't be cheated. So he cursed them. He made them eternal as the sand, and now they relive the horrors of their final hours, day after day."

Another bang came from the door and I flinched. Goose bumps covered my arms.

"The thing behind that door is neither man nor spirit," he continued, shaking fiercely. "It's something in between … much worse." His face went pale.

I wanted to reassure him that such things didn't exist. But how could I, after all I had seen in the last few days? So, instead I held his hand. "Carter, whatever is in this city, we'll face it together. And we'll find Katie."

Outside, the wind ceased howling. A hint of sunlight snuck through the grime-dappled windows and landed upon Carter's cheeks.

"Looks like the storm's ended." He rushed to the knapsacks lying at the foot of the altar. "Time to find the others."

I glanced at the chamber door. Whoever had been pounding on it had given up. Not a single sound came from the room.

"What if you're wrong about who's in that room?" I asked. "We can't ignore someone who may be trapped or hurt because of a bad dream."

"Yes, we can." He hurriedly repacked the supplies into the knapsacks. "Honey, my priority is to get you, Bryce, and my sister to safety."

"And Baxter," I added. "We can't leave him here."

"That Red Band's wellbeing is no concern of mine." He hoisted the bulkier of the two knapsacks onto his back and made his way toward the exit. Katie's herbal concoction must have worked because he no longer limped.

"You're impossible sometimes." I hurried toward the chamber door and placed my ear next to its wooden panels. "Hello? Is someone in there?"

Carter turned back toward me, shouting, "What are you doing? Let it be."

I removed the door's crossbeam from its brackets, but left a chain-linked bolt in place for safe measure. Opening the door to a crack, I peeked inside the small room. Light entered through a window on the far wall. With the exception of a pile of sand on the floor, the space was empty.

"That's strange," I whispered. "I know I heard something."

"Dammit." Carter joined me, slammed the door, and shoved the crossbeam back into place. "I said, let it be."

"Calm down," I said, raising my voice. "No one's even in there."

While he hastened back toward the exit, I gathered Miss Meow, who was huddling on a bench. Her puffed tail swatted back and forth, but she hopped into my knapsack without a fight. I slipped my arms through the straps and hurried after Carter.

Before I made it halfway down the aisle, the front door swung open. Bryce stood in the frame hunching, surrounded by a faint cloud of dust. Sand caked in his hair and clung to his cloak. His makeshift mask hung loose around his neck. Scratches marred his cheeks. He fell to his knees, panting.

"Oh no!" I raced to my friend and knelt in front of him. "Are you all right?" I brushed his hair off his forehead, scanning him for injuries.

"I'm fine," he croaked. With a downcast gaze, he lowered his head. "I couldn't find them."

I glanced at the door, searching for Baxter and Katie, but only a faint, brown haze entered the temple. I swallowed a lump. Time was running out for Katie, if it hadn't already.

Carter stormed toward the door and looked outside. "Couldn't find them? What do you mean you couldn't find them?"

Bryce looked at him with glassy, bloodshot eyes. "I'm so sorry, Carter. I searched everywhere."

"No!" Carter ran outside.

Bryce stood, but I grabbed his arm.

"Drink something first." I unhooked the canteen from his belt and removed the cork. The vessel felt full. No doubt he was saving the water for Katie once he found her. He took a few gulps as we emerged from the temple.

Once outside, my eyes strained against the sunlight as I took in the aftermath of the storm. Dusty fog lingered in the air, smudging the city with a filthy tinge. Two-foot-tall drifts of sand gathered between beaten-down buildings. Above, a blood-red sun hovered high in her noon position, burning through the murky clouds. The scent of dirt and seawater hung in the air.

Carter rushed ahead at a quick pace. "I'll kill that damned Red Band when I find him."

Under normal circumstances, I was sure Baxter could defeat Carter without breaking a sweat. But as Carter strode ahead calling his sister's name, his eyes flashed with such anger that I suspected he'd prove a challenge for any opponent—including the captain.

"Carter, slow down," I said, trailing him. "Baxter was only trying to do the right thing."

"Right thing?" Redness bloomed in his cheeks. "Not that man. He's the tyrant's blasted kin!"

"Tyrant's kin?" I looked at Bryce. "What's he talking about?"

Bryce sighed. "Robert Renselar is Black Valley's tyrant. All of his children are deceased, so Baxter must be his nephew." He drew closer and whispered, "I'm sorry, Ri, but that's why I didn't bring up the inscription on your compass last night. I wasn't sure what you'd do, and I didn't want to see you get hurt."

I froze and raised my palms. "Hold on. You're saying that the man who rules Black Valley is the same man whose name is etched on my compass?"

Bryce stopped walking, remaining at my side, while Carter hurried onward. "Yes, that's what I'm saying."

"Of all my blasted luck." I shook my head. The only man that might have had knowledge regarding the origin of Samuel's ailment and its cure was a wicked tyrant. "I can't believe that you weren't going to tell me."

"Ri, what would you have done? Barge through Gray Towers' doors looking for answers?" He started to rub my arm consolingly, but I swatted it away.

"That's absurd! I wouldn't barge through the doors. Please, I have some tact." Heat crept up my neck and into my cheeks. Had he truly planned to keep Robert Renselar's identity a secret? If so, I might have remained in the dark if Baxter hadn't shown up.

From the corner of my eye, I noticed Carter glaring at us from twenty-feet ahead, hands on his hips. "Can you two please concentrate on finding Katie? There are very evil things in this city." He spun on his heels and walked off before either Bryce or I could respond.

"Evil things?" Bryce raised an eyebrow at me.

I shrugged. "I'm not sure. We thought we heard something banging on a chamber door, but when I opened it, no one was there."

Bryce nodded, pursing his lips.

"Plus, he had creepy nightmare," I added. "I'll feel a lot better once we find the others and leave this dreadful place." I strode onward to catch up to Carter.

Bryce followed closely behind me. "Ri, wait. I really am sorry for not telling you about the inscription. "But you strike me as a little impulsive."

"I'm not impulsive, you're ridiculously overprotective."

He looked at the ground, nodding. "You're right. But I'm trying to keep you—keep everyone—safe." He sighed. "I hope you can forgive me. And I promise that once we all get to safety, I'll tell you everything I know about Black Valley and Robert Renselar."

I took a breath, attempting to let go of my irritation. After all, we had large problems to solve. "All right."

We made our way down the cobbled streets, searching buildings in case Baxter and Katie had fallen unconscious. I investigated a two-room shack. Light fell through a gaping hole in the peaked ceiling. Smashed furniture coated in sand lay toppled over throughout the building. A variety of woodworking tools hung on a wall. But other than that, the rooms were empty. I moved onto the next building only to discover a similar sight.

We carried on like this throughout the day as the sun descended toward the horizon. By late afternoon, the dry heat wore on me. I dragged my feet as if they weighed fifty stone. Each time I licked my lips, my tongue met a film of sand. My throat burned from calling Baxter's name.

Exhausted, I sank to my knees and rummaged through the knapsack for a canteen. Miss Meow hopped out and collapsed on the ground, panting. Her pupils were thin slits in wide eyes. After taking a gulp of water, I poured a bit in my palm and offered it to her. She weakly lapped it up. Bryce joined us with sweat beading on his brow.

"How are you feeling?" he asked.

"Just a bit parched." I handed him the canteen and he took a sip while scratching Miss Meow behind the ear.

Carter emerged from a cluster of ruins, cursing. Dust covered his face, except for two tracks that started beneath either eye and ended at his jawline. Throughout the afternoon, I had noticed him wiping tears away. Without stopping to rest with us, he entered the next building screaming Katie's name. His voice cracked dry and hoarse. His desperation broke my heart.

"Come on." Bryce stood, offering me a hand.

Once on my sore, blistered feet, I stared up at the sky. Most of the dust had settled, leaving a clear view of a blazing sunset that striped the sky in red, gold, and pink. On any other day, I would have called the display beautiful. But at that moment, the fierce colors announced the day's inevitable close, and nightfall would undoubtedly slow our search.

"I'm afraid we're not going to find her in time." I collected Miss Meow, and she sprawled in my arms like a limp blob of matted fur and heat.

"We will, Ri," Bryce said. Pink cheeks abused from the sun showed through smudges of dirt on his face. His lips were chapped and rough. "I'm not going to let her or Carter down."

While Carter searched the last few buildings at the end of the lane, Bryce and I rounded the corner of a fieldstone building at the intersection. A gust of wind plowed through the street, gathering sand off the cobblestone. Murky clouds swirled in the air, and though I covered my face, I managed to peek ahead through a narrowed eye. Shadows and light played against the clouds, forming shapes that soon morphed into recognizable, human silhouettes. A horde of people made completely of sand raised sand weapons, hacking at each other. A dusty ax flew toward my face and I ducked, barely saving myself.

"Bryce!" I turned toward him, but he just stood there, gawking at me. He spoke, but I couldn't hear his words over the clash of weapons and cries of anguish.

Then, the wind ceased. The sand settled to the ground and the horde disintegrated as suddenly as it had appeared. Heart pounding, I eyed the lifeless dunes scattered on the road.

"What just happened?" I asked.

A terrified Miss Meow had pinned herself to me with splayed claws, burying her head under my arm.

"It was only a little wind." Bryce looked around, slack-jawed. "Why are you acting so spooked?"

"Wind? Didn't you see it? Hear it? There was a whole army of sand people." I glanced down at Miss Meow. Her puffed tail wrapped around her tense body. "See, even your cat saw it. Look how scared she is."

"Ri, everything scares Miss Meow. Especially the wind." He stared at me as if I had gone mad. "There are no sand people. You're severely dehydrated and exhausted. Your mind's playing tricks on—"

A loud boom cut off his words. As its accompanying rumble vibrated under my feet, Miss Meow's claws stabbed through my shirt. Bryce pulled me into a building and scanned our surroundings for danger. Nothing came at us except for a panicked Carter. I failed to hear his approach due to the ringing in my ears. He dashed into the building to join us.

I carefully eased Miss Meow's claws off my shirt and poked my head outside. A few hundred yards away, a thread of black smoke rose into the western sky.

"Do you think Baxter did that?" I asked. "Perhaps he's trying to send us a signal?"

We emerged from our hiding place to get a better look.

"There's only one way to find out." Carter took off in the proper direction.

Bryce and I soon caught up, and we raced down the dusty cobblestone past skeletal frames of buildings that burnt down long ago. Ahead, beyond clusters of gabled, red-tiled roofs, flames waved in the wind, spewing black clouds. The dry scent of smoke thickened in the air, choking me. We rounded a corner, and I nearly collided with Baxter on the opposite side. He held an unconscious Katie over his shoulder. Blood spatter and dust covered his face and dappled his hair. His sword was drawn. A stream of crimson dripped off the blade.

His gray eyes shone with alertness, and the muscles in his jaw were rigid. "The Culling. It's here."

CHAPTER 16

Shadows cloaked the alley that Baxter had fled. Breathless, I scanned the area for the Culling's beasts, but could see nothing through the darkness. The fire raged on behind clusters of tiled rooftops, puffing coils of smoke into the purple sky. The last hints of daylight were slipping away, providing the ideal hunting ground for our pursuers.

Miss Meow squirmed in my arms. I loosened my grip so the poor cat could breathe and placed her into my knapsack.

"Take the girl and run." Baxter eased Katie off his shoulder and handed her to Carter.

Carter cradled his sister in his grasp and gently shook her. Tears rolled down his cheeks as he rambled, "Katie wake up, please wake up. Come on, you're all right. Just open your eyes."

"The Culling's beasts will be here soon," Baxter interrupted. "Find a safe place to hide while I hold them back."

Two pairs of eyes—red as hot embers—glared at us from the far end of the road.

"Go now," Baxter ordered, turning toward the flame-colored eyes. "Another sandstorm is coming, and the girl won't survive the next one."

"You heard him." Carter exchanged a glance with Bryce and me. "Let's go." Without waiting for us to respond, he took off in the direction of the temple.

Bryce drew his dagger. "Ri, go with Carter." He moved alongside Baxter and faced the beasts.

I slid my dagger from my belt. "No, I'm not leaving you behind," I said, despite the tremors racing up and down my legs.

Baxter looked at Bryce from the corner of his eye. "Katie told me you're a healer. She needs you." His voice was calm and steady. "Go. I'll catch up."

The wind shrieked, casting swirls of dust into the air.

I tugged Bryce's sleeve. "He's right. Katie needs us."

Bryce rubbed the back of his neck, passing Baxter and me a skeptical glance. Finally, he tucked his dagger under his belt and gave Baxter a nod of appreciation.

With that, we both darted off, attempting to catch up to the siblings who were roughly thirty feet ahead. Charred frames of buildings and their blackened, stone foundations stood on either side of us. The thick beams no longer supported roofs, but they rose toward the dusk sky, straight as soldiers. Gusts of sand blew through the skeletal structures, creating an eerie whistle that soared over the familiar rumble of the approaching storm.

Bryce took my hand as I pulled my scarf over my nose. A cloud of dust rolled into the street and instantly swallowed everything. Grit pelted me with the force of a heavy rain.

Squinting, I spotted Carter ahead. He maneuvered around two battling sand people that manifested in the murk. I tugged Bryce to the side to avoid them.

"What's wrong?" he shouted.

"Didn't you see them?"

"See what?"

This was the second time Bryce hadn't noticed the sand people. Was there something wrong with his eyes or was I hallucinating?

Ahead, Carter dodged two others. So the things weren't figments of my imagination! But why could Carter and I see them when Bryce couldn't?

A sand woman appeared out of nowhere, bumped into my shoulder, knocked me back a step, and then ran off. My hand slipped out of Bryce's, but he quickly regained ahold of it. Apparently, these beings could touch us, which meant they could also harm us.

Ahead, Carter waved from the doorway of a squat building. A metal sign shaped like a boot violently swung back and forth above him, squealing over the roaring wind. We reached the building and squeezed inside all at once. Carter slammed the door behind us.

I grabbed Carter's shoulder. "Those things ... those sand people ... are they the cursed you spoke of earlier?"

"Yes, but we'll discuss it later." He placed Katie on the ground near a stack of wooden crates. A faint patch of light fell from a single window, illuminating her ashen, sweat-dappled skin. Bryce joined the siblings while I removed my knapsack. Miss Meow hopped out and dashed to the edge of the room, crouching beneath rows of empty shelves. I quickly found Bryce's wooden box and a canteen in the sack.

Bryce accepted the items. He popped the box open and selected a vial filled with golden liquid. Meanwhile, Carter knelt on the floor, gently rocking Katie in his arms. He dabbed a bit of the herbal remedy onto his finger and placed it in her mouth, begging her to wake. She did not.

"She's badly cut up." Bryce poured a few drops of the liquid between Katie's parted lips. "This will help bring down the fever, but she's going to need stitches."

While they tended to the poor girl, I found a cloth in the knapsack, moistened it with water, and placed it on her forehead. Her eyelids twitched.

Small objects clanked against the rooftop. I glanced out the window, but dust obstructed the view. I fidgeted with the button that clasped my cloak, watching the murk outside thicken.

"We have to signal Baxter somehow," I said. "He'll never find us in here."

"Good," Carter said. "Let the storm take care of him. It'll save me the trouble."

I exhaled an exasperated breath. "You need to end this grudge. Even you have to admit that we'll need his help now that the Culling is here."

"He's likely the reason it's here," he scoffed. "We wouldn't be in this mess if it weren't for him."

Katie mumbled.

Carter frantically tapped her on the cheek. "Wake up, wake up."

Her eyes opened halfway. "Carter?" Her voice was slightly louder than a whisper, but we all sighed with relief at the sound of it. She smiled and raised a bony hand to her brother's forehead, brushing her fingertips against his stitches. "Oh, Carter. Are you all right?"

He grinned, clutching her hand in both of his. "Never better. Don't you worry about me one bit." He kissed her knuckles.

I glanced out the window again, searching for Baxter.

Bryce threaded a needle and eyed a gash on her forearm. "You have a few wounds that I need to tend, but I think you're going to be all right."

"Use this." Carter presented the jar of the herbal concoction.

"After I stitch the wound," Bryce said. "I prefer to rely on the tested and true over magical potions."

I gnawed on my lip while the two of them helped her. Did Baxter defeat the beasts? Was he searching for us, dodging the sand people? Perhaps he was blind to them like Bryce. My gaze slid toward the window again. I had to do something.

Miss Meow mewed and sniffed a coil of rope at the far side of the room.

I hurried to pick it up. At least sixty feet of sturdy cord rested in my hands. I tied one end of the rope into a lasso and slipped it around my waist.

Bryce paused from stitching Katie's wounds and stared at me. "What're you doing?"

"I'm going out there to see if I can find Baxter." Tethered, I could venture outside without getting lost in the storm.

Both he and Carter gawked at me, while Katie propped herself up and scanned the room.

"Oh my. He's still out there?" she asked.

"Ri, no," Bryce said. "It's too dangerous. I'll go."

"No. Stop acting so overprotective of me. You need to take care of Katie. The wind has died down, and I'll have the rope to guide me back."

His brow wrinkled as he glanced out the window. Objects no longer clinked against the glass panes, proving that the strong gusts had indeed slackened.

"The Culling's beasts may still be out there," he said.

"And we're no match against them without Baxter," I said. "We have to find him."

"Did you get knocked on the head?" Carter narrowed his eyes at me. "I can't believe you fancy that blasted Red Band."

"Don't be ridiculous! I don't fancy him. We need to look out for each other if we want to survive." I pulled my scarf over my nose and opened the door to a crack.

"Ri, wait," Bryce said.

I looked at him over my shoulder. "I'm going."

Sighing, he ran a shaking hand through his hair. "All right, go. But if you're not back in five minutes, I'm coming to get you."

I held up the coil of rope. "Just follow this. I won't be far."

After slipping out the door, I fastened the opposite end of my rope to the door latch and crept toward where we had separated from Baxter. A stagnant cloud of dust lingered in the air, allowing only a few feet of visibility in any direction.

Staying near the buildings, I inched forward while looking for signs of movement ahead. A cluster of sand people appeared in the brown fog. They were so fixated on killing each other that they failed to notice me as I slunk along the remnants of a stone building. One in particular sent shivers through me. Built nearly seven feet tall, his muscled arms bragged of a life spent hauling stone, or perhaps crushing it. He wielded an ax, and with each swing one of his adversaries disintegrated in a puff of dust. Not a hint of remorse existed in the dark holes that made up his eyes, or lack thereof. His voice, roaring victoriously over his rivals as he claimed his territory, sounded like animalistic growls.

The sand people had already proven they had human strength. Did their blades, formed of grit and debris, rival the sharpness of steel as well? Best not to find out. I snuck past, drawing my dagger for safe measure. Once they faded in the haze behind me, I called to Baxter. No answer came. I tried again.

Without the wind, all was quiet. My shoes were filled with sand and crunched with every step. Dust and dry air blurred my vision. A slight tug jerked my waist. The rope stretched taut with no more give. Unable to go any farther, I continued to call to Baxter.

Ahead, came a flash of movement.

"Baxter?" I squinted at a fast-approaching, dark-colored smudge in the haze. As it neared, the figure took shape. Standing tall as a wolf, it charged toward me on four muscular legs while whipping its reptilian tail from side to side. Red eyes locked onto me.

I gasped, sucking down a gulp of dusty air. Just as I turned to run, the beast pounced on top of me. The impact knocked me backward. I slammed against the hard cobblestone and coughed the air out of my lungs. Two rows of ebony-colored fangs snapped in my face.

Sprawled on the ground, I pressed my feet into the beast's scaled stomach to hold it back, but my legs buckled like twigs ready to snap under the creature's weight. Razor-sharp talons slashed at me, missing my nose by mere inches. Hot spittle dripped from its forked tongue and splattered onto my cheeks. I thrust my dagger, and a shock rippled up my arm as my blade plunged into its three-fingered hand. Blood gushed from the wound, drenching my weapon in crimson. I locked my grip on the slickened hilt and yanked my dagger free. The blade ripped through the beast's knuckle joint. It yelped and stumbled back.

I ran back toward my companions. My pulse throbbed in my ears, but I could still hear the beast's growls a few feet behind me. If I returned to the others, it would surely follow me and rip everyone apart. So instead of returning to them, I ducked into a rundown shack and hid behind a toppled-over desk. My shoulders and arms stung fiercely. I slipped my fingers through my torn sleeve and felt a jolt of pain when I touched parted, bloody flesh. In those terrifying seconds, I didn't realize how many times the beast's claws had slashed me.

A snarl came from outside. Holding my breath, I peeked over the desk, watching the dark silhouette search for me in the fog. My hands trembled, grasping my dagger—a pitiful weapon against such a monstrous beast. It was mere luck that I had even stabbed the creature in the first place. I was going to die. I was never going to see Samuel, Bryce, or home again. If only I had a powerful blade like Baxter's and the strength to use it. But I didn't, and I was alone.

"Pull yourself together," I told myself. "There's a way out of this. Think."

In the distance, another triumphant roar echoed from the man made of sand. I took a calming breath and set my jaw. Perhaps I didn't have the power to kill the beast, but I knew someone who did: sand giant.

I cut the rope off my waist and bolted into the open. Within seconds, the beast pursued. Its claws scraped the cobblestone behind me. I bumped into two sand people, shoved them out of the way, and kept charging onward. My plan was foolish. It was never going to work. In a few short moments, either a blade would split me in half, or fangs would sink into my flesh.

The ax-wielding sand giant materialized in the dust. I smacked into him. He turned his frightful, eyeless face toward me. His lips curled back, baring his teeth. He jammed the blunt end of his weapon into my gut. I fell to the ground, clutching my stomach, trying to refill my lungs with breath.

He lifted his weapon over his head, growling. The Culling's beast lunged on top of me. Hot breath reeking of blood brushed against my nape. The ax came down. Squeals pierced through my temples like knives. The beast collapsed alongside me, writhing and wailing.

I fumbled to my feet and dashed away. Every part of me ached. My shoulder blades stung from countless gashes. From behind, I heard the blade hack through the beast once more, permanently ending its high-pitched squeals. I stumbled onward without looking back. Spots danced in my vision. The entire front of my shirt was soaked in blood. The world was spinning. My legs went weak. Dying ... I was dying. Bleeding out. One more step, just one more step.

Someone rushed toward me.

"Ri," Bryce shouted. He joined me just as I collapsed into him.

"What happened?" he asked. "You're covered in blood."

"It's dead ... don't worry, it's ..." I slumped in his arms and closed my eyes. Suddenly, I was sitting on the sun-warmed cliffs back home, admiring the evergreen vale. Mist rose up in careless swirls. Soft bird chatter carried me off, farther and farther.

A voice called. The image of the valley disappeared. I opened my eyes, blinking away dust. Bryce was carrying me, rushing toward our shelter.

The voice called again. Louder. Closer. Baxter?

"Stop," I muttered.

Bryce stopped running and turned around. Baxter was hurrying toward us, fuzzy in the haze. I would have called back to him, but the energy to keep my eyes open dwindled away. I let them close. The spruce-filled valley welcomed me back. The birds drowned out Bryce's voice as he shouted, "Ri, wake up. Stay with me."

***

I awoke, propped against the wall of our shelter.

"She's awake!" Katie, sitting in front of me, waved a canteen in front of my face. I swatted it away.

"Don't move," Bryce said to me. He was kneeling at my right, armed with a needle and thread. "This is the last stitch. Almost finished."

I clenched my teeth as the needle's sharp point poked into my flesh. Three sets of black stitches marred the arm he worked on.

Carter was to my left, smearing the herbal concoction onto wounds Bryce had already mended. "Don't worry, Buttercup. By tomorrow you'll be good as new." The mixture cooled my shoulder, relieving the throbbing sting.

A few feet away, Baxter sat on a wooden crate. He rested his elbows on his knees, watching everyone fuss over me. For the first time, a hint of concern warmed his gray eyes as he stared at the threaded tracks upon my skin. Perhaps he thought I risked my life solely for him. Or, perhaps, he felt some level of responsibility for my near-death encounter. Either way, I hoped he would see me as an equal, rather than a weak inferior that he could order around.

"I was told you've been hunting the Culling on your own," I said. "What can you tell us about it?"

"It seeks to slaughter humanity." He stared down at his clasped hands. "My uncle always believed isolating the city would protect us—as if the beasts would forget about our small city in the northern corner of the world. A foolish idea. I left Black Valley six years ago against my uncle's wishes to search for the Culling's source so I could destroy it once and for all."

"A lot of good that did," Carter interrupted. Katie swatted him in the arm.

Baxter glared at him for a moment before continuing. "During my travels, all I encountered was the aftermath of the Culling's attacks. Dead cities. Occasionally I crossed paths with small bands of survivors. They told me that Harbingers spilled out of lakes, streams, rivers—killing everyone."

"I discovered dead cities during my travels as well," Bryce said. "I always assumed that they fell victim to war or famine." He looked down and shook his head. "It's surprising that Black Valley hasn't been attacked until now."

"Mere luck," Baxter said.

"We need to get somewhere safe." I turned toward Baxter. "Since we arrived, you've seemed familiar with this place. Where are we?"

"Sea Dragon's Point," he answered. "I lived here as a child."

"Oh." With the condition the city was in, it was difficult to imagine anyone had once called it home. Baxter must have left prior to the violence Carter had spoken of earlier. Or, perhaps, he left because of it. Either way, it was no time to ask such questions.

"So how far are we from Black Valley?" I asked.

Baxter raised his eyebrows. "It's simple geography. Even someone from the Slag would know."

"Don't be so hard on her," Bryce interrupted. "She's suffered a lot of injuries and is obviously not coherent." He locked eyes with me, delivering a clear message. I needed to watch what I said around Baxter. If he learned that I came from Warning Rock, it'd raise a lot of questions. Those questions would lead to Samuel.

"Sea Dragon's Point is directly south of Black Valley," Baxter explained. "It'd be a two-day trek if not for Funeral Peaks."

Two days? But it was so hot here and so cold there. It made no sense.

"No one's ever survived the journey through Funeral Peaks," Katie chimed in, clutching the front of her cloak. "It's rumored that cannibalistic tribes live there."

Cannibalistic tribes. The Culling. Sand people. Why couldn't we encounter something pleasant for once?

"So what do we do now?" I asked.

Bryce completed my stitch. "The original plan was to stay here for a few days until the waterfall can deliver us somewhere safe, but Baxter believes that the Culling will find us."

Carter scowled at our silver-haired companion. "Thanks for leading them here, Red Band. You've ruined everything."

"It's not his fault," Katie said. "We'd have swarms of those beasts on us if Baxter hadn't set that explosion off at the alchemist's shop. You should be thanking him."

"Would you stop talking about him like he's some sort of hero?" Carter scrunched his face in disgust. "He nearly got you killed."

Baxter opened his mouth to speak, but I cut him off. "Please, everyone stop arguing." Turning to Bryce, I asked, "Can we travel through the waterfall tonight?"

He shook his head, holding up his journal. "The waterfall on the opposite side is frozen."

"So we chop through it," I said.

"No, I've done that before and I'll never do it again." Bryce packed his supplies into his wooden box. "Once we destroy a frozen waterfall, it damages the passage. We'd be trapped wherever it delivers us, and chances are it'd be a cold, unlivable place."

I slumped against the wall. "So we'd all freeze to death."

Everyone sat quietly for a moment. Apparently, not even Carter's Whisperer spoke to him, because he just stared at the dollop of herbal concoction remaining in the jar.

Finally, Baxter stood. "I know a way out of here. Pack your things."

CHAPTER 17

Baxter's escape route brought us northward. The storm had cleared, and only the occasional swirl of dust cascaded from the rooftops when the night breeze stirred. Above, the clouds parted, revealing a star-sprinkled sky and a sliver of a moon.

My feet pounded the cobblestone road as we raced through the narrow alleys. Bryce and Baxter led the way, hauling the knapsacks while Carter and I lagged a few feet behind. Carter's chest heaved with labored breaths as he lugged his sister on his back. Sweat rolled down his face, creating streaks on his dust-coated skin. Katie's eyelids fluttered as she drifted in and out of consciousness.

We passed the charred buildings and arrived at an area filled with rundown gabled homes. Between the crumbling walls, heaps of scattered debris, and toppled over pillars and beams, the area offered too many places for the Culling's beasts to hide. At any moment, they could have leapt from the shattered windows to snatch us from behind. I shivered, imagining those drool-soaked fangs ripping through my neck ... feeling the razor-sharp talons slash at my stomach's soft flesh ... lying in the street, watching the blood draining out of me and webbing between the cobbles ... listening to my companions cry out as they suffered the same cruel death.

I tugged Carter's arm, urging him to run faster.

Finally, the alley widened and brought us to a large square framed by colossal homes. Carter let out a low whistle as he gawked at an estate's marble walls, elegant arched windows, and rooftop terrace. Ornate motifs crowned each building's entryway. The carvings, embellished with gold inlays, were so expertly crafted that I could almost smell the flora they represented.

We dashed across the square. Baxter stopped in front of a home with a large red door set behind a trio of columns. He led us up the steps, opened the door, and waved us inside.

Moonlight trickled through the front windows, lending a soft glow to the remains of luxury. The walls climbed at least thirty feet before reaching a ceiling decorated with murals of nature scenes. Thick drapes, dulled from age and neglect, drooped from rods with fern-shaped finials. Though sparsely furnished, recessed shelving housed hundreds of fragile books along the back wall. Perhaps the evil things had something to do with the city's downfall.

Bryce joined my side and whispered, "Such an excessive way for a single family to live while so many others starve."

"A single family?" I swatted away the dust motes, crinkling my nose at the musty-smelling air. "My whole village could fit in this place."

A massive oak table stretched across a chamber to our right. Most of its twenty chairs were toppled over. Remnants of daily life haunted the room: a pewter goblet on the floor, broken gold-trimmed plates and bowls, and a lopsided portrait on the wall.

Carter set Katie down and picked up the goblet. He rotated it in his hand, admiring the gems embedded below its lip. "Apparently, Baxter's family was quite well-to-do. And now the spoiled child is all grown up, leading Black Valley's oppressive regime." He smirked at Baxter. "How proud you must be."

"You know nothing." Baxter strode to a cabinet at the room's far end.

I gaped at Baxter. "You lived here?"

"Yes, until I was thirteen." He retrieved an oil lantern from the cabinet and with a click of the knob soft light illuminated our surroundings. Shadows pooled in the recesses of carvings upon the walls that featured men riding mighty hooved animals I had never seen before.

I glanced at the portrait again. Though dust coated the artwork, smudges of color poked through. The eldest male donned a rich purple vest. A gold broach adorned the woman at his side. The couple rested their hands on the shoulders of two children standing in front of them. Each boy had pale-silver hair. Baxter stalled in front of the painting.

"Is that your family?" I asked.

He jerked his head and glanced at me, as if surprised that I noticed him staring at the artwork. He cleared his throat and nodded slightly. "May they rest in the light of the Violet Star." Lowering his gaze, he rushed out of the room. "Follow me."

Instead of following, I placed my hand over my chest and watched him head back into the main room. Bryce, Carter, and Katie remained alongside me.

"How sad," I said softly. "Baxter lost his entire family."

Carter rolled his eyes. "Don't feel so sorry for him. Plenty of folks in the Slag have lost their families to Red Band filth like him."

"Carter!" Katie scowled. "Don't be so cold."

"Agreed," Bryce added. "Let's go, we're wasting too much time here."

We entered the main room where Baxter waved us to follow him up a spiral staircase with ornate iron railings. He hardly seemed like the type of man who would murder innocent families in the Slag. I wanted to know his story.

Taking two steps at a time, I followed him with the rest of my companions. A stretch of hallway met us at the top. Broken glass and tiles crunched beneath our feet as we hastened toward a double door at the end of the corridor.

Baxter swung the door open and entered a spacious room. "This was my father's workshop."

"Workshop?" I asked, close behind him.

A few steps past the entry, two large cloth-covered objects awaited us. One rose waist high, while the other towered a foot taller than Baxter. Beyond those, a desk stretched across the length of the back wall. Brass tools, bolts, spools of wire, and scraps of metal lay scattered on its surface. Drawings of contraptions with gears, wheels, and blades covered most of the walls. The only wall free of diagrams stood opposite the entryway. There, an expanse of windows provided a view of mountains and the endless, starlit sky.

"This is incredible!" I swiveled around, taking it all in. How I would have loved to rummage through every bin in that workshop, explore all the unusual tools, and study the drawings. "Your father was an inventor?"

"My father was a genius." Baxter proceeded to the rear of the room. "But he wasn't tidy, so watch your step."

I hurried to the largest covered item. I had to step over a few pipes and wrenches scattered on the floor before removing the sheet. Perhaps it was rude to do so without asking first, but that thought crossed my mind a moment too late. My breath hitched at what stood before me.

The base of the contraption resembled a canoe supported by three wheels: one at the pointed stern and two at its rear. A pair of canvas wings—retracted like a resting bird's—canopied over the base, fastened by a frame of metal pipes and sprockets. Inside, a plush seat faced a wheel and various knobs, levers, and switches. The mahogany and metal surfaces probably glistened in the sunlight once, but at that moment, a thin layer of the desert's golden-brown sand coated all of the parts.

I glanced at the others. "Isn't this amazing?"

Carter waited near the door. He waved his hand in front of his mouth and yawned. "I suppose. If you like this sort of thing."

Katie scowled at him. "You're acting jealous. Stop it."

Bryce joined me next to the contraption. I hopped inside and sank into the seat. The wheel begged me to grasp it, so I did.

Bryce knelt at the side of the contraption's base, resting his arm on its rim. I wiped away the grime from glass plates that shielded needles and symbols. My foot caught on something. Pedals? What did they do? I passed Bryce a sideways glance and our eyes met. Had he been watching me the whole time?

"What?" I asked.

Looking down, he shrugged. "Um … it's nothing. It's just … your sense of wonder is cute, that's all."

"Oh." My cheeks warmed.

Baxter approached. He rubbed his fingertips along the edge of the wing. "The flying machine."

"Flying machine?" My heart felt like it might flutter out of my chest. I pictured those wings spread, soaring toward the horizon, clouds brushing against my skin with the softness of wishing flowers. "That's your plan? We're going to fly out of here?"

"No," he said matter-of-factly. "The flying machine puzzled my father his entire life. He never finished it. Instead, we will use this." He pulled back the cloth from a nearby object, revealing a simple, yet well-crafted, fifteen-foot-long rowboat.

"Oh." My exhilaration plummeted from the clouds and crashed into the workshop's drab slate floor.

"You sound disappointed," Baxter said with a slight smirk.

"Um … well, no." I stepped out of the flying machine, still staring at the collection of switches. My fingers itched to flip one. "It's not that I'm disappointed."

"You don't need to explain yourself, Buttercup," Carter broke in, leaning against the doorframe. "I'm sure Baxter always disappoints the ladies."

Katie smacked her brother in the shoulder. Baxter tilted his head, squinting one eye, but he made no response.

"Where are you suggesting we row to?" Bryce eyed the boat.

"Black Valley. We must return at once to protect our city." The lantern light shone upon Baxter's deadpan expression.

Gaping, I exchanged a glance with Bryce and Carter.

Even Bryce's eyebrows shot up at Baxter's answer. "Excuse us for a moment," he said to Baxter. Bryce, Carter, Katie, and I huddled together in a circle.

Bryce leaned in and whispered, "Normally I wouldn't agree with a Red Band, but returning to Black Valley might be our best hope. Those beasts are likely in our pursuit, and we'll have a better chance of surviving in numbers. I'm sure Baxter won't let the City Guard harm us now."

"You can't be serious," I said. "You were so certain that we would be killed if we stayed in Black Valley, and now you want to go back? Baxter seems honorable enough, but he can't protect us from the City Guard if he's busy fighting the Culling. Let's use the boat and go west. To Warning Rock."

"No, Ri," Bryce said. "We've been through this. You've seen how dangerous the sea is. That little boat will make it to Black Valley because it's a straight shot north and we can row close to shore. But west? There's no way that dinghy would survive deeper waters."

"Either way, we can't stay here," Carter interrupted. He sucked on his lower lip, glancing behind him at the expansive hallway. "Let's get the boat to sea. I'll come up with something."

"Come up with something?" I asked. "Are you sure? We can't aimlessly float around in the water."

"Don't worry, Honey." He clasped my hand and grinned mischievously. "I wouldn't dare get you all wet and not deliver."

"Ew," both Katie and I said in unison. I pulled out of his grip.

"Is there a problem?" Baxter spoke over our hushed discussion.

Carter pulled Bryce and me close. "Trust me. I'll come up with something."

I hardly trusted Carter, but since the sea seemed safer than a monster-infested city, I nodded.

Carter then looked up at Baxter, smiling his phony smile. "No problem at all. Black Valley it is."

"Good." Baxter gave a terse nod. "Katie, are you well enough to walk on your own?"

She glanced at Carter before answering. "Yes, I think so."

"I will keep the path clear." Baxter gestured at me, Bryce, and Carter. "The three of you will carry the boat."

"A little demanding, isn't he?" Carter made his way toward the vessel.

I ignored him and searched the rear of the boat for blades or gears. "So does it do anything special?" I asked Baxter.

"Special?" He looked at me as if I was the village fool. "No, it's a rowboat. You dunk the oars in the water and row."

I scrunched my face into a scowl. "You don't need to be so rude about it. I was curious because it was surrounded by all these other unusual things."

A whirring sound came from the far side of the room. Baxter, Bryce, and I turned to look. A potato-sized mechanical bunny hopped across the desk. Katie stood next to it, gawking at us with wide eyes. "I'm sorry. I didn't mean to poke around." She picked the bunny up, placing her palm over its feet until the noise stopped. "Did your father make this too? It's marvelous."

"No, I built that toy as a child," Baxter said. "You may have it if you like."

"Oh, how kind." Katie showed it to her brother.

Carter looked down his nose at the toy. "Oh, yes. I owned something like that once. It broke. Cheap things they are."

She swatted him. Again.

"I think it's amazing," I added. "I've never seen anything like it."

"I believe I have another." Baxter strode to the desk, picked something up, and then approached me. In one hand he held the lantern, and in the other he held a small metal wolf.

"Oh." I accepted the gift. An odd crank protruded out of the toy's back, and when I wound it the feet moved back and forth. I smiled at the pair of crossed eyes etched into the metal.

"Baxter, these are more than toys," I said. "They're a memory from your childhood. You should keep this."

He dismissed my concern with a wave of his hand. "Don't be silly. Keep it."

"Thank you." I clasped the wolf, holding it to my chest. "I've never owned something like this. I'll treasure it always."

Bryce cleared his throat loudly, startling me. "We should get moving."

"Right." I placed the metal wolf into the knapsack in a separate compartment from Miss Meow. She mewed, letting me know that I disrupted her sleep.

With Baxter leading, we tipped the rowboat sideways and carried it out of the room. My muscles strained to lug its bulk.

Single file, we maneuvered the rowboat down the staircase and then headed into the night, leaving Baxter's childhood home behind. Baxter gripped the boat's stern with one hand while grasping his drawn sword with the other. Behind him, Bryce, Carter, and I carried the remainder of the dinghy's weight. Katie followed, too sick to assist us. She rested her hand upon the bow, struggling to keep up.

We cleared the square and then retraced our footsteps through the foreboding alleys. Our feet clomped upon the cobbles and our panting became hoarse thanks to the dry air that parched our throats. I doubted the Culling had ever stalked such noisy, easy prey.

"Get ready and stay close," Baxter ordered.

I peeked around him. Ahead, a beast's dark silhouette charged toward us, growling through its massive fangs. This was it. Time to fight.

No. Time to die, a smaller voice inside of me corrected. Tremors rippled through my limbs.

With sword raised, Baxter rushed toward the creature and sliced it across the chest. The beast's fiery eyes went dark as it sank to the ground in a lifeless heap.

Not far ahead, columns of black smoke rose into the sky, blotting out the stars. The fire Baxter started earlier had spread, engulfing dozens of neighboring homes in a ruthless blaze.

"Has Baxter gone mad?" I asked my boat-hauling companions. "Why would he lead us this way?"

"It may be the safest route back to the sea," Bryce shouted over his shoulder. "The fire might scare the beasts off."

Doubtful.

A wall of heat rushed over me once we reached the row of burning buildings. The wind picked up, casting plumes of smoke in our direction. Ash fluttered through the air like snowfall. The dry heat invaded my nose, scorching my throat and lungs. Carrying the boat one handed, I pulled my scarf over my nose. It did little good. All around me, the fire roared, sending burnt boards and beams plummeting to the ground. The alley morphed into a maze with walls built of flames and smoke.

Katie coughed uncontrollably. Carter jerked to a stop to help her, which also forced Bryce and me to a halt. Perhaps Baxter didn't notice that we no longer followed, because he kept running, eventually disappearing into the gray haze.

"You two take the boat." Carter released the boat and lifted Katie into his arms.

The vessel's bulk instantly burdened my muscles, and my legs trembled with exhaustion. With the boat's weight digging into my palms, I trudged onward and called Baxter's name.

"I don't see Baxter anywhere." Bryce gagged from the smoke and perhaps from his ailment as well. Not a hint of color dabbed his pallid cheeks.

Behind me, Katie also continued to cough and wheeze. We needed to move away from the fire before one of them passed out. Of course, veering off our current path meant we would lose Baxter, but the ill Bryce and Katie came first. If Baxter failed to join us at the shore, Carter and I would have to return to search for him.

I glanced at Carter. "Let's take a different route."

Ahead, another alley intersected with ours.

"Bryce," I yelled, "we need to take the next turn. The smoke is too much for Katie." I knew he wouldn't switch routes and abandon Baxter if he thought we were doing this for his sake.

We were no more than a dozen feet from the crossing when a dark smudge cut through the smoke, racing toward us.

"Harbinger," I screamed.

Bryce and I raised the boat in front of us like a shield. Katie shrieked. On the opposite side of the vessel, the beast scratched at the hull, snarling, pushing us back. My strength melted. Knees buckled. Ears buzzed from lightheadedness.

Carter jumped in, gripping the middle of the boat. Growling, he clenched his teeth together so tight that they looked as though they might break.

The tendons pulsed in Bryce's neck. "Shove it against the wall." He nodded toward a nearby building.

Together, we plowed the beast back until we felt a thud. The creature writhed as we wedged it between the hull and a stone building. Keeping one hand grasping the boat, Bryce drew his dagger, poked his head out of cover, and swung the blade. The beast yelped, but so did Bryce. When he ducked back behind our makeshift shield, his hand bled from multiple scratches.

He noticed me staring at his wounds. "I'm all right. Carter, grab Katie, we need to run now."

Quickly, we backed away from the beast. The creature barked, likely calling to its pack. I peeked over the boat. Bryce had slashed the beast across the eyes, soaking its face—like the diamond head of a snake—in a mask of crimson. It staggered for a moment on its powerful legs, whipping its tail. Then, its slit nostrils flared as it caught our scent. It turned in our direction just as Baxter rounded the corner of a burning building.

He stormed toward the creature. Small flames flickered on the hem of his coat. The creature sniffed and then lunged toward him, hissing through bared fangs. Baxter swung his blade in a wide arc and whacked the beast in the throat. He finished the move with a quick roll on the ground to extinguish the flames in his coat. The beast's head tilted backward on its half-severed neck. It fell to the ground—dead—stirring a cloud of dust from the sandy cobbles.

"There's dozens of them that way." Baxter pointed in the direction he came from. Soot and blood covered his face. He glanced at Carter, who was cradling Katie in his arms and then Bryce, who covered his mouth to muffle his coughs. Baxter cursed under his breath.

Without another word, Baxter took hold of the center of the boat. Immediately, the weight lightened, easing the strain on my muscles. "This way." He guided us into the alley at the crossing.

My lungs screamed in pain, abused from both exhaustion and smoke. But the gray haze dissipated the farther we sprinted, allowing me to seize a few breaths of fresh air. Baxter turned us right at the next crossing so that our route ran parallel to the fiery alley. The city's arched exit taunted us from a few hundred feet ahead. Behind us, the Harbinger's chants overpowered the roar of the fire. The haunting chorus sent a shiver rippling through my body.

"Get the boat to the water," Baxter ordered. "I'll catch up."

The boat's heft sank over Bryce and me as he released the dinghy. Dashing to our rear, he slid the crossbow off his shoulder and shot a few arrows off into the darkness. Without his help to carry the boat, our pace slowed. The city's exit seemed unreachable.

"Not much farther," Carter shouted, jogging alongside us. "Don't give up now."

Bryce straightened his posture at the reassurance, picking up speed. Our stagger turned into a hard run.

As we zipped through the arched exit, the continuous snap of Baxter's crossbow faded. Our feet met the plush ripples of desert sand. About three-hundred feet downslope, the golden landscape met the sea's black waters. The crashing tide rumbled in the distance.

Coughing, Bryce crashed to his knees and lost his grip on the boat. Our dinghy fell to the ground with the hull pointing toward the sky. Carter set Katie down and immediately presented Bryce with a canteen. He downed a few gulps, but mostly choked on the water. Carter and I crowded him, but he waved off our concern.

"I'm fine." Having subdued his cough, he handed the canteen back to Carter and turned around. Baxter was nowhere in sight.

"I'm going back in." I drew my dagger.

"Ri, wait." Bryce whispered something into Carter's ear and then pulled his dagger from his belt.

"No," Carter shouted. "You're not going after that blasted Red Band. We can make it. Just the four of us." He flipped the boat over, sliding it back and forth over the sand with ease. "See, it's a straight shot down from here."

"We're not leaving him behind." Bryce hastened toward the city. When I joined him, he passed me a solemn look that I couldn't quite figure out. He turned toward Carter once more. "Please, do as I asked."

"Dammit! I wish you would listen to me for once." Carter chased after us and grabbed ahold of my arm. "Katie, get in the boat."

She did so without question.

"What are you doing?" I squirmed, but he managed to secure my arms by my side. "Let go of me."

Bryce twisted the dagger out of my grasp and tucked it back under my belt. "Sorry, Ri. I need you to be safe."

"What?" I kicked at Carter to no avail as he dragged me backward. Bryce spun around and headed toward the flames and smoke.

"I hope you enjoy sledding, Honey." Carter whisked me off the ground and tossed me into the boat. I landed hard on my rump next to Katie. Then, grasping the bow, he pushed us down the desert's slope. After a few seconds, we gained speed and he jumped into our makeshift sled.

"No!" I screamed watching the city shrink away as we skidded down the hill. "We have to go back." I shoved Carter to the side, but he embraced me, pinning me in place. "Let go of me!"

"Trust me, this wasn't my idea."

"Damn you, let go! Let go!"

I wriggled, but his arms were too strong. The slope leveled out roughly two-dozen feet from the ocean, where the boat slowed to a stop. I clawed my way out of Carter's grip and started to race back up the hill. My feet sank in the powdery sand. He grappled me from behind. Off balance, I fell to my knees and so did he. Somewhere at the pinnacle of the slope, over three-hundred feet away, the Culling was likely closing in on Bryce and Baxter.

"Let go!" I leaned down and bit his hand.

"Ow! I didn't realize biting was your thing, Sunshine." He moved his arms toward my waist, still holding me like a snake coiled around its prey.

The city blurred as tears collected on my lashes. "If something happens to them, I'll never forgive you."

Without a word, Katie knelt by our sides, locking an anxious gaze on her brother.

"Tell him to let me go," I said to her.

She made fleeting eye contact with me, but then looked down and fiddled with her cloak. How could she accept what he was doing? I continued to twist and kick. The struggle irritated the wounds I received earlier, making my skin feel like it was on fire. After what seemed like an eternity, someone shouted from upslope.

"Get the boat to the water," Baxter called.

I stilled, blinking the tears from my eyes. Two figures were racing toward us. A surge of hope blossomed in my chest.

Carter released me. "Forgive me now?"

"No." I stood, brushing myself off. "I'm beyond angry at both of you."

"Then we'll have to spend more time making up later." He winked at me.

I shoved him as I strode to the boat. "I don't think so."

We each gripped a side of the vessel. Once Katie settled in we pushed it to the shoreline. Foamy ripples rolled up to meet the stern. Pausing, we watched Baxter and Bryce hurry down the hill.

"Come on, come on, come on," Carter said through clenched teeth. "Hurry up."

Baxter said something indiscernible to Bryce and they separated. While Bryce continued toward us, gripping his ribs and coughing, Baxter turned around to face a Harbinger in pursuit.

"Carter, start rowing," Bryce ordered, wheezing.

"Get in." Carter pulled my arm, directing me into the boat.

I sat down alongside Katie, heart racing while Carter dragged the boat into the sea. Once the vessel wobbled on shallow waves, he hopped in, taking the front-most seat and unfastening the oars. His cheeks flushed a deeper shade of pink each time he rowed. We rocked wildly. Waves slammed against the hull, drenching us in spray. I looked back to Bryce. He was swimming toward us, burdened by the weight of his knapsack.

I scooted to the rear of the boat and reached for him. He latched onto my hand. The bow dipped dangerously into the water as he pulled himself up. Miss Meow scampered out of his knapsack and hid under Katie's seat. Soaked, he flopped into the boat hunched over.

I hugged him. "Are you all right?"

He bobbed his head. "Fine. Just a little winded."

"Good." I smacked his chest and scowled at him. "Never do something like that again!"

"Ri, it's my responsibility to keep you safe. You're in this mess because of me."

"Stop acting so chauvinistic. Next time, we stick together. Promise me."

"All right, all right. I promise." He squeezed my shoulder and looked me in the eye with genuine sincerity. "I'm sorry that I upset you."

I blew out a breath. "Apology accepted."

With that, I slipped past him and searched the beach. Baxter was dashing toward the shoreline. The beast lay unmoving behind him.

A wave splashed over the boat and I lost sight of him for a moment. When the water settled, I looked back. He dove into the water and swam toward us.

"Slow down," I said to Carter.

He stopped rowing, panting. No longer guided by the oars, the boat swayed, giving up control to the sea.

Baxter grabbed ahold of the rear of the boat. Bryce and I both grasped his shoulders to pull him up. Water dripped off him, adding to the inch or so already on the floor of the boat. A few of the poisonous darts had impaled his coat, but fortunately none pierced his flesh.

Catching his breath, Baxter pointed in the direction of the Violet Star. "That way's north."

"Change of plans, Red Band." Carter pushed the oars into the water, leaning his body forward and backward with each stroke, powerfully propelling the boat farther into the ocean. "We're going to Warning Rock."

"What?" I gaped at Carter. Of all my companions, I had hardly expected him to side with me when all his luxuries awaited him in Black Valley.

"Satisfied, Buttercup?" He offered me a lopsided grin.

I nodded, still unsure that I had heard him correctly.

"We're not going to Warning Rock." Baxter lurched toward Carter, nearly flipping the boat over. I grabbed Katie before she hit the water. Baxter, apparently thinking better of his plan, returned to his seat at the rear of the vessel. Nausea brewed in my gut as the dinghy tottered from side to side.

Baxter glared at Bryce. "Change of plans? I knew I shouldn't trust a fugitive."

"I'm as surprised as you." Bryce passed a disapproving glance at Carter and me. "We'll never make it to Warning Rock. Our best hope lies in Black Valley."

"Sorry, but you two are outvoted." Salt water glistened on Carter's face as he pulled back the oars. The stern rose to meet the crest of each wave, tilted at a terrifying angle, and then crashed back down, descending into the trough.

"Outvoted?" Baxter scoffed. He turned his back to Carter and faced Bryce. "Get him in line or I will."

The boat jerked out of control again. Katie and I clutched each other and the seat with all of our strength. From the corner of my eye, I noticed Carter remove one of the oars from its holder. He raised it in a swinging position.

"Stop!" I shouted.

The paddle swooshed over my head. I ducked and heard a cracking sound. When I looked up, Baxter was slumped over unconscious.

"Carter!" Katie screamed. "That was uncalled for."

Her brother quickly secured the oar back into its holder. Both Bryce and I scrambled to Baxter to inspect his wound. A splotch of blood spread over his silver hair. Quickly, I grabbed the herbal remedy and began to apply it over the split skin along the back of his scalp.

"Dammit!" Carter yelled. "Don't waste the medicine on that blasted Red Band."

"There's more than enough," Katie said. She joined me and then dabbed a bit of the remedy under Baxter's nose. "That will keep him at rest until we get to safety."

Good idea. The last thing we needed was Baxter gaining control of the oars and forcing us back to Black Valley.

"Bryce," Carter said, "I want you with me on this. If we return to Black Valley, we will die. Your new Red Band friend can't protect us."

"I believe him," I added. "Every time we don't listen to Carter, something bad happens. I'm not returning to Black Valley. Ever. Samuel needs me." I clasped Bryce's hands, still bloody from his wounds. "I want you with us on this too."

He stared at our interlocked hands for a long moment, inhaled a deep breath, and pressed his lips into a thin line. "All right. All right, I'm with you."

I exhaled, releasing my built-up tension. I was going home. It was about time!

"As for the Red Band," Carter interrupted, "shall we throw him overboard or take him with us? I think you know which way I lean."

CHAPTER 18

I awoke the next morning to the sound of gentle waves splashing against the hull. To the east, the sun rose over distant mountains, casting light upon the gray, murky sea. The scent of saltwater lingered on the westward wind. I propped myself up with a groan. My body ached from an uncomfortable sleep on the floor between the center and rear seat of our cramped dinghy.

I glanced behind me toward the front of the boat. Bryce had taken over rowing duties. Sea mist soaked his clothing, and dark circles lent a hollow look to his eyes. The breeze tousled his hair in all directions. He wished me a good morning with a kind smile.

I acknowledged his greeting with a nod and then turned around, watching the mountains in the east shrink away with each thrust of the oars.

Carter sat alongside me on the boat's floor, leaning his back against the center seat. He held a sleeping Katie in his arms. Muck transformed his auburn tendrils into drab, tangled clumps. His tailored clothes were dirtied from dust and blood. He flashed me a grin full of white teeth. "Good morning, Honey."

"I'm not your Honey." Wincing, I rubbed a knot from my neck.

He wiggled his fingers. "I can help with that. Would you like a massage?"

"Definitely not!" I leaned away from him toward the edge of the boat. The waves spat cold spray onto my arms and face, but I preferred their chill over his wandering palms.

"Your loss." He interlaced his fingers and cracked his knuckles. "My hands work magic."

"Stay on your side of the boat." I glared at him.

He rolled his eyes. "Sheesh, I can't believe you're mad at me."

"Well, believe it. You could've seriously injured Baxter with that oar."

At the rear of the boat, Baxter slumped over the seat, still unconscious.

"You may not like my methods," Carter continued, "but you can't deny that you're happy with the results. We'll reach Warning Rock by nightfall."

Though I kept my gaze locked on the ocean, I felt his unwavering stare on me.

"Besides," he said, "the Red Band will wake up good as new thanks to my sister's concoction."

"At least one of you has a conscience."

He exhaled loudly. "Would you let it rest already? We have much to discuss."

I glanced at Bryce once more since he hadn't said anything in a while. Given that Carter and I sat with our backs to him, I doubted he could hear our conversation over the waves. "Then we should move closer to the front so we can include Bryce in our discussion."

"No, later. First, I want to know what you plan to do once Baxter is on the same island as Samuel. A captain of the City Guard, who also happens to be the tyrant's nephew, will definitely carry out the punishment the Stained Wall demands. And second, we really need to talk about the connection between us."

"Connection?" I jerked, causing the boat to rock.

"Everything all right?" Bryce shouted.

"Wonderful," I answered. Then, narrowing my eyes at Carter, I whispered harshly, "First, I'm sure once we arrive at Warning Rock, Baxter will row straight back to Black Valley to fight the Culling. He'll never even get close to Samuel. Second, there is absolutely, positively no connection between you and me."

Carter tilted his head back and laughed. "That's not the sort of connection I meant, but I could see how you would think that given all the romantic tension between us."

"There's nothing romantic about the tension between us." I mustered my best back-off glower.

"The connection I'm referring to relates to the sand people." His face drooped into a solemn expression as he looked at his sister and brushed loose strands of hair from her face. Her filthy curls matched the color of mud. "Katie repeatedly woke last night from nightmares. When I asked her what troubled her, she told me she had seen sand spirits at Sea Dragon's Point. She feared that her illness had finally reached her brain because Baxter couldn't see them."

"Oh." The horrible image of the sand people surfaced in my mind. "Perhaps your Whisperer knows why we could see them while Bryce and Baxter couldn't?"

He shook his head. "My Whisperer has been unusually silent. All that I can come up with is that there must be some link between the three of us."

"Perhaps I'm your long-lost cousin," I said, half-joking.

"Unlikely." He remained straight faced. "Charm runs in my family's blood."

"Watch your tongue. I'm charming!"

From behind, Bryce coughed loudly as he strained to pull the oars against the waves.

"Well, I think that's my signal to take over." Carter eased his sister from his arms so as not to disturb her and gently placed her head on the softer of the two knapsacks. Then he leaned toward me and whispered, "I'm afraid I must leave you with less enjoyable company. Just for now."

He crawled over the center seat toward the front of the boat. The dinghy tottered from side to side as he and Bryce switched positions.

I offered Bryce the canteen as he wedged between Katie and me. "How are you feeling?"

Smiling, he nodded, muffling his coughs with his hand.

"Perhaps a dose of Katie's herbal remedy will help that cough." I grabbed the knapsack, but he held my hand back.

"I'm all right, really. We should save the medicine for Katie since there's not much left."

"But—"

"Ri, it's nothing more than a cough. Once we arrive at Warning Rock, I'll ask Katie to bless more plants and I'll be fine. But I do need something for this." He showed me his red-raw palms. "Traveling through waterfalls beats rowing any day."

He rummaged through the knapsack and retrieved his wooden box. The glass vials within glistened in the sunlight when he popped it open. He selected a bottle filled with a thick, milky-white liquid.

I scanned the collection of vials before he closed the box. "I'm surprised that with all the medicines you carry, you don't have something for a cough."

He averted his gaze, plucking the cork from the vial. "I suppose I forgot to pack it."

That was a lie if I ever heard one. He had packed resolutely the day we left Black Valley. What if he carried no remedy because none existed? Clearly, if I wanted to know the truth about his ailment, I would need to ask elsewhere. I peeked over my shoulder at Carter, who in turn gave me a wink. He would tell me.

Bryce fumbled with the vial, applying the remedy.

"Let me help with that." I took the bottle from him. Cradling one of his hands in mine, I dabbed the oily concoction onto his swollen palm. A wave jerked the boat, causing me to slide closer to him. The last time I had held his hand so intimately was the night we almost kissed. My cheeks warmed at the memory. I spread the mixture, tracing the curves of his fingers, remembering how strong they had felt interlaced with mine. This close, his earthy scent mixed with the saltwater tang of the sea. A light breeze stirred loose hairs that tickled my neck, and I recalled how his breath had tickled my lips just as softly.

What a mistake that kiss would have been!

"You would make an excellent healer," he said.

I glanced up from my task and forced a smile. "It doesn't require much skill to spread around some ointment."

"You have a tender touch." He shrugged one shoulder. "It feels nice."

I released his hand and bit my lip. "There's something I have to tell you."

"What is it?" He gave me his other hand.

"When we reach my village, you need to avoid me, as if we never met." I concentrated on smearing the medicine over his palm. It was easier than meeting his eyes.

"Why?" He chuckled. "Do I embarrass you or something?"

"No, of course not." I finished applying the ointment and corked the vial. For a long moment, I fiddled with it, staring at the sunlight tracing its edge as I rotated it back and forth. My throat tightened. "Samuel and I are outcasts, and if people knew that we're friends—"

He lowered his head to meet my gaze. "Then we'll be outcasts together."

I shook my head. "I can't let you do that. I want you to be happy."

"Well, considering everyone in Black Valley wanted to kill me, living as an outcast in your village improves my situation. I think I'll be perfectly happy."

He had no idea what he was getting himself into. I pulled away, busying myself by returning the vial to the wooden box. If he wouldn't back off, then I would. It was in his best interest.

"I promised Carter that I'd join him up front," I said.

"You did?" His posture stiffened.

"So he doesn't doze off at the oars."

"All right." His lips pressed together into a firm frown. "I should probably catch some rest anyway." He slumped into the boat, shifting around until he found a comfortable position in the cramped space.

I slid onto the center seat and faced Carter. Fortunately, he whistled a cheerful melody and left me alone with my thoughts. I didn't want to give up Bryce's companionship, but I had to. So I stared ahead to where the morning light finally reached the western sky and filled it with wisps of pale blues and purples.

After a long while, Carter broke the silence. "What's on your mind?"

"I don't want to talk about it." I folded my arms, clutching my elbows.

"I think there's something you want to talk about."

"Actually, there is." I turned around and glanced at Bryce. His hands rested lightly on his stomach, and his eyelids twitched in dream state. Good. Asleep. I turned back to Carter. "The day we met in the cave, you brought Bryce some tea. Katie blessed the leaves, didn't she? You've been trying to cure him."

"You caught me." He stared vacantly at distant waters, sucking on his lower lip. "I'm not going to let my closest friend die."

"So he is dying ..." An unbearable ache touched my heart as he confirmed my fears. I slumped as the weight of that reality sank over me. "I can't believe that you would allow him to live in that dank cave instead of inviting him into your home."

He lowered his head, concealing his eyes behind disheveled bangs, and rowed with more force. "Do you think I enjoy seeing him live underground like some filthy rodent? I needed to keep him and Katie separated to protect them both."

"What are you talking about?"

"They are both so naïve and righteous. If I ever introduced them they would've started talking about changing Black Valley. And with their gifts they would've been foolish enough to think they could." Imitating Katie's voice, he said, "We can end poverty in the Slag." Then mimicking Bryce, he added, "It's time we stand up against the Red Bands."

He shook his head. "No one can change Black Valley. If they had ever tried, it would've led to their execution. My Whisperer warned of it countless times."

"Bryce would never put Katie in harm's way. He's far too overprotective."

"He's human and he makes mistakes just like the rest of us. He has lots of blood on his hands."

I raised my eyebrows. "Blood on his hands?"

He peeked behind me, making sure the others were still asleep. "Bryce's own village fell apart much like Sea Dragon's Point. But instead of droughts, they had floods that wiped out the fields and destroyed the crops. Things got bad, but most folks remained in the village, hoping things would get better—including Bryce. He was sixteen, still at the orphanage looking after all the younger ones. They were the only family he had ever known."

He cleared his throat and stared at his feet. "When the violence finally broke out, Bryce evacuated with as many as he could, taking them to the waterfall. But the waterfall on the opposite side was frozen."

I gasped. "That's the one he mentioned while tending my wounds in Sea Dragon's Point. He chopped through it?"

Carter nodded. "At the time, he didn't know any better. He trapped himself and a dozen of his orphan companions in a frozen wasteland. They wandered for months, surviving on what little food they found. In the end, Bryce was the only survivor. That's the reason he acts so protective of you. He can't bear to lose another person that he feels responsible for."

"That's so sad." I placed my hand over my heart. Bryce remained at rest, eyelids fluttering. Were his dreams pleasant, or haunted by those he had lost?

"You wouldn't have recognized him the night he first arrived at Black Valley. When he crawled out of the crypts, he was unwashed, straggly hair and beard, clothes worn down to threads. He may think I only cared about having a knapsack filled with expensive plants, but I gave him a chance to start over. I gave him a purpose. I gave him the opportunity for redemption that he thought he needed." His eyes watered to the point that I could hardly make out his clover-green irises.

Carter's personality had more layers than the papery skin of a garlic bulb. One minute I hated him, the next, he seemed like the sweetest man I'd ever known.

"I know that you care about him," I said.

"Please don't tell him that I told you. Some memories shouldn't be allowed to resurface."

"Of course. I won't say anything."

For the rest of the afternoon, Carter and I alternated at the oars so Bryce could recover. My pace hardly compared to Carter's, but at least it provided him the opportunity to stretch his arms and rest. After about three rounds of rowing, I drifted off to sleep, watching the sun edge closer toward the western sky.

***

"Wake up, wake up!"

Someone was nudging me in the leg. With a groggy mumble, I opened my eyes. Carter pointed toward the west, where dozens of evergreen humps stretched across the horizon. A gauzy haze smudged their bases, creating a brush-stroked effect that reminded me of Carter's paintings. The sun dipped behind the mountains, and storm clouds roamed freely against the cobalt heavens.

"We're almost there!" I placed my hand over my heart as if it might leap out of my chest from the excitement. Bryce, Katie, and Baxter still slept.

Carter smiled. "I should have us to shore within the hour." He paused a moment to wipe the sweat from his forehead and then reclaimed the oars with red, swollen hands.

"You've been rowing for hours. I should take over."

"Buttercup," he lowered his voice and raised a suggestive eyebrow, "I don't mind a little strenuous activity now and then."

"Ew." Folding my arms, I backed away from him, but my cheeks tugged my lips into a slight smile. Not even Carter's crude jokes could dampen my mood at the sight of my homeland.

For a long while, I sat quietly and watched the shoreline draw near with each pull of the oars. The height of the waves increased and the boat bobbed over each one. Water splashed the sides of the dinghy and burst into spray. Miss Meow cowered near Bryce's feet, wrapping her tail tightly around her body.

I gripped the seat, trembling. "The water is getting kind of rough."

"Don't fret, Sunshine. My Whisperer has promised safe passage to the island, and I don't doubt him for a second." He grinned.

A wave jumped into the boat, soaking my legs and feet. "Dammit." I wrung the ice-cold water out of my pants. "I suppose he didn't promise we'd arrive warm and dry."

When I looked up, my heart thumped to a halt. Roughly fifty feet ahead, clusters of boulders rose above the whitecaps. Gasping, I pointed. "Look out!"

Carter turned around, cursing. He pulled the oars hard, attempting to turn the boat.

The waves, gaining in ferocity, pushed the boat backward. Bryce and Katie stirred from slumber. Their eyes widened at the turbulent, boulder-filled waters ahead.

"Let me take over." Bryce crawled toward the front, but as he fumbled over the center seat, a wave shoved the hull, spinning us.

Instead of facing the island, the boat pointed east. My heart leapt into my throat.

"Everyone hold on!" Bryce shouted.

Clutching the seat, I glanced at Baxter. He slid side to side at the rear of the boat, remaining unconscious even in the chaos.

The boat dove into the trough of a wave. Water rose in peaks around us. We were spinning and sinking. A few inches of water filled the dinghy and more rained down on us. The shore teased us from a few hundred feet away.

From behind, the sea sucked its water back and formed a colossal wave. Towering fifteen feet high, it surged toward us as if it harbored a deep hatred for our dinky boat and punched us forward. The stern tilted toward the heavens. I lost my grip and plunged into the sea. The cold water sent a shock through my body. I clawed to the surface. The boat had flipped over, showing its hull. Ten feet away, Carter and Katie's heads surfaced.

Flailing, I attempted to swim toward them, craning my neck to keep my nose above the frothy waves. Saltwater found its way into my nose and mouth, burning my throat and sending nausea to my gut. The cloak tangled around my legs, so I wiggled out of it. Carter grabbed me a second later. Katie gripped his shoulders.

"Hold on tight," Carter shouted. "I'll get us to shore."

"Where's Bryce?" I scanned the surrounding waters. About twenty feet behind me, the crown of Bryce's head poked above the water. He hooked his arm around an unconscious Baxter.

"He'll be fine," Carter said. "Now grab ahold of me."

As soon as I clutched his shoulder, he propelled us through the torrents as expertly as he had at Sea Dragon's Point. Katie clung to him, bunching his shirt with her bony fingers. Her lips quivered, cooling to a deep shade of blue. Keeping one hand on Carter, I held onto her with the other, fearful that she might slip back into unconsciousness.

Though the waves climbed over my head, I caught glimpses of the shoreline growing closer with each stroke. Soon, my feet brushed against the sea's sandy floor and, after finding purchase, I stood, legs shaking from the force of the tide. Carter and I each wrapped Katie's arms over our shoulders and clomped toward the beach until we collapsed exhausted on dry land.

Bryce followed, dragging Baxter as he sloshed in knee-deep water. Miss Meow—clearly an invincible cat—shot out of the sea and ran toward the spruce trees lining the edge of the beach.

Breathing a sigh of relief, I dug my fingers into the sand. "We made it. I'm almost home."

"Woo!" Carter raised his fists in the air, grappled his sister in a hug, and planted a kiss on her cheek. Though she sneezed twice, she returned his enthusiasm with a soft smile. Then he turned to me.

"We made it, Buttercup." Grinning, he leapt to his feet and pulled me up with him. Before I could collect my bearings, he lifted me in his arms, twirled with me once, and then set me back down.

I trembled from a mixture of exhaustion and excitement, but I smiled back at him.

He released me and then stared at my chest. "My, my! Those clothes look better on you than they ever did on me."

I looked down. The soaked clothing clung to my body, revealing my form. Heat flooded my cheeks. "Stop staring at me like that." I folded my arms to cover myself.

Bryce joined us, dropping Baxter onto the beach as he fell to his knees. Hunched over, he wheezed harshly. I knelt next to him. From the corner of my eye, I noticed one of the knapsacks wash up on shore, along with shards of our boat.

"Carter, quickly see if the medicine is in the pack," I said.

He raced off and returned a moment later with the knapsack in hand.

"I'm fine," Bryce said. In between gasps, he pointed to Baxter. "I don't think he's breathing."

I lowered my ear to Baxter' nose and mouth. No breath tickled my cheek.

Looking at Bryce, I shook my head. "What do we do?"

"We let him be," Carter said, rummaging through the knapsack. "If he dies, he'll never meet Samuel."

"We're not going to let him die." Bryce nudged me aside and rolled Baxter flat onto his back. Then he tilted Baxter's chin.

Katie sat nearby, wringing her hands.

"No, stop." Carter crowded Bryce, wedging himself between the two. "This Red Band will cause us nothing but trouble. I'm sure of it."

Bryce shoved him out of the way and then pinched Baxter's nose while exhaling two breaths into his mouth. Baxter didn't wake. Placing the heels of his hands over Baxter's breastbone, Bryce pushed downward a few dozen times, choking the entire time. Then he puffed two breaths into Baxter's mouth again. Nothing.

Carter crawled over to me. "Honey, you have to stop this. Baxter's stuck with us now. He can't row back to Black Valley. He'll end up traveling with us and, I promise you, when we reach your village he'll make Samuel face his past. My Whisperer is screaming right now."

I watched Bryce pump Baxter's chest. His death would ensure Samuel's safety—at least from the laws of Black Valley. And we wouldn't even need to kill him. He would likely pass on his own if Bryce ceased what he was doing. But Baxter wasn't an evil person. He saved my life. How could I turn my back on him when he needed help?

"We'll have to deal with that when the time comes," I said. "I can't let him die."

"Dammit!" Carter marched off, pacing the beach. "You have no idea the trouble you're making for yourself—and me."

"She's right, Carter," Katie called after her brother.

Baxter coughed. Sputtering, he propped himself onto one elbow, spewing saltwater. Bryce, Katie, and I encircled him while Carter crossed his arms a few strides away, casting a vindictive glare.

"Where are we?" Baxter scanned the beach, the sea, and then the thick inland forests.

Bryce, Katie, and I exchanged a look.

Bracing myself, I answered, "Warning Rock."

"Warning Rock?" He eyed the remains of our boat, then flopped onto his back, staring at the stars poking through the clouds. His damp, silver hair spread out over the sand. In his usual monotonous tone, he cursed, "Bollocks."

CHAPTER 19

The following morning, the scent of roasted meat lured me from slumber. We had taken shelter where the beach merged with the forest under a cluster of spruce trees that canopied us with needled branches. I sat up and wiped a layer of sand off my cheek. The sun peeked over the horizon, blushing the pale-blue sky with the first hints of dawn.

To my left, two skinned squirrels cooking above a campfire caused my stomach to growl. To my right, Bryce and Katie slept with sand crusted on their skin and clothes. Between them, Miss Meow lay curled up with her tail wrapped around her body. Carter sat on a nearby tree stump, brushing himself off. Fifteen feet away from him, a Baxter-sized compression dented the beach.

Dammit. Where was he? I stood and grit sprinkled off my damp clothes. Though we were far from my village, I wanted Baxter within my sight at all times. If he wandered off on his own, he might reach Samuel before I did.

"Where's Baxter?" I asked.

"He was gone when I woke," Carter said nonchalantly, glancing at the squirrels on the spit. "I'm sure he'll be back since he caught breakfast."

"Do you think he's still upset with us?"

"Probably," Carter scoffed. "The food must be a courtesy to Katie and Bryce. You and I are likely on his disfavored list."

"You and I? It wasn't my idea to hit him in the head with an oar!" From the corner of my eye, I noticed a trail of footprints leading into the forest. I followed them toward a trampled path.

"Where are you going?" Carter asked.

"To find him so I can make amends. It's best we stay on good terms with him."

"Make amends?" Carter laughed. "Good luck."

Ignoring him, I stepped into the forest.

"Wait, Honey." He chased after me and grabbed my arm. "If making amends is your plan, I can't let you go on your mission looking like you do." He plucked a couple twigs out of my hair and corrected some tangles.

"What are you doing?" I backed away from him.

"Take it from a seasoned con-artist, if you're going to work your charm on him, you should look somewhat presentable." He swatted sand off my shoulders.

"I'm not trying to work that sort of charm." I smacked his hand away. "It doesn't matter how I look."

"Yes, it does. He's a man." Tapping his finger against his mouth, he leaned back, eyeing my clothes. His hands came at my shirt. "You should unfasten this top button."

"No!" I shoved him back.

"You're right," he said, smirking and raising his palms defensively. "That was more for me."

"Ew!" I stomped farther into the forest. "Stay here and make sure breakfast doesn't burn. I'll be back soon."

My feet sunk in the muddy earth as I followed Baxter's footprints into the woodlands. The scent of evergreens replaced the tangy aroma of the sea. Nocturnal and morning forest chatter melded together. Larks whistled above, urging the last few stubborn crickets to end their evening melody. Soft sunlight slanted through the branches, illuminating clouds of dust motes. Dragonflies whirred in the golden rays, occasionally drifting downward to tap the surface of a stream that meandered around birch trees and shrubs.

Twenty feet ahead, I spotted Baxter near the stream unclothed above the waist. Water glistened on his freshly washed skin. He was fastening his belt, but his coat and boots still lay on a nearby flat rock. Other girls might have admired the rippling of sinew and muscle, but all I saw was a man very capable of killing Samuel if he chose. He glanced in my direction and greeted me with a curt nod. I looked away, realizing that I had been staring at him.

"Good morning." I walked along the opposite side of the stream to join him. "Breakfast smells delicious!" My tone reeked of false flattery. "How did you ever catch two squirrels so quickly? I'm impressed."

He glared at me with a tensed jaw. "You should wash up or do whatever it was you came here to do." Turning away from me, he picked up his coat and beat the dust out of it.

Clearly, making amends wouldn't be easy.

I crossed the stream and stepped in front of him. "I came here to talk to you."

He slipped his arms through the sleeves of his shredded coat and passed me an irritated glance.

I sighed. "Fine. You have every right to be upset with me."

He cocked his head and then shook it. "Ri, it's my responsibility to protect the people of Black Valley, and now I can't do that because I'm stuck on this blasted island."

My stomach twisted. His need to protect his city was no different than my need to protect Samuel.

"It's my fault you're here, and I want to make this right," I said. "But Black Valley is a deathtrap."

"I'm aware of the dangers, Ri. I have to return."

I nodded. "I wish there was a way I could help you."

"Unless you happen to be a shipwright, I don't see how you can help." Bitterness seeped into his words.

I knew nothing of building boats, but the villages to the south of mine were situated near a wide river and the villagers often built small canoes to travel back and forth. But if I told Baxter this, I would reveal that I hailed from Warning Rock. He might ask questions that would lead to Samuel. Surely helping him wasn't worth the risk.

Closing my eyes, I took a deep breath. "I know where you can get a boat."

He raised an eyebrow. "Oh? And how would you know that?"

Dammit, what was I getting myself into? I knelt next to the stream to collect my thoughts. I was too impulsive. Why couldn't I think things through for once?

"Because …" I stared at my reflection in the water. My hair looked like a skein of yarn destroyed by a kitten. I finger-combed a tangle from my strands. "This island is my home. There's a village south of mine that has boats."

His jaw went slack for a breath, breaking his usual deadpan expression. "You live here?"

"Yes." I kept my gaze fixed on the stream. It ran clear to the bed of brown pebbles at its bottom. "Bryce and I met six days ago in the forest outside my village. He saved my life from the Culling's beasts by transporting me to Black Valley through the waterfall." I splashed cool water on my arms, and beach sand slid off my skin. "The night you found me in the Abandoned Quarter was the first time I had ever stepped foot in your city."

"I see." He sat on a nearby boulder and leaned closer to me. "Did the Culling attack your village as well?"

"I don't think so. Carter believes the Culling won't attack my village. He has this uncanny ability to predict things, but—"

"You have your doubts." He frowned.

I nodded. "I'm worried about my friends and family. That's why I had to return when the opportunity presented itself. I'm sorry, I know bringing you here was wrong and—"

He ended my apology with a wave of his hand. "I understand. You were merely trying to protect your own. I can't be angry with you for that." The tension in his face softened.

"So you and I are friends?"

"That depends," he said flatly. "How quickly can you find me a boat?"

"Well, um ... the journey will take a couple of days."

"Ri, I'm joking." He smirked and his eyes brightened with a playful glimmer. "You and I are friends."

"Oh." I let out breath. "Good."

"Finish up so we can be on our way." He fastened his boots.

One problem solved, but I had created another. In order to reach the villages to the south, we would have to first pass through my village to cross the mountains. I needed a plan—fast—or Baxter would discover Samuel.

"Ri?" he interrupted my thoughts. "You look troubled."

"Me? Troubled? I'm not troubled." Quickly, I dunked my head in the water, freshening my long locks.

When I lifted my head from the stream, Baxter was studying something in his hand. It reflected the sunlight onto his face. Perhaps a piece of metal or glass? I gasped and patted my pocket. Empty. My compass must have fallen out while I was washing. I stood, wringing water out of my hair. Sure enough, my most treasured position rested in his palm. If he flipped it over, he would discover the inscription and my connection to Samuel.

"I'm ready to go now." My heart beat fast, making me breathless.

"This is well made." He glanced up at me. "Where did you get it?"

"I found it in the Slag. I want to leave now."

He tilted it and the needle wiggled slightly. "It's broken."

"What do you mean it's broken?" Did Parkin pass off shoddy work? Using the opportunity, I grabbed my compass from him and examined the glass. Light shined across its smooth, flawless surface. "It looks fine to me."

"The needle points southwest instead of north," Baxter explained.

"Oh."

Bryce had seemed perplexed by the direction the needle pointed as well.

"Well, I like it fine—broken or not," I said. "Can we go now?"

"Of course." He stood, watching me as I shoved my compass into my pocket.

Had he read the inscription? No, he would question me if he had … unless he was keeping quiet about it in hopes that I would lead him to Samuel.

I cleared my throat and brushed off my clothes. In the calmest voice I could muster, I said, "Food sounds like a wonderful idea. Let's go."

***

When we returned to camp, Bryce nearly bumped into me as I emerged from the forest.

"I was just coming to look for you," he said. Despite a night's rest, the color in his cheeks had faded to a pallid tone, while the circles beneath his eyes had darkened to a deeper shade of blue. No doubt our journey was wearing on him. How would he ever make it up the steep mountain to my village?

I glanced at Katie, who sat a few dozen feet away next to her brother. She was mashing leafy plants together inside of a curved strip of bark. Good. She was already preparing medicine. Hopefully, her remedy would be potent enough to cure Bryce's illness.

Bryce shot Baxter a suspicious look and then his gaze whisked over my wet hair and freshly washed skin. "So where were you two?"

"We were just washing up," I said.

"Oh."

A brief moment of silence ensued as the three of us awkwardly stared at each other.

Finally, Baxter broke the silence. "Hmm. Breakfast looks ready." He made fleeting eye contact with me before heading toward the campfire.

Once Baxter had roamed out of earshot, Bryce leaned toward me and whispered, "Ri, I think you should avoid talking to him alone in the forest. What if you were to slip and mention Samuel? Or what if he ever got a look at your compass? I'd be too far away to help you."

"Well," I drew out the word, digging my toe in the sand, "he already saw my compass."

Bryce's eyes widened. "He did?"

I nodded. "But I don't think he noticed the inscription. Or if he did, he's keeping quiet about it."

Bryce looked over his shoulder at Baxter, who was removing the meat from the skewers and spreading it onto a flat rock to cool.

"There's more," I continued. "I told him I'm from here."

His brow furrowed. "You told him you're from Warning Rock? Why?"

I quickly explained the conversation I had with Baxter. "It was foolish. I wanted to help him and now I've put Samuel in danger."

He patted my shoulder. "Don't worry. I'll make sure he never finds Samuel."

I offered an appreciative nod, but Bryce needed to concentrate on recovering, not solving my problems. I would have to deal with Baxter on my own.

"Katie's preparing more medicine," he said. "Why don't you have her tend to your wounds and then we'll eat."

"All right." I joined the siblings while Bryce sat near the campfire with Baxter.

Carter glared at me and folded his arms as I approached. "Did you enjoy bathing in the stream with the Red Band? My Whisperer told me of your little arrangement."

I sat next to him and huffed, "Did your Whisperer give you any advice?"

"It just so happens, he did." He cupped my shoulders and looked me firmly in the eye. "You're going to have to kill the Red Band."

"Kill him? Have you gone mad?"

"Don't listen to my brother," Katie piped up. "I think Baxter will show Samuel mercy if they meet, but if you have any doubts, you should wish upon the stars. Everything will work out."

"Wish upon the stars?" I released a desperate laugh. "I need more help than that!"

Carter leaned closer to me. "We can stop him together. He'll never suspect you're up to something. Shove your dagger through his chest, and then I'll grab him from behind before he can retaliate."

"No!" Katie said. "We're ending this talk of murder."

I nodded. "She's right, I can't do it. What if Katie's right? What if Baxter would show mercy?"

"That's a gamble I wouldn't make," he snapped back. "Samuel is wanted for inciting a massacre in Black Valley. Hundreds died. Baxter will want justice for those who were slaughtered."

"Samuel's innocent. He'd never do those things." I glanced at the campfire. Bryce and Baxter appeared to be having a serious conversation. Unfortunately, the crackling fire drowned out their words.

Katie dipped her fingers into her makeshift bowl and gathered a clump of muddy leaves. She spread the remedy onto my wounds. "I'm telling you, wish upon the stars."

Did she bump her head? "I don't think wishing on the stars will solve my problems."

"It will. It worked for Carter and me. We wouldn't have our gifts otherwise." She smiled at her brother. Perhaps it was the early morning light, but her cheeks looked less sunken and a dab of color blushed her nose. She had not coughed since the night before.

"You received your gifts by wishing on the stars?" I asked.

"Yes. You see, growing up, Carter and I celebrated our birthdays on the same day because we were very poor. He always scraped up enough money to buy a pastry that we would share under the night sky while wishing on shooting stars."

"That's very sweet," I said.

With a solemn expression, Carter stared down at his clasped hands.

"On the day that Carter turned fifteen and I turned nine, a solar eclipse blacked out the sky. So instead of waiting until nightfall, we ate our pastry that afternoon in the Rose Quarter. No one shooed us away since everyone was hiding inside. They thought the eclipse was a bad omen, but we didn't care. We had the chance to celebrate our special day in the stone gardens of Black Valley's finest quarter. Of course, there were no shooting stars that day, but we wanted to carry on our yearly tradition. So instead we made our wish upon the dark sun. Carter wished to live in the Rose Quarter one day, while I wished for a way to help others in the Slag."

She finished applying the mixture to my wounds. "The next morning, Carter started to hear his Whisperer. And a few days after that, I started to feel this ... energy."

"So I need a dark sun, not a shooting star." I buried my face in my palms.

"Nonsense." She wiped her hands clean on her tattered cloak. "There are positive energies all around us, helping and listening to us. I'm not sure, but perhaps it's the gods who hear us. Either way, have faith. And stay optimistic—always."

Carter exchanged a glance with both of us. "It will take more than optimism to work this out."

"Ladies," Baxter called. "The food is ready."

"Did he just call me a lady?" Carter's lip curled, slightly baring his teeth.

"Calm down," I said to him. Then to Katie, I said, "I hope you whipped up some of your remedy for Bryce."

She presented a curved strip of bark filled with blueberries. "He doesn't like to be fussed over. I've blessed these to be less conspicuous."

"Thank you."

I offered Bryce the berries as I settled down next to the fire.

"Oh, thank you." He smiled and scooped some into his mouth.

I held my breath, expecting an immediate sign of recovery. Instead, he swallowed the berries and then muffled a cough with his hand. Perhaps I just needed to give it time. The medicine would work.

"After breakfast we'll travel west toward Ri's village," Baxter said as he watched the four of us seize a portion of meat. He tore a leg off the squirrel and bit into it, ripping flesh from the fragile bone.

I took a deep breath. Two days. I had roughly two days before he would wander into my village, catch a glimpse of Samuel, and kill him.

CHAPTER 20

Glimpses of the setting sun poked through the tangle of branches, bleeding crimson into the sky. My legs ached from our daylong, uphill hike. Regardless, the five of us continued trekking the forest's steep incline, past scattered spruce trees feathered with pale-gray lichen. Dark soil softened from a constant supply of decaying pine needles padded our footfalls. The scent of wet bark and moss reminded me of home. We neared my village with every step. I felt it.

And that meant trouble.

For the past few days, all I had wanted was to return to Samuel. But the thought of stepping into the village—with Baxter joining me—made my hairs stand on end.

Baxter maintained a steady pace a few feet ahead of our group, while Bryce and Carter (who still carried his sister) marched alongside me. Everyone looked spent, but Bryce heaved with labored breaths and his legs shook with each stride. Though Baxter had relieved him of the cumbersome supply knapsack some time ago, we still paused frequently so he could rest. But since dusk promised to overtake the sky within the hour, I knew Bryce would pass out before he'd admit he needed another break.

"Let's stop for a while," I said.

Carter set Katie down and pulled a handkerchief from his vest pocket. He shook dust out of the cloth and dabbed the sweat off his forehead. Katie leaned against a tree near a stream. Perhaps it was the lighting once again, but her cheeks looked fuller, void of sickly shadows. The dark smudges that were beneath her eyes the day before had vanished.

"How do you feel?" I whispered to Bryce. Miss Meow stirred in my knapsack at the sound of my voice.

"Fine." He waved off my concern. "We should keep moving. We're losing daylight."

Threads of light speared through the branches. Some of them faded as a cloud drifted in front of the sun. "Nonsense, we have a few moments to catch our breath."

"Ri, I know what you're trying to do."

I sat down on a fallen tree trunk and rested my elbows on my knees. "I'm not trying to do anything except take a break."

"You're fussing over me." He took a seat next to me, inhaling raspy breaths.

Why weren't the berries working? What if Katie's healing abilities were too weak to cure him? After all, Carter said that she couldn't heal fatal illnesses. No, I couldn't think like that. She was going to heal him. The medicine just needed more time to work.

"You don't need to worry," he continued. "I'm a little winded, nothing more."

I wished he would stop acting so prideful.

"Ri is right," Baxter interrupted. "This is a good place to camp for the night." He glanced at me, nodding his head slightly. Perhaps he sensed my worry for Bryce and had decided to offer support. But it would likely be the last time he would stand with me. The next day we'd be pointing our blades at each other. I folded my arms over my stomach, sickened by the thought.

"I'll catch us dinner upstream," Baxter added. "You four build a fire." He tossed the supply knapsack on the ground and then wandered off.

I removed my knapsack. Miss Meow hopped out, slinking off into the brush in search of her own meal.

Once Baxter had roamed out of earshot, Bryce said, "Great, you all must think I'm weak."

"Don't be silly," I said. Considering how hard Bryce pushed himself despite his ailment, he had proven he was far from weak. "We can't build camp or catch a fish in the dark. Best to use the last of the daylight we have to prepare for the night."

"And best to use this time to discuss what we're going to do about the Red Band," Carter broke in. Both he and Katie sat on the ground across from Bryce and me.

"I'm not going to murder him." I glared at Carter.

"What?" Bryce's jaw dropped. "That was your plan?"

"You should've let him die on the beach," Carter said.

"Carter!" Katie smacked him on the shoulder. "We're not going to kill anyone."

"We have to." Carter glowered upstream to where Baxter was sharpening a stick into a spear. "But I suppose we should let him catch us dinner first."

"No." Bryce lifted his hand as if he were about to chop something in the air. "I have an idea. Soon as we arrive in Ri's village, the three of you will find Samuel and keep him inside and out of sight. I'll lead Baxter to the southern village, find him a boat, and help him carry it back to the sea. If we limit the amount of time he's in Ri's village, he'll never have the chance to meet Samuel."

The plan could work as long as Baxter hadn't already read the inscription on my compass.

"We'll have to arrive during early hours so he doesn't choose to stay overnight," I said. "But I should go with Baxter, not you."

"You think I won't make it?" Bryce asked.

"I'm just concerned —"

"Oh, would you two quit squabbling," Carter interrupted. His brow, bunched with worry lines, hinted that his concern for Bryce matched mine. "I'll lead Baxter to the boat."

A generous offer, but it was hard to believe that he'd part from his sister. I narrowed my eyes at him. "How can I trust that you won't shove your dagger into Baxter's back once you're outside of my village?"

Carter flinched, placing his hand over his heart. "I can't believe that's what you think."

"It's exactly what I think. Bryce and I will go with Baxter. Together." I squeezed Bryce's hand to reinforce that my decision was non-negotiable. Of course, I had no intention of bringing him with me. He needed to remain in my village so he could recover. I grabbed the knapsack and rummaged through it until I found the tinderbox.

"We should build the fire before our discussion starts to look suspicious."

"You know," Katie said, "I still think Baxter's a good man and won't hurt Samuel. I'm sure everything will work out."

Naïve optimism. Carter had sheltered her for too long.

"Oh please. Don't tell me you fancy him." Carter threw his hands up. "He's not the type of man for you. You deserve to be courted by a gentleman who will shower you with expensive gifts, recite poetry to you over candlelight, feed you divine delicacies, muse with you under the starlight while gobbling up your every word—"

"Carter, stop!" Katie shook her head, but a smile tugged at the corners of her mouth. "Those are quite high expectations. I'll die an old maid before I meet a man like that."

"I don't think those expectations are too high." Bryce's hazel eyes met mine. "Perhaps expensive gifts and divine delicacies are out of the question, but snuggling with your true love under a canopy of stars—" he looked off into the distance, apparently losing himself in his own romance, "—that should be expected. Along with reciting poetry."

My heart quickened. Was he suggesting that he'd recite poetry to me under starlight? And what in the world was poetry? The word, seductively low on its first syllable, rose to a mischievous pitch on its last. It promised to send me spinning. I wished he would understand that we couldn't be together. Samuel needed my care, and I had no intention of pulling Bryce into our complicated life as outcasts.

Katie clasped her hands in front of her chest and tilted her head as she looked at Bryce and me. "That's so romantic. You two are adorable."

My cheeks warmed. Why did she assume we were already a couple?

"Well, you'll never get that romance from the Red Band," Carter told her.

"I don't fancy him," she said calmly, and it sounded like an honest answer. "I simply know how to spot someone of good character."

"Good character?" Carter scoffed. "My Whisperer continues to repeat, loud and clear, that he'll make Samuel face his past. That Red Band's rotten and I'll prove it. Tonight, I'll get him to admit his bloodlust."

I went cold. If Baxter confessed that he planned to kill Samuel, I would have to act long before we reached my village. But murder him? Could I bring myself to do it? Perhaps if I worked toward befriending him, he would drop his vendetta against Samuel once and for all. It was unlikely, but I had to try.

I grabbed a package of bread from the knapsack and tore off a small piece. "I'm going to help Baxter catch dinner."

"I don't like the idea of you alone with him," Bryce said, passing Baxter a fleeting look. "I'll come with you."

"Actually, I was hoping you could build the fire and spit. I'll only be twenty feet away. If he starts asking too many questions or gives me any trouble I'll signal you. Um … I'll scratch my ear like this." I demonstrated. "And of course, if he tries to kill me, I'll scream."

"That's not funny."

"You know he's not going to try to kill me," I said.

"Because he doesn't know your connection to Samuel yet."

"Well, I'm not going to walk over there and tell him."

Bryce pressed his lips together. "All right, Ri. Go. I'll keep an eye on you. But watch what you say to him."

With bread in hand, I followed the grassy bend of the stream. Wildflowers along the bank bobbed in the breeze, emitting a melody of sweet scents. Along the way, a couple of young catfish bumped their noses against the stream's surface, nabbing unfortunate insects that skimmed the water too closely. It wasn't worth going after them. My guess was that larger fish lurked in the depths.

I approached Baxter, remaining silent as he lined up his spear with its target. A foot-long catfish hovered over the stream floor, nearly camouflaged if not for the occasional glimmer of its amber eyes. Fins and whiskers rippled in the gentle current. I held my breath while the unsuspecting fish rounded its mouth and pumped its gills.

Baxter threw the spear and it struck the water with a loud whap. A cloud of sand erupted from where the tip impaled the stream floor. The fish darted away in a flurry of sediment and hid underneath a cluster of rocks. My stomach growled as if decrying the failure. There were better ways to catch a fish.

I rolled my pants above my knees. Though I preferred fishing with a pole, I caught plenty of fish in the past by hand. I slipped off my shoes and stepped into the stream. Its chill skittered up my legs, sending a rush of goose bumps over my skin.

I crept into the deepest section of the stream where the water's surface grazed my kneecaps. A water snake slithered by like a ribbon of glistening scales. I didn't flinch. They were harmless things. Not far, three gray fish rippled to and fro at the base of a rocky outcrop. From the corner of my eye, I noticed Baxter watching me. He stood parallel to me near a patch of reeds at the stream's edge.

"You intend to catch us dinner with your bare hands?" he asked.

"I do." I tore off a chunk of bread and placed the remainder in my pocket. Gripping the bait between my thumb and index finger, I placed my hand into the water slowly. A large fish jerked its nose in my direction. "It does not take much wit to outsmart a fish."

"So if I were to wager on this match of wit, I should place my bet in favor of the fish?" he asked.

His sarcastic remark burned me. But for Samuel's sake, I had to maintain a friendly attitude. I clenched my jaw and released an irritated breath. The fish sensed the slight twitch of my muscles and darted a few feet away. Dammit! "You can bet that I will have a fish in my hands long before you have one on the tip of your spear."

"Challenge accepted," he said.

"Huh?"

"Bet's on." A playful glint flashed in his eyes. "What shall we wager?" He wandered downstream where his spear still buried its nose in the sand.

"I have nothing of value."

"That's not true." He leveled the spear, training it on a batch of fish that looked like a swarm of shadowy ghosts from where I stood. "But I understand if you're afraid to lose."

Heat rose into my cheeks. How dare he assume that I was afraid of losing?

"I'm not afraid," I snapped back. "There's always the slight chance that you'll encounter a clumsy fish that accidentally impales itself on your spear, and if that happens I would have no way to pay you. Not even these clothes belong to me. They belong to Carter."

"He wouldn't mind if you lost those clothes."

"Carter's a pig, and you won't dare take these clothes!" I said. Once again, my stomach stole the last word with a rumble.

"There is one thing that you could wager," he said. "Something you always seem to have an abundance of."

I chuckled. "And what is this invisible thing I apparently have an abundance of?"

"Talk."

"I don't understand."

"Assuming I win," he started, "I'd like to talk to you after the others fall asleep tonight."

I bristled. Surely he had noticed the inscription on the back of my compass and planned to confront me about it. What else could he have wanted to talk about? Alone. At night.

"We can talk now," I said.

He shook his head and smiled. "Tonight."

The last time I made a deal over a fish, the exchange hadn't gone as well as planned. I doubted this instance would go any better.

"Ri?" He raised a brow. "What do you want from me if you win?"

I mulled over how I could phrase the request.

Well, Baxter, the man accused of inciting a massacre in Black Valley happens to be the most important person in my life. I'd appreciate it if you could refrain from killing him if the two of you meet.

Lowering my head, I placed my hand over a hollow ache in my chest. The thought of him murdering Samuel squelched my appetite. "I don't want to play."

"There is something you need from me." He lowered his spear, no longer interested in the fish teeming in the water. The gleam in his eyes shifted from playful to duty-driven as he gave me his attention. "The anxiety is all over your face."

I dug my toes into the pebbly stream floor. The water rippled over my feet. "I can't tell you what it is."

I glanced in Bryce's direction. He was securing the support sticks of a spit with rocks. As if he sensed my worry, he glanced up and met my gaze. I wondered how many times he had looked in my direction while I spoke with Baxter. Perhaps he forgot our agreed signal, because he abandoned his project, letting the sticks topple over as he hurried toward me.

"Whatever it is, consider it done," Baxter said. "Whether you win or lose."

"What?" I asked. "But you don't even know what I had in mind."

"Clearly it's something important and I fear nothing you may ask of me."

Bryce joined us, remaining on dry ground adjacent to me. "Ri, I could use your help building the spit." He extended his hand to help me out of the stream, but I was still staring at Baxter, stunned by his offer. Katie was right. He was a good man.

"Ri?" Bryce prompted me again.

"We don't yet have a fish to roast on the spit," I said, shaking my head. "It's all right."

"Are you sure?" He shot Baxter a suspicious look.

"I'm fine," I answered.

He nodded respectfully. "Very well. I need to find a damp stick for a skewer anyway. I'm sure I'll find one near this streambed." He glared at Baxter, before poking around in the reeds. There was a perfectly good stick ten feet downstream, but he opted to keep his search nearby.

Baxter made a quick, thoughtful grunt and turned away from Bryce. His muscles and expression were relaxed. "Ri, have you changed your mind regarding our bet?"

Bryce's attention snapped to me. "What bet?"

"Ri believes she can catch a fish with her bare hands before I can strike one with my spear."

"Oh." Bryce raised his eyebrows in surprise, but a supportive smile crept onto his face. "If she says she can, then I believe she will."

"We will see," Baxter said. "Her prospect has already fled underneath a rock." The corner of his mouth twitched upward.

"What?" I glanced at the rocky perimeter of the stream and spotted the flicker of a fanned tail poking from a crevice.

"What are you wagering?" Bryce asked.

My heart stopped. He would not be happy if he knew that I would owe Baxter a private conversation if I lost.

"The loser cleans the catch," Baxter lied.

"Well, I'm not sure I even want to play," I said.

"She's afraid she'll lose."

"Ri, I know you can do it," Bryce said.

"I'm not afraid of losing," I said through a growl.

Baxter remained straight-faced, though I knew he was gloating on the inside as if he had already won. This match wasn't fair. Not only did he have a head start, his new target swam in plain view, suspended in the water like a drifting cloud. He angled his spear, keeping his gaze locked on the fourteen-inch catfish.

A wave of competitiveness struck me. I sloshed toward my timid fish and dropped a couple of bread chunks into the water, hoping to lure him out. The bread went ignored. The tail fanned back and forth before disappearing deeper into the rocky crevice. I heard the whoosh of Baxter's spear hitting the stream, but instead of turning to look, I lowered my hand into the water, positioning it a few inches outside of the hole.

"I'm not going to lose this bet due to your stubbornness," I mumbled to the fish.

I sensed the whiskered creature inside of its hiding place, as if an invisible string connected me to it, reverberating with each twitch of movement. The surrounding world dissolved.

In a burst of movement, I shoved my fist into the crevice. I immediately felt the gritty texture of the fish's miniscule teeth clamp down on my hand as it attacked to defend itself. With four fingers inside of its mouth and my thumb pressing against the top of its flat head, I gripped my catch. It flapped and struggled as I pulled it out of the stream. I hurled it toward the bank. Bryce jumped out of the way. The fish landed on the ground flopping madly. I tackled it.

It had a lot of fight. Kneeling on the ground, I clutched the slippery body. I noticed Baxter's spear a few feet away next to a large catfish. Dammit. I lost.

Smirking, Baxter knelt in front of me and grabbed my fish's head. "It looks like you need some help."

"I have it under control."

He reached his finger into my fish's gill slit and jerked the head back, breaking the neck instantly. "I'll see you tonight," he whispered, leaving me sitting in the cool grass clutching my lifeless catch.

CHAPTER 21

Night rolled over the forest. Inky silhouettes of spruce trees rose from tangles of bramble, stretching toward a sky speckled with stars. Our campfire crackled, and the air smelled of fire and roasted fish—a welcome aroma after a week of being cold, damp and hungry. I savored the dry heat from the flames as it seeped into my muscles.

The five of us sat in a circle around the fire: Carter to my left, then Katie and Baxter, and closing the circle to my right sat Bryce. Miss Meow lay curled at his side while the two of us shared a portion of fish spread atop a flat rock. We didn't say much as we enjoyed the succulent meat and its sweet, earthy flavor. Sometimes our fingers touched when we both reached for a piece at the same time. When that happened, he would hold eye contact with me for a moment and smile before offering the portion to me.

"Don't you think you've had enough, Red Band?" Carter's voice cut through the silence. The last scrap of fillet sat on a rock slab between him and Baxter. It glistened with juices. Both of their hands hovered over it.

Baxter grabbed a knife and cut the fillet in half. He glanced at Katie and me. "Ladies, would you like more?" When we both shook our heads, he grabbed the larger half of meat and left the remainder—a charred, unappetizing strip—for Carter.

Carter took the meat, frowning as it shed dark flakes.

"You need to be faster." Baxter shoved the meat into his mouth and grunted as he chewed it.

"Carter, I'm full," Bryce said. "You can have the rest of mine."

Carter waved away the offer and smirked. "It's all right. Those with no manners always get what's coming to them."

Baxter's brows knotted together as he swallowed the last of the fish. He groaned and massaged the center of his chest with his fist.

"Heartburn?" Carter asked, mouth twitching to hold back laughter. "I could have warned you about that." He plucked the burnt edges off his food nonchalantly before taking a bite.

Katie glared at her brother. "Stop being rude." She offered a handful of berries she had blessed to Baxter. "These will help."

Baxter nodded in appreciation.

"Would you stop being kind to him?" Carter shook his finger in Baxter's direction. "He's ruined everything."

If Carter's words angered Baxter, he failed to show it. His expression remained cool and patient, as if he were waiting for a child to tire of a tantrum. "Whatever you hold against me, it'd be in your best interest to set it aside."

"Or what?" Carter leaned in.

"Carter, stop," Bryce broke in. "Now."

"Yes, please stop," Katie added. "I may not have a Whisperer like you, but I'll tell you what my illness has taught me. Fate owns all of the tomorrows, and we take them for granted because she gives them so freely … until the one day she doesn't. I can't tell you the last time I've felt this healthy, and I'd like to enjoy tonight without your childishness. Can't you put this grudge or whatever it is aside for one night?" Her lower lip quivered.

I shifted uncomfortably, wanting to sneak away from their argument. I glanced at Bryce, who offered a shrug. Clearly, he wasn't good in these types of situations either. Baxter, on the other hand, scowled at Carter with a clear message in his eyes: fix this.

Katie wiped a tear off her cheek and then looked down, fiddling with her sleeves.

"I'm sorry." Carter pulled his sister into a tight hug. "You know I didn't mean to upset you."

She looked up at him with moisture in her eyes. His face scrunched up as if someone whacked him in the ribs.

"You win, I've completely caved," he said, grinning. "What would you like to do now? Rest? Huddle around the campfire and tell ghost stories? Perhaps you'd like me to catch you another fish?" He picked up Baxter's makeshift spear and held it high, puffed his chest, and jutted out his jaw in an attempt to look valiant.

Katie giggled melodiously. "That's something I'd love to see. But I'm not hungry or tired."

"Let's tell stories," I interrupted. Perhaps a good tale would lift everyone's spirits.

"Good idea," both Baxter and Bryce said in unison.

"Perfect." I straightened my posture. "I know the perfect scary story. Prepare to be terrified."

Katie beamed. Carter raised a skeptical eyebrow. Bryce offered a supportive smile and scooted closer. Baxter leaned his back against a tree, folded his arms, and eyed me with amusement.

I lowered my voice. "It was a full moon—"

"Why are you talking like that?" Baxter smirked.

"It's a ghost story," I said through a growl. "So I'm talking spooky."

Baxter chuckled. It was a pleasant laugh—the sort that could draw folks in. But since he was making fun of me, I threw a twig at him. He dodged it easily enough.

"Like you could do better," I said.

"Are you suggesting another wager?" A mischievous glimmer flashed in his eyes.

Bryce cleared his throat loudly, eyeing the two of us. "I thought you did fine."

"Honey, why don't you let me tell the story?" Carter touched my shoulder. "For once, I agree with the Red Band. You're not a very good storyteller."

"But you didn't even let me finish my sentence!"

Carter whispered in my ear, "I can get that blasted Renselar to admit his lust for vengeance. Let me take over before you warm to him any further."

"Warm to him? Oh please," I whispered back, shaking my head.

"Don't doubt me, Buttercup. In a few minutes, you will hear the undeniable truth from his own lips."

Earlier, Carter had boasted that he would prompt Baxter to admit his desire to kill Samuel. Not knowing whether he would raise his weapon to Samuel's throat or show mercy was the only thing holding me back from taking action.

"So, will you be sharing this story with the rest of us or only Ri?" Baxter interrupted.

"Carter was asking me for advice in choosing a story," I said. "I doubt the one he picked will deliver on its promise, but let's hear it anyway."

"Oh, it will deliver." Carter edged closer to the fire so that the light roamed over him, creating dark shadows that bounced around his face.

"There was a seamstress who lived in Gray Towers. The day I crossed paths with her, I sensed a dark memory in the far recesses of her mind. I couldn't stop myself from asking my Whisperer about her past."

"Like you ever stop yourself," I said under my breath, but loud enough for Carter to hear.

"Honey, I'm telling a story. The right way." He took a deep breath and made brief eye contact with each of us. "It was one day after the massacre incited by Samuel Perrington."

"Stop," Bryce jumped in. "This story is hardly appropriate."

"Many of my predecessors died that day protecting our fine city," Baxter added in a threatening tone. Any trace of former good spirits vanished, leaving a hard glint in his eyes.

"Perhaps you should just speak of the seamstress," Katie urged her brother.

"Yes, it seems some of us are overly sensitive tonight," Carter said.

Though I wanted to learn more about the massacre Samuel had been wrongly accused of starting, I didn't want to test Baxter's patience. His chilling expression was enough to frighten anyone. If Carter kept it up, he might find himself with a blade through his chest.

"Perhaps we should tell a different story altogether," I said.

"Nonsense. I'll be more conscientious of those with fragile feelings." Carter lifted his chin with a cocky smile, but his appearance soon became sinister as he angled his body toward the fire once more. Deepening his voice, he spoke slowly.

"The clouds were preparing to unleash a storm, thickening into a dark gray murk that blotted out the moon. And the wind howled like starving wolves. Deep in the basement of Gray Towers, the seamstress sat in her candlelit, dank chamber, fastening adornments to a burial gown. Her bony fingers quivered through their work, and she flinched at every sound that echoed in the corridors beyond her door. Little did she know a dead woman would be visiting her that night."

I found myself leaning in closer. Katie looked hypnotized.

"Gray Towers is not haunted," Baxter said.

"Shhh." Katie crossed her finger over her lips.

"When her last candle died down to smoke, she retired to her bed," Carter continued. "All the sounds beyond her chamber door intensified. Of course, they were the typical sounds: footfalls from the floor above, murmurs from the adjacent servants' quarters, boards settling and creaking. Yet, that night they were painfully unsettling. So, in her fright, she lit another candle and lay in her bed staring at all the items in her room. Mannequins draped in half-finished garments stared back at her, their dresses and cloaks swaying like ghosts stirred by the draft slipping under the door."

"Carter!" Katie squealed. "Did the mannequins come to life?"

"Of course not, sweet sister." He patted her hand. "They were nothing more than wood and cloth."

"Oh." Her shoulders slumped.

I was glad the mannequins didn't come to life. It would have been a dull climax to the story.

"The seamstress was nearing slumber when something moaned in the corridor. At first she thought it was some sort of animal. But then she made out words. It was a woman calling for her baby.

"So the seamstress tiptoed out of her door. Her candle partially lit the black hallway. Carefully, she made her way toward the woman's voice. 'Hello?' the seamstress called. But the woman continued to wail, 'He has taken my baby from my womb.'"

Katie gasped.

A shiver raced up my spine. Just then, Carter grabbed my arm and I squealed. I never squeal! To my dismay, he and Katie chuckled. Even Bryce smiled, but then he rubbed my back as if I needed comfort.

"That wasn't funny," I scolded them, folding my arms.

Carter looked away, attempting to conceal his mirth. Baxter had been quiet for some time. He glared into the fire. Chaotic flames reflected in his eyes. What was he thinking about?

"The seamstress paused at an oak door at the end of the hallway." Carter brought my attention back to the story. "The wailing carried on from the opposite side. At first she knocked, staring at an eye-level motif of a wolf's head bearing its fangs carved into the center panel. It looked as if it might leap forth and make a meal of her."

"Oh my!" Katie said through a shriek. "Did it?"

"No sweet sister," Carter said. "It was merely a door. A very creepy door."

"Oh." She plucked a piece of grass out of the ground and twirled it between her fingertips. "Well I wish you'd get to the point already."

"Ah, but the climax is not something to be rushed." He placed his hand on my knee and in a husky voice, said, "It is much better to the take time and enjoy the way there."

"Ew!" both Katie and I said in unison. I smacked Carter's hand away.

Carter raised his palms defensively. "You all need to get your minds in a clean place. I was simply talking about the art of storytelling."

"Finish the story," I said.

"The door whined as she pushed it open." His voice sunk into a chilling whisper. "Inside, cobwebs clung to wooden crates stacked to the ceiling. The room smelled of grain and rot. The seamstress stepped inside. In the corner, propped against a crate, rested the corpse of a naked woman. Water dripped from a crack in the ceiling and slid down the ashen body. A gash split her in half from the breastbone to the abdomen. Her hand clutched the wound to hold in her organs. A rat nibbled on the bits that escaped her fingers. The corpse turned her head and spoke to the seamstress, 'He ripped my baby from my womb.' The seamstress paled to the color of snow, for she recognized the woman and the voice. After all, she had toiled over her burial dress all day. Sera."

"That's enough of this story," Baxter interrupted. "Any stories the servants might have told about Sera visiting them after her death is nothing more than gossip and rumors."

Carter playfully nudged me in the side with his elbow. "Gossip and rumors are two of my favorite things."

"I think we've had enough storytelling for the night," I said. "It's not appropriate to speak of someone's deceased relative right in front of them."

"I agree," Bryce added.

"You're right." Carter nodded and then smirked at Baxter. "I didn't realize you were close to your step-aunt. But I completely forgot that she wasn't the only one in your family who died the day of massacre. I'm sorry if I offended you."

Who else had Baxter lost? His gray eyes found mine.

"I lost three of my kin that day," he explained. "My step-aunt, her unborn child, and my only cousin from my uncle's first marriage. I never met Sera personally and I met my cousin only once, but they were still family. And the man responsible for their deaths still lives. His face has not disappeared from the Stained Wall." His lip curled in anger. "One day I will find him and return to Black Valley with his head."

I froze. Both Carter and Katie stared at me.

"That's rather brutal." I rubbed my neck. "Are you sure this man did those things?"

"Yes. Survivors of that horrid night attest to it," Baxter replied. "The people of Black Valley deserve to see Samuel Perrington brought to justice. He must pay for the lives he took."

A breeze rustled the leaves.

"Well, it's certainly been a long day," Bryce said nervously as he interlaced his fingers and stretched. "Why don't we call it a night?"

Sleep? How could I sleep? Carter was right. Baxter would slash Samuel's neck at the first opportunity.

Across from me, Carter pulled a blanket out of the supply knapsack and sprawled it on the ground for Katie. He fixed his clover-green eyes on mine. I knew the question he wanted to ask. Would I kill the Red Band? I answered with a nod.

"Very well," Baxter said. "I do want to be at the top of this mountain before sunset tomorrow. You four rest up, I'll keep watch tonight."

Bryce fluffed up the knapsack that we had carried Miss Meow in and offered it to me as a pillow. I rested my head, feigning indifference to Baxter's threats.

"Ri," Bryce whispered, lying a few inches away from me. Miss Meow rested at his side. "I won't let him hurt you or Samuel. Ever."

Neither would I. Since I lost our bet, I owed Baxter a private conversation. So, that night, under the silver moon, I would make my move. I patted my waist. My dagger, sharp and ready, waited beneath my belt.

CHAPTER 22

I closed my eyes and pretended to doze off while the others settled in. Carter complained about sleeping in the dirt and all of the six-legged things that might crawl over him. But after tending to Katie, he found an acceptable position and fell into slumber. Next to me, Bryce rested his head on his knapsack with Miss Meow contently snuggled under his arm. For a long while, I suspected that he remained awake in case trouble arose. But eventually his breath slowed, turning into soft snores.

I sat up once I was sure he was asleep. Six feet away, Baxter kept watch propped against a tree. After glancing at our three dozing companions, he stood and tossed a handful of sticks into the campfire. The flames roared up, crackling with life. He waved at me to follow him. Since refusing would raise his suspicions, I did so. If I was going to kill him, I needed him to trust me.

I patted the hilt of my dagger with sweaty palms. No longer was my blade a means of protection or a handy tool. It had transformed into a horrible thing that was going to take the life of someone I had grown to respect and admire. I felt like throwing up, but Baxter would discover Samuel and execute him if I didn't act. I had to remember that.

He headed toward the area where we fished earlier. I glanced back at the others. If Baxter figured out my plan and drew his weapon first, I doubted that my companions would wake in time to help me. Fear wormed through my insides.

I stopped walking. "We shouldn't go any farther."

Baxter looked at me over his shoulder.

I fidgeted with my sleeve. "I mean ... we should keep an eye on camp. Just in case."

He nodded and turned to face me. "Draw your dagger."

"What?" My heart came to a stabbing halt. Clearly, he knew about Samuel, but in his pursuit of morality and justice, he must have preferred to challenge an armed opponent.

"Ri," Baxter said. "Your weapon. It's time you learn how to use it."

"Learn how to use it?" I said with a rising pitch. "Um ... what?"

He stepped closer to me. A hint of moonlight shone on his face, highlighting his silver hair. I froze as my eyes locked on his. Traces of blue surrounded his pupils like slivers of sky poking through storm clouds. His expression lacked its usual hardness.

"In a few days I must return to Black Valley and leave you and the others on your own. I wouldn't feel right if I failed to show you how to protect yourself."

"Um ... protect myself? You want to show me how to protect myself?" A lump formed in my throat. I was an awful person to plot his murder. Perhaps there was still a chance that he would drop his vendetta against Samuel if they met. After all, how could anyone execute a feeble old man? But what if I was wrong? To assume that Baxter would show Samuel mercy would be naive.

"Let me see how you hold your weapon," he said.

I drew my dagger, holding it in the same manner as I would to gut a fish. "Why now? You could've given us all a lesson around the fire tonight."

He considered me for a moment. A lonely owl hooted, filling the brief silence.

"Bryce knows what he's doing, I taught Katie in Sea Dragon's Point, and Carter would never accept a lesson from me," he said matter-of-factly.

"Oh." Though he answered my question, a private lesson while my companions slept seemed unusual, especially since he had won our bet. How would teaching me to use a dagger be a prize for him? Perhaps he was up to something.

"Come." He walked farther from camp. "Let's not wake the others."

I trailed him to a patch of grass that brushed against my ankles. He placed his calloused hands on mine, wrapping my fingers under the belly of my weapon's handle. Despite the chilly air, his palms were warm. He positioned my thumb so it touched my index finger. Held like this, the blade face-up, the dagger felt like an extension of my arm.

"This is a forward grip. It's comfortable for most and will give you reach." He pulled his dagger and demonstrated with a quick thrust. "However it will also leave you wide open and may limit the amount of force you can apply."

Mimicking him, I stabbed the air with a quick blow.

"Not bad," he said, amusement flavoring his tone. He eased the dagger out of my grip. "Now, try holding it like this." He pointed the blade down with the sharp edge angled away from me. Again, he arranged my fingers around the belly, but my thumb pressed against the butt of the handle. "There are many advantages to this grip."

He cupped my elbow in his palm and then moved my arm in a sweeping motion, like a cross-body punch. "You can rake your blade across an enemy like this, or," he extended my forearm, "stab like this with good force."

He went on showing me other attacks and positions, occasionally grabbing me one way or another and showing me the proper way to get free. Normally, I would've never allowed him so close, but he stepped back after each lesson: a complete gentleman. He patiently noted my mistakes as well as my successes during the hour-long instruction.

"I'm quite good at this," I boasted, smiling after breaking out of his hold for the tenth time. My veins pulsed with exhilaration. Brushing myself off, I straightened my crumpled clothes.

"You still have much to learn." He scowled. "Let me make something very clear. If you encounter the Harbingers of the Culling, I want you to run. I was impressed that you managed to kill one in Sea Dragon's Point, but you won't be that lucky next time."

My high spirits dissipated. "I didn't kill that beast by mere luck alone. I had a plan and it worked."

"Ri, I mean it. That dagger is your last resort if you're pinned or cornered. Your best hope is to slash the beast, preferably across the eyes, and get away fast. Understood?"

"Yes." I wished he would stop expressing concern for me, considering what I had to do. Guilt churned in my stomach. "What if my opponent is not one of the Culling's beasts?"

The cleverness in his storm-gray eyes hinted that he understood what I was asking: how do I kill a man? "If your opponent is human, your size and inexperience puts you at a disadvantage."

"Perhaps, but I'm quick."

"You'd still do best to slash and run." He raised his coat and pointed to a position under the last rib. "But if you can't run, stab here, upward into the kidney."

My hands shook as I imagined my blade sinking into his muscular flesh.

"You can also slash here." He lowered his collar and placed two fingers on the right side of his neck. "With a cut through the jugular, your opponent will drop after a breath or two."

My knees went weak as saplings. Another image flickered in my mind of Baxter gasping, clutching his neck while blood reddened his fingers. I cleared my thoughts. Samuel first. No guilt.

"And if you're unable to reach the neck, you can aim for the heart." He unfastened the top buttons of his coat and, with a hand placed on mine, he guided my dagger's tip to a hollow spot below his breastbone. His pale skin glistened from the day's sweat. "Thrust up and in with all the force you have. Twist on the way out."

My weapon caught the moonlight, sharp and ready while my stomach coiled in knots. This man saved me from the Slag-guard, protected me in Sea Dragon's Point, and gave me his mechanical wolf, such a special trinket from his childhood. How could I fathom killing him?

"Ri?" he asked.

"Um ... what?"

"Twist when you pull the dagger out. I have seen men last a few minutes after a clean cut through the heart."

My weapon was lined up perfectly. I could do this. Push, pull, twist, and the threat standing in front of me would fall. Samuel would be safe. A cool sweat broke out on my forehead. The forest was spinning and thickening nausea in my gut weighed me down.

I staggered backward, lowering my weapon. Baxter caught my arm when I tripped over a fallen branch. Our eyes met. I couldn't do it. I couldn't kill him. Somehow he had snuck into the realm of friendship. I tucked my dagger under my belt.

"I need to sit down." Crossing my arms over my middle, I sat on a nearby rock. I stared at the stream as Baxter seated himself on an adjacent fallen tree trunk. He offered me his canteen, but I waved it away. I couldn't accept any more kindness from him after the murderous thoughts that had swirled in my mind. He remained quiet, waiting.

"I'm overwhelmed, that's all," I said.

The stream babbled, skipping over smooth stones and piles of drift. I was sure that he continued to watch me, though I couldn't bring my eyes to meet his.

"Return to Black Valley with me," he said, interrupting the stream's peaceful melody. "The Culling will strike this island, and I've seen what it can do to small, remote villages. But if you come with me, I'll house you and your friends in Gray Towers. There is no safer place."

I turned toward him. "In Gray Towers? With your uncle? I'm told he's a tyrant."

He tilted his head from side to side, as if half agreeing with me. "My uncle has kept the people of Black Valley under control. We can fight the Culling today because we did not destroy ourselves yesterday. At Gray Towers, you'll be my guests, and my uncle will treat you as such."

I wrapped my arms tighter around me. "I'm not going to Gray Towers."

"You've never met my uncle, and yet you fear him so?"

"I don't fear him, but he is a cruel man. He allows a corrupt City Guard to harass the people, and he ignores the starving and suffering in the Slag. How can you support a man like that?"

I wanted to shake some sense into Baxter.

"It's complicated, Ri. If I were to turn against my uncle now, chaos would break out and leave Black Valley's people incapable of defending themselves against the Culling."

I straightened my posture and gaped at him. "You plan to overthrow your uncle?"

He frowned and looked away. Perhaps his words were a slip of the tongue, or perhaps they were a secret plan that he had intended to leave unspoken.

"I will not lead a rebellion against a man who took me as a ward and treated me as a son. But I do have a vision for Black Valley, and if I save it from the Culling, I will also save it from oppression."

"But how will you do that without rebelling against your uncle?"

"Diplomatically, I hope. I've seen enough bloodshed." Lowering his head, he rested his elbows on his knees and stared at a stone near his feet. "I will not see Black Valley suffer the same fate as Sea Dragon's Point. So many people died at the hands of their neighbors, just like my family. The riots were nothing less than a slaughter."

So his family had been killed in the violence Carter spoke of. Leaning forward, I clasped his hand. "I'm sorry about your family."

Though it was dark, I noticed a slight glimmer of moisture in his eyes. He stared at my hand atop his. His finger twitched as if he were contemplating whether to pull away or draw closer.

"It was a long time ago," he finally said in a melancholy tone.

"Would you like to talk about it?"

He shook his head. "Perhaps another time."

Sadness emanated from him, and my insides caved with the weight of it. But continuing to bond with him would only make it harder when the time came to protect Samuel. And then there would be no room for pity. Slowly, I released his hand.

He knit his brow. "Please, Ri. Return to Black Valley with me." His eyes searched mine, looking for agreement.

"I can't."

"You can bring your family. Surely we can find a large enough boat."

I shook my head. "My family died many years ago, but the man who raised me ..." What was Samuel doing while I spoke to the man who wanted to kill him? "He's very ill." My voice cracked, and my eyes burned, threatening tears.

"Is he too ill to make the journey?"

I nodded, gazing at the dark soil.

"I see." His pitch dropped to a defeated note.

We sat quietly for a long while. Nearby, river reeds whispered in the light breeze.

"Ri, I owe you an apology. I treated you rudely the night we met because I thought you were nothing more than a troublemaker breaking curfew. But I know the truth now."

"That is the truth." I dug my toe into the sand. "I've caused you much trouble, don't you think?"

He looked at our surroundings with a slight smile. "Perhaps. But you also saved my life that night."

I shivered as images of that terrifying night flashed in my mind. I joked to relieve the tension, "Yes, I saved you even after you wrapped me in a blanket full of frozen spiders."

He smirked. "You stayed warm, didn't you?"

Our eyes met, but I quickly looked away at a pair of moths fluttering over the streambed.

"That night, you ordered a young guard to escort me home," I said. "What was his name?"

Baxter tilted his head, as if surprised by the question. "His name was Evan Corkern."

I fiddled with my fingers. "He was brave. And kind. I stayed with him until he …" I covered my mouth, stopping a sob.

"You stayed with him instead of running?"

I nodded, keeping my attention on the stream. I sensed him staring at me.

"Ri," he finally said, "once my city is safe from the Culling, I will return to check on you and the others."

A jolt skittered through me. "What? No!" If luck befell me, and Baxter left my village oblivious to Samuel's existence, he needed to stay away for good. "It's too dangerous for you to cross Fool's Last Sail again."

"Don't be silly. I can't forget about you—" He cleared his throat. "The four of you, I mean."

Why did he have to be so noble? If he left permanently, both he and Samuel might be safe. "I don't think it's a good idea."

"There's no need to fear for my safety. I've survived worse things than the sea."

I didn't doubt his statement. If he survived the Culling, he would return to Warning Rock. And though I wanted him to prevail against the Culling, I didn't know how I would protect Samuel if Baxter strode unannounced into my village one day. Of course, that situation might never arise if the Culling slaughtered us all first. I slumped, overwhelmed by all the threats I had to face.

"Ri, don't worry. We will know peace again." He stood and offered me his hand. "And when we do, I hope you'll visit me in Black Valley. I have a small workshop there—not as impressive as my father's—but I used to tinker before duty led me elsewhere. I think you'd like it."

Under different circumstances, my heart would have burst from the excitement of visiting a workshop full of wonderful inventions. But that reality would never manifest. A darker fate awaited the two of us. We headed back to camp and settled in. While he kept watch, I closed my eyes, dreading all that the next day would bring.

CHAPTER 23

I stood in the center of a field, staring at the spiked tops of distant spruce trees. The breeze rippled the grass into golden waves that beat against my legs and fingertips. But I couldn't breathe. I felt like it was an ocean, and I was drowning. Blood spattered the tussocks surrounding me. Clouds churned into a gray whirlpool that swallowed the sun. I touched my lower back, slipping my fingertips into the warmth of a ragged, crescent-shaped gash.

"Ri, wake up." The field swirled away as I woke to Carter shaking my arms. "We have to go, now."

Traces of dawn filtering through the branches illuminated our camp. Carter scrambled over to assault Bryce with the same level of agitation he showed me. Miss Meow, startled, swatted at Carter before scurrying away. Bryce bolted awake, wide eyed after being severed from dreams and cat warmth.

I drew my dagger expecting an attack. Was it a puma, a bear, the Culling? My heart thumped loudly. Katie was stuffing our supplies into the knapsack. Her eyes, alert with panic, searched the camp for any items she might have missed. Baxter was nowhere in sight.

"What's going on?" I asked.

"The Red Band found something." Carter pointed northward and then stood, yanking me to my feet.

"Is he all right?" Pulse racing, I scanned the surrounding forest, but only wisps of fog slithered amongst the thick evergreens.

Carter shoved the supply knapsack at Bryce and the smaller one at me. "I see you've had a change of heart toward him," he whispered in my ear with a sharp tongue. "Did the two of you have a nice chat under the stars?"

Bryce approached us. "Where is he?"

"I'll explain everything on the way." He whisked Katie onto his shoulders and she yelped. Then he grabbed my sleeve and dragged me along.

"Wait!" I smacked his hand away. "I thought you said Baxter was in the other direction."

"Yes, he's that way." Carter nodded toward the north. "That's why we must go this way." He pointed his thumb toward the west. "My Whisperer says that if we go now we'll make it to your village before sunset."

Before sunset. The words were tempting, but I stopped myself from going with Carter. "No, we have to stick together."

"She's right," Bryce said. "Let's find him and then we can go."

"No." Katie trembled. Her blond hair, rumpled and dirty from sleeping on the forest floor, lent her a hysterical appearance. "Baxter wanted us to get to safety."

"He'll catch up," Carter added, tugging me. "Come on."

Perhaps Baxter would return to our campsite, follow our tracks, and find us. But then, Carter cared nothing for him and would probably lie to protect himself from whatever danger was discovered. Baxter may have been a skilled fighter, but he wasn't invincible.

"I'm not running off like a coward." I freed myself from Carter's grip and glanced at Bryce. "What if Baxter's needs help?"

Bryce nodded. "Agreed." He scooped up Miss Meow and placed her into my knapsack. Without waiting for Carter's response, we headed toward the northern section of the forest.

"The two of you should know to listen to me by now!" Carter shouted.

Bryce turned around, walking backward. "Wait for us. Hide near those rocky outcrops." He pointed toward the area where Baxter and I had spoken the night before.

"You two are impossible," Carter yelled after us. "I'm done protecting you."

"He'll get over it," Bryce said to me with a shake of his head.

We raced through the woods, stomping through brambles. The density of the forest increased the farther we strayed from our streamside camp. Overhead, the branches blocked the sky, allowing only filaments of sunlight to trickle through. Twigs snapped and pinecones cracked underfoot, but other than that, the forest was eerily quiet. A horrible odor thickened in the air, overpowering the scent of wet bark and dirt.

I called Baxter's name. My panicked voice probably alerted some vicious creature of my location, but I didn't care. I had no idea where to look for him. My Fireflies had yet to return to me.

"Ri," Bryce called from behind me, panting.

He propped himself against a tree with one hand and clutched his side with the other. Shadows smudged the area underneath his eyes. His freckles, which had handsomely dappled his nose the day we met, now looked too dark against his sallow complexion.

My hopes plummeted. He couldn't go any farther. Though I could continue the search, I would have to do it alone. Perhaps Carter was right. I was putting both Samuel and Bryce at risk for Baxter's sake. Had I lost all sense? Baxter wanted to execute Samuel. I needed to let that sink into my brain.

I hastened to Bryce and touched his shoulder. "We should head back."

He pointed southward, gasping. "Let's look there first."

Roughly thirty feet away, an orange glow illuminated a small section of the forest. The light didn't create bouncing shadows like a campfire would. The radiance remained constant, like sunlight on a cloudless day. I drew my weapon for safe measure. Bryce did the same.

We crept toward the light. Though we moved with caution, brambles snapped underfoot, destroying any possibility of surprise. As we neared, I heard a squish followed by a wheeze. It sounded like a knife had stabbed a watermelon. The noise came again and again. The glow dimmed slightly with each occurrence.

The stench—like a combination of fish and rotting flesh—grew more powerful. Bryce gagged, blinking moisture from his eyes. I pressed on even as the odor congealed on the back of my tongue. A rotten tomato toasted in a sweaty boot would have been more palatable.

I touched Bryce's arm. "I've smelled something like this before."

"Poor girl." Choking, he pressed his nose against his forearm. "What is it?"

"The day we met in the forest, I found a human jawbone that was covered in ooze that had the same odor."

He pivoted in front of me. "A human jawbone? Why are you just telling me this now?"

I shrugged. "Sorry, but between traveling through waterfalls, fleeing from Black Valley's guards, fighting the Culling, and avoiding Carter's advances, it slipped my mind."

Bryce sighed. "I'm sorry. I didn't mean it like that. I know you've been through a lot." He braced my shoulders. "Stay here. Let me go ahead and I'll signal to you if it's safe. But if it's not, run. Don't wait for me."

He marched onward with sure and steady steps. The eerie glow shined in front of him, diluting his back into a featureless silhouette.

I was not going to wait alone in a dark patch of brambles while he strode farther away. Something might leap from the shadows to snatch me up. Or some horrendous beast might charge from the glowing patch of trees and swallow Bryce in a mouthful of fangs. I caught up to him, tripping on his heels.

"Wait for you? I don't think so." I kept pace alongside him. "We stick together, remember?"

Frowning, he maneuvered back into the lead. He held his weapon in reverse grip, exactly like Baxter taught me the night prior. I mimicked him, holding the blade parallel to my forearm with the sharp edge facing outward. A flurry of butterflies swarmed in my stomach.

We reached the source of light. Bryce lowered his weapon before I had the chance to peek over his shoulder. When I scooted around him to steal a look, my hand flew to my mouth to muffle a gasp.

Baxter stood—unharmed—amongst a dozen ten-foot-tall cocoons latched onto the surrounding trees with claw-like appendages. It looked like the bark had bubbled with enormous swollen blisters. Veins webbed through the fleshy husks, bulging over skin that was pink, smooth, and moist as an earthworm. A repetitive ba-dump came from each one, timed in unison; their collective heartbeat. It was a disturbing sound that made my own heart pound harder against my ribs.

An ambient glow like a miniature sun radiated from inside half of the cocoons. The other half, gray and dull, appeared to have already suffered the steel of Baxter's blade. He plunged his sword into a cocoon alight with life, scattering a swarm of blue-winged butterflies that had been nestling on the tree. It was an odd sight, because despite the cocoons' grotesque appearance, lovely plants sprouted along the trunks, wreathing each husk in vibrant-green patches sprinkled with violet flowers.

"I told Carter to make everyone wait at camp." Baxter scolded us with a quick sideways glance. He pulled his sword out of the cocoon, and it made a sickening slurping sound. Strings of slime clung to the blade. The collective heartbeat softened, lessened by one, and the cocoon paled to the color of cool ash.

I stood, unable to speak as I watched a stream of goop as thick as dripping honey slowly flow out of the gash.

"What are these things?" Bryce asked.

"During my travels, I met some survivors who fled their city after the Culling attacked. One told me that the Harbingers eventually go through a metamorphosis."

He stabbed another, jumping back to avoid the splash of goop that shot out of the puncture. Another light dimmed. "I had never seen any proof of that until now."

"Metamorphosis?" I asked, shaking. "They turn into something worse than what attacked us?"

Baxter affirmed with a grunt.

Bryce pulled me close. His gaze flickered around the forest before settling on me. "There may be others guarding this nest."

"It's possible," Baxter said, keeping his attention on his task.

"Well, I prefer to know what we're up against." I wriggled out of Bryce's grasp and strode to one of the dim husks. The veins had darkened into inky threads webbed beneath a thin layer of dull flesh.

"Wait," Bryce called, catching my wrist as I raised my dagger to slit the cocoon open. "Whatever was growing inside of that thing might be poisonous like the darts." He tugged me back, making sure I stood a foot away from the expanding puddle of slime collecting on the ground.

"Good point," I said. Why didn't I ever think of these things?

"There's no poison." Baxter buried his sword tip into a pallid husk and sliced downward.

Two figures tumbled out of the slit, limp as dolls. The first was an emaciated, juicy human corpse. I spun around, covering my mouth to fight the urge to vomit. I swallowed, took three deep breaths, and turned back around. The corpse looked waterlogged, as if it had been rotting in a river for a month. Shreds of clothing lay plastered to the body, clumping in the recesses of furrowed flesh. The three of us stood in stunned silence. Then, without warning, the thing gasped, opening its mouth into an elongated oval. Bryce and I staggered backward. Baxter didn't flinch.

Though the man was alive, he was in no condition to save. He moaned, obviously in great pain.

"May Death give you peace." Baxter thrust his sword downward, impaling the corpse—the person—through the chest. The blow was quick and merciful.

Using the flat side of his blade, Baxter rolled the dead man onto his stomach. A cord, roughly the width of a rope and made up of black, insectoid segments, stretched out of the man's lower back and connected to the abdomen of the dead beast that had fallen out of the cocoon with him. The creature—twice the size of a man—sprawled on the ground. It had a body like a praying mantis, except that the two prominent front legs had talon-tipped claws, and the head had a powerful jaw filled with ebony fangs. A hollow cavity started in the center of its chest and spanned the length of the torso. Millions of silver-white threads spilled out of the opening like the filling of a torn stuffed toy.

"Perhaps the Culling uses this island as its nesting ground," Baxter said quietly, more to himself than to us.

I trembled, chilled from fear. If more cocoons existed on the island, it was only a matter of time before they hatched and made their way to my village—and Samuel. Carter was wrong. We wouldn't be safe from the Culling.

"The man I met told me that the Harbingers of the Culling collect a live human to feed on while they cocoon," Baxter said. "They drain their victims of their souls." Using the tip of his sword, he pried the cord out of the corpse's back. A crescent-shaped hook capped the end of the cord, leaving a matching wound in the flesh. I slipped my hand under the back of my shirt and traced the smooth texture of my scar with my fingertips. My lower back throbbed, as if in rhythm with the collective heartbeat of the remaining beasts.

A wave of anxiety rushed through me. Surely, it was mere coincidence that my scar mirrored this man's gash in both size and shape.

Though I couldn't remember how I received my wound, Samuel would have told me if he rescued me from such a beast, wouldn't he? Of course, he would ... unless he couldn't remember due to the Sickness. I shook the paranoid thoughts from my mind. I was never attacked by one of these beasts or trapped inside of a cocoon. It wasn't possible.

"I want to leave," I said, distancing myself from the monstrosities attached to the trees.

Bryce placed a reassuring hand on my shoulder. He said something, but my ears rung over his words.

"I want to leave," I repeated.

Wind sliced through the forest, stirring loose leaves and shrubs. My attention twitched in all directions before settling on Baxter and the three cocoons still aglow.

Bryce squeezed my hand and his eyes lit up with determination. "Ri, whatever happens, we'll fight these things together."

I glanced at the wretched creature once more. Its front claws could easily rip through a grown man's chest with a single blow. Bryce and I would die together, more likely.

Baxter finished off the remaining cocoons with powerful strikes into their luminescent hearts. "Let's return to camp."

CHAPTER 24

We returned to find Carter and Katie's footprints surrounding the heap of charred twigs that had been our campfire. But our friends were nowhere in sight. The stream twisted through the black banks like a glistening ribbon in the morning sunshine. A pair of butterflies swirled together in flight, skimming the tops of willows. Nature went on, languid and peaceful despite the horrors we had just discovered.

Bryce hurried to the rocky outcrops, calling for the siblings. When no one answered, he turned toward Baxter and me. "I told them to hide here."

I imagined the Culling's horrid beasts, hungry and stalking through the forest. Perhaps one had caught scent of the siblings and crept through the boulders to where they both hid. A single slash of its claws could rip them in half. And if the beast alerted its brethren of our presence, the three of us could be next.

I examined the ground. No tracks from the Culling's beasts or wild animals imprinted the dark soil. But across the stream, a pair of footprints matching the size of Carter's feet wandered upslope in a westward direction.

"I think Carter and Katie ran off," I said, pointing at his tracks.

"Bollocks," Baxter said under his breath.

"All right, calm down everyone." Bryce raked his hand through his hair as he scanned the area. "They couldn't have gone far."

"I'm not so sure," Baxter said. "That coward runs faster than a cat from a wash bucket."

Miss Meow stirred in my knapsack, as if hearing of a bath made her nervous.

Baxter stepped across the stream to where Carter's tracks began. He waved us to join him. "Come on. Let's find them before that damn deserter gets his sister killed."

We followed the footprints, alternating between a walking and jogging pace. Morning mist smudged the bases of trees and carried the scent of bold evergreens. Bird chatter filled the branches. Since the larks sang contently, I thought our route might be free of predators. Even so, I jerked toward every unusual sound.

Before long, brush and weeds grew thick over the forest floor, obscuring clues of the siblings' course. We slowed our stride to better hunt for any trace of their presence. A few trampled shrubs and partial footprints led us to a steeper slope. My leg muscles burned from the climb. From the corner of my eye, I noticed that Bryce's body quivered each time he inhaled. His gasps had turned into barking coughs, and a sweaty luster moistened his cheeks.

"We should rest." I rummaged through my knapsack, searching for the herbal remedy. My heart sank when I uncorked the jar. No medicine remained.

"Ri," he said, his voice breathy and weak, "I'll be fine. We'll rest once we find Carter and Katie." Waving the empty jar away, he continued onward, stumbling over rocks and gnarled tree roots.

"I wish you would stop acting so prideful and take a break." Following, I offered him the canteen.

He drank conservatively, no doubt rationing in case we didn't find another stream along our path. "I'll be all right, don't worry."

Don't worry? Impossible.

We continued the search all day. The sun climbed to its zenith and then, as if bored watching our endless wanderings, she began her descent. Our shadows grew long, but we hiked on without pause.

The sky had transformed into a blaze of fire when something hit my shin with a light tap. I stopped walking and looked down to see a pinecone lying near my toes. Another one shot toward me from the direction of a tall, plump pine. The tree's lowest row of branches, plush with needles, sagged toward the ground, creating a canopy that surrounded the base of the trunk. The limbs were shaking. I went for my dagger. Baxter and Bryce turned around, glancing at me and then the tree.

"Ri," called a faint female voice. "Is it safe?"

"Katie?" I squinted at the pine. A flash of blond hair moved behind the branches. "Yes, it's safe. You can come out."

Two of the needled sprigs parted and Katie's head peeked through. "Carter refuses to come out."

Baxter strode toward the tree, shaking his head. Cords bulged in his neck. "I'll get him out of there."

"No! Wait," Katie squeaked, raising her palm to halt Baxter's determined pace. "Perhaps Ri could talk to him first. His Whisperer has told him horrible things." She waved me to join her.

Bryce tilted his head at me and shrugged with a sigh. "See what you can do. Baxter and I will keep watch."

I huffed toward the tree. "His antics will cause us nothing but trouble."

"If he doesn't come out on his own in five minutes," Bryce called after me, "Baxter and I will drag him out."

Baxter grunted. "One minute. We're losing daylight."

I shuddered, terrified of encountering more cocoons, or worse, the things that hatched from them after dusk. The crisp scent of pine greeted me as I poked my head through the siblings' shield of branches. Carter lay in a fetal position on top of a blanket of rust-colored needles. Forest debris and smudges of dirt covered his clothing. With his eyes closed and arms wrapped around his waist, he gibbered while slightly rocking himself.

I glanced at Katie. Strands of her hair sprung out of a sloppy bun in all directions. She fidgeted with a twig as she stared at her brother. Her eyes, glassy and bloodshot, hinted of the tears she shed before our arrival.

"Is he injured?" I asked her, scanning Carter for wounds.

"No, but he's so upset. I can't talk any sense into him."

I groaned. "Carter, come out from under this tree. Right now!"

"Buttercup," he said, weak as an old man on his deathbed. "Is that you?" He raised a hand, blindly reaching for me.

"My name is not Buttercup." Tension mounted in my temples. I crawled through the branches and sat with the siblings underneath their evergreen tent. "Nor is my name Honey or Darling or Sunshine—"

"You are hardly sunshine right now." He hid his face under his forearm.

Miss Meow growled from within my knapsack.

Katie tapped my shoulder and whispered, "Perhaps you should try a more sympathetic approach."

I smacked Carter's thigh. "Stop being so dramatic. Get up."

"Honey, you're so cruel." He sat up, slouching. Dead pine needles clung to his cheek. He looked at the ground like a child mourning over a broken toy. "I've been used, horribly used. What have I done to deserve this?"

"What are you talking about? No one used you." It was time for Bryce and Baxter to pull Carter out of his hiding place. I turned to leave, but he clutched my arm and pulled me toward him.

Tears rolled down his cheeks, carving paths through the grime. "This entire time, I've been nothing but a pawn. A pawn! It's so unfair."

"We don't have time for this," I said to Katie. "What's he talking about?"

Katie opened her mouth to speak, but Carter hushed her with a raise of his hand.

"I'm nothing but a horse pulling a carriage," he started, "and when my driver whispers a command, I whinny and follow. Why would I question him? He has rewarded me with sugar cubes and many sweet, luxurious things."

"Did you bump your head?" I asked, shifting away from him. "You sound delirious."

"His Whisperer spoke to him a few hours ago," Katie said quietly into my ear. "And now he thinks his Whisperer is leading him toward Death."

"My Whisperer must be a cruel spirit! I know it!" He wiped the tears from his cheeks, smearing the dirt on his blotchy, puffy face.

Katie and I watched him in expectation of another outburst. But he sat there, staring down at his trembling hands.

As angry as I was at Carter for abandoning us this morning, I hated seeing him in such torment. "Why would you think your Whisperer is leading you toward Death?" I brushed leaves and pine needles out of his hair, smoothing his auburn tendrils.

He shook his head, staring vacantly at the ground. "Because he plans to desert me when I need him most."

"What you're saying makes no sense," I said. "Your Whisperer has given you angora, fine cheese, and plush slippers ..."

"He lives inside my head. He gets to enjoy all of the things that I enjoy." He looked at me with pained eyes that were green as spring ferns collecting rain.

"Ri's right," Katie interrupted, holding her brother's hand. "Your story makes no sense. If the spirit—or whatever it is—lives inside of your head, then why would he want to lead his host toward Death?"

"Because his work is almost done and my body is far too limiting. That's all I know."

He delivered his words with such conviction that the hair on my nape stood up. It was as if the spirit in question settled next to me and sent shivers through my body by tracing its wispy fingertips along my spine. Carter's gift came from somewhere. But a spirit?

I braced his shoulders and looked him in the eye. "Carter, I think you're crazy, but I'm not going to let you die."

Of course, that was an impossible promise to keep considering what lurked in the forest, but I needed to comfort him somehow so we could be on our way.

"You're kinder to me than I deserve." He grappled me in a hug and wept harder, pressing his face against my shoulder. Moisture from his tears dampened my neck and hair. Katie rubbed his back and murmured comforting words.

"Ri, is everything all right?" Bryce peeked into our pine-needled shelter. His eyes widened as he looked at Carter falling apart in my arms.

"One moment," I mouthed to him.

He nodded and gave us privacy. To my surprise, Katie did the same. She crawled out from under the tree, leaving Carter and me alone.

"Carter," I said, patting his shoulder. "You have to pull yourself together. We can't stay under this tree."

He gripped me tighter. Embraced as we were, I felt his heart hammering against my chest. His tears soaked through the shoulder of my shirt.

"I don't want to die, Honey. I'm so much more than a lowly con-artist," he said, sniffling. "Really I am."

"I don't know," I said. "You're a difficult person to trust."

He let go of me and sat back on his heels, gaping. "I can't believe you think that. Everything I've done, I've done for others, especially my sister. Haven't you noticed how healthy she looks since coming to this island?"

"She does seem better," I said. Katie's melodic voice murmured beyond the branches.

"She derives good health from nature, but when nature withers around her, she withers with it." His voice was dry and hoarse from crying. He looked at the ground and divided clusters of pine needles into piles. "Black Valley was the worst place for her since nothing blossoms there anymore. That's why I put my share of Bryce's harvest in her room each month. While it wasn't much nature, it was enough to keep her alive."

I raised an eyebrow. "Bryce told me that you sold your share to support your luxurious lifestyle."

He swallowed hard. "I did sell some of it, but only because I wanted to give Katie nice things." Another round of tears flowed from his eyes. Once again he was clinging to me, gripping bunches of my shirt. "I need to make sure that your village is a safe haven for her in case something happens to me."

I petted his hair, parting his curls with my fingertips. "I told you, I'm not going to let you die."

He continued to weep as if he didn't hear me. "I've wanted to bring her here ever since I met Bryce and learned of his power. But every time I spoke to Katie about leaving, she refused. I didn't have it in me to force her. She would've resented me forever. People needed her healing gift in Black Valley, and there was nothing I could do to convince her to put her health before theirs."

"Your sister has a selfless and compassionate heart," I said. "You should be proud of her."

He leaned away from me, curling his lip in disgust. "I don't want a corpse that I can be proud of. I want a living, healthy sister. When you and the Red Band arrived, opportunity presented itself. The two of you were the catalyst I needed."

My stomach hardened. "What are you talking about?"

He slid both palms down his face, clearing the moisture from his cheeks. With a deep breath, he ceased sobbing and took my hands into his. They were wet from tears. "I have a confession."

"A confession?"

He closed his eyes. "The Red Band was never a threat to us in Black Valley. We didn't need to leave."

"What!" I smacked him in the chest. "Why would you lie about that? We nearly died in Sea Dragon's Point. And the ocean! Carter, we could have drowned."

His nostrils flared with heavy breath. "But we didn't die. We didn't drown. The only way Katie was going to leave Black Valley was if she thought we were all in mortal danger. A captain from the City Guard was the perfect prop to convince her of that threat."

"We deserved to know the truth."

"No." He pointed a finger at me. "Everyone believes lies are inferior to the truth, but they are both flames that can either save or destroy you. It all depends on what you've used to fuel them. And my lies have always been fueled by love. Katie deserved a cure. Bryce deserved to live like a human being. You deserved a way home. I thought that leaving Black Valley was the only way to get those things for all of you."

"Ri," Baxter shook a branch, "I'm dragging the coward out of there in ten seconds."

"One more minute," I said sharply. Heat crawled up my neck and face as I turned back to Carter. "I can't believe how you try to justify yourself. Does Katie know?"

"I told her a few moments ago. She understands that my heart was in the right place and she forgave me. But I'm coming clean because I need you to trust me. The Red Band wasn't a threat to us in Black Valley, but he certainly is now. He will make Samuel face his past. My Whisperer promises it."

"What nonsense! You've hated him from the start. How can I believe anything you say? And even if you are telling the truth, why would you believe anything that your Whisperer tells you if he's a cruel spirit?"

"Because Red Bands always ruin everything!" Spittle flew off his lips. "We have to kill him. Tonight, right before we reach your village, you distract him and I'll shove the dagger into his back."

"We're not going to kill him. You need to calm down."

From behind, Baxter's hands poked through the branches and clutched my waist. I yelped as he dragged me out from under the tree.

"That wasn't necessary," Bryce said, glowering at Baxter while offering me a hand.

Waving away his help, I stood and wagged my finger at our silver-haired companion. "I was in the middle of a conversation."

"Sounded like the end of it to me," Baxter said in a gruff tone. "If we don't move now, it will be dark long before we reach the mountaintop."

"We can camp here and start fresh in the morning," Bryce said.

"Here is no good." Baxter eyed our surroundings. "We'll have a better vantage point up higher."

Carter emerged from hiding, rustling the pine's branches. Katie rushed to his side and offered him a canteen. Her forehead was creased with worry. Though the hem of her tattered dress was muddy, and her cheeks were smudged with dirt, she stood tall, radiating with good health. By bringing her to the island, Carter had indeed cured her. After taking a sip of water, he pulled the collar of her cloak around her neck to protect her from the chilly air.

I would never resort to Carter's level of dishonesty. Lies of that scale, even those fueled by love, would burn someone eventually.

Bryce cupped my shoulder as I glared at Carter. "Is everything all right?"

I nodded. Revealing Carter's confession would only slow our journey, and Baxter had raised a valid concern. A faint white moon had already appeared in the sky.

"Well, I think I've wasted enough of our time," Carter said with a smile that didn't reach anywhere near his eyes. "Let's finish this trek, shall we?"

Bryce patted his shoulder. "I'm proud of you, Carter. We'll get through this together."

***

We had been hiking for an hour when the slope steepened to a near sixty-degree angle. Tree roots veined the forest floor like lacework, preventing the formation of paths. Needled boughs of spruce trees fanned overhead, leaving the black soil untouched by sunlight. Only a few lonely patches of weeds poked through the dirt.

We proceeded in silence to listen for possible predators. While the trees provided excellent cover, they also offered hunters ample concealment for a sneak attack.

Bryce lurched alongside me, his breath growing raspy as he made the climb. Perspiration beaded on his forehead and above his lip. Each time he wheezed, my chest tightened with worry.

"We should rest for a moment," I whispered to him. My legs were also burning from the steep climb.

He quickened his pace. "Not safe here." He punctuated the end of his sentence with a gasp. "Almost dark. I'm fine."

The sky was cooling to cobalt, and clouds rumbled with approaching thunder. Bryce went a few more steps and then fell to his knees.

"Bryce!" I knelt on the ground next to him, clutching his arms. Miss Meow yowled in my knapsack.

Carter joined us with eyes round as those of a startled fish. He felt Bryce's forehead. "He has a fever." Looking at his sister, he ordered her to make more remedy.

Though Katie had been supplying her concoctions to Bryce since our arrival, his condition hadn't improved. Perhaps the medicine was useless against his illness, but at that moment it was our only hope.

"There aren't any more medicinal plants in our supply pack." She clasped her trembling hands together.

Frantically, I scoured the area and found a patch of golden weeds. "Will those work?"

She glanced at the stalks, most bent in half or withering. "Those plants are nearly dead."

"Try," Carter said in a firm tone that I'd never heard him use before. He grasped Bryce's face between his palms. "Slow down. Inhale. Exhale. You can do it."

Baxter, whose steady stride always placed him at least ten feet ahead, turned toward us. "We're not far from the pinnacle," he called out and began jogging upslope.

"Where're you going?" I called after him.

He didn't respond.

Katie blessed the weeds and placed them inside a canteen. Carter ripped the vessel out of her hands and placed it to Bryce's mouth. He took a few sips, pausing to cough. Once finished, he shivered and murmured something indecipherable.

A few minutes passed before Baxter returned. "I've spotted a village."

"A village?" I looked toward the peak and, after days of absence, the Fireflies appeared, drifting down from the treetops. My heart jumped. It was about time they showed up.

Without explaining, I chased them up the incline. A clap of thunder boomed, releasing a downpour that pummeled the needled branches above. The forest ended ahead, and the trees stood against a roiling backdrop of storm clouds. Raindrops broke through the canopy overhead and found my cheeks.

I reached the edge of a cliff that cascaded into a valley filled with the spikes of dark spruce trees. Evergreen-covered mountains encircled the valley dappled with mist. A red rock ledge snaked along the side of a nearby slope—we were no more than an hour's journey away. Upon that ledge, a thatch-roofed village spun threads of smoke from its chimneys. And there, alone on the westernmost side, was my home.

The glow of hearth fire lit its windows. I closed my eyes, grateful that Samuel was likely safe if someone was keeping our home warm.

I returned to my companions with heart pounding from excitement and fear. Baxter and Carter helped Bryce to a standing position. He staggered and his eyes took on a vacant, glassy stare.

"That's my village," I said. The rain came down harder, leaving large splotches of moisture on my clothes. Before long, the downpour would soak us all through. "I know a healer."

Bryce's pupils rolled back into his skull and he slumped over unconscious. If not for Baxter and Carter holding him upright, he would have crashed face first into the mud.

I hastened to him and patted his face. "Bryce! Bryce! Wake up, wake up!"

Rain plastered his dark bangs to his forehead. His breath came faint. I trembled as a heavy feeling overtook me.

"We're almost there," I told him, my voice quivering. I moved closer to block him from the wind and wiped raindrops from his face. His skin burned hot against my palm. "Please, wake up. We're so close."

Closing my eyes, I rested my forehead against his and begged, "Please don't die."

"I will get him to your healer," Baxter said, his tone resonating with resolve. He heaved Bryce over his shoulder, and his cheeks grew pink from the strain of the weight. He marched upslope, though his legs shook from the effort.

Arriving to my village at night, instead of day like Bryce and I originally planned, increased the odds of Baxter discovering Samuel. But Bryce needed shelter. We couldn't stay in the wet forest until morning.

Once Baxter roamed out of earshot, Carter whispered, "When we reach the perimeter of your village, we take him down. He'll be tired from carrying Bryce. It's our best chance."

I pushed Carter so hard that he stumbled backward into a mud puddle. "We're not going to kill him," I whispered back harshly.

Carter's Whisperer was a liar. How could Baxter, who continuously helped the four of us, kill the most important person in my life? He was not going to make Samuel face his past. Our friendship meant something to him. I felt it. No longer did he fill me with anxiety. Instead, his presence filled my heart with reassuring warmth. Leaving Carter and Katie behind, I rushed ahead and caught up to him.

"Thank you," I said, touching his arm.

We shared a long, silent look. How could I have ever interpreted his eyes as cold when we first met? It wasn't the chill of ice coloring his irises, but rather the gentle heat of a lake glistening at sunset. He set his jaw and nodded. His determination gave me hope. Together, we would save Bryce.

CHAPTER 25

By the time we reached the pines that I'd explored since childhood, the storm had stolen the color from our world. Only faint traces of light remained to outline spruce trees and shrubs in silver.

The rain battered us. Droplets the size of blueberries bombarded the puddles underfoot with a sound like thousands of beads spilling onto a slate floor. Damp cold seeped into my bones. The storm had soaked me through from my dripping hair to my soggy shoes. I clenched my jaw in a poor attempt to keep my teeth from chattering.

Baxter led the way, trudging through mud. Over his shoulder he lugged Bryce, who hadn't stirred since he passed out nearly an hour before. We had draped Katie's blanket over him, but the soaking quilt sagging over his body offered little protection from the elements. His arms dangled limply, and I caught glimpses of his fingertips poking from underneath the fringe of the blanket. The way we had him covered reminded me of the way the people of my village shroud the dead. I shivered at the thought.

Quickly, I jogged to Baxter and searched under the quilt until I found the crown of Bryce's head. Heat poured off him. His fever had worsened. Baxter must have sensed my anxiety, because he sped his pace.

Carter followed, carrying his sister on his back. Katie huddled closely to him, tucking her face against his neck with quivering lips. I kept a close eye on them both, ready to warn Baxter in case Carter drew his dagger.

Our path led to the entrance to my village. Baxter nodded, suggesting that I take the lead. My stomach somersaulted. He was in my village, a few dozen yards away from Samuel. Images of him slicing Samuel's neck flickered in my mind. But I had made my choice and all I could do at that moment was take every precaution to keep them separated.

I guided my companions through narrow alleys flanked by the cob walls of thatch-roofed homes. Strips of hearth fire shone through the slats of wooden shutters. The bad weather had driven everyone indoors, sparing my band of outsiders from the village's scrutiny.

We arrived at Kaylan's door soaked, cold, and with mud caked on our shoes and ankles. Though a thread of light slipped out from under the door, the racket of the storm made it impossible to hear any sounds from inside. Before knocking, I stole a glance at my home on the western edge of the village. The busy hearth still illuminated the main room's window, reassuring me that Samuel was safe inside. Though the light called to me like a flame summons a moth, Bryce needed tending to first. I pounded on Kaylan's door until it opened.

Kaylan's eyes bulged. He pulled me inside, and the pleasant sensation of dry warmth welcomed me. He then waved my companions to enter.

Coren, Kaylan's son, sat at the table near the hearth, enjoying a bowl of stew. He was two years younger than me, but his stubble and height made him look two years older. His identical twin brother, Kai, was nowhere in sight.

"Ri! Where've you been?" Kaylan spread his arms to hug me, then apparently thought better of dampening his clothing and patted me on the shoulder instead.

"No time to explain." I ripped the drenched blanket off Bryce. "My friend needs your help."

Kaylan glanced at Bryce and then turned to his son. "Don't just sit there. Gather up some blankets and dry garments."

Coren knocked over his chair as he leapt to his feet and raced down the dark corridor that led to a storage room. Tendrils of steam rose from his unfinished stew, curling like fingers beckoning his return.

Kaylan waved his hand toward two beds at the far side of the room. "Set him over here. Quickly!" Though he didn't speak in the Crooked Tongue, Baxter figured out what he was being asked to do and carried Bryce toward the beds.

As Baxter wandered out of earshot, I leaned toward Kaylan and whispered, "Is Samuel all right?" I held my breath, awaiting his answer.

"No need to worry. Kai's watching over him." He patted my shoulder and then rushed to Bryce.

Good. Samuel was safe, which meant I could concentrate on helping Bryce. I trailed Kaylan to where Baxter had set Bryce next to one of the two beds. Wooden frames raised both straw-padded mattresses a few inches off the ground, keeping the wool blankets free of dust. "He has a fever," I explained. "But it's the result of a much more serious illness that he refuses to admit he has."

The main room in Kaylan's cottage was double the size of any other in my village since he needed the space to tend to the sick and injured. One wall had recessed shelving that housed countless clay bottles, cloth bandages, and supply boxes. Bunches of herbs dangled from a rack along the opposite wall, freshening the room with pleasant scents.

Baxter stepped out of the way as we approached so we could kneel next to Bryce. I removed my knapsack and released the squirming Miss Meow.

Kaylan placed a hand on Bryce's forehead. "You could roast potatoes on this boy."

Coren returned with a stack of dry clothes in his arms. "Ri, who are these people?"

Keeping my voice low so Baxter wouldn't hear, I said, "I know it's hard to believe, but my companions come from Samuel's homeland."

"Explain later," Kaylan interrupted. "Help me get this lad out of his soaked clothing." He unbuttoned Bryce's shirt and then glancing at my companions, he spoke in the Crooked Tongue. "No point in standing around with your teeth chattering. Get yourselves warmed up."

Baxter and the siblings settled beside the hearth while I remained near the bedside. Not even the fire and its promise of warmth were capable of luring me away from Bryce. He slept peacefully as he always did. I held his hand, hoping my touch might speed his wakening. The corner of his mouth twitched, but other than that he didn't stir.

"What's that girl doing?" Coren pointed a thumb at Katie. She had found a mortar and was grinding something that smelled like basil and rosemary near the fire. Carter sat next to her, staring at the mortar with glazed-over eyes. He seemed lost in distant thoughts. Baxter sat across from the siblings, thawing his hands near the flames. For the first time since he followed us to Sea Dragon's Point, he showed exhaustion, slouching.

I looked back at Coren. "She's preparing medicine for Bryce."

"That won't help," Kaylan muttered. "The boy needs some yarrow tea to help him sweat the fever out."

"Let her try," Coren said.

Kaylan smacked Coren in the shoulder. "Stop gawking at the girl and help me." He pulled Bryce's arm out of the drenched sleeve with his old, gnarled hands. With the shirt half removed, the amulet resting on Bryce's chest was in plain view.

Coren let out a low whistle, studying the translucent stone. "That's some piece of jewelry."

"Get the dry shirt on him," I ordered, glancing at Baxter. Though we had grown close, I didn't want him to see the amulet and suspect that it was the source of Bryce's power. After all, I gave Bryce my word that I would keep his secret.

Baxter noticed me glance at him and straightened his posture. "Ri, do you need something?"

I shook my head and turned back to Kaylan and Coren. "You mustn't mention Samuel around Baxter—the silver-haired one," I whispered. "He thinks Samuel committed a horrible crime where he comes from, and I'm not sure what he would do if they met."

Kaylan finished buttoning Bryce's new shirt. "If that man intends to harm Samuel, I can fix him some tea to knock him out for good."

"No," I said. "It's complicated. Baxter's a good person ... I wouldn't be here without his help." I inhaled a deep breath. "We found these beasts in the forest, like nothing I've ever seen before."

"I know what you speak of." Kaylan unbuckled one of Bryce's shoes.

"You do?"

"A man killed one in the Dark Woods while you were—wherever you were." He patted my arm. "Don't worry, Ri. These things will not destroy our village. We'll fight back."

Clearly, those in my village had not yet seen the bloodshed that I had. Perhaps they were lucky enough to kill one of the Culling's beasts, but they had no idea what they were up against.

Katie joined us, carrying a bowl of green goop. "Ri, place a dollop of this under Bryce's nose. It will help sooth his lungs and fever."

"That concoction won't do a damn thing," Kaylan told her, "although it smells delicious. Are you trying to lure him out of slumber by encouraging his appetite?" Kaylan chuckled. Part of me wanted to smack him. Couldn't he see that Bryce was dying? It was no time for humor.

Katie offered a polite, though thin-lipped smile. "You're quite funny," she said with a hint of irritation in her tone. "But certainly it will do no harm?"

Kaylan's expression softened. "Well, I suppose."

I scooped some of the mixture onto my index finger and plopped it under Bryce's nose. Then Katie and I joined the others near the fire, giving Bryce privacy while Kaylan and Coren slipped dry pants onto him.

Baxter offered me a towel, and I dabbed my soaked hair, staring at the flames flickering in the hearth. What if Bryce didn't pull through? My heart ached to see Samuel, but I couldn't pry myself from Bryce's side. I glanced at Carter, who was rocking back and forth. One hand clutched his stomach while the other cupped his mouth.

"He was never supposed to catch fever," Carter mumbled into his palm.

Coren and Kaylan tucked Bryce under the blankets and I returned to sit on the floor next to his bedside, as if his mere presence could soothe my worry. I placed my head next to his atop the pillow. His damp hair smelled of rain and spruce.

"I'll brew some tea to warm you and your friends up," Kaylan said. "Then you can tell me what happened."

Kaylan went about preparing tea while Katie sat next to me with her hand on my shoulder. Coren approached us and offered Katie dry clothes. I recognized the garments. He had bartered with the best weaver in the village last summer to acquire them. They cost him a bear pelt and were the nicest things he owned. The linen shirt, dyed soft green with stinging nettle, complemented the pale-colored pants.

"How lovely," Katie said. "Thank you."

"He can't understand you," I explained. "Only Kaylan speaks the Crooked Tongue."

"Oh," she said, and then offered him a smile and a nod.

Though Coren was obviously interested in Katie, Carter, strangely, did nothing to intervene. He stared at the floor and wrung his hands. Meanwhile, Baxter looked at me. Some people might shift their eyes when caught staring, but not him. He held my gaze as if he was expecting me to request something. Perhaps that was his way of offering comfort. The fire reflected in his eyes, warming them to the color of a sun-drenched ocean.

"Ri," Coren said forcefully. It made me wonder if this was the third or fourth time he had called to me. "Please, tell me what she said."

Startled, I looked away from Baxter. "Um ... she said, 'thanks.'"

He pursed his lips, shaking his head. "That was a lot of words for thanks."

"Coren!" Kaylan shouted. "Get over here and chop these carrots for more stew."

"Yes, father." Coren hurried toward the table where Kaylan had stacked a heap of vegetables.

"He likes you," I said to Katie once Coren stepped away.

She rolled her eyes. "Well, I have work to do. This is hardly the time to think about such things."

Most girls might have smiled from the attention, but Katie locked a compassionate yet determined gaze on Bryce. "I'll do everything I can to cure him. You have my word."

Her resolve continued to impress me. "Thank you, Katie. Bryce and I are fortunate to have you as a friend."

She patted my hand and offered a reassuring smile. "Now, let's discuss Samuel. I know you're worried, so I'll keep an eye on Bryce if you'd like to check on him."

"But if Bryce wakes and I'm not here—"

"Then he'll understand. At this point, there's nothing you can do except be patient. Trust that Kaylan and I will do what we do best. And if Bryce wakes while you're gone, I'm sure that I can ask Coren to fetch you." She said the last sentence loud enough for Coren to hear. His face split into a grin at the sound of his name coming from her lips.

"Thank you Katie," I said. The gratitude ran down to my bones.

"I'll be back shortly." I headed toward the door. Rain pelted the shutters and roof, but my home was only a short run away.

"Ri's going home to check in," Katie explained to everyone.

Baxter stood. "I'll go too."

"No," I said, my hand gripping the door handle. "Um ... I mean—"

"I'll go." Carter snapped out of his trance and joined me. He wiped tears off his cheeks. Regarding Baxter, he added, "You're the strongest one here. I'd prefer if you stayed with my sister and Bryce in case the Culling shows up."

Baxter glanced at me, but sat back down. "I plan to check on you if you're not back in a few minutes."

Kaylan poured tea into a couple of mugs. "No need for that, they'll be with the strongest in our village."

Neither Kai nor Samuel was known for his strength, but Baxter sipped his tea, appeased by Kaylan's fib. Carter and I hurried outside. The storm swallowed us in a torrent of rain and wind. Mud squished beneath our shoes, and the puddles underfoot frothed from the relentless downpour. We reached my door and I swung it open with a loud bang.

Inside, Kai accidentally dropped a bowl as he leapt up from a stool near the hearth. Ricky dashed toward me from his bed at the corner of the room, and then jumped on his hind legs to lick my face. He greeted Carter with the same enthusiasm.

"You scared the life out of me, Ri," Kai said in our village's native tongue. He held out a spoon, his bowl of stew lying toppled on the floor near his feet. He raised his hands and let them flop to his side, gawking at his ruined dinner. Ricky sniffed the floor until he found the puddle of broth and steaming vegetables. He lapped it up with a snort of delight.

"Sorry," I said. "I didn't mean to startle you."

"Where've you been?" Kai's gaze flicked to Carter, who closed the door behind me. His mouth turned downward as he measured Carter up. "And who's he?"

"I'll explain later." I hurried past him and Carter followed. "Where's Samuel?"

"He's fine." Kai held me back by the arm. "Wait, Ri. You can't disappear for days like that. You've always been impulsive and, well, reckless, but you outdid yourself this time."

"What's he saying?" Carter eased me out of Kai's grip, offering a rigid smile.

"He only wants to know where I was," I translated. "Like I'm going to tell him that I met a boy who could travel through waterfalls and spent the past week trying to get home from Black Valley. Come on, let's check on Samuel."

I waved Carter to follow me down the narrow corridor. The firelight illuminated only the entrance of the hall, leaving the far end shadowed. I heard Samuel searching the storage closet past our bedrooms.

"Something doesn't feel right." Carter cupped my shoulder, walking so closely that his toes caught on my heels.

"Samuel?" I called, squinting in the darkness.

He ceased rummaging and the corridor went quiet, save the crackle of the fireplace and Carter's heavy breathing. Then, the thump of a boot-clad foot echoed in the closet, followed by another. My heart stopped. Five feet in front of me, the silhouette of a tall man stepped into view. I peeked into Samuel's room directly to my left. He lay on his bed with his blankets tangled around his waist. His chest rose and fell with breath. He seemed safe.

"Who's there?" I asked.

The man answered with a disturbing chuckle. "Well, well. It looks like little bird found her way home." The deep, familiar voice grated against my ears.

"Mallory." My voice withered to a whisper.

"Mallory? Did you say Mallory?" Carter grabbed my arms, twisting them behind me in his haste, and dragged me back into the main room. The intruder's footfalls approached us.

A moment later, Mallory's scarred face emerged from the dark corridor. He held a bottle of dandelion wine and a mug. Since our last meeting, he'd gone from a grubby madman to someone who seethed with importance. He had traded in his dirty, worn garments for crisp linen that mirrored the colors of the storm outside. A wool cloak fringed with bear fur fanned behind him as he strode forward.

I broke out of Carter's grip and met him halfway with my neck craned up to look at him. "Why are you here?"

His powerful eyes looked into mine. They glinted with wicked amusement. "There was a sudden vacancy."

I glanced at the sword and the dagger strapped to his hip. The hilts of both weapons gleamed from recent polishing. "I swear if you've harmed Samuel—"

"You'll what?" He shoved past me toward the table where a loaf of acorn bread and a knife awaited. He sliced himself a piece of bread.

Though I could do little to protect Samuel from a man twice my weight and who had likely fought—and killed—countless opponents, I stormed to him. "I won't cower from you, Mallory."

Carter kept a safe distance near the hearth. "Honey, we need to talk. Right now."

"Later," I said. No intruder, no matter how intimidating, was going to enter my home and threaten Samuel's safety. "I'm not leaving this man alone with Samuel."

Mallory laughed as he sat down and poured wine into his mug. "Relax, little girl. I've no interest in killing a frail, old man. There's no sport in it."

Kai's confused gaze bounced between the three of us since we were speaking in the Crooked Tongue. He touched my arm. "Ri, be at ease. This man is a hero and he's treated Samuel with nothing but kindness."

"He's up to something," I replied. "Just look at him."

Mallory's expression never changed. His snide grin hinted that he thought himself superior to everyone else in the room. He pointed a thumb at Carter. "So is this the boy who travels through waterfalls?"

"Travel through waterfalls?" My heart thumped against my ribs, but I squared my shoulders, maintaining backbone. "What sort of nonsense are you talking about?"

Carter waved his palms in the air and added, "I'm nobody important."

Mallory looked down his nose at him. "I can see that." Then, turning to me, he added, "Don't play games with me, girl. I heard you loud and clear. Where's this boy who travels through waterfalls?"

The door swung open and all of us flinched, except for Mallory. Baxter stood in the doorframe with water streaming down his face.

My legs went weak as he stepped over the threshold and entered my home. My home! With Samuel, just a few feet down the hall. How could I deal with him and Mallory at the same time? Carter looked like he might bolt at the first opportunity. Ricky cowered behind Kai, whining with his tail between his legs.

Baxter glanced around the room, first at Carter, Kai and me, and then at Mallory. He narrowed his eyes at him and then slowly brushed back his coat to clutch his sword's hilt. "You live with this man, Ri?"

"What? No!" I raised my palms. "I only met him once in the forest, and his being here is as much of a surprise to me as it is to you."

"I see." His hand tightened around his hilt as he scowled at my unwelcome guest.

At the table, Mallory remained seated, but he slipped the knife next to the acorn bread into his hand, hiding the blade parallel to his arm. He kept his dark eyes trained on me, smirking, while I stood a couple feet away panicked as a mouse that had wandered into the path of snake.

Mallory glanced at Baxter's weapon and then back at me. His mouth curled upward, creasing the scar on his cheek. "Consider your next move carefully, Red Band filth."

My breath hitched. If Baxter drew his weapon, that knife would surely find its way to my throat within seconds. I froze, unable to turn my head away from the blade. From the corner of my eye, I noticed Baxter release his weapon.

"So honorable." Mallory smiled with satisfaction. "But also pathetic. You miss your opportunity to strike me for a simple village girl without a hint of noble blood in her veins. What low standards you have in women, cousin."

"Cousin?" I whispered through a trembling breath. Baxter had said that his only cousin—Robert Renselar's son—had died during the massacre. "Robert Renselar is your father?"

"That's right, girl. But he looks more like my father's son than I do." He nodded toward Baxter. "And judging by that captain's coat, he happily follows the tyrant's orders without question. Worthless dog."

"We believed you to be dead." Baxter's tone boiled with hatred. His piercing stare fixed on Mallory while his hand remained tense, obviously itching to draw his sword. "Why are you here?"

"I'm visiting an old acquaintance," he replied.

Baxter exchanged a look between Mallory and me. "It's time for you to leave."

Mallory turned his head toward me, and once again I was caught in the snake's paralyzing stare. "You haven't told him, have you?"

Baxter questioned me with a raised eyebrow. Even if I could have thought of an explanation, my throat tightened so much that I could only release a pitiful sound.

Mallory snickered at me. "You certainly brought the wrong man home to meet your pop."

Footfalls approached from the hallway. "Mallory?" Samuel called.

No, no, no. I spun toward the hallway just as Carter hurried to block Samuel's path.

Raising his arms, Carter maneuvered in front of Samuel so he couldn't slip past. "You need to go back to bed."

Samuel swatted at Carter. "Get off me, lad. Who are you? Where are your manners?"

I wanted to hurry to him, but dared not move lest I drop my guard in front of Baxter and Mallory. "He's a friend," I said to Samuel, voice cracking. "Please, go with him. I'll tuck you in shortly."

"Ri? You're home?" Samuel peeked around Carter's shoulder. The firelight shone on his heavily lined face. His sparse hair stuck out in all directions, and though it might have been the lighting, I swore his cheeks looked thinner and his limbs frailer. He grinned in a way that lifted his drooping skin.

Carter pushed him back down the hallway offering comforting words. Though I cringed at the way he shoved Samuel, it was the only way to get him out of Baxter's sight.

Baxter stared at the hallway, breathless, with his mouth hanging open. "Samuel Perrington," he whispered. Slowly, his hand grasped the hilt of his sword as if it had a mind of its own.

"Heartbroken, cousin? Tsk, tsk." Mallory leaned back in the chair and sipped his wine. "What will you choose? Love or duty?"

"Quiet," I snapped. His malicious comments were growing tiresome. Clasping my hands, I turned to Baxter. "Please, let me explain."

He raised his hand to hush me and shifted his gaze downward as if I was the most despicable thing he had ever set eyes upon.

My heart, my spirit, dropped to the floor, leaving an enormous cavity inside of me. Our friendship was over just like that. "Please, Baxter."

Without even glancing at me, he shook his head.

Mallory grunted with amusement. "He's too much of a gentlemen to have words with his girl in front of others." He discarded the knife on the table, staring at me with bitter joy. "You're no longer useful leverage."

Baxter glared at his cousin. "You and I need to speak. Outside." He swung the door open and left. The wind slammed the door shut.

Mallory rose. He stood taller than Baxter, taller than any man I had ever known. He strode toward the door, but paused in front of me.

I grasped the hilt of my dagger, though the steel hardly offered me any sense of security around him.

He smirked. "Renselar men are not known to forgive." Then he left, following Baxter into the storm.

I turned toward the hallway. "Carter!"

He returned from Samuel's room within seconds, his eyes wide. "Honey, this is bad, very bad."

"Tell me something I don't know." I dashed toward the window and opened the shutters to a crack so I could keep an eye on the Renselar men. Rain slipped through, splattering my cheeks with ice-cold droplets. I saw nothing through the darkness.

Carter and Kai joined me, squinting as they looked through the shutters.

"My Whisperer repeats the same thing," Carter said. "Baxter will make Samuel face his past. He says nothing of Mallory."

"Dammit," I said under my breath. Could Carter's Whisperer even be trusted? As much as I didn't want to believe those words about Baxter, I had to consider the possibility of their truth.

A streak of light branched through the sky, followed by a clap of thunder. Samuel called these streaks lightning, but our village knew them as Collectors: servants of Death who gathered additional souls when the god felt certain quotas weren't being met. Another flash lit up the sky and in that brief second of light, I saw neither Baxter nor Mallory anywhere.

"Ri?" Samuel hobbled out of the hallway. "Who was that young man in the doorway? He looked so familiar."

"No one to worry about," I lied, hugging Samuel. "He's gone."

I looked Samuel over. He did appear thinner, and his pale skin and dark circles hinted of lack of sleep. "When did you last eat?"

He waved his hand, dismissing my concern. "How could I eat with you missing? Not that Mallory would let me go hungry. He's a good lad." He scanned the room. "Where did he wander to?"

"Samuel, listen to me." I gripped his shoulders, meeting his eyes. "Mallory shouldn't be trusted."

"Don't be silly, sweetie." Samuel chuckled. "He might have been troublesome as a youth, but long ago I taught him morals back home. He fought for what was right. He fought for the people."

Perhaps he did at one time, or perhaps Samuel's mind, deteriorated as it was, created a false memory. "Well, Mallory is not that man now."

Regarding Carter, I said, "We should all return to Kaylan's home for the night. I don't want to leave Bryce and Katie alone with those two wandering about." I then translated my plan to Kai.

Though I hated to drag Samuel into the rain, we had a better chance of survival in numbers. And if the Renselar men returned, I would be ready. I shoved the soft spot I had for Baxter deep down inside me. Hopefully, it wouldn't resurface when the time came to draw my weapon against him.

CHAPTER 26

Sunrays snuck through the slats of my bedroom shutters, disturbing my slumber. Judging by their brightness, dawn had passed hours ago. The noisy bustle of life roared outside: men hammering and chopping, women gossiping, and goats bleating. But neither the racket nor the light could pry me from the warmth of my bed.

"The world can wait five more minutes," I mumbled. With a lazy stretch, I rolled over and ducked my head under the pillow. My wool blanket promised a quick journey back into dreams. Ah!

No!

I bolted upright, heart drumming. How did I get in my room? Did someone carry me to my bed? The last thing I remembered was sitting on a stool in Kaylan's home, guarding the door in case Mallory or Baxter returned. I threw the blanket off and hurried down the hall toward muffled chatter.

The savory aroma of potatoes and eggs greeted me as I entered the main room. Katie and Samuel sat at the table as Carter whisked around them pouring tea. Samuel wore clean clothes and a smile, while both siblings donned new garments. Katie wore a green dress, and flowers poked out of the braids wrapped around her head. Carter's pale linen shirt and pants boasted of softness as they flowed around him. Red embroidery adorned the cuffs of his sleeves.

"What happened last night?" I rushed toward the window, scanning the village for the Renselar cousins. In addition to the typical crowds and activities, a group of men were building what appeared to be a tall fence.

Carter rested his hand on my shoulder. "You passed out just before dawn, so I brought you back here to get some proper rest. Baxter and Mallory never returned, and everyone is safe, including Bryce."

"He is?"

"Yes, perfectly." He dragged me away from the window. "Let me keep watch for a while. I've placed a wash bucket and fresh garments in your room. Go clean up and then join us for breakfast."

Four plates of beautifully arranged food waited on the table. Scrambled eggs mixed with sausage crowned a spiraled base of thinly sliced potatoes. A sprinkling of goat cheese, fresh herbs, and red sauce topped the mound. My stomach whimpered like a begging puppy.

Samuel took a bite and grunted with approval. "Best potatoes I've ever tasted—" He paused mid-chew and gawked at me. "Oh, except for the ones you cook for me, sweetie."

I smiled. "You don't need to flatter me. I'm just happy you're eating." Turning to Carter, I asked, "How did you get all this food?"

Grinning, he pushed me toward my room. "I made a new friend."

"A new friend?" I eyed him. Part of his shirt wasn't tucked in and the buttons were misaligned, suggesting that he had dressed in haste. Strange, considering the attention he had given his appearance when we first met. Unless …

I shoved him away. "That sort of friend? Already?"

He glanced at his shirt and snickered, correcting his buttons.

"You don't even speak my village's language," I added.

"The language of love is universal, Buttercup." He wiggled his eyebrows. "But if you're not fluent, I'd be happy to teach you sometime."

"Ew!" I spun around and hurried down the hallway. When I reached my room, I paused a moment, listening to make sure he wasn't following. His voice soon addressed Katie and Samuel, and the three of them resumed their conversation.

Atop the chest at the foot of my bed sat a pile of unfamiliar clothes, a brush, and a red-beaded barrette too fancy for my tastes. Next to those, a bucket of water and a small slab of soap waited. I quickly washed and put on the new clothes. The garments consisted of a pair of brown linen pants that fit surprisingly well, a lightweight shirt, and a new belt with an attached sheath that would hold my dagger. Swiveling, I grabbed my weapon from the side of my bed and slipped it into place.

Leaving the barrette behind, I left my room while twisting my hair into a braid.

"I'm going to visit Bryce," I interrupted as I returned to the main room. "I'll be back in ten minutes."

Carter pointed at one of the plates. "Eat something first. You need to regain your strength."

I glowered at the food, but I figured I could spare five minutes to eat. Lack of nourishment and exhaustion had left me lightheaded. Besides, I missed Samuel's company. He had fallen asleep shortly after arriving at Kaylan's the prior night, leaving no opportunity for chitchat, and I had questions.

"Samuel," I said in a much sweeter tone than I had used with Carter, "how long did Mallory stay here while I was gone?"

Samuel shrugged. "Oh, I don't quite recall. Perhaps three days ..."

Three days? Three whole days? Who did Mallory think he was, sleeping in our home, eating our food, and drinking our wine like he owned the place? I jabbed a cluster of eggs onto a potato slice and shoved them into my mouth.

Oh!

A melody of savory flavors hit my tongue at once. Time slowed. The red sauce started off sweet before sharpening with hot spices, complementing the buttery taste of the eggs.

"Has my cooking made you weak in the knees?" Carter asked, licking greasy potato juice off his fingertips.

"It's a little dry," I answered. "But I can't let food go to waste."

Samuel chuckled. "There's no need to be jealous over Carter's skill. Show some appreciation. He woke at dawn to assist one of the village's widows in order to earn this fine food."

Carter grinned. "Yes, it was strenuous work, but I believe she was quite satisfied with my efforts."

Gross. Both Katie and Samuel munched on their food, oblivious to Carter's true meaning. I narrowed my eyes at him before returning my attention to Samuel. "So what did you and Mallory talk about?"

Samuel furrowed his brow and concentrated on his plate. "Hmm. What did we talk about? Blast this forgetful mind of mine. I know he spent a lot of time searching for you. I was so worried." He patted my arm.

I was sure that Mallory only offered to look for me to earn Samuel's trust. He was up to something.

I layered my hand atop Samuel's. "You don't need to worry about that ever again. I'm staying right here from now on."

His eyebrows knotted together, once again looking down at the table as if it might speak the memories he had forgotten. "He had a lot of questions too, I remember that."

"What sort of questions?"

"Just catching up mostly. And he was looking for something, but I can't remember what it was." Scrunching his face, he jabbed at his temple as if to bore the memory out. When his hand began to tremble, my appetite withered away, despite the delicious scents of food that surrounded me.

"That's enough talk about Mallory for now," I said, not wishing to press him any further.

"I have an idea," Katie broke in. "Samuel mentioned his garden to me earlier." Smiling, she nudged his shoulder. "Didn't you say the daffodils were blooming?"

"Oh yes." Samuel grinned.

"I would love to see them after breakfast." She beamed.

For me, the garden would have to wait. I stood and kissed Samuel on the cheek and then headed toward the door. "I'll be back in a few minutes."

Carter followed me, carrying my plate of unfinished food. The brisk morning air skittered against my skin as I stepped into the daylight. It was a beautiful morning even if danger lurked beyond my village. Carter joined me and closed the door behind him.

"If you're not going to finish this marvelous breakfast I prepared, at least give the rest of it to Bryce," he said. "That is if he's awake yet."

"Well, since you worked so hard for it." I took the plate. "Don't you think it's a little inappropriate to be frolicking with women when the Culling and the Renselars are out there?"

"Frolicking? Is that what you call it? Cute."

"I'm serious." An irritated sigh ripped through my throat.

"So am I." He leaned in. "And I plan to live everyday as if it's my last because it very well could be."

How could I argue with that? I wanted to tell Carter that I wouldn't let him die, but each day I felt more and more powerless to protect anyone. "All right, do you think you could just stay here for ten minutes and watch over Samuel?"

"Of course. But before you go, I heard some talk about Mallory this morning."

"Oh?"

"Your village considers him a hero because he rescued a small child from one of the Harbingers of the Culling. And later that same day, he killed one of the creatures that hatch from the cocoons. Kaylan told me that your village calls them Nightmares."

"Nightmares?" I cringed, recalling the horrible things that Baxter had discovered. "That's a good name for them."

"Anyhow, I think Mallory could be useful."

"Useful? Oh please, he didn't save a child and protect my village out of the kindness of his heart. Whatever his motivations are, I doubt they're in our interest." I glanced around as if Mallory might appear. "Stay here. I'll send one of Kaylan's sons over to help you guard Samuel."

At his nod, I hurried off. I passed the men who were building the fence. The posts towered three times the height of a man, and their tops had been sharpened into spear-like points. Nearby, Coren was hauling two of them toward the perimeter of the village.

"What is this?" I asked.

"Barricade," he said, breathless. "To keep the Nightmares out."

I doubted it would work, but at least a fence would offer some protection. I asked him to watch Samuel for a few minutes, and he bobbed his head, eager to take a break.

We parted and after a short run I arrived at Kaylan's door. I reached for the latch just as it swung open.

Miss Meow bumped into my legs as she raced outside. Bryce stood in the doorframe, the sweat of panic beading on his forehead. Kaylan stood behind him, trying to tug him back indoors.

"What are you doing?" I asked. "You should be in bed."

"I just woke up and didn't know where you were." He looked me over, relaxing his rigid stance. "I thought you were in trouble."

"I'm fine. Everyone is fine," I assured him, raising the plate of food. "And I brought you breakfast."

"Oh." He stepped aside to let me enter.

"He refused to stay in bed." Kaylan passed Bryce an accusing glance. "Everyone thinks they know better than the village healer. After all, what do I know? I've only been doing this my whole life."

"Sorry." Bryce sat down on the bed as if that would get him out of trouble.

"Kaylan, could you give us a moment?" I asked.

He nodded. "There's more tea in the kettle." After fastening his satchel of supplies to his hip, he headed outside, leaving Bryce and me alone.

"You need to listen to him." I handed Bryce the plate of food and then placed my hands on my hips. "You have to rest."

He slid some eggs and goat cheese onto a potato slice and plopped it into his mouth. "Did you make this? It's the best thing I've ever tasted."

"You're changing the subject, but no. Carter made it."

He savored another scoopful. "Well, it's delicious."

"Bryce, please." I sat next to him. "I don't want you pushing yourself. Promise me that you'll stay in bed until you recover."

He swallowed his food, planting a downcast gaze on the floor. In a tone that implied I had crushed all the joy in the world, he said, "All right. I promise." He chewed for a moment. "So what happened after I passed out?"

I explained that Baxter carried him all the way from the forest to my village, despite the downpour. "Once you were settled in bed, I left to check on Samuel, and Baxter followed without my knowing."

He paused, setting a half-finished potato back on his plate. "But everyone is safe?"

If I told Bryce the truth about Mallory and Baxter, he would barge out of Kaylan's cozy home, retrieve his dagger, and insist on keeping watch. He wouldn't recover if he was worried about protecting me.

"Yes." I stared at my hands and fiddled with a loose thread on my sleeve. "Baxter saw what a frail man Samuel had become and couldn't bring himself to hurt him or me."

"Really?"

I cleared my throat. "Yes. I guess Katie was right after all."

"I guess so," he said, digging back into his food. His forehead wrinkled, as if something troubled him. Whatever it was, he kept it to himself while he finished the last of his grub.

Hoping to add more credibility to my fib, I added, "He left this morning to retrieve a boat with another man in my village."

"Well, I'm glad that Baxter showed mercy, but I'm ashamed that I was in no condition to help you deal with the situation." He rose, standing with a slight hunch, and placed his plate on the table. Pouring himself some tea, he added, "I should've been there for you."

"Don't be silly," I said. "You needed rest."

He returned and sat himself closer to me. Our shoulders touched. His body radiated heat. No doubt he still suffered from fever. As he sipped his tea, the sweet scent of yarrow reached my nose.

"There's so much I could do if I didn't have this illness," he said. "As foolish as it sounds, I once dreamed that I could change things in Black Valley. Rally the people, urge them to rebel against the Red Bands' injustices."

Baxter had denounced rebellion, wary of possible bloodshed. But after all the misery Bryce had witnessed in the Slag, I understood why he would lean in the opposite direction.

"I don't think that sounds foolish at all," I said.

"It is. The people need to be led by someone who can fight for them." He shook his head, glaring at the opposite side of the room. "I can't even run for five minutes without feeling winded."

"You shouldn't be so hard on yourself." I rubbed his back.

"Perhaps you're right." He coughed and raised his arm to cover his mouth. It was a dry, hoarse sound that made my insides twist together. Once he regained his composure, he lowered his arm enough for me to see a small splotch of moist crimson dabbing his sleeve.

Panic rolled over me. He had hacked up blood. Blood! All of the care, rest, and medicine prepared for him were useless. He was getting worse.

Shifting away from me, he finished his tea in a single gulp. "I must have dripped some of the red sauce on me while eating."

Did he think me a fool? I knew blood when I saw it.

"Would you mind getting me more tea?" He shoved the mug toward me and then lowered his arm to hide his sleeve.

I could have challenged him, but instead I did as he asked. Samuel often attempted similar lies to cover up the deteriorating effects of the Sickness. I wasn't sure if it was to ease my worry or to maintain his dignity—or both. Perhaps Bryce felt the same way. And what good would it have done to force him to admit that it was blood? I couldn't heal him. Not even with Katie's remedies.

At the table, I poured tea into the mug. Keeping my back to him, I looked up, hoping to stop myself from crying. Seeing my hurt would only make him feel worse. I set the teakettle down, took a deep breath, and returned to him.

"Thank you," he said, warming his hands against the mug. "I could get used to this. Being here, in your village with you."

A breeze blew in through the window, rustling shrubbery leaves outside. He inhaled, filling his chest with the fresh air.

"It's peaceful," he continued. "So unlike the life I knew in Black Valley. Almost like a dream."

I placed my hand upon his and rested my head on his shoulder. "It is like a dream." If only I could have lingered in that moment for hours.

"But the peace is temporary, Ri. We need to discuss the Culling."

I rubbed my fingers against his, yearning to ward off reality and all its awfulness for a few more seconds.

"There's something I've been thinking about ever since we arrived here," he added. "And now I know it's the right thing to do." He removed his amulet. "When Baxter passes back through your village with the boat, I need you to give this to him."

The space at the bottom of my throat tightened. He placed the cord around my neck and the pendant dangled, so, so heavy.

"No, Bryce ..." I blinked, forcing back tears. "You're getting better."

"Listen, I'm too weak to bring peace to Black Valley, but I believe Baxter can. Even though he's the tyrant's nephew, he's proven himself to be fair and just. And he'll stop the Culling. I know it."

Though Baxter and I were at odds, I knew he would use the amulet to do the right thing. But how would I even find him, and how would he treat me once I did?

"I think you should wait before making this decision," I said. "In a few days, you may feel much stronger."

"Please, I need your support on this. Give the amulet to Baxter. Explain to him how it works. My journal is still in the knapsack. The pages got wet, but they're still legible."

I bit my lower lip to hide that it was quivering. Closing my hand around the cold amulet, I slipped it under the collar of my shirt.

He brushed a strand of hair off my face, and I searched his eyes for the honey tones and inner light they had possessed when we first met. But both were gone, drained from his dull irises.

"Thank you, Ri." He leaned closer until our faces were so close that the breath escaping his lips brushed against my own. "I know I promised I wouldn't try this again … but …" He kissed me, and this time I let him.

His lips were warm and slightly bitter tasting from the yarrow tea. He traced the side of my face with his fingertips, downward to my neck. The touch was tranquil as the morning breeze. I pulled him closer, pressing my lips firmly against his, as if my desperation could steal more time—more life—for the boy I was falling for. Our first kiss and likely our last.

The door opened and we jerked apart. Carter stepped inside. "Sorry for the bad timing."

"You're supposed to be watching Samuel!" I jumped up from the bed.

"He's in good company, Buttercup." Any trace of his earlier light-heartedness had vanished from his expression. "I need to speak to Bryce. Privately."

Bryce and I glanced at each other, still breathless from our kiss. What did Carter have to tell Bryce that he couldn't say in front of me?

"Um ... all right." I hugged Bryce.

"Visit me later," he said with a soft smile.

"I will." I headed toward the door, but paused to whisper to Carter. "I told him that Baxter dropped his vendetta against Samuel. I don't want him to worry about a thing."

"Understood." Carter offered a sympathetic smile and patted my shoulder.

I then stepped outside and all the tears I had held back poured forth, streaming down my cheeks. Bryce was dying and there was nothing I could do to help him. I couldn't even be honest with him. I lied about Baxter and failed to tell him about Mallory altogether. How would I fulfill his wish—possibly his last wish—and give the amulet to Baxter? I had to do it somehow. I owed it to him. And even though Baxter despised me, Bryce was right. He was the world's best chance against the Culling.

A glimmer in the distance caught my eye. The Fireflies whizzed around a cottage toward me. They circled my waist once and then whooshed toward the village's perimeter.

"Now?" I said under my breath, wiping my face dry. I glanced at my home. Both of Kaylan's sons had joined Katie and Samuel in the garden. They were safe.

The Fireflies waited near the village's log entryway. Their energy slipped inside me, warming my heart with gentle waves of comfort. What had they discovered? Something that might help me protect Samuel and my friends? Something that might cure Bryce? I rushed after them into the forest.

After following a deer trail for a few yards, the Fireflies guided me around a blind bend. Two feet ahead, seated on a tree stump, was Mallory. I stumbled to a stop. The Fireflies circled around his head once and then vanished, leaving me alone with him in the shadowed forest.

He stared at me, chuckling with a soul-chilling look in his eyes. "Welcome to where the monsters lurk, girl."

CHAPTER 27

My skin prickled at the sight of Mallory sitting in a shadowy patch amongst the evergreens. He was tearing into a strip of venison, pulling the flesh away with a wolfish snarl each time he bit into the meat. I backed up a few steps and bumped into a tree.

"Relax, girl." He pointed his thumb at his chest. "This monster has no interest in harming you today. It's no fun fighting someone who can't fight back." He glanced at the dagger on my belt and smirked before stuffing the last hunk of meat into his mouth.

Shaking, I squared my shoulders. "If you come near Samuel again, you'll see that I can fight back."

He chuckled, a menacing sound that urged me to run. "You're nothing but a kitten with her tail puffed, swatting at a big grouchy dog." He shifted his weight, and the gleam of his sword hilt caught my eye. A splotch of blood stained the ornate filigree.

"Where's Baxter?" I scanned the area, but he was nowhere in sight. Anxiety rolled through me.

He rested his elbows on his knees and stared at me for a long moment. His black eyes glinted with cruel satisfaction. "He's a long, long way from Samuel now."

I couldn't breathe. What was he implying with that cold sneer? Had he fought his cousin? Was Baxter lying in the woods with a stab wound through his chest? I darted my gaze around the forest.

Mallory leaned back, straining to conceal his mirth. "Calm down, I didn't send him to the Violet Star if that's what you think. We parted ways after our discussion. By now he's deep in the Dark Woods."

"Dark Woods?" Odd that Baxter chose to venture deeper into the forest rather than find a way back to his homeland. "Why did he go there?"

"To either hunt the Culling or get killed by it. Which one makes no difference to me."

"You're an awful person," I snapped. "He's your cousin."

"I'm a Renselar. Awful runs in my blood. The question is whether that will stop you from making an arrangement with me." He gestured toward a tree stump opposite him. "Have a seat."

I remained where I stood. "An arrangement?"

"We both want something that the other can provide." He studied me for a moment and seemed to savor my unease. "I know how to cure Samuel."

My spirit jolted with a burst of hope that vanished as quickly as it had appeared. I couldn't trust Mallory. After all, the previous night he held me hostage at knifepoint. "I don't believe you."

"Then run back to your village, scared little kitten, and watch the Sickness torment Samuel for the rest of his days."

Scared? I called it common sense. "For all I know you're bluffing."

"We'd both be taking a risk in trusting each other, girl. But I'm willing to take the chance to get what I want."

A flash of light near the treetops caught my eye. The Fireflies drifted downward and settled behind Mallory. His gaze followed my line of sight, and he looked over his shoulder, arching his eyebrows, blind to the glowing orbs hovering near his head. How could my Fireflies side with him? Clearly they had gone mad.

I stormed to the tree stump opposite him and sat down, glaring into his black eyes. "I need more information to even consider working with you. Prove to me that you know something about the Sickness."

He leaned in. With his face mere inches from mine, I could smell the scent of venison on his breath. He stared at me as if searching for all my insecurities. I clenched my jaw and held my ground.

"Samuel read from a book," he said. "That's how he inflicted himself with the Sickness."

"A book?" I recalled the leather-bound volume that Samuel owned when I was a child. The wilted pages had fluttered, threatening to tear, when he hurled it into the valley.

"You know what book I speak of."

I nodded. "Samuel called it an evil thing and discarded it years ago."

"Evil? Perhaps." His smirk spread, creasing his scarred cheek. "It had the power to give and take life. And it's the reason you sit before me now."

"What are you talking about?"

"Samuel told me stories while you were gone. Many, many stories. After he left Black Valley, he wandered for years before arriving here. And when he did, he discovered a devastated village to the west and a little girl lying dead, face down in the mud."

"Oh please!" I stood to leave. "Samuel did not bring me back from the dead if that's what you're suggesting."

He rose and snatched my arm, fast as a snake claiming its prey. The Fireflies scattered. "It's true, girl, whether you like it or not. Samuel's past is haunted by dark magic. By now, I'm sure you've also learned of the crime he's accused of."

"I have and it's a lie." I pulled free of his grip and rubbed the white compression mark from my wrist. "Samuel never started a massacre."

"He did, but there's much more to the story than that. Make this deal with me and I'll tell you everything I know."

The Fireflies settled on his shoulder, soft as drifting leaves. Their energy latched onto me, tugging at my core with invisible threads. Static shocks tingled in my fingertips. It was clear what choice they wanted me to make.

"Do I need the book to cure him?" I asked.

He nodded.

"And you know where it is?"

"No, but Samuel tells me you're quite good at finding things."

Why was I even entertaining this idea? His promises were useless if I didn't have the book in hand. If the volume hadn't rotted away, someone else had probably claimed it by now. "I track well enough, but—"

"I'm not talking about your tracking skills, girl. I'm talking about Fireflies."

The world went cold. Time stopped. My breath and heart with it. "How do you know about the Fireflies?"

"Samuel's more perceptive than you think."

The last time I mentioned the Fireflies to Samuel, I was six years old and I had assumed he thought them nothing more than imaginary friends. So why would he share this information, and with Mallory of all people?

"I'm surprised Samuel brought them up." I folded my arms.

His mouth curved into a lopsided grin. "Shall we discuss my terms?"

Though I never expected Samuel's cure to arrive in a charming box fastened with a bow, I never expected it to arrive with a madman either. I nodded.

"You will ask your Fireflies to lead us to Oblivion, and once they do, I'll tell you how to cure Samuel," he said.

"Oblivion? Are you crazy!"

"I have a score to settle with Fate. And I have reason to believe the entrance to Oblivion is on this island."

"Oh my, you're serious." I closed my eyes and took a breath. When I opened my eyes, I said, "Take a moment to think about this. No one can survive a journey to Oblivion, and challenging a goddess will surely damn your soul."

Leading him to Fate would likely damn my soul as well. Not that I planned to agree to his foolish plan.

He straightened his posture, pushing his shoulders back with his chin tipped upward. "Girl, my soul is already damned. I'm not afraid." The Fireflies continued to rest on his shoulder. Apparently, they were happy to accept damnation as well.

"You should be afraid," I said, passing my glowing companions a reprimanding glance. "What do you have against Fate?"

His smirk vanished. He cast his gaze downward, and all the forest seemed to quiet. "She took something from me."

With sympathy in my tone, I said, "That's her nature. But if you go to Oblivion, you'll die."

"Are you in or not?" His black eyes lifted to meet mine.

"I can't leave my village now. Haven't you heard the Culling is coming? I need to protect Samuel."

He laughed. "How will a scrawny girl like you protect him if the Culling strikes? Come with me and I'll eradicate every trace of the Culling we find along the way. At least that'll give your village more time to prepare themselves."

"I need to think." I stepped away from him and paced, clutching my forehead. If I made this deal, I might cure Samuel and delay the Culling's arrival to my village. And I might also find Baxter, mend our friendship, and give him the amulet. But how could I abandon Samuel when evil lurked so near? And to possibly damn my soul by leading this killer to Fate? If I remained home, I could protect Samuel and my friends somehow, couldn't I?

No, I couldn't. I was a weak, scrawny girl. I was no match for a Nightmare, but Mallory was. This was my chance to protect those I loved.

"I want the Culling stopped. Permanently. Can you do that?"

He shook his head. "I don't know its source, so I can't promise you that. But if we happen to find it—you have my word that I'll destroy it."

I exhaled, releasing my apprehension. If a duck doesn't dunk her head in the water, she misses dinner. "All right," I said, shaking slightly. "I accept."

The Fireflies swirled about as if in celebration.

"But I need to say goodbye to Samuel first. Wait here for me."

He sat down on the tree stump. "Be back within the hour."

***

I returned to my village and dashed through the courtyard toward my home. What had I agreed to? Had I lost my mind? I could still back out of the arrangement. If I didn't return to the forest within the hour, Mallory would likely wander off alone on his quest. I passed the men building the fence. They had only added a dozen more posts since I left. At that pace, it would take them days to finish the project. If the Culling arrived that night, all their work would be for naught. I had to stall its arrival.

"No more second thoughts," I told myself. "I have to go with Mallory."

When I arrived home, Coren and Katie were sitting in the garden listening to one of Samuel's stories. I would have loved to join them since I had spent hardly anytime with Samuel at all since returning home.

"Where's Carter?" I asked them.

Katie pointed a thumb at my home. "He went directly inside after visiting Bryce."

I nodded a thank you and then rushed inside. Carter was frantically wrapping a loaf of bread in brown cloth. Our half-stuffed knapsacks sat on the floor.

"What're you doing?" I asked.

"Packing." He shoved the bread into the knapsack. "My Whisperer told me about the deal you made. I'm going too."

"What? No!" I joined him at the table where he had moved on to covering a bundle of dried meat. "Yesterday you were convinced that your Whisperer was leading you toward Death, and now you want to venture into a forest filled with monsters? You need to stay here."

He kept his head down, hiding his face beneath his curly, auburn bangs. "No need to worry. It seems my future has changed. My Whisperer will remain with me, and I will die an old man. You'll be stuck with me for many years to come, Buttercup." He passed me a grin as he placed the package of meat inside the knapsack. Unfortunately, he turned his head before I could determine whether it was a fake or genuine smile.

"I don't trust your Whisperer."

He rose to his feet and gripped both my hands between his. Small cuts and callouses marred his palms. "This morning, when you were angry with me, I realized I was trying to recreate the life I had in Black Valley. I thought if I surrounded myself with good food, wore fine clothes and ... um ... frolicked, that I would feel almost normal again. I wanted my life to return to how it once was, but I now know it never will."

He closed his eyes and inhaled deeply before continuing. "Honey, if I don't go, you'll fail. You need someone like me to go with you."

"Someone like you?"

He nodded. "Someone who can con Mallory into destroying the Culling for good, before he abandons this realm for Oblivion."

"Good luck!" I scoffed. "He's not the sort of man you can con."

"I can con anyone." His determined eyes stared into mine, even as sweat beaded on his brow and his hands trembled. "If the Culling arrives to your village, my sister won't be able to protect herself. I must do whatever it takes to keep her safe."

He lowered his head and delivered his next words in a strained voice, as if holding back sobs. "All I wanted was for her to be happy. I need to do this. I need to go."

"All right," I said, softly. I had to admit, I'd rather have him by my side than go with Mallory alone.

"Wonderful," he said, standing back up. "Will you send Katie in while I continue packing? This news will be difficult for her to hear." He stared at the knapsacks and shook his head, as if lamenting how little they'd help with the conversation.

A sick feeling gnawed at my gut. It wasn't going to be easy to tell Samuel that I had to leave again.

"I'll send her in." I patted his shoulder and then headed toward the door.

"Oh, one last thing," Carter called after me. "If we find Baxter, don't give him that amulet. My Whisperer still tells me that he'll make Samuel face his past. We must kill him before he does."

We were not going to kill Baxter. But there was no point in arguing about it now. We were wasting too much time. So, without answering, I slipped out the door.

CHAPTER 28

Not even the spring air or the sun upon my cheeks could lighten my mood. In the courtyard, two men covered in dust and sweat shoved another massive post upright to join the others in the barricade. Meanwhile, groups of women carved spears and sharpened arrowheads with their playing toddlers nearby.

I sulkily made my way toward the garden where Samuel sat with Katie and Coren.

"The south side needs more daffodils," Samuel said. He tried to keep the conversation light, but his brow crinkled as his gaze slid toward the activity in the courtyard. He rubbed the stub of his missing arm—a nervous habit he had developed years earlier. "Yes, yes. Definitely needs more daffodils."

Katie listened to him intently while Coren kept scanning the nearby forest as if the Culling might charge from the trees at any moment. At Samuel's feet, Ricky rested in the grass, slapping his tail against the ground.

I joined the three of them and said to Katie, "Carter needs to with speak with you right away."

"Of course." She stood, staring at my hands as I wrung them nervously. "Is everything all right?"

I dried my sweaty palms on the waist of my shirt. "Carter will explain."

Biting her lip, she backed up two steps, staring at me as if I might say something else. When I didn't, she hurried off. An empty feeling formed in the pit of my stomach.

Coren pointed at the men in the courtyard. "I should return to help."

Once he roamed out of earshot, I sat down on the log next to Samuel and stared at the surrounding daisies. Since childhood, I favored daisies amongst all other flowers, so Samuel planted them each year without fail. Their sweet fragrance lingered on the breeze.

"The flowers are lovely," I said.

"Yes." He scooted closer to me and rested his hand on my shoulder. "But you want to talk about something other than flowers. Your left eyebrow wiggles when you're worried."

Did it? I massaged my eyebrow. "I have to leave again."

He patted his vest pocket and offered me a handkerchief. "And why's that?"

I dried my eyes. "I spoke to Mallory and we made an arrangement."

"No, Ri." He clasped my wrist. "Please, I'm begging you to stay here. I once thought of Mallory as a son—and a part of me still does, though I remember so little of him. But his fearlessness borders on insanity. He'll drag you into places so dark that you'll forget that light ever existed."

I didn't doubt that.

"It's complicated, Samuel. Something bad is coming to our village, but Mallory can help me stop it."

He hugged me fiercely and my heart wilted. "What if you don't come back? I'd rather lose my other arm than lose you." Through my tears, his face warped into a distorted blob.

"Samuel, please. I have to do this … for you and Bryce and Katie. Everyone. The whole village."

His Adam's apple bobbed as he turned his head and stared at the bustle in the courtyard with watery eyes.

"I wonder if I ever possessed a fraction of your bravery." He offered a sad smile as he brushed a strand of hair off my forehead. "Growing up, you climbed more trees and bluffs than I could count, and you wore your bruises like marks of honor. Of course, I was always too frail to stop you from doing such things. As I am now." He looked down at his withered hands.

"But I always had faith that Eisanea protected you. I must find that faith again." He scratched at the stub of his missing arm as footfalls approached.

"Are you ready?" Carter asked in a flat, monotonous voice. He stood a few feet away with one knapsack loaded on his back and the other in his hand.

Samuel remained seated on the log, staring at the flowers sway in the breeze. He wiped his eyes, plucked a daisy, and placed it in my shirt pocket. "Be careful. Come home to me."

"I will."

Then, without looking back, he hobbled toward our home. Ricky leapt up, licked my hand once, and followed him inside.

I accepted the other knapsack from Carter as we strode off past my home. From inside, I heard Katie weeping and Samuel consoling her.

"They'll take care of each other," I said, but Carter said nothing and kept his gaze forward until we reached Kaylan's home.

"One goodbye left," he said.

With cool sweat on my forehead, I opened the door and it scraped against the warped floorboards. Miss Meow was curled on the bed near Bryce's feet. She acknowledged our entrance with a lazy stretch. Bryce didn't stir. Neither Kaylan nor Kai were home.

"Bryce?" I knelt next to the bed and clasped his wrist. Though he didn't wake, a gentle pulse beat beneath my fingertips.

"You'll see him again, Buttercup." Carter sat down and wrapped his arm around me.

I rested my head on his shoulder. "I'm not so sure." I studied Bryce's face, memorizing his features. When the cold night came, I wanted the image of his charming smile and warm eyes to bring me comfort. "What if we defeat the Culling only to return to find him ..."

"Don't talk like that." Carter lightly touched my chin, turning my head so my eyes met his. "You will see him again. Alive."

"But if he wakes and finds out that we left, he'll come searching for us."

"I've already planned for that. Katie will prepare a concoction that will keep him knocked out for a few days. With any luck, we'll return by the time he wakes."

"She plans to drug him like she did to Baxter on the boat?"

He tilted his head from side to side. "Well, yes, but you make it sound so harsh."

"It feels wrong."

"It'll keep him safe." Carter stood, offering me his hand. "Come, we mustn't keep Mallory waiting."

He was right. If we were going to convince Mallory to fight the Culling, we needed to be on our best behavior. Closing my eyes, I leaned down and kissed Bryce's lips.

"This isn't goodbye," I whispered. Then, I hurried outside with Carter and we dashed into the forest.

We followed an animal trail through thick brush. Spears of light shot though the needled branches above. After racing a short distance, the Fireflies swooped down and joined us in the lead.

Carter stopped running.

I turned around to face him. "What is it?"

Gawking, he answered, "I can see them too. Seven glowing orbs. They're beautiful."

"You can see the Fireflies?"

He nodded. "Honey, there must be a connection between us. Fireflies. Sand people. Why can we see them when everyone else is blind to them?"

"I don't know, but there's no time to figure it now." I grabbed his hand and pulled him along. How strange that we shared this same ability. I doubted that we were blood related, but …

We rounded the trail's blind curve and it delivered us right into the path of a Harbinger. It lay sprawled on the ground with red eyes trained on me. I stumbled backward into Carter. "Run!"

But the beast didn't move. Dead. It was dead. My breath slowed. I swiveled around in search of Mallory. His laughter echoed in the distance.

Both Carter and I froze, holding our breaths and listening. I slipped my dagger out of its sheath in case more Harbingers lurked nearby. Footfalls approached. Mallory appeared from the shadows. He glanced at the dead beast and then at us.

"These weak imps waste my time." He kicked the creature and its limp body rolled over.

"The Harbingers of the Culling are far from weak imps," I said. "I've seen what they can do."

He leaned toward me. Fresh blood spatter glistened on his face. "You haven't seen what I can do, little girl." Glaring at Carter, he added, "Why are you here?"

Carter placed his hand over his heart and gasped. "I'm surprised you ask. All morning, I've heard the great stories of Mallory Renselar. And though I'm hardly the superior man that you are, I hope you'll allow me to serve you on your mission. You see, we share the same enemy: Fate. That miserable goddess has interfered with the lives of men long enough. She's nothing but a jealous hag. If a man takes anything other than sadness for company she shows him wrath. I say it's time to put an end to her reign."

Mallory squinted one eye at Carter. "Try your speeches on the Nightmares when they come. I'm only interested in keeping one little girl alive. She's useful to me. You're not."

How I hated Mallory's scarred face and mocking sneer, but I held my tongue.

Flashing his fake smile, Carter grasped my shoulders from behind. "Well, I can help you keep her alive. Ri is impulsive and never listens." He placed his hand alongside his face, hiding it from me. Whatever expression he made caused Mallory to chuckle. When he lowered his hand, he added, "I'll make sure she follows your orders."

I shook Carter's hands off me and shot him a warning look. He answered me with a wink.

"Fine," Mallory said. "Run when I tell you to run, hide when I tell you to hide, and shush up when I tell you to shush up. That will be most of the time because your voices irritate me."

Surviving Mallory's company would be more of a challenge than surviving the Culling.

"Time for a lesson. Pay attention." Mallory lifted the dead beast's head to reveal its neck. There was a small hole in its throat. "Only young Harbingers attack to kill. The older ones will attempt to paralyze you so they can take you captive and feed off your soul while they cocoon."

He stuck his finger into the hole and pulled out a thorn-like dart, identical to the one that had struck me the day I met Bryce. Though it dripped with yellow liquid—the poison—Mallory suffered no effects.

He held the dart in front of us. "Don't get hit by one of these. I will not be happy if I have to carry you around until you recover."

Carter and I nodded.

"A Nightmare—as your village calls them—needs to feed off of souls to survive," Mallory continued. He reached into his pocket, pulled out a clump of silver fibers, and handed them to me.

The fibers matched those that lined the inner cavity of the Nightmare that Baxter had discovered. Thin and smooth as onion grass, they sparkled with light and sent tingles through my fingertips.

"What is it?" I gave the fibers to Carter to examine.

"Starlight," Mallory said. "Thousands of those strands fill an opening in the Nightmare's frontside." He placed one hand below his breastbone and the other over his lower stomach to demonstrate.

"The fibers light up to hypnotize the beast's prey. Once a Nightmare dazes a target, it will cage the poor bastard inside its hollow space to feed. But it takes a long time to drain a man of his soul. He could suffer a few days before Death grants him mercy." He wagged his finger at both of us. "So don't look at the Starlight. Two pathetic weaklings like you won't be able to break away from the spell."

"We are not pathetic weaklings!" How could I maintain good behavior around a man that continued to insult me? "And I'm not going to do whatever you say like some puppet."

Carter pivoted in front of me. "Now Honey, don't be foolish. Mallory is far more knowledgeable about the Culling than we are. It will do us best to learn from him."

I let out a breath. "Go on."

"The Starlight will speak to your soul," Mallory said. "It'll show you what you desire most, and it'll feel better than your most pleasant dream. It took me years to build a resistance to it."

"Fine," I said. "I won't look at the Starlight."

"Good," he said with a curt nod. "Are your Fireflies ready to lead us?"

As soon as he mentioned them, my glowing companions whooshed from the treetops and glided westward toward the Dark Woods. I took a deep breath to calm my nerves.

"This way." I marched after them.

Behind me, Mallory's heavy boots cracked brambles and pinecones. I didn't hear Carter's footfalls, so I turned around. He stared into the forest, breathing heavily, with his hands jammed into his armpits.

"Are you all right?" I asked.

"Um ... yes, yes." He shook his head as if I had asked a silly question and proceeded to follow. "Just a touch of cold feet."

"It's not too late to stay in the village if you'd like," I whispered.

"No. I have to go on for Katie." He puffed his chest and straightened his shoulders. "Let's do this."

CHAPTER 29

The Fireflies weaved around the trees, guiding us westward. With Mallory and Carter following me, I plowed through brambles, swatted away low branches, and maneuvered around rocks. I wouldn't allow fear to wiggle into my thoughts. Stop the Culling. Find Death's book. Cure Samuel. No turning back. Not even when the Fireflies crossed into the Dark Woods.

The sun disappeared behind the coverage of black branches. In the dim lighting, my other senses heightened. Loam and fungus thickened the air with a scent that was almost suffocating. In the distance, crows squawked, as if celebrating the gloom of the low-crawling mist.

"Stop," Mallory called to me.

I did as he asked and so did the Fireflies. They hovered twenty feet ahead, shining upon a cluster of trees finned with shelf-like fungus.

Mallory strode into the lead, casting me a disapproving glance. I folded my arms and glowered back at him. Drawing his weapon, he paused and scanned the forest. It made the faintest sound as the steel slid against leather. Carter joined me, his face flush from the run. He looked over the expanse of sunless forest.

"Don't worry," I told him. "Mallory will do everything he can to keep us safe."

"Only you, girl," Mallory called in our direction. "The sooner he dies, the sooner I have one less fool slowing me down."

I opened my mouth to fire back at him, but Carter touched my shoulder and shook his head.

"It's all right," he whispered. "We'll get what we want from him. Patience."

Unlikely. Mallory was an ass who cared only for himself.

We waited for the scoundrel to signal our next move. Perhaps he sensed an adversary that we didn't, because the only wicked thing in our presence—other than him—was a fist-sized spider stalking along a web that stretched from one tree to another. With its furry foreleg, it poked at a moth that was struggling to free itself from the sticky fibers. The spider looked ready to sink its minuscule fangs into its catch when an owl swooped from the treetops and snatched it.

I shuddered.

Creatures in the Dark Woods only harbored the instincts to hunt, kill, and eat. And I was sure that beasts lurked in the shadows, drooling over the prospect of human flesh.

Mallory waved us forward. "Slow your pace and stay close."

I reclaimed my place in the lead and Carter strode alongside me. Occasionally, he flinched at typical forest sounds such as birds chattering or insects chirping. I squeezed his hand.

We trekked in silence for an hour. In that time, we encountered a snake camouflaged among fallen branches, black-shelled insects that swarmed the remains of a hog carcass blossoming with maggots, and countless bats. Not a single Nightmare sniffed us out. My steps came easier. Carter's posture relaxed as well, though his eyes remained alert.

I looked over my shoulder at Mallory. "Now's a good time for you to tell me everything you know. Let's start with the Sickness."

"No," he answered, keeping his gaze locked on the distance.

"Why not?"

"We'll talk tonight. When you're too far from your village to cower home."

Of course he would withhold information to keep me baited. I turned around with an exasperated sigh. "You better keep your word."

The birds quieted. The insects ceased chirruping. Even the breeze died down, stilling branches that had been clawing at their neighbors. All that remained was the sound of our footsteps softly pressing dead needles into the earth.

Carter stopped and tilted his head. "Do you hear that?"

A clicking sound broke the silence—exactly like the one I heard when I first encountered the Culling. Mallory grinned and his eyes brightened. No doubt he craved the sport of battle. This was it. Our first fight with a Nightmare. I swiveled around, searching for the beast. Nothing. Where was it? My heart thumped, drowning out all other sounds.

Cracking branches drew my attention upward. A Nightmare broke through the needled canopy above, descending the tree with the speed of a hungry puma. It pounced on the ground directly in front of me. Carter yanked me backward as the creature hissed hot breath into my face, revealing rows of ebony fangs. Terror shocked my limbs, seizing every nerve. The Nightmare reared up, raising its talon-tipped forelegs. Massive claw-like appendages interlaced down the length of its underside. Shaking, I slid my dagger from its sheath.

"Run," Mallory ordered.

A glimmer of steel flew past my head. Wind brushed my cheek. Mallory's dagger landed in the Nightmare's throat. Screeching, the creature reeled back. Mallory shoved Carter and me out of the way.

"I said move!" Mallory ordered, lunging at the creature with his sword raised. "I'll take care of this."

Needled sprigs showered from above. Two more Nightmares crept down the lengths of nearby trees. Run? Where? The whole forest could have been teeming with Nightmares.

Carter grabbed my hand. "You heard the man! Let's go."

The Fireflies circled around my head, snapping me out of my petrified state. They whisked through the dense growth of trees, cutting the fog. Carter and I chased after them. Without slowing, I glanced back at Mallory. Through the haze, his silhouette lunged and ducked as he thrust his sword. A flurry of sparks erupted as his blade sliced across the beast's chest. Meanwhile, another Nightmare skulked toward him. Where was the third beast?

I looked around unable to hear anything over my panicked breath. Then, from the corner of my eye, I noticed the beast's dark figure running parallel to us, fifteen feet away. It charged and rammed Carter with the crown of its head. He bumped into me, and the impact hurled us both to the ground.

I leapt to my feet and tugged Carter's arm. "Get up!"

He groaned, having taken the brunt of the attack. No more than ten feet away, the Nightmare rose on its hind legs. All at once, the claw-like appendages retracted into its ribs, exposing its cavity. A human corpse, soggy and wrinkled as the one we had pulled from the cocoon, fell out of the hollow space. No doubt the beast was making room for a fresh meal.

I yanked Carter's arm more forcefully. "Come on. Get up! Get up!"

A flash of blue light burst from the beast as thousands of silver, thread-thin fibers blossomed out of its cavity. Shimmers of light raced up and down each one, glistening like millions of tiny stars.

Beautiful.

I released Carter's arm. The clumped fibers promised the softness of unspun cotton. How wonderful it would have felt to sink into that luxury. I stepped toward it. My muscles relaxed and my eyelids grew heavy. Then, in that light I saw it ...

Samuel's cure.

But how was that possible? So hard to think. Clearly, the cure was in front of me. Why question it? Joyous tears moistened my eyes. After all these years, I had finally found it. My journey was over. The rest of the world faded away. Nothing else mattered.

Another step closer. Weightless, I drifted like a leaf on a calm stream. But another light competed for my attention. Seven amber orbs swarmed in front of my face, blocking my view of the sparkling threads. I wanted to swat at them, order them to leave, but my energy was slipping away.

The strands reached out to explore my face. Soft tickles filled me with warmth. Then, as if startled, the fibers recoiled.

My starlit sky blackened with clouds. I was standing before a monster. Its powerful front leg whacked me, casting me aside. Pain shot through my arm as I crashed to the ground. What happened? I shook my head, clearing the fog from my mind.

Mallory charged through the trees with his sword drawn. He raced past me. "Dammit girl, I told you not to look at the Starlight."

Time sped up. The fog left my mind. Samuel's cure—or rather the hallucination of it—had been nothing more than the Starlight's spell.

The beast snapped at Mallory. He ducked the attack and then drove his blade into the cluster of sparkling threads. Slinking backward, the beast swung its massive talons in defense. Mallory's black eyes glared at me as he pivoted to avoid the attacks. "Girl, go wake up your friend."

To my right lay the human corpse with brown, mottled flesh. The stench of rot struck me. I scooted backward, gagging. The corpse's face caved inward, moist and gooey from decay.

The Fireflies whizzed past me and guided me toward Carter. His half-closed eyes gazed at the Starlight. Even as Mallory's blade clacked against the beast's hard shell, Carter continued to stagger toward it. Mallory kicked him in the stomach, forcing him back while shoving his weapon upward into the creature's jaw and through the top of its head. The Nightmare fell to the ground. Its Starlight went dim.

I rushed to Carter and shook his shoulders. "It's not real. Whatever you see, it's not real."

He remained spellbound, looking through me as if I wasn't there.

I tapped his cheek repeatedly. "Wake up. Wake up."

Mallory joined us. "Use more force."

I nodded and then slapped Carter across the face. No response. I smacked him once more, harder, and then raised my hand for a third time. His eyes widened and he stumbled backward, waving his palms back and forth.

"Stop!" He rubbed his reddened cheek. "I ... I ..." He looked around, scratching the back of his neck. "What happened?

"You two fools looked at the Starlight." Mallory sheathed his sword. "That's what happened."

Carter looked at his empty palms. "No, I had it right here in my hands." He looked at me and slumped, defeated. "I found these special plants and Katie was going to use them to save Bryce. It was real!"

The Starlight managed to con the con-artist. It was powerful stuff indeed.

Mallory yanked Carter by the shoulder and turned him toward the corpse. "That's the only reality you'll know if you look at the Starlight again."

Carter covered his mouth and went pale. He hurried to a nearby shrub, bent over, and vomited.

Mallory turned to me. "After looking at the Starlight, you won't be feeling right for the next few hours. You can expect sweats, chills, and irritability. And you won't even want to look at food."

"I feel fine." No chills. No sweats. I looked forward to a meal later. And irritable? Well, Mallory was making me plenty irritable already. I hastened to Carter.

"You feel fine?" Mallory's ugly smirk crept upward. "How intriguing."

I patted Carter's back as he straightened his posture and wiped his mouth with his sleeve. His body quivered.

"Why's that intriguing?" I asked.

"I've never met someone who broke out of the Starlight's spell without experiencing some effects." Mallory rubbed his chin, squinting one eye nearly shut. "But more interesting is that the Nightmare didn't want you."

"What do you mean?" I asked.

"I saw its Starlight latch onto you and then jerk away as if it touched a hot pan. It swatted you aside like trash."

I folded my arms. "Well, I should count myself lucky."

The Fireflies swirled around, luring me toward a faint orange glow roughly thirty feet away. More cocoons.

"We have a job to finish." I hooked my arm around Carter's, maneuvered around the dead beast, and strode toward the nest. Mallory followed.

After a few steps, the breeze blew the cocoon's stench toward us. Carter's hand flew to his mouth.

"Just hold on," I said, grasping his arm tighter. "It'll pass."

We reached the nest where three pink husks bulged upon the trees. Like those we had discovered with Baxter, an abundance of violet flowers wreathed each one. But the scent of rot overpowered any trace of floral fragrance. The silhouettes of the creatures and their trapped victims showed through the cocoons' thin flesh.

Mallory shoved past us and stabbed his sword through the nearest cocoon. A wail followed the blow, and it took me a moment to figure out that he had struck both man and beast with a single thrust.

"Wait!" I rushed in front of him, blocking him from the next cocoon. "The people inside might still be alive."

With dagger in hand, I hurried to the cocoon and lined my blade up with the beast's radiant heart. With a quick thrust of my weapon, I pierced the fleshy shroud, plunging my arm inside until my blade impaled my target. It felt like I had stabbed a sack filled with warm jelly that had a tender roast in the center. I heaved, tasting bile, but I managed to subdue the urge to vomit. The cocoon went dark. I withdrew my weapon and shook the slime off my arm.

Mallory chuckled. Ignoring him, I sliced the husk open, freeing the man and the dead beast. Both tumbled to the ground in a heap. The man, shiny with goop, landed face first in the dirt. Mud coated his hair, hiding its color, but he wore a City Guard coat.

"Baxter?" I yelled. Unable to breathe, I collapsed to my knees and rolled him over. He had been stripped of his weapons. "No, no, no."

"There're no chevrons on the sleeve," Carter sat on the ground and pulled his knees to his chest, shaking. "It's not him. Can we hurry up with this and go?" he snapped.

I wiped the slime off the man's face. He had a wide nose and unruly thick brows. The pace of my heart slowed. It wasn't Baxter. The man gasped once. Then his chest didn't rise or fall again. No pulse.

Mallory stared at the dead man and roared with laughter. "Looks like my pop is losing his dogs. Nightmares kidnap their victims and then cocoon somewhere they think is safe. They travel through water, just like my cousin. I wonder where he obtained such a power."

I tilted my head, taken aback by what he said. Of course Mallory would have assumed that it was Baxter who had the ability to travel through waterfalls. He had no idea of Bryce's existence. Best to keep it that way.

"I have no idea how Baxter does it," I said. "He never told me."

Mallory leaned down, his face inches from mine. "You're lying."

"Can we go?" Carter interrupted, grasping both sides of his head. "The whole forest is spinning. And I'm freezing. And it stinks. I want to leave. Now!"

With a nod, Mallory pierced the last cocoon, the same way as he did the first. A human whimper followed.

"Dammit!" I leapt to my feet. "You killed them both."

"Girl, there's no point in trying to save whoever's inside. Their minds are mush by now."

"I want to know who's inside." I cut open the cocoon that Mallory had first struck, and a woman fell out. Crimson spread from the stab wound through her chest.

Mallory slid his sword through the last one, and an old man dropped to the ground. "No Baxter here either."

I exhaled with relief.

Mallory sneered at me. "Why do you care so much about a man who despises you?"

"I don't want to talk about it." Nor did I want to think about it. I located the Fireflies quickly and waved my companions to follow. "This way."

CHAPTER 30

We trekked through the forest until moonlight shone on our path. The Fireflies led us into a swamp where mud and rotting trees covered the ground. Nearby, a platter-sized snapping turtle rested in a puddle. It retreated into its shell as we approached. Mallory grabbed a stick and poked it repeatedly in the nose. With a hiss, the turtle extended its head from protective cover and latched onto the stick. Mallory swung his dagger and beheaded it. A spray of crimson shot out of the neck, spattering his hands and sleeves. The head, gaping with wide eyes, sunk into the murky puddle as Mallory carried the body off by the tail. Blood gushed from the turtle's neck before slowing to a steady drip.

Though I was glad to have food for later, watching the turtle bleed out reminded me that the Culling's beasts could end our lives just as easily. The gods would protect us no more than they'd protected that turtle. We were on our own, and survival was a desperate, brutal thing.

By the time we took shelter in a shallow cave, my swollen feet were squeezed against my shoes, irritating scattered blisters on my toes. I gathered some dry kindling and built a fire. Meanwhile, Carter rocked back and forth, shivering, still suffering the effects of Starlight.

"It's reckless to have a campfire," Carter said. Sweat on his forehead and upper lip glistened in the firelight. "Why not send a smoke signal to every Nightmare in the forest?"

"Let 'em come." Mallory sat across from us cleaning the turtle. He sawed through the lower portion of the shell with a serrated knife. "The Culling won't stand between me and cooked turtle meat."

"We'll make ourselves sick if we eat raw turtle," I said. "Once it's cooked, we'll put out the fire."

"Fine." Sulkily, Carter slouched and wrapped his arms over his middle.

Turning to Mallory, I said, "I've kept my word so far, now it's time for you to keep yours. Tell me more about the Sickness."

He tossed a handful of sticks on my lap. "Make some skewers."

"You can't ignore my questions forever." I began shaving the end of a stick into a point, but it broke in half from the force I applied. "Dammit." I grabbed the next stick.

"Do you always have such a temper?" Mallory shook his head, rolling his eyes. "Fine. I'll tell you something before you destroy every stick in the forest."

He removed the turtle's lower shell and moved on to slicing off the legs. "Someone once told me that when you die, Death offers your spirit a choice. You can either remain here in the earthly realm or ascend to the Violet Star for judgment. Many choose to stay. Either they can't accept that they're dead or they remain to look after loved ones. But others, who had lived sinful lives, fear their final judgment a great deal. For them, it's better to remain in the earthly realm than face Death's punishments."

"Interesting story," I interrupted, "but I don't see what it has to do with the Sickness." I dunked a couple of skewers into a canteen to soak.

"Patience, girl." He placed the limp turtle limbs on a flat rock next to him. Guts and blood covered his hands. "When spirits—good or evil—decide to stay here, Death refuses to give them a second chance to enter the Violet Star's light. So they wander about, trapped as wayward spirits in our realm for eternity. Their existence is torturous and lonely. Eventually, they go insane."

He tossed the tail onto the growing heap of meat. "The hallucinations Samuel sees aren't figments of his imagination. They're spirits."

"Spirits? How absurd." I glanced at Carter, wondering if his Whisperer could confirm or deny Mallory's claim, but he just stared at the ground quivering.

"You're telling tall tales," I continued. "First, you tell me that Samuel brought me back from the dead and now this? Perhaps you're leading me on so I'll continue to help you."

"Perhaps." He sneered. "But you've no choice but to stick with me now, little girl. You and your Starlight-stricken friend would never make it back to your village alive."

"Let's say you're telling the truth." I gathered the skewers and began threading them with the moist, yet slightly tough meat, and positioned the food over the fire. "Why would spirits haunt Samuel for all these years?"

"Because the book that gave him the Sickness once belonged to Death. And when he spoke the passages, every spirit within miles heard him. Since Death had ignored their pleas for years, their hopes were raised when they heard someone else speak the god's powerful words. So they swarmed to Samuel like flies on a dead rat. Now they haunt him because he can't give them the salvation they seek."

I stared at the flames browning the meat. The idea that spirits tormented Samuel was far worse than mere hallucinations. If Mallory spoke the truth, I had to help Samuel. No matter what.

"How did Samuel get possession of Death's book?" I asked.

"Sera brought it with her when she arrived at Black Valley," he answered.

"Sera? Your father's second wife?" I shuddered, recalling the statue's chilling smile.

He nodded.

"Well, where did she get it?" I leaned closer to him. "And did she have the Sickness too?"

"She stole it from Death himself as a means to protect herself." He shrugged one shoulder nonchalantly. "Little good it did her. She might've had the Sickness."

"You know so much about Death and spirits, but you don't know whether your step-mother had the Sickness?" I removed the skewers from the fire and set them on a flat rock. The meat sizzled, oozing juices.

"I didn't pay her much attention. I was a sixteen-year-old boy and found one of the young ladies she brought with her much more interesting." For a brief moment, he stared into the flames and smiled.

I knew that expression! Plenty of smitten boys in my village had worn it when gazing at their true love. Unbelievable. Mallory—rude, heartless Mallory—had loved someone.

"You loved this young lady, didn't you?" I asked through a surprised chuckle.

He frowned and waved his hand over the skewers, swatting the steam away. "It's time to eat."

"You're changing the subject!"

Carter, who'd been unusually quiet, nudged me with his elbow and shook his head.

Oh. How quick my mouth had been. If this young lady was no longer in Mallory's life, then there was a strong possibility that something bad had happened to her.

"I'm sorry," I said. "I shouldn't have pried."

We ate in silence. It was the first time I had eaten a snapping turtle. The texture was a mixture of stringy, chewy, and tough, and it tasted like turkey and fish mashed together.

Mallory finished the last scrap of his food and then gestured at me. "I have a theory as to why the Nightmare had no interest in you."

I slowed my chewing to listen.

"When Samuel brought you back from the dead," he continued, "I believe you lost your soul."

"What?" I choked on my food.

"Think about it," he said. "The beast hunts to eat. A glutton wouldn't want an empty plate, and a Nightmare wouldn't want a soulless body."

"She has a soul," Carter piped up. "Don't say such cruel things."

"It's all right." I glanced at Carter. "It's a silly idea and I won't give it a second thought. Without a soul, I'd be an emotionless monster. Obviously, I have one."

"Believe what you will," Mallory said.

His theory was rubbish and it was time to return to the discussion that truly mattered. "So once I have the book, how do I cure Samuel?"

"Chitchat's over. It's time for sleep." He stood and stomped out the dying remains of our fire.

"Sleep? Are you really going to make me wait until we reach Oblivion before you tell me?"

"That was our deal." Without the fire, my companions morphed into dark silhouettes. Mallory leaned against the cave wall and said nothing else.

"I can't believe he's going to sleep," I said to Carter.

"Let him be," Carter said. "You'll get your answers."

"Girl, I'll tell you how to cure Samuel tonight if you tell me how my cousin travels through waterfalls."

I would never reveal Bryce's secret to him. "I already told you that he didn't tell me."

"And I already told you that I know you're lying."

"Why do you want to know anyway? I doubt there're any waterfalls in Oblivion."

"You don't understand."

"Then help me."

"I want closure."

"Closure for what?"

"That's none of your concern. Now if you're not going to talk about waterfall travel, go to sleep. We have a long day ahead of us tomorrow." He inclined his head, and within moments a heavy snore came with each of his breaths.

"He's impossible," I said to Carter.

"Patience, Honey. I know I'm not myself tonight, but I have a plan. We'll get what we need from him."

I sighed. "Very well." Scanning the dark forest, I added, "One of us should keep watch. I'll cover the first half of the night, and depending on how you feel, perhaps you can take over later?"

He nodded, then fluffed his knapsack to use for a pillow. I removed the amulet from under my shirt and packed it deep within my knapsack. Such an unusual pendant would draw Mallory's curiosity if he caught sight of it, and I couldn't expose Bryce's secret. Not to mention, I owed it to Bryce to keep my word and give the amulet to Baxter—if I ever saw him again.

CHAPTER 31

I awoke the next morning to something nudging my thigh. I shot upright, smacking away Mallory's boot. He stood over me with his back to the mouth of our shallow cave. Behind him, the sky hinted of approaching dawn. A faint pink glow traced the peaks of the eastern mountains.

"Are you always so jittery when you wake?" Mallory asked.

"Do you always wake people by kicking them in the leg?"

"I've woken folks in worse ways." He strode into the open, puffed his chest with a deep breath, and scanned a forest not yet warmed by sunlight.

I rubbed grit off my clothes. My body ached after sleeping on the hard, cold ground, but it was a miracle that I slept at all given the beasts that lurked in the woodlands. I struggled to doze off, spending more time worrying for Samuel and my friends than sleeping.

Carter sat next to me near the ashes of last night's fire. Slouching, he shoved the canteens into his pack. The whites of his eyes were bloodshot, and his irises had dulled to the color of drab swamp vines. With bristle along his jaw, mud smeared on his vest, and his auburn curls hanging in tangles, he looked like a vagabond.

"How do you feel?" I asked.

Keeping his gaze downward, he shrugged. "I have a stabbing pain in my forehead." He fastened his knapsack and slung it onto his back. "My feet are cold and blistered, and my shoulders ache from carrying this sack."

It was too soon in our journey for him to break, so I reached for his hand and squeezed it. "I need you, Carter. I can't do this alone." Keeping my voice low, I added, "We must get Mallory to help us stop the Culling."

Without looking at me, he pressed his mouth into a poor attempt at a smile. "It will be the greatest con I've ever pulled."

"And your cleverness will see the plan through." I patted his arm, then slung my own knapsack over my shoulder. "Come on. The sooner we get on our way, the sooner we can return home."

"Home." He swallowed hard and closed his eyes.

"Yes, home." I picked up a small stone and offered it to him, just as he had done the first night we met. "I never properly welcomed you to my village, but no matter where our journey takes us, what is mine is yours. We're in this together."

He studied the black speckled stone until a hint of moisture formed in his eyes. Quickly, he stuffed it into his pocket. "Thank you, Buttercup," he whispered so quietly that I could barely hear his words. "I won't let you down."

With that, we exited the cave together.

Mallory eyed him suspiciously as we walked into the open. "What's eating at you? The Starlight's effects should be long out of your system by now."

"Let him be," I said through a growl. "This journey has been taxing on all of us."

"Speak for yourself." Mallory looked toward the forest. "Which way are we heading?"

Roughly a dozen feet away, the Fireflies drifted from the sky and hovered over a collection of puddles, waiting for us. Their amber reflections danced in the murky water.

"This way." I waved my two companions to follow.

We walked for an hour mostly in silence. Carter remained melancholy, hugging himself as we trekked over the damp earth. The farther we went, the more fidgety he became. Occasionally, he parted his lips as if he wanted to say something, but then he opted to retreat back into his thoughts. Mallory on the other hand, strode along, taking everything in with his vigilant black eyes. I doubted a Nightmare could sneak up on us under his guard.

The Fireflies led us westward into the depths of a gorge carved in half by a shallow river. We hiked along the muddy bank down current. Gnarled trees thrived in the dark, wet soil. Their roots veined the ground while their flat, wide leaves fanned overhead. On either side of us, red rock bluffs loomed over the lush gulch and stretched toward a stormy sky. Mallory shoved into the lead, using his dagger to hack through vines. Eventually, the river widened and Mallory stopped to stare at the opposite bank.

I followed his line of sight to where a pair of boot prints and trampled shrubs littered the ground. Hope jolted through me. The footprints, detailed with tread, were likely only a few hours old. They disappeared under the ferns and then reappeared, heading west just as we were.

"Those tracks must belong to Baxter!" I said.

Mallory chuckled. "You sound awful giddy to run into your enemy."

"Giddy?" I scoffed and folded my arms. "I don't sound giddy."

I scanned the forest in hopes of spotting a glimpse of a black coat or silver hair. Surely, Baxter would put aside his vendetta if we came across each other. There would be something other than disgust in his eyes. I quickened my pace.

Mallory passed me a sideways glance and shook his head. "You should find love elsewhere, girl. Falling for him would be like falling for me. We're the same type of man."

"What?" My voice reached a high pitch. How could he compare himself—mean and selfish as he was—to Baxter? "He's nothing like you. He fights to protect his city, not to satisfy some crazed need for vengeance." Heat rose into my cheeks. "And I'm not in love with him."

Mallory pressed his lips together, suppressing laughter. What an ass.

"Furthermore," I continued, "he actually cares about people—he may not say it in so many words—but it shows in everything he does."

He grinned and nodded. "You've proved my point. You're smitten."

"I am not!"

Perhaps I admired Baxter, but love him? How absurd. I couldn't be falling for both him and Bryce at the same time. That would be wrong—plain and simple.

I glanced over my shoulder at Carter. He nervously folded and unfolded his arms a few times, darting his gaze around the forest.

"Are you all right?" I asked.

He continued to stare into the forest as if he didn't hear me.

I tapped his shoulder. "What's wrong?"

His attention snapped to me. "Oh, nothing. I'm fine, just fine." He quickly went back to scanning our surroundings.

That was a lie. Perhaps the Starlight's effects hadn't worn off of him.

By noon, a cool fog crawled into the gorge and sprinkled the forest with a light drizzle. The bird chatter ceased. Only a lone crow squawked in the distance. The Fireflies' amber light struggled to cut through the mist.

Behind me, Carter slipped in the mud. He cursed under his breath.

"Let me help you." I took his hand and his cold, trembling fingers met my palm. His face had gone ashen, and his widened eyes hinted that he might lose his wits at any moment.

"We need to stop," I said to Mallory's back.

Carter sat down on a fallen trunk, pulling me down beside him. His grip squeezed my fingers. Meanwhile, Mallory huffed and leaned against a tree fifteen strides ahead. "Two minutes," he ordered.

"Carter," I whispered. "What's bothering you?"

He clasped his hands together into a ball, as if he were praying. He stared into the fog that shrouded us, bouncing his knee and gnawing on his lip.

"Carter?" I bumped my leg against his, urging him to answer.

He lowered his head, and his auburn tendrils fell over his eyes. After glaring at the ground for a moment, he wiped his sweaty hands on his pants and took a deep breath. "Honey, I'm terrified. I know I talked like some valiant warrior the day we left your village, but right now I'm terrified."

I wrapped an arm around his shoulder. "Well ... I'm scared too. For all of us. But I promise you that whatever awaits, we'll face it together."

He took my hand and fiddled with my fingers. For a long while he said nothing. His breath came in quick gasps until he finally spoke. "I'm grateful we got to know each other. You mean so much to me, and I don't need my Whisperer to tell me that you care for me too—as a friend of course."

I placed my hand on top of his. My palms stuck to his clammy skin. "If you don't want to go on, perhaps we can find you safe shelter—"

"No," he said. For the first time all day, his eyes met mine. "I'm going to do what I have to do."

"You're going to save the world," I said, hoping to cheer him. "You'll be the most popular man in my village."

He let out an unnatural laugh, the sort people do when they really want to cry. "Yes, yes. The masses will sing of my bravery." He looked into the distance.

I smacked him playfully on the shoulder. "Your bravery? What about me?"

He turned his head back toward me and though his facial muscles remained tense he managed a smile. "You'll sing of my bravery too."

I laughed. "I don't sing."

"I can make you sing. In fact, I think we'd reach an exciting crescendo together." A glimmer flashed in his eyes. "If you know what I mean."

"Ew, Carter." I squirmed out of his grasp and stood, but I offered a smile. Listening to his sick humor was better than watching him sulk.

From the corner of my eye, Mallory strode toward us. "You ninnies done with your chitchat, or do you plan to pull out some crumpets and tea and have a picnic?"

"What's a crumpet?" I asked.

He exhaled loudly through his nose and then turned around and marched forward. "Are the Fireflies still heading this way?"

Ahead, the Fireflies' diluted glow bounced off the mist. "Yes," I muttered.

"Then onward." Mallory glared at us both. "Quit wasting time."

Carter pulled at his vest, straightening the fabric with force. "Grouchiness runs in the Renselar family, doesn't it?"

Mallory marched ahead without answering. Carter and I exchanged glances and then trailed our rude companion. After some time, the drizzle and fog dissipated, allowing sunrays to pierce through the gray cloud cover. Patches of light dappled the forest floor, giving the gorge a dreamlike appearance. Despite the evident danger, it was beautiful.

The path sloped downward, and the river dipped with it, forming a waterfall that was more like a slick veil than a tumble of froth. We made our way down the bluff and continued onward until the Fireflies whooshed around a blind corner. A rock outcrop blocked our view, but the thick, putrid scent of cocoons loomed in the air.

Mallory turned and looked at both of us. "Do exactly as I say. I'll keep the instructions simple so you two can follow them."

As much as I hated his tone, Mallory knew more about the Culling than I did. If Carter and I were going to survive, we had to listen.

"We're not a pair of fools," I said. "What do we need to do?"

"Stay," he ordered us and made his way around the outcrop. A moment later, he hooted in laughter from the opposite side.

Carter and I rushed to join him, maneuvering around rock, river, and plush vegetation. When we reached him, Mallory had already plunged his sword into a cocoon. Unlike the cocoons we had encountered previously, this one was nearly transparent—more of a gooey film than an earthworm-colored shell. The Nightmare inside writhed at the tip of Mallory's blade. A talon-tipped claw sliced through the shroud, flailed for a moment, and then went limp. Mallory withdrew his sword, and the Nightmare's luminescent heart went dark.

Ahead, dozens of roiling cocoons clung to the trees.

"I think they're hatching." I staggered back a step.

"Of all the girls in the village, I brought the smart one." Mallory stared at me, shaking his head.

"Stop being so damn mean to her." Carter leaned toward him with clenched fists.

Mallory ignored him and pointed toward a spot in the bluff roughly fifty feet away. "You two see that crevice? You'll be safe hiding there while I take care of this." Then, his lip curved into his familiar sneer as he turned toward the cocoons. Draped in his bear-fur fringed cloak and holding his gleaming sword, he looked quite capable of destroying every beast in the forest.

A cluster of branches shook. A Nightmare leapt out of cover, eyes on Mallory. Then another. Rows of gills flapped along their flanks, reverberating with their signature click. The two snapped at each other, flashing their fangs. Mallory let out a whoop. When a third stalked toward him, his eyes sharpened with excitement. With his sword angled across his body, he widened his stance in preparation.

Carter pulled me in the direction of the bluff. "Come on, Honey. Move."

I staggered after him, looking over my shoulder at Mallory.

"Don't worry about him." Carter yanked me onward. "Killing things is his favorite pastime."

We ran a few bounds before a Nightmare pounced in front of us, reared up on hind legs, and revealed a plume of glistening Starlight.

I shoved Carter ahead before it could entrance him. "Run!"

He slipped past the creature. When I tried to follow, the Nightmare jabbed its front leg in my path, causing me to stumble backward and fall onto the ground.

Carter glanced at me over his shoulder, but didn't stop running. "I'll find help." He disappeared into the thick forest.

Help? Help from whom?

I glanced at Mallory. Five were on him. Two lay dead at his feet. I was on my own.

The Nightmare rammed its nose toward my chest and sniffed. Its slit-shaped nostrils flared large enough to swallow my fists. I scooted back against a tree and fumbled for my dagger. My fingers, clumsy as puppet limbs, managed to grab hold of the hilt. I drew the weapon but was unable to steady the blade. My lungs threatened to explode.

Using reverse grip, I swiped at the beast, aiming for the eyes as Baxter had taught me. The Nightmare jerked its head back, avoiding the blow. For a few breaths, it considered me, blinking. Its lids slid out from the corners of its ink-colored eyes. I took a breath to calm myself and braced the dagger. Then, with a snort, the Nightmare backed away and turned its attention toward Mallory.

I let out my breath, shaking. The creature stalked toward Mallory, its claws threshing through bramble. Along its armored back, splotches of cocoon goop glistened in the sunlight. My head hummed from my heightened panic, but finally I pieced together what had happened. The Nightmare didn't want me.

"No," I said to myself. "I have a soul. I have a soul." But why didn't it want me? The forest was aglow with Starlight, none of it capable of luring me as it had during my first encounter.

The Nightmare that had turned its back to me neared Mallory, watching him strategically stab its brethren in vital areas. Sunlight raced down the edge of his blade. The beast crouched, ready to pounce. At the top of its cavity, beneath clumps of Starlight, a slimy sack marbled with glowing veins withered and expanded, withered and expanded. Its heart.

If this Nightmare joined its pack, Mallory would have six vicious beasts snapping at him. Too many.

Clutching my dagger, I sprinted after the beast. I jumped and slid across the forest floor, glided underneath the Nightmare's hollow chest, and drove my blade into its heart. A spray of blood burst from the organ, spattering on my shirt. Starlight clung to my arm like static-charged hair until I pulled back. The creature reeled onto its hind legs screeching. It flailed and whacked me with its front leg. I saw stars. The creature continued to wail. My vision cleared, and I caught a glimpse of something that made my blood turn to ice. On either side of the heart I had impaled, two more beat, pumping ferociously.

CHAPTER 32

The Nightmare charged toward me, huffing steam from its nostrils as it swept its massive forelegs downward. I turned and ran. With the beast's legs pounding the ground so close behind, a gust of wind brushed against my neck each time it swung its claws.

My ankles turned as I rushed through the overgrowth of ferns and brambles. I tripped over a tree root and pitched forward onto the muddy ground. The impact knocked the air out of my lungs. I scrambled to my feet and swerved right, but the beast pivoted in the same direction. The dagger-length talons slashed through my knapsack and my supplies tumbled onto the ground. I soon followed.

I rolled over. Though slick blood coated the Nightmare's Starlight, the luminescent strands continued to sparkle through the layer of crimson. The beast swayed and panted, clearly spent, but it roared a howl that echoed through the forest. Trembling, I braced my dagger, eyeing the two throbbing hearts. I had to strike them. Somehow I had to, or I would die.

I stood and steadied my legs. All my muscles tensed in preparation to lunge. But then something whooshed overhead, cutting through the air. I ducked expecting an attack from above, but the object's flight ended with a moist clunk. The beast staggered and then fell to the ground clawing at the four-foot-long blade wedged in its neck.

The weapon, with its plain yet sturdy craftsmanship, could only belong to one man: Baxter. I scanned the forest until I caught a glimpse of silver hair poking through the cover of vegetation. Baxter barreled through the tangled forest growth toward me.

Meanwhile, the Nightmare shrieked and writhed on the ground. Its Starlight rippled, graceful as ribbons in a breeze. Even this close to death, the beast attempted to lure a victim with its luminous bait. Was Baxter immune like I was? Probably not. I dodged the beast's flailing legs and stabbed both spare hearts. My blade sunk into them as if they were overripe melons. The Nightmare wheezed a final breath, and its limbs went limp.

Baxter joined me a moment later. Anchoring his foot on the creature's neck, he pulled his sword free with both hands. The blade made a sickening slurping sound on its way out of the wound. "Dammit, Ri. You shouldn't be out here. With my cousin of all people."

His brow lowered over his storm-gray eyes as he glared first at me and then in Mallory's direction. Though Mallory was hidden by tree cover, the sound of his sword clacking against the beasts' armored shells pierced through the forest.

For the moment at least, Baxter was angry with me for something other than my connection to Samuel.

"I couldn't just wait in my village for the Culling to attack," I said, out of breath. "I had to do something."

He answered with a gruff reprimand. "You're lucky Carter found me when he did."

My heart jolted. "Carter! Is he safe?" I looked across the stream to where the crevice zigzagged up the bluff roughly fifty feet away.

Carter poked his head from cover, waved, and then slunk back into hiding.

"Come on." Baxter yanked me in the direction of the bluff. "Hide with Carter until I return for you." He flashed me a scolding glance.

"Let go!" It was the demeaning treatment rather than the idea of hiding that scorched my cheeks. I struggled to free myself, but he gripped my wrist with the same relentlessness that Ricky often displayed during a game of tug-the-rope.

He clomped into the stream and I was forced to follow. "Is Bryce out here too?"

"Of course not! He's too ill." I dug my heels into the soft sand at the water's bottom. "Stop treating me like a child!"

He had reverted into the cold officer who had humiliated me the night we met. How dare he think this type of behavior was appropriate?

"Dammit, Baxter," I yelled, squirming. "Let go."

We had nearly crossed the stream when the sound of heavy stomps and snapping branches came from behind us. We spun around just as a Nightmare leapt from the cover of trees and splashed into the water. The beast reared up, displaying its plume of Starlight.

Baxter shoved me behind him with such force that I crashed into the water. Without looking at the Starlight, he swung his sword. His blade slid against the armored body, and the clash made a high-pitched screech like a bat at dusk.

Unlike Mallory—who began his attacks with his eyes trained on a vital target and ended them with a precise thrust—Baxter hacked blindly. His massive weapon swept through the beast's right foreleg, slitting it at the joint. The limb dangled useless as a spray of blood showered from the wound, tinting the water crimson.

I sprang to my feet as the beast lunged toward us again. Its claws swooped downward and we jumped back to avoid the attack by mere inches. The waterfall's rumble grew louder behind us. Each time Baxter deflected the massive claws, the beast advanced, snapping its fangs, and we would retreat another step back. Before long, the waterfall's mist chilled my body, and froth gathered around my calves. Cornered. We were corned.

The corded hook burst out of the beast's abdomen, quick as a frog's darting tongue. Baxter swerved, shielding me. The tip of the hook caught his shoulder and ripped through his coat. He groaned through clenched teeth, lowering his sword for a second.

The Nightmare lashed at us again, chomping its powerful jaw. Hot breath that stunk like rotting flesh wafted in my face. With one hand grasping my waist, Baxter maneuvered us into the waterfall. Our backs slammed against the rock wall of a small nook behind the cascade. On the opposite side of the veil of water, the blurry silhouette of the Nightmare sprang in our direction.

The beast's head broke through the cascade. Baxter shoved me to the side as he thrust his sword into the Nightmare's lower jaw, piercing upward into the brain. The beast shrieked and then all went quiet save the rumble of the falls. I pressed my back against the ice-cold rock in the nook, expecting the creature to slash at us once more. But after a few seconds of twitching, its body sagged like a soaked cloth doll. Baxter pressed his foot against the creature's collarbone and pushed the dead body away as he withdrew his sword. The beast fell beyond the curtain of cascading water.

We stood side by side, panting, separated from the rest of the world in our secret nook. My body shivered in the cold and perhaps also from Baxter's hard expression. Would I ever know him as a friend once more, or had he saved me merely out of duty? He stepped forward to leave the nook, but I grasped his arm. In the distance, Mallory's whoops of victory carried over the sounds of the ongoing battle.

"I know you're still upset with me," I said.

His eyebrows squished together as he clenched a muscle in his jaw, keeping his gaze forward. "Upset puts it lightly, but I've decided to leave you and Samuel alone. I can't do any more than that."

"Do any more than that? What's that supposed to mean?"

"It means that if we defeat the Culling I'll return to Black Valley and that will be the end of," he waved his hand back and forth between us, "whatever this is."

"It's called friendship." I moved in front of him so I could look him in the eye. Only a narrow space separated us in the cramped nook.

"We've risked our lives for each other. Doesn't that mean anything to you?"

He released a pent-up sigh. Standing rigid, he stared down at me with a blank, emotionless expression. "It does mean something to me. That's why I won't execute the man who raised you, even though the people of Black Valley deserve justice. I can't hurt you. I could never hurt you."

"Baxter ..." I placed my hand on his, but he brushed it away.

"But you must understand that we can't remain in contact. You'd be a constant reminder of my failure to do what's right by my city. Parting ways will be best for your safety and my sanity."

I lowered my gaze and swallowed the lump in my throat. "I understand, but I wish you'd consider that Samuel may be innocent."

"I'm sorry, Ri, but you'll need to accept the truth eventually."

Far beyond the waterfall came a yelp. Mallory? I turned my head to listen. A Nightmare wailed and then racket of battle faded. All went quiet.

"Girl, where are you?" Mallory shouted, his voice clear though he must have been dozens of feet away. "Come out of hiding. Now!"

I looked back toward Baxter. "It sounds like he defeated the last of them. I'm going to join him. Let me look at your injured shoulder. It'll get inflamed if you let it go."

He cleared his throat and broke eye contact with me. "I'll tend to it myself."

Sadness rushed through me.

"Um ... of course. If that's what you prefer." I turned to leave, but the wall behind him caught my attention. Layers of ice, not rock, cascaded from the ceiling to the nook's floor, like cooled candle wax.

"Ice?" I touched it, and the chill bit into my palm. "It should be melted by this time of year."

Baxter turned around and slid his hand down the slab while I looked around. Adjacent to me, a hair of light ran up the rock wall, across the ceiling and down the opposite side. The glowing seam divided the nook into two halves. The waterfall occupied the front half, while ice covered the rear half.

"I think we traveled through the waterfall and are now in between two," I said. "But one is frozen."

I patted my shredded knapsack. Empty. The amulet was still lying on the ground next to all the other supplies that had fallen out of my sack. "How's this possible?"

"Let's see what's on the other side." He slipped my dagger out from under my belt and chiseled the ice.

"No, wait." I grabbed his arm. "Don't you remember what Bryce told us at Sea Dragon's Point? He said that destroying a frozen waterfall destroys the passage. You could trap us at whatever place is on the other side."

"Then I'll only make a small hole." He thrust the blade through the ice. After tucking my dagger back under my belt, he closed one eye and peeked through the walnut-sized peephole. His head flinched back.

"What is it?" I nudged him out of the way so I could look. Chill air slipped through the hole and brushed against my face.

On the opposite side of the frozen barrier, countless strands of Starlight vined along the gray brick walls of a massive room, glistening in an illuminated splendor enhanced by the frost. The ceiling rose twenty-feet high before curving into a dome supported by gnarled, wooden beams. An iron door tapered to an arch loomed fifteen strides ahead, daring only the most brazen to enter.

Baxter touched my shoulder, pulling me away from the ice. "How are you able to look at the sparkling threads without going into a trance?"

There was no point in explaining Mallory's theory. Maybe two Nightmares had turned their noses away from a Ri dinner, but that didn't mean that I lacked a soul. I shrugged a shoulder and said, "Strong will power I suppose."

"Hmm." He raised an eyebrow.

Mallory called for me once more.

"Come on, we should go and discuss this with the others," I said. "Hopefully you and Mallory had a chance to reconcile your differences."

"Not quite, but I can refrain from killing him," he said, deadpan.

I had one foot through the waterfall when a shriek came from behind the wall of ice. We both spun around just as the slender foreleg of a Nightmare stabbed through the frozen barrier. The leg latched around Baxter's waist and smashed him against the ice with his arms pinned to his sides. He jerked his shoulders, struggling to free himself. I drew my dagger and stabbed the leg at its unarmored joint. The beast squealed, but instead of releasing Baxter, it punched its other foreleg through the ice and hooked him around the neck. A chunk of ice broke free and fell to the ground, leaving a gaping hole in the frosty barrier.

"Ice about to break," Baxter said, straining for air. His cheeks and lips turned purple. "Get out. Now."

"No, I'm not leaving you." I pulled and stabbed at the leg that was choking the life out of him. Cracks webbed through the ice. Shattered fragments fell around us.

"Go," Baxter said again.

"No! If it takes you, you'll be trapped on the other side!" I shouted back. Blood droplets smothered my hands as I knifed the beast. The leg twitched. More ice broke away, creating a crack that stretched from floor to ceiling. "I'm not letting it take you."

"Ri!" Baxter wheezed my name repeatedly until I made eye contact with him. He whispered, "Take care of yourself." Then, he kicked me through the waterfall out of our nook.

I landed rump first into the river next to the beast he had killed minutes earlier. The Nightmare was bleeding out, tinting the waterfall's foam in scarlet. I leapt to my feet and pushed my hand through the cascade. My palm met solid rock. The nook—and the passage to the frozen waterfall—was gone.

"No, no, no," I screamed, slapping the rock so hard that my palm burned. The amulet. I needed the amulet.

I rushed out of the river and up the bank to where all my scattered supplies lay in the mud. A glimmer in a nearby tussock caught my eye. The amulet shimmered in the sunlight. I grabbed it and raced back to the waterfall, passing Mallory along the way.

"Girl, come with me!" he shouted. "Now."

"No, Baxter's in trouble." Grasping the amulet in one hand, I shoved my other into the waterfall, punching solid rock. "No, dammit!"

Somewhere, Baxter was fighting a Nightmare in a cold room filled with Starlight. I imagined a pile of crumbled ice—once a waterfall—lying near him. The passage was destroyed, and even with the amulet in my possession, I was powerless to help him.

Mallory stomped into the river and grabbed my arm. Blood soaked the fringe of his cloak. "My cousin can wait."

"No he can't! He's trapped!" I screamed as he yanked me to dry land. "We need to help him. Let go!"

"There's no time." He pulled me upslope, past the heap of Nightmares he had slaughtered. They lay in a tangle of limbs and dull Starlight, with blood glistening on their ebony-shelled bodies.

"Let me go! I have to save him! I have to save him!" My wrist burned from the friction of trying to pull free of his calloused grip.

He released my arm and pushed me ahead of him. "Look."

Fifteen feet ahead, Carter lay on the ground with one of the beast's thorn-like hooks puncturing his side. The dead monster it belonged to sprawled near him, blood oozing from a gash through its neck. A dreadful cold chilled my core.

Trembling, I rushed to his side. "Carter. Oh no, Carter." The words came through wisps of panicked breath. "What happened? You were safe at the bluff. I saw you."

"Hello, Buttercup." His eyes fluttered open, weakly.

"He jumped right out in front of one," Mallory explained.

"If I didn't, you'd be lying here instead of me," Carter said through labored breaths.

"No I wouldn't," Mallory shouted. "I had it under control. You should have stayed put."

"Stop yelling at him!" My hands shook like rickety shutters holding back a storm. I peeled away the blood-soaked fabric of Carter's shirt. The tip of the hook protruded out of his flesh between his middle ribs. I placed my hand over the wound, attempting to staunch the blood flow.

"I always knew you'd tear my clothes off one day." He winced through a pained chuckle and struggled to lift his head. He gaped at his wound, and his gasps turned into sobs. Tears slid down his cheeks as his head collapsed back into the mud. "The greatest con I've ever pulled ..."

"Don't talk, save your energy." I leaned down and held him, cradling his head to keep it off the cold ground. Then I commanded Mallory, "Quick. There's a jar of herbal concoction where my supplies are scattered. Find it."

"No," Carter said. "Katie's powers ... too weak to heal me." His breaths sawed in and out of his mouth.

"Why Carter? Why didn't you stay near the bluff?" My tears fell onto his cheeks as I tried to wipe his beautiful auburn tendrils clean of mud.

"Not much time. Please listen." He grasped the back of my head and drew me close. "Fate weaved yours and Mallory's threads short. Both of you ... were meant to die today." He sputtered, coughing up blood. "But my death instead of Mallory's foiled her plans. Both of your life threads have disintegrated, and it will take her three days to weave you new ones ... new deaths. Until then, your destinies are of your own making. Move fast. You two are humanity's—Katie's—best chance against the Culling. And Fate ... she wants you to fail."

I clasped his hand, holding him closer as I heaved with sobs. "No, there had to be another way."

His body shook as shock began to set in. "So cold …"

"I'm here, Carter. I'm not letting go."

Mallory walked off.

"Honey," Carter said, "My Whisperer told me what connects us … why we're able to see the things we can. We've all been touched by Death's magic."

"What?" I stared at him through tear-blurred vision.

Instead of answering, he gazed toward the sky. His pupils dilated, leaving only a sliver of his clover-green irises showing. Blood continued to seep out of his wound. There was nothing I could do but hold his hand.

Mallory returned with a clump of Starlight, and though it hung limp as damp grass, most of the strands still sparkled. "He's talked enough. This will do something for the pain."

"Starlight?" I jerked my head.

Carter's muscles relaxed when he accepted the Starlight. He glanced up at me, with eyes glistening from both tears and the Starlight's euphoria. "Tell me a different future, Buttercup. A better future."

I wiped my eyes on my sleeve. "Look at the Starlight, Carter. And I'll describe it so you can see it, clear as a dream." My words came through a shaky whisper.

"Thank you." He looked at the Starlight. His eyelids half closed.

"We return to my village and …" I cleared my throat. It tasted salty from crying. "Katie looks beautiful and healthy. You don't have to worry about her anymore."

"Look after her." He smiled, petting my hand. "See that she marries a good man. Someone that I would approve of."

"I will. I promise."

"I'd like to live in your little cottage. It's simple, but …"

"Beautiful. You live a beautiful life, Carter. And sometimes I do sing for you." I hummed a song, voice cracking.

"You sound lovely." He closed his eyes. "I could listen to you forever, but I'm so tired."

"All right, Carter. That's all right. Just outside of my village, there's a place the sun warms just right. Next to a maple and a small pond. It's peaceful. Let's rest there for a while." I could no longer see him through my tears. I held his hand tighter and felt something hard in his palm.

"You're right. It's warm. Peaceful." The corner of his mouth curved upward. "But I'm afraid I must depart and leave you with less enjoyable company …"

"Just for now …" I finished.

"Just for now."

After that he said nothing else. His chest rose and fell a few times, then stopped. The item I felt him holding rolled out of his palm as his body went limp. The small stone I gave him—the promise of a new life for him and Katie—fell onto the ground. I stared at our hands. Mine trembled while his lay unmoving.

CHAPTER 33

A pallid color replaced Carter's sun-warmed complexion, and smudges of crimson dabbed his mouth. When I squeezed his hand, he didn't squeeze back. His fingers grew cold. My tears came through quiet sobs, and droplets fell from my lashes each time I blinked. I squeezed his hand again. Nothing. Just the stillness of death.

"Say your final words." Mallory wiped the sweat from his forehead. "Then we'll bury the body." He strolled toward the river, maneuvering around the pile of dead beasts.

Nothing seemed real. I brushed the debris out of Carter's hair.

"You were right when you said that you'd steal my heart one day," I said, clutching my chest. "I can feel a piece of it missing." I bent down and kissed his forehead. His skin felt cool against my lips. "And that piece will be yours, Carter. Always."

I removed the hook from his side as if I could make him whole again by discarding the thing that killed him. It scraped against bone when I pulled it out of his flesh. I threw the wretched thing as far as I could.

I took a deep breath. "May you find peace in the light of the Violet Star."

Honey, I imagined him saying, *I'll have peace once the Culling can't kill my sister.*

With that thought, I stood. Down the bank, the river babbled, breaking waves into bouquets of foam. Mallory was washing the blood from his arms and face. I joined him. All his features, but especially his eyes and cheeks, took on a drooped, downturned appearance. His ever-present sneer had vanished.

"Tell me what happened to my cousin," Mallory said.

The waterfall tumbled down the bluff, gurgling a serene melody as if it had nothing to do with Baxter's disappearance.

"He's gone." I placed my hand through the cascade and rested it upon the bluff. The rough stone dug into my palm, pushing back. Fighting the urge to cry, I explained that a Nightmare had pulled Baxter through a frozen waterfall, and that the passage to return to us was lost. Closing my eyes, I gripped the rock tighter. If only Baxter's hand would have appeared and latched onto mine. But the seconds passed.

"Don't fret, girl," Mallory said. "He can't be dead yet. There's nothing Fate enjoys more than feeding the Renselar family misery, and Baxter's too young to have had his fill." He gave me a hard pat on the back that jerked me forward. "Dry your eyes. We have a job to finish."

How could he be so cold? Carter was dead. Baxter was trapped. And all he cared about was his own ludicrous quest.

"Of course," I said through a growl. "We must find your precious Oblivion."

His familiar sneer returned. "Not yet. Carter said that Fate didn't want me to stop the Culling, so let's go stop the Culling. I'd like to piss the hag off before meeting her face to face."

"You want to stop the Culling?" I asked, gaping, unsure if I had heard him correctly.

"That's what I said." He clomped out of the river.

"Dammit, Carter," I whispered. "Always a trickster. Even with your last words, you manage to con Mallory into helping us." More tears rolled down my cheeks.

Mallory headed up the bank, pausing near my scattered supplies. He picked up a blanket and then pointed at the rest of the items. "Pack all this up."

I stared at my hand still grasping the rock through the falls. The chilly water numbed my fingers.

Honey, I imagined Carter saying, *Stop worrying about the Red Band.*

At that moment, there was nothing I could do to help Baxter. I patted the rock before releasing it. "Hold on Baxter. Just hold on. I will find you."

I raced up the bank. Along the forest floor, packages of food and other supplies poked out of the mud. I removed my knapsack, but the tear down the center made it useless.

"Use this one," Mallory shouted. He removed the knapsack from Carter's dead body and tossed it to me. Crimson stained the straps.

I closed my eyes and took another breath. "Pack one thing at a time. You can do it."

I opened my eyes and picked up the tinderbox nestled in a patch of weeds. "Pull it together, Ri," I said, continuing to coach myself. "Everyone's counting on you. Samuel, Katie, Baxter, the village. Take inventory of supplies first."

I scoured through Carter's knapsack. Inside laid a package of dried meat, bread, a lantern, a decent length of rope, and a pair of shackles. I dangled them in front of me.

"Toss 'em. They're not needed," Mallory said. He wrapped Carter's body in the blanket.

I didn't want to know why Carter owned a pair of shackles, but I told Mallory, "If Carter packed them, then we need them for something."

"Do I look like the sort of man who arrests people? I prefer swift resolution, girl." He patted the hilt of his sword.

I stuffed the shackles into the knapsack to defy him, if nothing else. Then I collected the canteens and food lying on the ground. Mallory joined me with Carter cradled in his arms. I stiffened my chin and fought my sorrow.

"The ground's too rocky to dig a hole here," Mallory said.

I swung the knapsack onto my back and looked around for the Fireflies. They swooped down from the treetops and chose a westward path.

"The Fireflies want to continue that way." I hurried in their direction and Mallory followed.

***

Mallory carried Carter's body over his shoulder until we reached a meadow with a grand maple tree at its center. The sinking sun dyed the sky orange. A calming breeze rustled through leaves and grass. Mallory laid Carter under the tree and then chose a spot undisturbed by roots to dig a hole. With dagger in hand, he chopped the ground to loosen the soil.

I followed suit, alternating between cutting and digging through the wet, chunky dirt. My movements came mechanically, like the wind-up wolf that Baxter gave to me. I kept my thoughts on what I had to do. Dig a hole. Bury Carter. Find Oblivion. Cure Samuel. Stop the Culling. Dig a hole. Bury Carter. Find Oblivion. Cure Samuel. Stop the Culling …

Once the hole was so deep that we could stand inside of it, Mallory signaled me to stop. We pulled ourselves out of the hole, and then he placed Carter—still wrapped in the blanket—inside. He quietly waited for me to toss the first scoop of soil over the body.

Instead, I reached into my pocket and retrieved the stone that I had given to Carter. For a long moment I clutched it, staring at my deceased friend. I inhaled, but rather than fresh air, the scent of death crept into my nose.

"Remorse is nothing but a thief, girl," Mallory said. "It steals time better spent hunting down those responsible."

The taste of tears lingered in my throat. "Goodbye Carter."

I tossed the stone into the hole and then scooped some soil into my palm. Carter disappeared into the earth one handful of dirt at a time.

***

For the next day, Mallory and I paused only for short breaks to catch our breath, fill the canteens, hunt, and eat. The Fireflies led us long into the night. They flew in tight formation and amplified their glow, guiding me as well as a torch in those dark hours. After we had a short rest, their insistent glow woke us before dawn.

We traveled downslope through lush forests, where every direction embraced shades of green. Clusters of leaves blocked the sky, leaving us only tiny gaps to peek through. Below, ferns covered the ground and brushed against my ankles like feathers. Ahead, moss clung to the trunks of old, gnarled trees like fur cloaks.

The thick forest growth blocked most of our view ahead, but on the second morning, the ground leveled out. We had reached the foot of the mountain. The Fireflies continued to lead us west and we followed.

***

By late afternoon, the density of the trees tapered off, allowing the warmth of sunlight to fall onto our shoulders. The Fireflies swerved into a clearing, and I stopped in my tracks.

Ahead, a dozen broken-down cottages rose above plumes of ferns. With slanted walls and decaying roofs, the homes slumped in the overgrowth of vegetation like defeated soldiers. Moss feathered their cob walls in tufts of green, and vines snaked up from the earth and through the windows. Busted doors hung from loose hinges, allowing the plant life to flourish over thresholds and invade the homes' interiors.

I drew my dagger. There were too many hiding places for the Culling's beasts to lurk.

Remaining quiet, I listened as we followed the Fireflies into the village center. Our presence disturbed a few ravens perched on an exposed roof beam. They watched us for a moment and then resumed pecking at what remained of the thatching. Mallory peeked inside a home that housed no one except for a young tree that had broken through the stone floor and now splayed its branches above the main room.

"Do you think the Culling attacked this village long ago?" I whispered.

"Probably," Mallory said as if he didn't care one way or another. "Let's go. Nothing of value is left and we're wasting time."

The Fireflies guided us through the village, and I glanced inside the homes we passed. Clay bottles and moldy wooden tools lay scattered on the floors. I imagined that one morning, everyone in this village started their day like any other. But then an unimaginable terror arrived.

"All of those poor families." I placed my hand over my heart. "I hope they were able to escape."

The Fireflies slowed their flight to a cautious hover when we were a few strides from the outermost cottage. A stone ax head draped in thistle caught my attention. I stopped walking and stared at the blade wedged in a damp, black log.

"Why you stopping? Let's go," Mallory said.

Ignoring him, I approached the abandoned tool. I knelt next to it and traced the flat side with my finger.

An image slipped into my mind. A man with broad shoulders and brown hair, his body slick with sweat, raised this ax over his head. With his gaze trained on the log, he drove the blade down in a powerful swing that ended in a burst of splintered wood. The scent of fresh-cut lumber filled the air.

About a dozen feet behind him, a woman sat on a stump in her garden tying together bunches of lavender for hanging. She smiled and hummed, joyously lost in the activity. Her waist-length brown hair flowed over her shoulders, bouncing slightly in the breeze. I wanted very much to hug her. She smelled like the daisies that sprouted in the surrounding garden.

"I think I know this place," I said.

"Dammit," Mallory said under his breath. "Of all the places we could have found. Come on, there's nothing but bad memories for you here."

"Perhaps, but they're my memories and I want them."

A cottage with a slightly lopsided—yet familiar—window lured me to enter. I stepped over the unhinged door rotting near the threshold. The interior of the one-room home resembled the other we had investigated, minus the tree. Leafy vines cascaded down the walls, and sunlight glistened on dew-coated spider webs. Weeds took advantage of the weak clay floors, poking through cracks and crevices.

"I do know this place," I said.

I envisioned this home—my home—as it once was: the fire reveling in the hearth, aromas of stew and baked things pouring through the door, and deer-hide blankets that kept me cozy at night.

But now, the bedding lay rotting. Years of abandonment had given vines the opportunity to crawl over the hearth and break it down bit by bit. Mallory's footfalls approached behind me.

"What happens to the souls that the Nightmares take?" I asked. "Do they find peace at the Violet Star? Or are they just gone ... forever?"

"I don't know." He cupped my shoulder. "But it's best we get moving."

The Fireflies drifted toward an old chest that sat below a window on the far side of the room. I didn't need their guidance. I recalled this spot. Once, I believed that the gap between the chest and the corner of the room was the perfect hiding place. My parents never found me there when we played hide-and-seek.

I had accepted the death of my family long ago. But seeing my first home in this decrepit state pumped a flurry of emotions through my veins. Sadness, anger, fear. My head spun. I hated the Culling. My mouth quivered, but I set my jaw so I wouldn't break into sobs in front of Mallory.

While Mallory waited in the doorframe, I rushed to the chest and found where a piece of the clay floor had broken away revealing the dirt ground underneath. I dug with my fingers, still marred with scratches from digging Carter's grave, into the hardened dirt. Pebbles and debris wedged under my nails.

About four inches in, I stopped digging. My fingers pressed against a plush object, and I removed it from the hole. The dark beaded eyes of a mud-colored doll stared back at me. Mold festered in the hair. Her arms dangled by threads. I wiped at the grime, but years had locked the filth in place.

The morning the Nightmares attacked, I needed to save something. Powerless to save anyone else, I hid my goose-feather-stuffed doll. Someone might find her one day. Someone might avenge the injustice that happened here.

"I remember." I looked up at Mallory. With his back to the sunlight, shadows hid the expression on his face. "I remember everything."

***

Fourteen years ago, a Nightmare had smashed through the door right where Mallory stood. When the beast locked its ebony eyes on me, my small, frail body went ice cold, as if dead already.

Trembling, I climbed on top of the wooden chest and scrambled out the window. The beast's claws scraped against the clay floor as it backed out the door and rounded the corner in pursuit of me. I ran barefoot, trampling the parsley and chives in my mother's garden.

Near the stump she had been sitting on moments ago lay a bunch of lavender with a half-tied bow around the stems. Neither she nor my father was in sight. I screamed and cried. Stones cut into my soles as I raced into the village center only to find Nightmares dragging terrified victims into their hollow cavities. Nearby, other beasts scoured the area for remaining villagers, clawing at closed doors and busting them down. Some poked their heads through windows, spewing drool as they snapped at the air.

I turned and bolted toward the forest. My lungs heaved, and my heart pounded. From behind came a loud shriek. Something whacked my back, and excruciating pain burned up my spine. I pitched forward. For a few breaths, I coughed up blood. My head swam along the brink of unconsciousness, and then I let go, plunging into the black depths of sleep.

When I opened my eyes, a tall man stood over me. His cloak rippled around him like a shadow. A hood draped over the top of his head showed only the tip of a narrow nose and a solemn mouth with lines on each side. His lips looked like two smudges of soot on his pallid flesh.

Nightmares surrounding us pursued their last victims in frenzied violence, but the chaos diffused into a fuzzy haze, as if it happened entirely in an alternate realm. This man claimed my attention. He exuded neither cruelty nor kindness. He was the unfair yet perfect system that ruled all things.

He extended a long-fingered hand toward me without saying a word. I reached my hand toward his, hypnotized by his presence. When his hand closed around mine, a flash of light blasted the world away and delivered me to a place of mist and starlight. The pull of reality let go, leaving my body—my spirit—weightless in the heavens.

"Dammit, Mallory." I shook the memory from my mind and tossed the doll on the ground. "You were right. Death has my soul and I want it back."

CHAPTER 34

We reached the forest's edge late in the day. Mallory swung his sword, clearing the last of the vegetation that blocked our path. We stepped out of the shadowed woodlands and into a golden field. The sun peeked through gray clouds, sinking lower in the heavens.

The second sunset. Only one day left to stop the Culling.

"We're not far from the sea." Mallory stared at an obnoxiously loud flock of white birds drifting in the stormy sky. "Your Fireflies better not have led us to a dead end."

The Fireflies waited in the field ahead, skirting the feathered tips of wheat grass. They swirled about, urging us forward.

"Carter told us to keep following them." I scanned the area for danger before hurrying onward. "They won't let us down."

My feet burned with blisters, my sides cramped from hunger, and my legs begged for rest, but I pressed on. Mallory followed. Thunder boomed overhead, and a light drizzle sprinkled from the clouds. Rain plastered my clothes to my sweat-drenched skin.

As I jogged on, I glanced over my shoulder at the spruce-covered mountains toward home. Poor Samuel and Katie. I was sure they feared for us as much as I feared for them. Heaviness sank over me each time Bryce crossed my mind. What if I defeated the Culling to find a fresh grave instead of his embrace? I ran faster. I couldn't lose anyone else. Each time I blinked, I saw blue—blue like Baxter's lips as the Nightmare strangled him. And each time a cool raindrop splattered upon my cheek, I felt a chill that reminded me of Carter's cold, dead hands.

We reached the end of the field and stood at the ledge of a small cliff overhanging a rocky beach. Wind blowing in from the sea tugged at my clothes and sent sprays of rain at my face. The Fireflies dove, following the cliff's slope until they hovered at the edge of the shore. We trailed them down the bluff, boots sliding over the pebbly terrain.

"There's nothing here." Mallory's eyebrows scrunched together as he cursed under his breath.

I swiveled around, but a growing fog obscured our surroundings. The Fireflies swerved up shore and I ran after them. The fuzzy silhouette of a bridge manifested in the haze.

"Mallory! This way." I hopped over the beach's slimy rocks, rushing toward my discovery.

Made of granite blocks, the bridge stretched over the sea until it eventually disappeared at the misty horizon line. Years of waves battering the deck and supports had gnawed away chunks of stone. Leafy sea plants nestled in cracks.

"This is incredible," I said as Mallory joined me. "It must've taken thousands of men to build this bridge." I squinted, searching for its end without success. How far west did it go? Hmm ... west. I recalled how perplexed Bryce and Baxter had been when they discovered that my compass had pointed west. Out of curiosity, I removed it from my pocket. The needle lined up with the bridge. How strange.

Mallory scrutinized the crumbling structure. Meanwhile, the Fireflies glided over the deck. Their amber light bounced off the rolling haze.

"They want us to cross it." I stepped onto the bridge. Waves lapped the stone, slickening the three-foot wide deck with water. I imagined that farther out, the whitecaps rose higher and stronger, promising a dangerous journey. But the answer to what lay beyond the bridge won over my fear.

I advanced a few steps. The heavy clomp of Mallory's boots followed close behind. Locking my gaze downward, I avoided the cracks in the stonework and tangles of plants. Before long, waves slammed against my calves, buckling my exhausted legs.

"You look like a drunken opossum waddling across a tree branch." Mallory chuckled.

"Be quiet and keep up," I snapped.

We had trekked at least thirty yards when a flash of light in the distance caught my attention. I stopped walking and placed my hand to my brow, blocking the rain from falling into my eyes. Directly ahead another streak of light plunged from the sky, followed by two more in close succession. The low rumble of thunder rolled toward us.

"Collectors," I said.

"Collectors? What nonsense are you talking about?" Mallory pushed me forward. "It's lightning, that's all. Keep moving."

I turned around to face him. "My village calls them Collectors. They're servants of Death that gather additional souls when the god feels he hasn't received enough. Don't you think it's strange that they're all striking the same spot?" A wave rammed into me, and I would have fallen into the sea if Mallory hadn't grabbed my arm.

"Collectors." He punctuated the statement with a skeptical grunt, narrowing his eyes at the flickers of light ahead. "I'll take the lead now. Get behind me and hold onto my cloak. You do me no good if you fall into the ocean and drown."

"I'm not going to fall in," I huffed.

I shuffled behind him, glancing back at the shore. Through the fog, a bulky, dark figure barreled along the bridge toward us. The shape took form—first, two prominent forelegs, and then a tapered head with large ebony eyes.

"Nightmare!" I shouted. It was no more than thirty feet away. Instead of revealing its Starlight, the beast kept its claw-like appendages interlaced, shielding its hollow cavity.

"Stay back." Mallory shouted as he rushed toward the beast. He drew his sword.

The beast swung its talons, slashing nothing but the air above Mallory's head as he dropped and skidded toward the beast, striking an unarmored joint in its hind leg. As the Nightmare staggered, Mallory rolled backward and leapt to his feet, repositioning himself for the next attack.

Mesmerized by his movements, I failed to notice the sea brewing a treacherous wave alongside me. It struck my hip and knocked me onto my knees. One leg slipped into the frigid water as the waves continued to drive me toward the bridge's edge.

Hunkering down, I dug my fingers into the cracks in the stonework to hold on. My arms strained against the sea's power, and the jagged stone cut into my palms. Below, the dark silhouette of a thirty-foot fish passed under the bridge. My heart hopped over a beat. I swung my leg out of the water and hooked my foot into one of the deck's many crevices. Staying low, I spat the briny taste of the sea from my mouth and looked back toward the battle.

Waves crashed against man and beast, bursting into mist. Both moved with agility and balance along the narrow bridge—a blur of steel, talons, and fangs. The Nightmare extended its neck to snap at Mallory just as he ducked. Mallory then lunged with the speed of a venomous snake and drove his sword into the beast's chest between its interlaced appendages. When he pulled his weapon free, the blade, slick with poppy-colored blood, screamed for notice against the gray haze and dull, churning sea.

Screeching, the Nightmare reared backward. It retracted its appendages and released a victim from its hollow cavity. The body—a man with dark hair—fell onto the bridge. My heart sank. Poor unlucky soul. Meanwhile, the injured beast swayed on the deck with blood staining its strands of Starlight. Finally, it toppled into the sea, flailing its legs and tail as it struggled against the tide.

The sea carried the beast twenty feet from the bridge before a massive, fang-filled mouth launched out of the water and clamped down on the Nightmare with a bone-snapping crunch. I flinched at the sight of the menacing sea creature. Its barbed scales were cragged as the stone bridge, as if the sea had weathered and shaped them for centuries. Both beasts splashed down into the depths while I clung to the bridge, gulping down panicked breaths.

"Girl, get over here," Mallory called. "Now!"

Keeping a firm grasp on the bridge, I scurried toward him. Waves continued to leap over the deck and pound my sides. As I made my way, Mallory bent down and lifted the dead man's shirt.

"No hook mark," he shouted over the roar of the sea, pointing at the corpse's lower back. "Strange, the Nightmare wasn't feeding off this one."

"It was probably carrying him off for some equally dreadful purpose," I said as I joined him.

The corpse lay on its stomach face down. As Mallory had stated, no puncture from the beast's hook marred the lower back. And unlike the other victims we had encountered, the smooth flesh appeared free of rot. Fresh, no doubt. A bloodstain spread over the upper region of the man's shirt. When Mallory plunged his sword into the Nightmare, his blade must have pierced through this man as well.

Closing my eyes, I bowed my head. "May you find peace in the light of the Violet Star."

When I opened my eyes, the body moved, struggling to lift himself on his forearms as waves flooded over him.

My hand flew to my chest. "He's still alive!" I knelt near the crown of the man's head and touched his shoulder. "Don't strain, we're going to help you."

"Ri?" Wincing, the man craned his neck to look up at me.

Time stopped.

Two hazel eyes accented with gold undertones stared back into mine. Bryce.

"No, no, no," I repeated. With trembling hands I brushed the hair away from his forehead, praying that the man before me was someone else. Perhaps the effects of hunger and exhaustion had reached my brain, creating the most dreadful hallucination my mind could conjure. But as my palms grasped his face, pressing against the slight stubble along his jaw, the gut-wrenching reality set in.

"Bryce, no." My voice wilted to a desperate plea.

"Bryce?" Mallory quickly knelt alongside us. He mouthed the name a second time and then his eyes widened, showing their whites. "Dammit!" He stood and paced the bridge, alternating between scratching the back of his neck and rubbing his hand over his mouth.

There was no time to worry about what troubled him. I looked back at Bryce.

"I finally found you," he said, coughing up blood.

"You shouldn't be out here. You shouldn't be out here." My entire body was shaking. "No, no. You shouldn't be out here."

"Katie told me that you left with the tyrant's son. I couldn't let you fight the Culling without me. We stick together, remember?" Groaning, he rolled over and flopped onto his back. A matching red splotch stained the front of his shirt. The stab wound went straight through him. "I searched nonstop, until ..."

"No," I whimpered. A tear escaped. Many more followed.

He closed his eyes, inhaling and exhaling sharp breaths. "Where's Carter?"

Dead. I failed him. I failed everyone.

"Rest, just rest," I said. Then, grasping my forehead, I whispered to myself, "Pull it together, Ri. Fix this."

I lifted his shirt, revealing a three-inch-wide puncture near his upper ribs. Kaylan told me that a fortunate man in our village once survived such a stab wound.

"All right." I hunched over to protect him from the constant waves and slung my knapsack off my back. "I have a jar of Katie's remedy. We can heal you."

"Won't work." He reached for me. His warm palm caressed my cheek as he pulled me toward him, leading my mouth to his. My lips quivered, holding back sobs.

"She's calling me," he said, his mouth still brushing against mine.

"What are you talking about? No one's calling you."

He stretched his arm toward the edge of the bridge and dipped his fingers into the sea. A faint blue glow radiated around his hand as it slipped out of this location and into another.

"That's impossible. It's not a waterfall. You're not even wearing the amulet."

I gasped. Slip of the tongue. I glanced at Mallory, wondering if he heard me, but he just stood over us staring. Perhaps it was the dim lighting, or the tears blurring my vision, but I swore his hands were trembling.

Quickly, I rummaged through the knapsack for the small jar of herbal remedy. Meanwhile, Bryce clutched the edge of the bridge and pulled himself closer to the water.

"Stop moving," I said, but he didn't listen.

"I have to go." The words barely carried over the crash of the sea and the growing thunder. "She's calling me."

I glared at Mallory. "Don't just stand there! He's delusional. Keep him still."

"This is Fate's work," Mallory said. "We can't help him now."

I shook my head. "Damn if I'm not going to try!"

I clutched Bryce's arm with one hand and continued to search the sack with the other.

"Ri, you have to let go," Bryce whispered.

"Stop talking nonsense. Stay still." My palm finally pressed against the cool glass jar of remedy. I released Bryce for a second so I could wrestle the cork free.

He stole that second to thrust himself into the sea. A flood of blue light flashed over the waves and then he vanished.

"No, no, no!" I pawed at the water, but unlike Bryce, my hand remained in the murky sea instead of disappearing in blue light. "This should work. I have the amulet. This should work." I sobbed hard, as if I were coughing up my own heart.

Mallory clutched the back of my shirt and yanked me to my feet. "Dammit, can't you see these waters are teeming with fang-scale sharks?"

Gray, barbed fins sliced through the surrounding waters.

"We have to go after him!" I clawed out of Mallory's grip and shoved my arm back into the water. Once again my hand failed to plunge into another land. "Dammit, why isn't this working?"

Mallory seized my knapsack, grabbed me by the waist, and slung me over his shoulder. "This is no time to fall apart."

The water had risen above the bridge's supports and coated the deck even when the waves receded. One of the sharks butted against the bridge, catching a glimpse of us before whipping back into the depths.

Carrying me, Mallory jogged onward.

"We have to do something." I pounded my fists against his back. It wasn't his fault that he stabbed Bryce. But cowering? Leaving Bryce behind? How could he? I struck him harder, but he didn't even flinch from my blow.

"Listen," he finally said. "That boy chose to transport somewhere else, and there's not a damn thing you can do to follow him now. You go back there, you'll be nothing but shark food."

I stopped smacking him. Samuel warned that if I went with Mallory, I'd discover places so dark that I would forget that light ever existed. At that moment, I couldn't fathom a darker place. The spot where Bryce had vanished grew small behind us until it disappeared in the fog.

"Girl, can you swim?" Mallory shouted. The waves buffeted his waist and splattered my face with spray. "There's a thirty-foot gap in the bridge ahead."

"What?" I twisted my body trying to see what lay ahead, but the way he gripped me made that impossible. "No, I can't swim."

"Then prepare to learn." Without slowing, he maneuvered me off his shoulder and held me alongside his hip as if I were a battering ram. The bridge ended no more than five feet ahead. Whitecaps rose like mountain peaks before crashing down in eruptions of froth.

"I can't swim through that!" Heart pounding, I squirmed to free myself from his grasp. But he launched off the bridge and threw me forward while in mid-air.

I plunged into ice-cold water, sinking beneath the waves. The unbearable chill burrowed into my bones and veins. It was so cold it numbed my flesh. Yet I moved, squinting in the blackness as I flailed my arms and legs. I clawed my way toward the light, but a whitecap smashed me back downward before I could draw a breath. My sides ached, screaming for air. When my lungs could suffer no more, I gasped. Pure reflex. The briny water burned my throat. My body convulsed, but I held my breath and continued to fight the chaotic current.

Before long, my kicks grew weak. My arms barely swung. The pulls of unconsciousness tugged at my mind as the sea sucked me downward. For a moment I drifted, unmoving until my hand brushed against rock. The feel of something solid against my palm awakened every nerve. I latched onto the stone, and though my arms shook from exhaustion, I heaved myself upward.

I broke the surface choking. Every breath was part pain, part relief. I opened my eyes to slits, enduring the harsh sting of the saltwater. The object I held onto took shape through my blurry vision. By some miracle, I had managed to grab onto the opposite half of the bridge. I thrust myself upward and flopped onto the deck, heaving to replenish my lungs with air.

I turned my head to the side and peered out into the sea searching for Mallory. The rain shifted to a mixture of snow and sleet. I shivered as the wind whipped against my face.

"Mallory," I yelled. My strained voiced failed to carry over the waves. I shouted his name once more.

A fin cut through the waves. It stalked the surface for a moment and then sunk out of sight. Crouching, I drew my dagger.

"Mallory," I called again. The fearless man could kill anything on land, but in water the sharks had all the advantage.

The fin emerged from the water once more, closing in. I tightened my frozen, raw fingers around my dagger's hilt, preparing.

"Dammit, Mallory, where are you?"

All was quiet save the crash of the waves and the grumble of thunder in the distance. I glanced toward the right, where the shark was a moment before. Nothing.

Then, a dark shape passed beneath the bridge. I tensed, readying. My heart threatened to explode. The shark's head burst out of the water. Its black eyes locked on me, and a stirring of air hit me as it snapped its mouth inches from my face. I scooted backward. Keeping myself low, I swung my dagger. The blade sliced the gill slit, and the shark dove back into the sea.

Luck. Pure luck. No doubt I had merely angered it. It would return to devour me whole. A splash erupted at the edge of the bridge. Flinching, I jutted my dagger toward it.

"Watch it." Mallory pivoted, dodging my blow as he pulled himself onto the bridge.

"You're alive," I said with a relieved sigh.

"Of course I'm alive." He stood and offered a hand to help me up.

Quaking, I rose to my feet, scanning the water for the shark. But when I looked back to Mallory, my breath hitched at the sight of his chest. His shirt had been torn from the collar down, and an amulet shard—just like Bryce's—was nested between his scarred pectorals. Instead of dangling from a chain, strips of his flesh, like stretched dough, held it in place. His purple veins webbed inside of the translucent stone.

"You have the missing piece of the amulet?" I touched my parted lips.

"No time to chitchat." He shoved me forward. "Move."

I turned and raced onward. No more than twenty feet ahead loomed a rocky, snow-coated island. Though the waves died as I neared land, the wind picked up, slamming against me. I folded my arms to hoard what body heat I could, but all warmth leeched out into the bitter air. By the time I reached the beach, I was shivering uncontrollably. I fell to my knees and rubbed my hands together, but there was no relief.

Hugging my limbs close, I stared at the sea. Waves carried on in their ebb and flow, indifferent to my pain. Mere moments earlier, I had heard Bryce's voice, held him, felt his lips upon mine. If only I had talked sense into him. Kept him on that bridge. Slathered the remedy on his wound in time. But I didn't. And he was gone.

Mallory squatted in front of me and looked me in the eye. Wind whisked snowflakes off his hair and cloak. "If you don't get up, you'll freeze to death."

The sun had already surrendered the sky to the moon, and just like the sky, I needed to endure another dark night. So I stood, holding onto him for balance, even though the emptiness inside of me rivaled the barren, snow-covered landscape ahead. But far in the distance on the horizon line, stood a lone building framed by spired towers. Dozens of Collectors lit up the clouds in webs of silver light, striking the place as if yearning to see it crumble.

"It looks like a temple of some sort," I said through chattering teeth. "Those Collectors are going to smash it apart."

"It's the only shelter we're going to find. Move."

He marched onward and I followed, maintaining a firm grasp on his arm. Snow seeped into my shoes, and the burn of frostbite crept into my toes. Sensation vanished from my nose, ears and fingers. One more step. One more step. Staggering, I repeated those words to myself. Pain stabbed through my skull. So cold. Step. One more. One. What was I counting? Steps. Steps. I was counting steps. Why was I counting steps? I closed my eyes and collapsed.

CHAPTER 35

I awoke to a crackling sound. Still exhausted, I forced my eyes open and found myself in a dark room, atop a pile of dusty rags and covered with an equally dirty blanket. To my right a campfire burned, barely lighting the enormous—and unfamiliar—stone room. Despite the flame's heat, a deep coldness chilled me to the core, and I was too tired to even work up a shiver. Figuring out where I was could wait. I closed my eyes and curled up for warmth. Even this slight movement sent stabbing pains through my joints. Wincing, I hugged myself tighter. My bare skin was nearly numb to the touch.

Bare skin?

Someone had stripped me to my undergarments! I jolted upright. Lightheaded, I scanned my surroundings, blinking away the spots that clouded my vision. Layers of dust coated broken furniture scattered throughout the abandoned space. My clothing and belt lay flat on the slate floor next to Mallory's shirt and cloak. The man himself sat propped against the wall on the opposite side of the fire. The amulet, bound to his chest by strips of his flesh, sparkled in the firelight.

I grabbed my shirt and covered myself. The damp fabric made me colder. "What's going on?"

He rolled his eyes. "Calm down. Your body temperature dropped and those soaked clothes weren't doing you any good."

Fuzzy memories pieced themselves together: ice-cold water, sharks, the snow-covered island, Collectors.

"Bryce." I jerked, placing my hand over my mouth. The image of his bloody wound shoved all other memories aside. Perhaps he had survived. Perhaps he had transported some place where he was receiving proper care. Perhaps, somehow, I could still reach him.

Such silly thoughts! He had lost far too much blood. He was gone. Gone. My breath came fast and everything inside of me crumpled.

Mallory moved closer. No compassion warmed his eyes, but the absence of his usual smirk suggested some concern. "Remember what I told you about remorse?"

I wiped a lone tear off my cheek. "It's nothing but a thief. It steals time better spent hunting those responsible."

He gave a terse nod. "Pull yourself together. You'll have your vengeance."

"Pull myself together?" Did he truly think I could forget the three friends I had lost and move on so easily? "Vengeance won't heal my pain."

"It will. You'll see."

"Doubtful." I pulled the tattered fabric around me, but it offered no more protection from cruel reality than it did from the room's biting chill.

He picked up a small pot from the fire. Then he mixed Katie's herbal remedy and the steaming water into a canteen. "You need to bring your body temperature up. Drink, and then we'll see what's been hiding in this temple." He handed the concoction to me.

Slowly, I sipped the medicine. Its heat thawed my frozen limbs. The steam soothed my nose and cheeks, which throbbed from the icy temperatures outside. Mallory settled back on the opposite side of the fire gnawing on a strip of dried meat as the light shone on the amulet poking through its grotesque weaving of flesh.

"How did you get the other half of Bryce's amulet?" I asked.

"Bryce's amulet? So it didn't belong to my cousin?"

"Baxter never even knew about it." No point in hiding the truth from him any longer. "I didn't tell you because I didn't trust you."

"Fair enough." He considered me, tapping his finger against his lips. "It's time I tell you about Samuel's past, but first, you need to tell me what you know about that boy."

Some sort of connection must have existed between him and Bryce. What if he was Bryce's father? He was in his late thirties, certainly old enough. Absurd! They neither looked nor acted anything alike.

"What does it matter to you?" I asked.

"It matters," he said.

Bowing my head, I closed my eyes to prevent another round of tears. "I met him in the forest the same day I met you. He was ill, but he risked his life every month to collect medicinal plants for the poor in the Slag. I thought that if we stopped the Culling, he might've had the chance to recover ... he didn't deserve ..." I covered my mouth, holding back sobs.

"Concentrate, girl."

I took a deep breath and then explained how Bryce had been abandoned at an orphanage with nothing but a blanket and the mysterious amulet. "He learned of its power by pure chance, and he eventually arrived at Black Valley after floods destroyed his home village."

"Hmm." Mallory leaned back, rubbing his chin.

"We were attacked by the Culling in the forest," I continued, "and he rescued me by bringing me to Black Valley. When we left, Baxter followed us. We didn't know until it was too late."

He made an irritated grunt at the sound of his cousin's name.

"I know you dislike Baxter, but he's a far better man than you give him credit for. I disliked him when we first met, but ..."

My cheeks warmed. I had grown fond of Baxter. Looking down, I fiddled with the matted threads along the fringe of the blanket. While half my heart longed for Bryce, the other half seemed to yearn for

Baxter. Clearly, cold and exhaustion had gotten to my brain. How could I care for two men so deeply at the same time? I cleared my throat.

"Two things puzzle me," I said. "First, I don't understand how Bryce disappeared in the ocean. The amulet is only supposed to transport people through waterfalls, and it was in my knapsack while we were on the bridge. And second, I can't explain how Baxter and I traveled through the waterfall without the amulet. It makes no sense."

"I can explain the latter." He pulled my compass out of his pocket.

"That's mine!" I lunged for it, but he jerked his hand out of my reach.

"Relax. I plan to return it."

Exhaling a nervous breath, I sat back on my heels.

Mallory held the compass to his nose, squinting at the horizontal ridges along the side of the casing. "I remember the day my father gave this gift to Samuel. That old tyrant loved puzzles."

"Puzzles? What does that have to do with my compass?"

"Patience, girl. I'll show you." He smirked with a knowing glint in his eye. "My father spent countless hours solving puzzles because he believed they kept his mind sharp. He needed to stay one step ahead of his enemies."

"Then he must have been solving puzzles all day, considering how many enemies he had," I said.

Mallory chuckled. "Believe it or not, he rose to power because he was charismatic, an effective manipulator. Even now, I'm sure he still has his share of supporters. My little cousin for example."

"Baxter didn't agree with your father's ways. He wanted to bring change to Black Valley. Peacefully."

"Peace?" Mallory laughed. "Only bloodshed can bring change to Black Valley."

"Well, if we stop the Culling and Black Valley still stands, someone must overthrow your father."

"Someone came close to overthrowing him a long time ago." Mallory held my compass up and tapped the inscription.

"Samuel?" My voice echoed in the huge room. "I knew it! I knew he never started a massacre! Your father made that story up to soil Samuel's reputation!"

"Don't be so quick with your assumptions, girl. I told you before that Samuel killed plenty of folks—my father's dogs and innocents alike."

"No, he would never do that."

"Do you want answers or not?"

"Go on," I said firmly.

The crackling of the fire filled a brief lull in our conversation.

"I was fifteen when droughts started withering far-off lands. For decades, Black Valley had been nothing more than an outpost for fur traders. But my father saw potential in the land and he developed it into a thriving city. Hordes of folks arrived seeking refuge, dreaming of a better life."

He wedged his fingernail into one of my compass's ridges and slid out a pin.

"You're going to break it!" I reached for my most treasured possession, but he closed his fist around it.

"I know what I'm doing."

"If you break it—"

"You'll what?" He raised an eyebrow. "I don't fear your claws, little kitten."

"Please, you know it's special to me."

"I'm about to make it a whole lot more special." He pinched the bottom of the casing, below the last ridge, and turned it.

I gasped. The ridges weren't engravings, but the spaces between multiple plates that could be shifted. "My compass is a puzzle?"

Mallory nodded as he continued to study the compass. I scooted closer.

"One day," he continued, "Sera strode into our city with eight young ladies in her company. Every man was in awe of her beauty, including my father. After a short courtship, they married. She was naïve, couldn't see past his false charm. A year later she was pregnant."

He shifted another plate, and two pins slid out of place. "The last few months of her pregnancy, he locked her in his estate with no other company than him and a handmaid. She loathed him for it. He frequently suffered bouts of paranoia and feared someone might steal her away. And someone did."

"Samuel?"

"No. Me."

"You?"

"Sera's eight young followers begged me to help her escape. They couldn't bear the thought of her trapped in my father's clutches."

I recalled the story Mallory told a few nights before that hinted of his lost love. "You couldn't say no to them, could you? Because you cared deeply for one of those women."

He stopped fiddling with my compass and glared at the fire, the light reflecting in his black eyes. With thick hatred resonating in his tone, he said, "It was a chance to spite my father. That was all the reason I needed."

He looked away from the flames and returned his attention to my compass. "When I snuck into Sera's chamber, she sat alone, weeping as she rubbed her swollen belly. Leaving all possessions behind except for a withered old book, she followed me through Gray Towers' secret passages until she stepped outdoors for the first time in three months."

"So Samuel didn't murder her?" I interrupted.

He shook his head. "She was murdered, but not by Samuel. Halfway through the Rose Quarter, we heard fighting. We didn't know that Samuel had planned a revolt that night. Dozens of Red Bands were charging toward the quarter's perimeter.

"Sera and I kept to obscure alleys, but we soon found ourselves in the middle of the slaughter. To make things worse, she went into labor. Fate, that wicked goddess, cursed us that day. It's her fault these things happened."

He clicked another plate into place.

"I did my best to quiet her, but two rebellion fighters spotted us. Bloodlust was in their eyes. They didn't care that I despised my father as much as they did. My words fell on deaf ears. I killed them quickly, but not before one drove a dagger into Sera's back."

I placed my hand to my mouth. "That poor woman."

"With the last of her strength, she removed an amulet she wore around her neck and slammed it against the cobblestone, breaking it in half. One half she gave to me, and she asked me to deliver the other to her true love." He twisted the top and bottom of my compass and the casing opened like a miniature chest. Inside lay a small shard that shimmered like ice.

Mallory returned the compass to me. "Bryce and I aren't the only waterfall travelers."

I picked up the shard, and strangely, the needle of my compass swung to point north as I separated the two. Sparkles of light traveled up and down the shard's length.

"Why does Samuel have a piece of the amulet hidden inside my compass?" I asked.

"Foolish girl, haven't you been paying attention? Samuel was her lover. They had been carrying on a secret affair for months. A little over nine months to be exact."

"Nine months? So the baby—"

"Was still moving beneath her dead flesh. I knew nothing about babies, but I thought I might be able to save the thing. So I took my dagger, made a few good guesses, and pulled a screaming boy from her womb. Tiny thing, he was. With hazel eyes that you've come to know quite well."

"Bryce," I whispered.

Mallory confirmed with a nod. "Samuel arrived shortly after that. He went hysterical as he looked upon his lover, cold as the cobblestones she lay upon. She still cradled the book in her arm, and Samuel picked it up. Opened it to a seemingly random page."

He paused for a moment, and I held my breath, waiting for him to continue.

"That book had a way of speaking to us. It promised to give life or death. I looked over Samuel's shoulder at the book, surprised that I could read the writing, even though the symbols were foreign to me. Understanding those passages was innate as breathing. I suspect that even an illiterate like you could have read from that book."

I tightened the blanket around me. "I could've learned to read if Samuel had taught me."

"Would you stop interrupting me?" He exhaled an irritated breath. "When Samuel read from the book, I thought he was trying to bring Sera back to life. But as he spoke the words, a dark energy emerged. It felt like something was pulling apart the threads of my flesh. And the baby screamed louder. So I rushed into a nearby shack hugging the child to my chest and waited for it all to end.

"When Samuel finally stopped chanting, the whole world went quiet, save for the wailing baby. I stepped outside and looked out of the alley. Dead men littered the square—mutilated in ways you couldn't fathom in your worst nightmares."

"Samuel would never have done that on purpose!" I shouted. "Obviously, he wanted to save Sera and that book fooled him."

"We'll never know for sure," he said in a solemn tone. "When Samuel found Sera dead, his heart raged. Vengeance rode in his eyes."

"No," I said, shaking my head. "I know Samuel. He wouldn't do that intentionally."

"Perhaps. Either way, Samuel and I couldn't stay in the alley. He was mumbling gibberish—the first signs of the Sickness—and that baby wouldn't quit its crying. We went into hiding. Sera had once explained the book to Samuel, and that night during his moments of clarity he shared those secrets with me. I thought we would work to cure him, but the next morning, I awoke and he was gone. Took the book and the baby with him. Figured he was long dead until the day I found you."

I set the empty canteen down and clutched the drape near my chest. "It's so sad. All of it."

"That's life for you. Our happy moments are merely the tangles in Fate's threads."

A week ago I might have disregarded such bitter sentiment, but at that moment nothing sounded truer.

"What happened to the eight ladies?"

His eyebrows twitched upward, as if he didn't expect such a question. He stared down at his clasped hands for a long moment. "I found them too late. Strung to the ceiling by their necks. Suicide. They left a note: 'We belong with Sera and the child.' They thought the baby had died with her. I left Black Valley after that, wandered for years ..."

"Oh, Mallory. I'm so sorry." I reached for his shoulder to offer comfort, but he waved me off with his palm.

"I don't want your pity."

I tucked my hand back under the fabric. Of course Mallory wouldn't want sympathy. Only one thing could give him peace: confronting Fate, the orchestrator of all his misery.

He tilted his head to the side. "Those Fireflies of yours ... Samuel said you started seeing them shortly after you settled in Red Ridge."

"That's correct."

"I have a theory as to what they are."

"Oh?" I raised an eyebrow.

"It's obvious, isn't it? They're the spirits of Sera's companions."

"What? That makes no sense. Why would they look after *me* all these years?"

"Mistaken identity. After their death they must've learned that Sera's baby had lived. They sought Samuel and finally found him years later caring for a little girl."

"They thought I was Sera's child ..."

The Fireflies suddenly appeared and hovered over Mallory's shoulders. They bobbed up and down as if nodding.

"I imagine at some point they figured out that you weren't who they were looking for," Mallory continued, "but by then they loved you too much and couldn't abandon you. So they remained, protected you, and shielded your village from the Culling. That's why your people have remained safe all these years. But the Fireflies have been fighting a long time, and the beasts are starving, desperate for food. It won't be long before those Nightmares sniff your village out."

The Fireflies continued to bob, as if confirming Mallory's story. Perhaps it was my imagination, but their amber light seemed fainter than when we set out on our journey.

"There're only seven Fireflies," I said. "Where is the eighth—" I gasped, recalling the lone Firefly in Black Valley that led me through the fence as that wretched guard pursued me. "I saw her."

Mallory narrowed his eyes. "You saw her? Where?"

"In Black Valley." But why would she remain there when the others left so long ago? Simple. She had to be the spirit of the girl Mallory loved. "What if she's been protecting Black Valley all these years from the Culling by herself? Waiting for your return?"

He shook his head. "I can't return until I kill Fate. My girl deserves retribution."

"You're being silly. You can't kill a goddess—"

"Watch me." He raised his voice. "Now do you want to know how to cure Samuel or not?"

There was no talking sense into him. "I do."

"Then you have to find that book and read from it. Only one person can carry the Sickness at a time."

"Only one person? So, to cure Samuel I must take the Sickness in his place?"

"Quite a conundrum, isn't it?"

I hugged my knees to my chest. Cursing myself with the Sickness meant that I would see horrifying visions for the rest of my life.

Eventually, my mind would wither away, as would the memories of those I held dear.

"I owe Samuel a cure," I said. "I'll do it."

Mallory leaned toward me. The salty scent of the ocean still lingered on him. "Girl, Samuel's forgotten about his days in Black Valley, Sera, and the massacre. If you cure him, those memories may come flooding back. I suspect they'll cause him a great deal of pain. Are you sure you want to make him face his past?"

"Face his past?"

"Yes, pay attention. Face his past."

Carter's Whisperer had promised that Baxter would make Samuel face his past. We misinterpreted the prediction. Baxter wasn't going to kill Samuel; he was going to cure him.

"I think your cousin has the book," I said.

"What gives you that idea?"

The Fireflies flew across the room to shine their light upon an iron door that looked identical to the one I saw through the frozen waterfall. Not only did Baxter have the book, but he was likely in this temple.

I shot up, legs still shaking from exhaustion. "It's a long story. We need to find Baxter before he reads from the book." I snatched my belt and dagger off the floor. "Let's go."

CHAPTER 36

As Mallory opened the iron door that complained with a rusty screech, a skin-prickling wind rushed into the room, carrying with it the scent of sleet. Shivering, I peered around Mallory's shoulder to see what lay beyond. An endless hallway stretched before us, lit only by slivers of light that fell from holes in the crumbled ceiling. Patches of snow covered the slate floor like scattered wool rugs, while the shredded remains of wall tapestries whipped in the gale.

The Fireflies whooshed down the hall and I squeezed past Mallory to follow. Snowflakes drifted from the damaged ceiling, melting into cool droplets on my cheeks. Above, a pale-pink sky illuminated the spaces between cracked tiles and splintered beams.

"It's dawn?" I spun around and smacked Mallory in the chest. "We're running out of time and you let me sleep until dawn?"

Mallory's eyebrows pushed low into the bridge of his nose. "You'll need your energy to get out of this place alive."

I craned my neck, glaring at him. "We have less than a day left to stop the Culling before Fate can meddle with our life-threads again."

He leaned closer. "Then quit your squawking and get moving."

"You're impossible." I turned around and trailed the Fireflies into the dim unknown. The tapestries fluttered in occasional gusts, brushing against my skin like spirits vying for attention. My stomach rolled. If I took on the Sickness to cure Samuel, actual spirits would torment me until my death. "Stop the Culling, worry about the Sickness later," I ordered myself under my breath.

Twenty feet ahead the Fireflies shifted downward and vanished. My heart stopped. They couldn't abandon us. I raced ahead kicking up snow. Mallory's heavy footfalls followed.

"Dammit, girl. Stop." He hooked his arm around my waist just as I pitched forward.

The tips of my shoes met the edge of a gaping hole in the floor. If not for Mallory's quick reflexes, I would have tumbled into its depths. He released me and I stepped back, regaining my balance. Below, the Fireflies swirled about in the blackness. I sighed with relief. They hadn't abandoned us.

"They want us to go down there." I knelt and peered into the abyss.

Mallory shoved his hand into my knapsack and rummaged around until he pulled out the small lantern. With two clicks of the knob, the wick flickered. He lowered the lantern toward the hole, and its golden light illuminated a stone floor eight feet below.

"Wait here." Mallory slid into the hole and landed with a thump. He swung the lantern to the right, and then the left. The halo of light brightened the brick walls and floor of a narrow corridor. He waved to me. "Come down."

I lowered myself into the hole and dropped to the ground. The thick scent of loam hung in the air. All was quiet, save the occasional drip of water droplets.

In one direction, uninterrupted darkness awaited. In the other, pale-blue light escaped from a room beyond an archway. The Fireflies chose that direction. As we hurried through the corridor, the lantern's glow drifted over fragments of bones and human skulls. Couldn't we receive a less ominous welcome for once? I maintained a steady pace. Hopefully, whatever beast stripped those bones of flesh had deserted this place long ago.

"Girl, if we find Death's book, I need your word that you won't curse yourself until after we find Oblivion."

I rolled my eyes. "Don't worry, I'll find your precious Oblivion."

He grabbed my shoulder and spun me around to face him. Deep shadows lingered in the hollows of his eyes. "I mean it. The first few days of the Sickness can turn even the bravest man into a hysterical mess. If Baxter already read from the book, he'll be in a far worse state than you've ever seen Samuel in. You might be tempted to take the Sickness in his place, but I need you to wait. Once you curse yourself, you won't be able to see the Fireflies through the hordes of spirits that'll haunt you."

I gnawed my lip. If the Sickness could break Baxter so easily, what chance would I have against its spell?

"All right," I said. "But as soon as we stand at Oblivion's edge, if we have the book, I'm taking the Sickness."

"We'll see." He motioned me to continue onward.

We arrived at the arched entry, and Mallory stepped into the room first. I trailed him.

"Oh my!" I swiveled around, taking it all in.

Strands of Starlight covered every inch of the massive chamber. The thin fibers sparkled, rivaling the beauty of frost webbed on a glass pane. Only hints of the stonework peeked through, revealing gold inlays of floral carvings.

Scattered throughout, five-foot-tall eggs budded in the plumes of iridescent threads. Their soft, transparent shells twitched with movements of life. I drew my dagger and approached one.

Inside the slimy shell, the dark silhouette of a Harbinger jerked about. It tucked its legs close to its chest and stomach, huddling in a fetal position. The lizard-like tail wrapped between its legs and over its shoulder. Its red eyes watched me, no doubt yearning to slice me limb from limb.

Shaking, I scanned the room. "There must be hundreds of them. We should kill them while we can." Angling my dagger, I aimed to plunge my blade into the egg.

Mallory grabbed my wrist. "There's a bigger battle to be fought. If we waste time here, then we risk losing the element of surprise."

"Fair point."

He watched me sheath my weapon. "These Harbingers will be more ferocious than any you've encountered before. They're too young to cocoon and they'll be eager to experience their first human kill."

My insides quivered at his words.

The Fireflies flew straight ahead toward a dark passage.

"Through that corridor." I pointed.

Mallory picked up a two-foot-long wooden beam along the way and handed me the lantern. He then ripped a clump of Starlight from the ground and wrapped it around the end of the beam, crafting a makeshift torch.

"Save the oil," he ordered.

I clicked the lantern's knob and repacked it into my knapsack. We navigated the twists of the narrow passage, but Mallory's tall frame blocked my view of what lay ahead. I continuously tried to peek around him to no avail. Finally, I gave up and watched his billowing cloak dust the slate floor.

He stopped short and I bumped into him. After an irritated shake of his head, he stepped aside. "Intersection. Which way?"

The Fireflies hovered in the center of the crossing, refusing to budge.

"I'm not sure. They stopped."

"Stopped? Well, tell them to get moving."

"It doesn't work like that. There must be something here. Something they want us to find."

Mallory waved the torch around, but nothing lay on the ground except for crumbled debris. We searched for a few moments until footfalls came from the passage branching off to our left. Whoever—or whatever—they belonged to was hurrying in our direction. Mallory swung his torch toward the passage and drew his sword.

"Baxter?" someone called. "Is that you?"

My heart jolted at the sound of the familiar voice.

"Bryce?" I shouted.

"Ri?" he yelled back. His tone reached a hopeful pitch. "Ri?"

I turned the corner, racing toward Bryce in the darkness. A second later, I fell into his arms. His warmth surrounded me as he pressed his soft lips against the crown of my head.

"You're alive, you're alive," I repeated, babbling though sobs and laughter. Nuzzling my face below his chin, I grasped him tighter, as if he might flitter away if I didn't. I breathed him in—his pleasant scent of sea and forest filling me.

"How's this possible?" I patted the area where his stab wound had been, feeling nothing but solid muscle beneath his shirt.

"It was Baxter," he rambled. "I know this will sound unbelievable—but somehow he healed me. Even my lungs, Ri. It's a miracle."

I placed my palms upon his chest. It rose and fell as calmly as ripples in a lake. No raspy sound. No wheezing.

I hugged him once more, savoring the sound of his soft breath flowing out each time he exhaled. But the moment was bittersweet—a cruel joke played on us by Fate. There was only one way Baxter could have healed Bryce: he read from the book.

I closed my eyes and swallowed hard. "Where's Baxter now?"

"He went hysterical and ran off. I've been searching these tunnels for him for hours."

"This is bad." Panic tightened my throat as an image of Harbingers shredding through Baxter's flesh crawled through my mind. "Baxter inflicted a curse on himself and he won't survive on his own."

"So my cousin has the Sickness." Mallory approached from behind and the blue torchlight fell upon Bryce's face. Bryce immediately turned his head, raising his forearm to block his eyes. Though Bryce had been touched by Death's magic, the Starlight's effect on him was proof that he still had a soul, unlike me.

I gestured for Mallory to lower the torch and quickly told him what Bryce had told me.

Mallory grunted. "You better not go back on your word, girl."

"I won't," I snapped. Baxter was cursed, but all Mallory cared about was reaching Oblivion. Heartless monster.

"You made a deal with the tyrant's son?" Bryce glowered at Mallory, leaning forward with balled fists. "He can't be trusted, Ri."

"Trusted?" Mallory smirked. "I've done a better job looking after your girl than you have."

Bryce opened his mouth to fire back, but I placed my hands on his shoulders and eased him away.

"Stop," I ordered. "We don't have time for this. I can't lose another friend to the Culling."

"*Another* friend?" Bryce's eyes went wide as he attempted to look behind Mallory. "Where's Carter?"

"He ..." I lowered my gaze, unable to get another word out. I could still feel the warmth of Carter's blood against my palms. And I could still see his green irises, dull beneath the shine of his tears.

Bryce gaped at me and then vehemently shook his head. "No. His Whisperer should've kept him safe. I promised Katie that I'd find him ... that I'd bring him home."

I placed my hand on his. "He sacrificed himself so we would have a chance to defeat the Culling," I said with shaking voice. We had to keep going, keep fighting. But each time the memory of Carter's death surfaced in my mind, I felt sadness wrap around me, draining my strength. With a deep breath, I pushed its imaginary binds away. "We can mourn later. If we slow down now, his sacrifice will be for nothing."

Bryce dragged his palms down his face. "I should've been kinder to him," he whispered. "I was always so judgmental."

I rubbed his arm. "Don't be so hard on yourself. He never thought you were unkind. You were his closest friend."

He nodded, though his downcast gaze suggested my words brought him little comfort.

"Kill the Culling. Protect his sister," Mallory broke in. "That will give his spirit peace."

Bryce set his jaw and offered a terse nod. "I can't believe I'm going to fight alongside Renselar's son."

"Few men are given the privilege." Mallory smirked.

The Fireflies reappeared and sped past us down the corridor. Bryce stumbled out of their way.

"Did you see that?" He turned and gawked at where they hovered at another intersection.

"They're our guides," I explained. Since Bryce had been touched by Death's magic, he could now see otherworldly beings like I could. I had so much to tell him, but it would have to wait until after we found Baxter. I hurried after the Fireflies and waved my companions to follow.

"There's something else I have to tell you," Bryce shouted over our footfalls. "The woman I heard on the bridge is in this temple. I think she summoned me here to help me, but Baxter beat her to it."

Normally I'd doubt that a random woman was holed up in a frozen temple, but after all I had witnessed during the last few days, little could surprise me.

"Where is she now?" I asked.

"In the room where I arrived, bound in those glittering threads. I think she's being held captive. I would've helped her if Baxter hadn't run off, but I had to go after him first. I feel awful just leaving her there …"

"Don't worry," I said. "Once we find Baxter, we'll save her too."

The Fireflies paused at another intersection and then darted from the entrance of one passage to the other.

"I think they're lost," I said.

Mallory cursed under his breath. I peered down one of the corridors. Nothing but darkness.

Then a chorus of chanting voices rose in the passage closest to me. My limbs locked up at the sound of the chilling melody. Dozens of red eyes appeared in the darkness, rushing toward us. More voices joined in from the remaining passages. Harbingers.

"This way." Mallory drew his sword and charged down the passage ahead.

Bryce and I followed, quickly sliding our daggers from their sheaths. My mouth dried as panicked breath raced in and out of my lungs. Images of the slaughtered guards in the Abandoned Quarter flashed through my mind: tangled cords of intestines spilling out of shredded flesh, the bitter scent of blood lingering on the frigid wind, the crimson slush that surrounded the dead.

We crashed into a pack head on. Mallory tossed the torch on the ground and pierced the first beast through the neck. He pulled his sword free with a spurt of blood and then thrust it through the skull of another. From behind came another pack. Trapped.

My legs tensed as one leapt toward my neck. I crouched and blindly drove my dagger forward. A shock rippled up my arm. The Harbinger landed on all fours, its razor-sharp claws scraping against the stone floor. Limping, it lunged at me again with strings of drool spewing from its curled lips. I spun around and its jaw latched onto my knapsack.

I fell to my knees and choked on dust. Wind whipped over my head as another beast slashed at the first. I ducked as the two Harbingers fought over which one got to kill me. Blood misted down, dampening my skin and clothes.

I scrambled away from them and glanced at my companions. Two snapping beasts had Bryce against the wall. The blue glow of the Starlight illuminated a stream of blood flowing down his face.

"Girl, you all right?" Mallory thrust his blade toward the beasts ahead and then pivoted to strike one of the monsters pinning Bryce.

His sword pierced through the Harbinger's stomach. The beast fell backward, crimson spraying from its wound.

"Yes," I called. My voice hardly carried over the racket of steel clashing against armored flesh.

Another beast lunged at Bryce. He fended off the first, his dagger waving wildly. I dove in, my grip tight as I shoved my blade into the newcomer's neck. The monster whipped its head in my direction, and my dagger slid from my sweaty palm.

I stumbled over a pile of bones. I landed hard on my back, and the knapsack dug into my flesh. With the kill in sight, the beast growled and pounced on top of me, but I grabbed a thick bone and knocked it across the head. The bone cracked in half, sprinkling the air with white dust that clung to my sweaty skin. The snarling beast shook its head and snapped at me. I rolled. The heat of its breath brushed against me as it chomped its jaw inches from my neck. Its weight pinned me against the ground. I reached for my dagger that was still lodged in the side of its neck. Claws raked across my upper arm. I screamed. The heat of blood gushed over my skin. I scrambled for another bone and jabbed it forward. Its knobbed end slid into the hole in the beast's throat. The Harbinger reeled back, gagging.

I scooted backward into a narrow crevice. The beast slammed against the wall, unable to fit inside. It slashed at me, but its reach was mere inches too short. Its red eyes gleamed with mad desperation and renewed fury. Each time it snorted, saliva flew from its fangs and laced my flesh with sludge.

No weapon. I had no weapon.

"Mallory!" I shouted.

No answer.

I pressed myself against the rear of the crevice. My hand fell upon a loose brick. I ripped it from the wall. A good, solid weapon. I drew a breath and met the beast's bloodthirsty red eyes. Its fangs gnashed at the air in front of me. I clutched the brick tightly and swung. A sickening crack echoed on impact. The beast slumped to the ground, still swatting at me with slow and uncoordinated strikes. I slammed the stone against its skull again. A mist of blood showered me. The creature whimpered.

Again: for Carter. Bone crumbled from my blow. The Harbinger twitched at my feet. Again: for my parents. Again: for the cocooned victims. The beast stopped moving. Blood soaked my hand. Red warmth ran down my fingers. This was vengeance. This was justice. Again. Again. Again. Until I finally hurled the stone at the mottled heap of flesh, skull, and brain at my feet.

Exhausted, I tugged my dagger out of the Harbinger's neck and slumped against the wall. An acrid scent like salt and bile filled the air. My hands were shaking. My ears humming. I couldn't stop trembling.

The torch went out. Pitch black. The sounds of Mallory and Bryce fighting continued.

Quickly, I shoved the rancid, brain-covered carcass out of my way and staggered out of the crevice. Four of the Fireflies zoomed past me, urging me away from the battle toward the quiet end of the corridor.

"Mallory!" I called. "Bryce!"

Their footfalls hurried toward me.

"Go!" Bryce said. "Go, go, go!"

I raced after the Fireflies through corridors so dark all I could see was their amber glow. They turned right, and I let out a whimper as I bumped my injured arm against the wall in my rush to follow. My head was still spinning from the loss of blood, and dots speckled my vision, mingling with the Fireflies' light. I tripped. Got back up. Tripped again. My knees landed against an angled edge. I patted the floor. Stairs.

"Careful," I called to the others. "There's a staircase."

Crawling, I made my way up. After reaching the top of the short flight of steps, I gulped down breaths, listening for my companions. Nothing.

"Bryce?" I said.

A few dozen feet away, someone mumbled. I removed my knapsack and rummaged inside until I felt the lantern. I pulled it out and after two clicks a circle of light surrounded me. It shined upon a dusty tiled floor and four pillars positioned in each corner of a large room. Chipped motifs of fish leaping over waves crowned the top of the archway above the staircase. Neither Bryce nor Mallory were anywhere in sight.

My stomach somersaulted. I located the herbal remedy in the knapsack and slathered it on as I hurried toward the archway. A voice drew my attention toward a crevice that zigzagged up the wall opposite the stairs.

"Hello?" I said.

More mumbling. I slipped into the crevice. A few feet ahead, Baxter sat on the floor with knees pulled up to his chest. With his gaze planted on the ground, he rocked back and forth clamping his hands over his ears. A worn leather-bound book lay beside him.

"Not real, not real, not real," he repeated over and over. The lantern light reflected off beads of sweat on his forehead.

"Oh, Baxter," I said with a gasp. Mallory warned me that the Sickness's torment would cripple even the strongest of men.

I sunk to the floor and set the lantern down. "Snap out of it." I touched his knee, but he shoved me away so hard that my back slammed against the wall.

"You're not real!" he yelled through a growl. Then he looked down, clawing at his cheeks. He shook with sobs so ferocious that I imagined his bones shifting within him. "I want you to be real. I want you to be real. Ri, please come back."

I crawled toward him. "I'm real. I'm right here." I gently lifted his chin and brought his eyes to meet mine. "Look at me, nothing else."

He shook his head. "I can't. They're so loud. They slaughter my family over and over." He choked for breath. "I'm reliving the riots, Ri. I can't help my mother. And I can't help you. They tear off your limbs, slice you in half until all I can see is your innards. I can't stop it."

"Listen," I said. "You're seeing spirits, and what they show you isn't real. They can't harm you. And they can't harm me."

He squeezed his eyes shut and dug at his scalp. "Stop saying that! Don't hurt her, please, don't hurt her."

I cupped his clammy face in my hands. "Please, open your eyes and look at me. You can block them. You need to concentrate."

He interlaced his calloused fingers with mine. His palms were soaked with tears. "The book," he nodded toward it, "it promised to save Bryce's life. I found it near this strange woman and did what it told me to do. But now I don't feel right, Ri. I don't feel right." He opened his eyes, trembling. "What do I do? How do I make it stop?"

The desperation in his voice gutted me. I swallowed hard and stiffened my lip. I could cure him that instant. The book, with its weathered pages and cracked leather cover, begged me to pick it up. Flip to a random page. Read a few words. Baxter's torment would end and mine would begin. I wiggled one of my hands free from his grasp and traced the book's spine with my fingertips.

"I can help you." I opened the cover. A biting chill rushed through my fingers and up the length of my arm. Samuel had never taught me to read, but I understood the symbols, just as Mallory said I would.

Baxter clasped my hand and brought it to his cheek. The book flopped closed. "No, leave it be. Leave it be."

Leave it be? He was suffering. It was my responsibility to cure Samuel and carry the Sickness. Not his. But I had also made a promise to Mallory.

"All right." I would leave the book alone. For now. I leaned closer to him, feeling the faint warmth of his body heat against me. "I'm going to help you. I won't rest until I do. But right now, I need you to pull yourself together."

He clasped my head, tangling his fingers in my hair. I didn't pull away. It was his way of climbing out of the Sickness's torturous depths and returning to reality. The last of his tears fell with a blink.

"Good," I said. "Concentrate on me and the spirits will vanish."

He bobbed his head, leaning in so close that only a sliver of air separated our faces. "Look at Ri. Look at Ri." He repeated the words a few times, his breath brushing against my lips.

He kissed me.

What was he thinking? I pressed my palms against his chest and pushed him away. He released me and for a long moment we stared at each other, breathless.

"I'm sorry," he said, averting his gaze. "This condition," he pointed to his temple, "it leaves me with no self-control."

"No, I um …" I waved my hand, dismissing his apology. A strange but pleasant heat burned through my veins. "It's all right."

"I've complicated things." He moved closer and traced my jaw with his fingertips. My skin tingled from the touch. "But I don't care. I feel something for you. I know you feel something for me too."

I flinched away from him. The world was spinning. "I don't know. I don't know what I feel. I just want to stop the Culling and go home. I can't do this now."

"Girl?" Mallory called. His footfalls echoed in the large room outside of the crevice.

I cleared my throat. "I found Baxter. Are you all right?"

"We're fine," Bryce called back.

I exhaled with relief and then gathered the lantern and the book. "We need to go," I said to Baxter. Without waiting for his response, I spun around and headed toward the crevice's exit. When I emerged, Mallory and Bryce were already rushing toward me.

Bryce gripped my shoulders, looking me over. Smudges of dried blood and dirt covered his cheeks. "Are you hurt?"

"No, just a little shook up."

"You look a bit red in the cheeks to me," Mallory said as Baxter joined us.

My face burned. Was he implying that he suspected that Baxter and I had kissed? How could he have known?

"I'm merely flushed from all the running," I said.

"Well, we're all together now," Bryce said. "Things are starting to go in our favor." He approached Baxter and patted his shoulder. "How are you feeling?"

Baxter shrugged nonchalantly and in a calm, monotone voice replied, "I could use something to plug my ears. Spirits make loud, obnoxious company."

Bryce smiled sympathetically. Perhaps Baxter's tough demeanor fooled him, but not me. Every few seconds, his pupils slid to the right, no doubt watching for ghouls the rest of us were blind to. He would fall apart again. It was only a matter of time.

While the two of them talked, Mallory leaned close to my ear and whispered, "You'll only know misery if you fall for a Renselar."

"You don't know anything." I jerked away from him, inviting curious looks from both Baxter and Bryce.

"I know plenty." Mallory smirked. "Which way?"

I glanced over the room. Three side-by-side arched passages occupied the wall to our left. A pile of crumbled stone lay in front of the first, while the other two offered nothing but darkness. The Fireflies whooshed over the heap of stone, diving into the cramped opening of the first passage.

Just my luck. How I hated tight spaces. I inhaled a calming breath and marched on with my companions close behind.

Mallory took the lantern from me and placed the metal handle between his teeth. He lunged up the stone pile, climbing until he disappeared into the passage. Baxter clambered through next.

Without the lantern light, all went dark. The faint sound of more chanting came from the direction of the archway. More Harbingers would arrive within seconds.

"Hurry." Bryce placed his hand on my lower back, guiding me toward the stone pile. "I'm right behind you."

Patting around, I grabbed an outcropping of stone and anchored my foot onto another. I crawled up and squeezed through the tight passage. Mallory and Baxter waited on the other side, standing at the bottom of the pile. I slid down the graveled heap to join them.

"More Harbingers are coming," I said.

Bryce descended the stone pile. "Go, they're on us!" he urged.

From the other side of the stone pile came the sound of digging. Within seconds the beasts would widen the gap enough to pursue. Both Mallory and Baxter drew their swords.

"You three, go." Mallory shoved the lantern into my hands and took the rear.

With Baxter leading, we rushed down a lengthy corridor. Bryce lagged far behind, dragging his leg.

"Are you hurt?" I asked.

"One of the darts hit me," he said through clenched teeth. "My whole leg is numb."

Without slowing his stride, Baxter glanced at the two of us. "The poison from a young Harbinger isn't strong. You'll remain conscious, but you'll probably lose the use of that leg for a few hours."

"A few hours?" Out of the question. "We don't have hours. If Mallory doesn't hold them back, that pack will be on us in no time."

The corridor led to another large room. At the far end, a closed double door rose twenty feet high. Intricate carvings of trees and birds adorned its mahogany panels. The Fireflies hovered near its two iron handles, both shaped like puma heads.

"Through there." Baxter dashed ahead and pushed the door open, leaning all his weight against it.

Its hinges screeched, shedding flakes of ice. Once the door was opened a few feet, cold wind and blue light slipped in. Bryce and I hobbled across the room as the sound of footfalls came from behind.

"Go, go, go!" Mallory's voice boomed out of the corridor.

I glanced over my shoulder as he entered the room. Scratches marred his face and hands, and blood tinted his shredded shirt. He took Bryce's opposite arm, hooked it over his shoulder, and dragged us through the door. Once the three of us were through, Baxter followed and we shoved the door shut. Claws raked against the mahogany from the opposite side.

Keeping our backs pressed against the door, we scanned the room. A rug of Starlight sprawled before us, climbing up the walls to the domed ceiling above. Thirty feet across from us, an archway opened to the snowy terrain outside. Wisps of powder blew into the temple, coating the strands of Starlight in sparkling frost. Collectors shot from the sky in branches of silver light.

Along the wall parallel to us, a short staircase led to a platform. At the top, a woman was cocooned to the wall by Starlight. Her arms were spread out alongside her at shoulder level, but her hands dangled limp. Slivers of flesh and strands of hair poked through the glistening fibers.

More thuds came from the opposite side of the door.

"There's too many," Mallory said. Sweat rolled down his forehead.

Mallory, the most fearless man I'd ever met, was admitting to a battle he couldn't win.

CHAPTER 37

I grabbed an iron crossbar off the ground and pushed it through the door's brackets. For good measure, Mallory and Bryce held their backs to the door. Even then, the force of the beasts' repeated slamming shoved them forward with each assault. Cords of muscle tensed in their necks and arms. My legs trembled as I imagined the horde of Harbingers busting into the chamber and shredding our skin with razor-sharp claws.

"Not real." Baxter sunk to the ground gripping his head as if it might burst. He squeezed his eyes shut. "Not real, not real, not real."

Dammit, the Sickness had the worst timing.

I squatted in front of him and clasped his cheeks, guiding him to look at me. "Come on Baxter, not now." I forced myself to speak calmly even as my breath came in frantic gasps. "Snap out of it."

"Ri?" He opened one eye to peek at me.

"Yes, yes, it's me." I tugged his arm. "Get up, we have to run."

He jerked away and curled into a fetal position. "Nowhere to run. Nowhere to run."

I glanced at the arched door that led outside. Dozens of Collectors filled the clouds with monstrous rumbles and flashes of light. One after the next, silver streaks shot down from the heavens and struck the ground, casting sparks into the air.

"We're trapped," Baxter continued. "The spirits are taunting me. I hear their voices. All that lies outside is Oblivion."

"Did you say Oblivion?" I looked at Mallory, who was still backed against the door. He glanced at me and then glared at the temple's exit. I could see a plan forming in his eyes. I expected him to bolt toward Oblivion without a second thought for the rest of us. Instead, he hooked Bryce's arm over his shoulder and hauled him toward me.

"Girl, get my cousin on his feet."

"I'm trying," I snapped. Once again I yanked Baxter's arm. "Get up! There has to be another way out."

He shoved me away.

Dammit!

I swiveled around to search the chamber once more. Nearby, a narrow crevice ran up the temple's crumbling wall. I raced into it, but met a dead end within ten feet. I cursed under my breath and hurried back to my companions.

"No other way!" Baxter hugged himself tighter, rounding his shoulders over his chest. "Carter says so himself."

"Carter?" My heart made a hard thump. "What are you talking about?"

"His spirit." Baxter fixed his half-mad gaze on an area to my left.

I gulped down a breath as I imagined Carter's spirit drifting alongside me amongst all the malicious ghouls. A loud thud hammered the door.

Bryce grabbed Baxter's arm. "We can't stay here. We'll have to take our chances with Oblivion."

"Wait." I clasped Baxter's face between my palms and looked him in the eye. If he could see Carter's spirit, it meant that Carter turned down his only chance to enter the Violet Star's light. Surely he did this for a reason: to help us stop the Culling. "What else does Carter tell you?"

"The Collectors ..." Baxter clawed at his head, digging bloody scratches into his scalp. "Carter says they can't harm you or Bryce. They're forbidden to take those touched by their master's magic."

"Collectors?" Bryce raised his eyebrows. "What's he talking about?"

"Lightning," I explained.

Baxter shut his eyes and began hyperventilating.

I clutched his shoulder. "No!" I shouted. "What else does Carter say? There must be more."

"Starve them, starve them, starve them." He buried his face in his palms and rocked back and forth. I pulled his arm, but he refused to budge.

A Harbinger busted a melon-sized hole through the door and shoved its head through the opening. Mucus dripped from its flaring nostrils. Mallory thrust his sword at the beast, forcing it back.

Bryce yanked me away from Baxter. "Ri, if the Collectors can't harm us, we may be able to shield the others. You and Mallory keep going, and I'll stay with Baxter until he's ready."

"You seriously want me to run into Oblivion without you?"

His eyes widened. "Would you rather stay here and be mauled to death?"

A claw smashed through the door. Dust and splinters flew through the air. Mallory impaled the beast's palm with a quick thrust of his weapon. Bryce tugged Baxter's arm again, but Baxter curled further inward, trembling.

"How can we run and just leave you and Baxter like this?" I yanked Baxter's opposite arm, but he was still struggling against whatever it was only he could see.

"Ri, please just run." Bryce wobbled, struggling to maintain balance on his injured leg. "Go with Mallory. Baxter and I will only slow you down."

"No, I'm not deserting either of you."

An unfamiliar voice called out, "I can help." Startled, we looked up at the woman cocooned in the Starlight. She strained against her iridescent shroud. "Cut me free."

Bryce and I spun toward her as Mallory continued to pierce the claws and snouts shoving through the damaged door. He could only fight so many. We needed the woman's help—whoever she was.

I broke away from Bryce and dashed toward her. The Fireflies swooped down from above and glided alongside me, casting a shimmering glow upon the surrounding Starlight.

"No, Ri!" Bryce called after me. His voice rose, high and panicked. "There's no time. You have to get out of here."

"Not without you and Baxter," I called over my shoulder. My breath came in short spurts as I raced through frozen Starlight that covered the floor like brambles. The strands crackled apart like fragile glass, disintegrating into a fog of crystalline dust.

Once I reached the platform, I drew my dagger and ascended the half-dozen steps. A collection of treasures lay at the woman's feet—gold tableware, jewels, and coins. I maneuvered around the heap and ripped away the mask of Starlight covering her face.

Her eyelids fluttered open as she lifted her head, revealing her milky-filmed, hazel irises. Wrinkles crisscrossed her skin like cracks in dried mud. Her hair hung in limp tangles that merged with the strands of Starlight encasing her.

Poor woman. I grabbed a clump of Starlight near her arm and sliced through it. She winced as if I had harmed her.

"Are you all right?"

"Keep cutting," she ordered through clenched teeth. Her voice was dry, like the sound of autumn's last leaves scraping across the forest floor.

Grabbing more Starlight, I sawed through the fibers. They immediately grew back, snaking around her arm thicker than before. Sweat formed on my brow as I tried again. But the fibers were sprouting in all directions, reclaiming their captive.

The woman cursed and tilted her head upward. At that angle, the curve of her lips and the slight slant of her eyes seemed familiar. So familiar. Her wrinkled skin stretched over prominent cheekbones, a small nose, and a pronounced jawline. Her features were hard—hard as those of a stone statue.

My jaw went slack. "Impossible."

Unease skittered through me, just as it had the night I stood amongst the carnage in the Abandoned Quarter staring into the blank eyes of Sera's memorial.

"You're Sera." I stepped back. It was her. It was definitely her. *The* Sera. The tyrant's wife. Samuel's lover. Bryce's mother.

She jerked her frail arm forward, attempting to free it from her binds. When only a few fibers snapped apart, she stopped struggling and looked at me. She offered a tight smile that didn't crinkle her eyes and said, "Dear girl, don't you recognize a goddess when you see one?"

"Fate?"

"How dare you mistake me for the repulsive hag," she spat. Then, sweetening her voice, she added, "No dear, I am Eisanea. Please, keep cutting your goddess free."

A hard feeling formed in my gut. Something wasn't right. "You're her, I know you're her."

Her lips pressed together. "I loved humanity so much that I masqueraded as a human for a mere minute of my existence. A mistake I've paid for! Now cut me free and bring me to my son. I've spent nearly two decades trying to bring him here."

Claws scraped against the door. A quake of anxiety rippled through me.

"Hurry," she shouted.

Quickly, I tore away the Starlight shrouding her chest, hurling wad after wad onto the ground. The Fireflies returned, spinning around my hand as if caught in a whirlwind. Their amber light reflected in her milky eyes.

"I hear my priestesses." She tilted her ear in their direction.

"Your priestesses?" My glowing companions continued their erratic flight.

Her mouth arched downward as if she had tasted something sour. "Their spirits. Servants eager to follow me into the afterlife. They committed suicide believing a mere human could kill me."

Another whack on the door. No time to ask questions.

"Hmm, it seems Priestess Justice is missing," she mused, the corner of her mouth tilting upward.

I ripped another clump of Starlight from her chest. The Fireflies swirled around me, their energy zapping my hands with static sparks. Each snap upon my skin sounded like the word "Stop."

Why were they protesting the rescue of their goddess? Hadn't they led me here to save her? I staggered back, heeding their warning. Eisanea writhed, and a large clump of Starlight fell from her front side. Instead of a heart, a tightly woven ball of Starlight resided in a hole in her chest. The ball expanded and collapsed, beating in rhythm to the pounding on the door. Each time the strange heart thumped, fresh Starlight sprouted out of it.

A bitter taste rose into my throat.

"Black Valley's tyrant cut out my heart," she explained. "I made a better one." She gazed at the door with her foggy eyes. "Hurry. There's not much time."

"Ri, stop!" Baxter stuttered, his voice more panicked than before. He knelt on the ground clasping Bryce by the wrist. "That heart … it's her hatred. She's no longer Eisanea … she's wrath … vengeance … spite!"

Given the distance, he couldn't have heard the conversation. Surely, that warning came from Carter.

Starlight continued to sprout from her heart, covering her chest and stomach. A single Firefly separated from the others and drew my attention to the treasures at her feet. Scratches marred their gleaming surfaces, and Harbinger tracks littered the dusty ground surrounding them. Had the beasts brought these treasures to her as gifts?

"Don't listen to him. Cut me loose!" The tendons in her neck bulged as she writhed in her binds.

I shook my head. How could this be possible? She was a goddess. I stepped back once more, heart thudding as a horrible thought occurred to me. "You're not the Culling's prisoner, you're its creator."

"Born of my tears, nourished by my hatred." She raised her chin, and a proud glimmer shone through her clouded eyes. "That tyrant still has my heart caged in a cold statue." She seized a clump of Starlight covering her stomach and clawed it away, revealing another hole. "And his son stole my child. Cut him right out of my womb."

"No, he saved your son's life," I said.

She released a sharp laugh that cut through the chamber. "Oh, the cruel things that tyrant did to me. I deserved better. So much better. But they'll pay. I'm coming for them, destroying one city at a time. Let that tyrant see what I can do. Let him stew in fear."

"You've gone mad. The Culling killed thousands of innocent people." I needed to hear her express remorse. For Carter. For my parents.

She smiled. "All of my children need to eat."

My mouth moved, trying to find words. Baxter was right. Without her heart—her true heart—she had transformed into a monster. She was no longer Eisanea. Or Sera. My hand clenched my dagger so tightly that my palm burned.

Footfalls echoed up the steps. Mallory grabbed my arm. "We have to go, now."

Eisanea's head jerked from side to side, her blind eyes searching. "Is that Renselar blood I smell?"

"It is," I answered coolly.

She writhed frantically. "Cut me free, cut me free, cut me free!"

"You've become a prisoner of your own hatred," I said. "Of your own obsession with vengeance." Turning to Mallory, I added, "I found the source of the Culling."

"Renselar filth!" She shouted, crimson creeping up her neck and into her cheeks. "My children will see you both dead! Dead! Dead!"

Without warning, Mallory lunged past me, cloak rippling behind.

Eisanea squirmed like a fly tangled in a web. "No!"

Mallory thrust his sword, driving the blade into her luminous, vengeful heart. She arched her back and belted out a skull-piercing shriek. A flurry of sparks burst from her chest and shimmered up the steel of Mallory's weapon. He pulled his sword out of her as her scream weakened.

Releasing one last breath, she slumped forward. Her heart withered into a dull skein of dead Starlight. Meanwhile, the threads surrounding her flickered and then dimmed until the strands looked like nothing more than dirty cotton. Within a few seconds, every strand of Starlight in the temple paled.

CHAPTER 38

I swallowed a lump. If I ever regained my soul, it'd likely be damned after this. Mallory grabbed my wrist and dragged me away from the crumpled corpse.

Stumbling after him, I looked over my shoulder unable to pry my gaze from the slain goddess. I feared her heart would re-ignite at any moment and drench the temple in its cool, white glow. She would throw her head back, laughing through a wolfish grin that would inspire fresh rage in her Harbingers.

But by the time we reached the base of the platform, Eisanea still hadn't stirred. Her waist-length hair swayed from the breeze blowing in from outside. Other than that, she was quiet as a forest after snowfall.

Another tug came from Mallory. Instead of heading toward Bryce and Baxter, he pulled me toward the temple's exit.

"Where are you going?" I asked, digging my heels into the ground.

Bryce sat with his half-paralyzed leg sprawled before him. He shook Baxter's shoulders and shouted at him, but Baxter continued to rock back and forth hugging himself. The door shuddered and splintered each time the Harbingers rammed against it.

"I kept my word," Mallory said. "Now it's time for you to keep yours. You owe me Oblivion."

"And I've led you to it!" I wiggled my wrist, but his grip was tight enough to cut off circulation to my hand. "Let me go, I'm not leaving them behind."

"They're fodder and I need you as a shield," he shouted. "The Collectors can't strike me without striking you too."

"Let go, you heartless monster." I bit his hand. The taste of dried venison—the last thing he must have eaten—assaulted my mouth.

His fingers splayed open. "Dammit, girl!"

I ran, but he chased close behind. Withered Starlight crunched under his boots. His fingers brushed against my back as he attempted to grab me. I sped up and the sound of his footfalls faded.

Ahead, Bryce had moved to the door. He stabbed at the claws and fang-filled mouths shoving through the busted panels. His eyes bulged when he noticed me running toward him. "No, Ri!" he screamed. "You have to get out of here."

"I already said I'm not deserting either of you." I crouched next to Baxter and lowered my gaze to meet his. "Baxter, I need you on your feet."

An explosion of splinters shot from the door as a Harbinger rammed its head through a panel. With the beast's body unable to squeeze through, Bryce thrust his dagger at its thrashing nose. He withdrew his weapon, and a claw raked his chest. He jerked back. A large crimson stain spread across his shredded shirt.

I shook Baxter. He kept muttering. Mallory's footfalls approached. Dammit. I couldn't let him drag me away again.

I cupped Baxter's shoulders and lowered my eyes to his. He stopped muttering. His pupils dilated.

"Good, good," I said with relieved breath. "Come on, Baxter. Get up."

He started rambling again, as if unaware of me.

"No, no, no." I shook him. "Please, Baxter. Ignore the spirits. You can do it."

From behind, Mallory grabbed my arm and hauled me to my feet.

"Let go." I clawed out of his grasp. My eyes burned with tears. "I'm not leaving them. You're better than this, Mallory. I know you are."

"Ri, go with him," Bryce said, bracing my shoulders. "Get somewhere safe. Baxter would want you to run too."

Shaking my head, I stared at Baxter through tear-blurry vision. If only he would snap out of it.

"The book," Baxter shouted. "They want the book to resurrect their creator."

The book. That was it. Why hadn't I thought of it sooner?

I slid my knapsack off my back and removed the book. "I can kill the Harbingers. Every last one of them."

Mallory looked at the worn volume of yellowed pages.

Bryce alternated glances between us, his mouth agape. "What's she talking about?"

"Hmm ..." The clever glint in Mallory's eyes suggested that he understood my intentions. The book gave life, but it took life too.

"Mallory, what's she talking about?" Bryce repeated, but then closed his eyes and waved his hands. "It doesn't matter. Just get her out of here. Now."

One of the door's hinges broke free and clattered to the ground.

Pushing down my fear, I rattled off my plan to Mallory. "You'll have to get Bryce and Baxter out of earshot, or the spell will kill them too. Bryce can be your shield against the Collectors. Take them as far away as possible before you cross into Oblivion."

"No." Bryce shook his head and then shoved me into Mallory. "Get her out of here."

Mallory stared down at me. "There are over a hundred Harbingers on the other side of that door. You'll kill yourself conjuring up the amount of dark magic needed to slaughter them all."

Bryce continued shaking his head, repeating the word, "No." And Baxter, he was so lost in the Sickness's depths that he didn't even recognize the threat that lay beyond the door. I had to save them.

I stood straighter and met Mallory's eyes. "Death." I forced a smile. "He only scares those who haven't seen him before."

Bryce stopped shaking his head, and his shoulders sagged. "Ri, I can't let you do this."

I kept my gaze locked on Mallory and he me. No backing down.

Another thud on the door. I bristled, every muscle rigid. Sweat chilled the back of my neck.

Mallory inhaled a deep breath. "I've got a better plan."

He grabbed Baxter by the collar of his coat and pulled him to his feet. Baxter looked around startled. Before he could draw a breath, Mallory was dragging him toward the crevice I discovered earlier. Baxter stumbled behind him, his toes catching on cracks in the floor. His gaze darted around the temple. Bryce and I followed.

"Girl, you still have the rope and shackles?" Mallory asked once we reached the crevice.

I rummaged through the knapsack, found the requested items, and held them in front of me. "What's the plan?"

"Heroics," he said. "Tie one end of that rope around your waist."

I stared at the rope. Should I trust him? He had kept me alive so far. If he wanted to, he could have easily clobbered me over the head with the blunt end of his sword and used my unconscious body as his shield against the Collectors. But he didn't.

"Dammit, girl, tie the rope," he repeated.

I lassoed the cord around me and began knotting it. He took the shackles.

"Cousin," Mallory smirked at Baxter, "I've been looking forward to this."

Baxter blinked at him. He gasped as Mallory's fist swung toward his face. He moved to duck, but his Sickness-dulled reflexes were too slow. The impact made a loud crack.

"What are you doing?" I stopped fiddling with the rope and caught the unconscious Baxter as he fell backward. His weight forced me to the ground.

"Keep tying the rope if you want your friends to live," Mallory shouted. Sweat dripped past the bulging veins at his temples. He grabbed Baxter by the arms and said to Bryce, "Help me hide him."

Perhaps concealing Baxter was the only way we could protect him. I nodded at Bryce and though he raised a suspicious eyebrow, he helped Mallory shove Baxter into the crevice.

When I finished knotting the cord, I tugged the rope, testing its strength. Solid. A click drew my attention back to my companions. Mallory had locked one of the shackle's clamps around Bryce's wrist.

"What the?" Bryce attempted to hobble away, but Mallory plowed him into the crevice too. They disappeared in its depths.

All the warmth drained from my face. I knew Mallory couldn't be trusted. I trailed them in to the darkness and hit Mallory in the back with my fists. I could hear Bryce pummeling his front side with a few well-placed blows to the face. But then a second click echoed in the narrow space.

"Dammit, Mallory!" Bryce shouted. "Unlock these shackles."

"Carter didn't pack a key." Mallory turned around and seized my wrists, pushing me backward until we both emerged from the crevice.

"You shackled them together?" I asked.

"I need them out of the way." He claimed the opposite end of the rope and raced toward the temple's exit.

Tethered, I had no choice but to stumble after him. The rope tightened around my waist, pinching my skin. "We can't leave. They won't be able to defend themselves."

"The beasts want the book." He lassoed the opposite end of the rope around his waist, leaving a taut ten-foot length of cord between us. "They'll follow us."

Arrogance! "You don't know that for sure. We have to go back." I clutched the rope and began sawing through it with my dagger. The rough cord burned against my palm.

"Dammit, girl." Mallory tugged the rope, jerking me forward. I lost my grip. "There's no going back."

From behind came another thud on the door, followed by the cracking and snapping of wood. I glanced over my shoulder. The door fell forward and crashed to the ground raising clouds of dust and swirling splinters. A swarm of Harbingers spilled through the haze, thick as ants on discarded food. Flaming eyes trained on us. The beasts clambered over each other, mashing bodies into the slate floor and shredding through armored flesh. A bloody mist thickened over the horde. Growls thundered in the chamber.

A burst of terrified energy rippled through me. The rope was digging into my ribs as Mallory sped onward. My feet pounded across the eroded tiled floor. We shot out of the temple and into the storm.

Sleet-laden wind howled over the barren landscape. Ice pellets stung my cheeks and gusts plowed against me. My clothes and hair whipped in all directions. I stumbled over choppy mounds of snow, sinking into white drifts that gathered around my calves.

The horde leapt over the dunes in long bounds, unfazed by the elements or harsh landscape. Ice clung to my eyelashes and blurred my vision, but I could still make out the beasts' razor-sharp fangs and claws as they gained ground.

"Please let Bryce and Baxter be all right," I said under my breath. But there were no gods left to pray to. Eisanea was dead. Fate wanted us dead. And Death ... his Collectors webbed the murky clouds like torn lace. They boomed and crackled, raging against the heavens. I imagined the god looking upon us, fingers tapping, eagerly awaiting our demise.

Mallory tugged the rope, dragging me closer until I caught up alongside him. Breath puffed from his mouth and into the frigid air. "Stop looking back."

"But they're trapped. Baxter's not even conscious. What if the beasts find them? This is a horrible plan." I tripped in the snow and fell to my knees. The cold bit into my legs. Mallory yanked me up. The Harbingers' growls rumbled over the wind. They were no more than forty feet away.

"Never mind those two. You need to come to Oblivion with me if you want to survive," he said.

About a hundred yards ahead, a wall of dense white clouds stretched across the entire length of the horizon. They billowed skyward, twisting and swallowing each other like waves in a violent sea. Ice droplets sparkled on the crests of each plume. The wind howled with a deafening hollow moan.

"Like you care if I survive!" I shouted. "You only want me to go because I may be useful to you. Don't you understand? I have to read the book. I have to kill all the Harbingers or they'll find my village." And discover Bryce and Baxter if they hadn't already.

We plowed into the haze. The temperature dropped, and dampness saturated my body and chilled me to my bones. I escaped the powdery dunes only to find slick, icy ground. My feet slid forward, promising to send me skidding into Oblivion. Hail darted sideways, pelting my face and clattering against the frozen ground.

I slipped. My front side smacked against the hard ground. I choked out a breath. Mallory kept running, dragging me behind him. Outcrops of ice punched and scraped me. Grabbing the rope, I pulled myself up. The cord went rigid as Mallory regained a fifteen-foot lead. Mist engulfed him, blurring his form into a ghostly silhouette that grew fainter with each bound forward.

The growls intensified behind us. A half-dozen pairs of red eyes glowed through the haze. Terror drove like nails into my gut. Breath rasped in and out of my parched throat. The terrain sloped downward. The soles of my boots slid over loose balls of ice and snow.

A Harbinger raced past me and pounced on Mallory. Both man and beast fell hard. As they slid, the rope cinched my waist and flung me forward. I tripped over my feet and toppled over. Pain rippled up my hip. I slid behind Mallory. He anchored his foot against a rock. Unable to secure my own footing, I whizzed past him. He threw the Harbinger over his shoulder, and it landed a few feet away from me with a hard thunk.

I slid alongside of the beast as the pitch of the slope increased. The Harbinger yelped, unable to gain traction as its claws scrabbled over the ice.

Then the ground disappeared. The rope strangled my waist like a vice, taking away my breath so that I couldn't even scream. My legs dangled over a massive abyss. Clouds curled out of its depths, swirling with ribbons of snow. The Harbinger plummeted past me. Its cries faded as it tumbled into the unknown.

"Mallory!" I shouted. "Help!" My heart pounded. "Pull me up, pull me up!"

I dropped another foot. Cool sweat chilled my neck. "Climb, Ri," I ordered myself with shaking voice. "Climb. Don't look down."

With both my hands grasping the rope, I pulled myself up. Dots danced in my vision as I sunk into deeper depths of pain. Groaning, I climbed onto the ledge and called to Mallory. The haze concealed him. "It's not Oblivion. It's just a cliff." The wind swallowed my words.

Using the rope, I clambered upslope until I could see the fuzzy stain of Mallory's silhouette through the fog. He pivoted as he thrust his sword at one beast and then the next. Perhaps he had chosen heroics over Oblivion after all.

Anchoring my feet against a protruding rock, I stabbed my dagger into the frozen ground. I heaved a breath, thankful for secure footing. Time to kill the monsters. Take the Sickness. I had to. I had to, or everyone I knew would die.

"Mallory, I'm going to read from the book!" I reached into my knapsack and pulled out the worn leather volume.

My rigid fingers fumbled to a random page. Sleet collected on the paper, wrinkling it with moisture. My lips trembled. My ears rang. "Don't be afraid. Just read it." I shoved my hand into my pocket and rubbed the smooth glass face of my compass. "For Samuel."

Mallory's heavy footfalls clomped toward me. He leapt in my direction and landed on a cragged rock next to where my dagger was lodged in the ice. Half his face was coated in a mask of scarlet and chunks of the Harbinger's viscera. His shredded shirt thrashed in the wind, revealing three bloody streaks running diagonally across his chest. He yanked my dagger out of the ground and hurled it at an approaching Harbinger. The blade nailed the beast in the eye. A spray of blood exploded from the socket. The creature fell backward and rolled off the cliff's edge.

"Cover your ears." I looked down at the book just as he tore it out of my hands.

"What're you doing?" I asked through a gasp.

He grabbed me by the collar and pulled me up, leveling my eyes with his. The corner of his mouth twitched into his familiar smirk, but it was the amusement in his eyes that sent a tremor through me.

"Best of luck to you, girl." He pushed me backward.

I fell on my side and slid downslope. He sneered as he clutched the book to his chest. The rope was no longer tied to his waist!

Scrambling, I clawed at the ground. Rough patches of ice sliced my palms, snapping my fingernails off. I slid faster. My heart thrashed. I screamed for help, but Mallory remained perched on the rocky outcrop like some stoic statue until he morphed into a smudge in the mist. Dozens of red eyes teemed behind him. He laughed as I tumbled off the cliff's edge.

Falling. A shriek ripped through me. My stomach slammed into my throat. Samuel. Bryce. Baxter. The kiss. Everything crashed into my mind at once.

Then the rope dug into my ribs. I stopped falling. Dangling, I coughed out a breath. Had Mallory secured me? Had the rope merely caught on something? No matter. Climb. I had to climb.

I grabbed the rope. Inhaled a deep breath. The slight expansion of my ribs sent daggers of pain piercing through me. Growling through clenched teeth, I pulled myself upward. The cord's frayed fibers stabbed into the cuts on my palms, itching and stinging. Sleet collected on the cord, and I fumbled to pull myself up.

"Woo!" Mallory shouted from above.

I stopped climbing. Looked up. He stood on the ledge. Collectors lit up the sky behind him.

"It's not Oblivion," I shouted, but it was too late.

He jumped.

Cheering, he plummeted past me, still grasping the book. "Try not to miss me ..." His words faded as he plunged into the abyss.

Gone.

Gripping the rope, I stared into the fog below. Mallory was gone. I was alone. Without the book, I couldn't kill the beasts. I couldn't cure Baxter ... if he was even still alive.

"Dammit, Mallory! You selfish ass," I shouted into the abyss, not that he could hear me. "Damn you, damn you, damn you."

A Harbinger yelped above and fell toward me. It bumped into my shoulder and sent me swinging. I lost my grip and slipped down the rope to where I had first begun my climb. More pain shot through me. The Harbinger smacked into the side of the bluff with a sickening crack before plunging to its death. Then another fell a few feet away to my right. Then another.

From the ledge came a deafening chorus of growls, yelps, and claws grating against ice. Five more beasts fell, smacking against the bluff's outcrops. Limbs broke, twisting at impossible angles.

Were the beasts chasing after the book, even at the risk of falling to their deaths? Or were they merely sliding off the edge, unable to save themselves from the icy slope above?

As I swung toward the cliff side, I clutched a rock and huddled close to shield myself. A half dozen more tumbled off the edge and then a dark shadow loomed over me. Dozens upon dozens of beasts rained down. They crashed into each other, clawing and biting before vanishing into the fog below. It seemed like eternity, but finally the stream of beasts tapered off. All went quiet.

"Climb." I clutched the rope once more and heaved upward. Climb. One more pull. One more pull. I closed my eyes. Move. Don't stop. One more pull.

Finally, I arrived at the top and dragged myself onto the ledge. The haze concealed the opposite end of the rope and whatever I was tethered to. Groaning and shivering, I crawled upslope. Score marks from the Harbinger's claws left long trails through the ice. The bumps and ridges pressed into my soles, providing some traction.

"No more beasts. Please let them be gone." My hands left scarlet prints in the snow. So cold. So much pain. I slumped to the ground. "No. Keep going. Keep going."

I reached the end of the rope.

Mallory's sword impaled the ground. He had knotted the rope around the hilt. Sleet droplets sparkled on the ornate filigree. I stared at the weapon, half-expecting its crazed owner to crawl over the bluff and make some snide remark.

But he didn't.

"You shouldn't have jumped." I looked down and clenched my fists. "You shouldn't have jumped, you crazy fool."

I anchored my feet on the surrounding rocks and tugged at the sword. My hands slipped and I fell backward. I yanked it again. Fell. A rock stabbed at my back. A sharp pain pierced my ribs and I yelped. I tried again. And again.

The blade slid out of the ice.

I stumbled out of the mist with sword in hand. The Collectors vanished from the clouds. My skin felt numb, yet each time the wind picked up, it was as if the gusts were flaying me. Harbingers that had been mauled by their brethren scattered the barren snow dunes. Most lay dead in heaps of blood-tinted slush. One lifted its head in my direction. With both his hind legs broken, it used its forelegs to drag itself toward Oblivion. Cords of intestines trailed behind it. Perhaps Mallory was right. The beasts craved the book's power, even at the risk of death.

I limped into the temple. The cold air burned my throat. My arms shook. Spots danced in my vision.

At least a dozen dead Harbingers littered the ground inside of the temple. Two lay near the crevice. The first sprawled in a pool of its own blood, its tongue spilled out of its gaping mouth. The second lay on its stomach with Baxter's sword wedged into its back. From within the crevice came a repetitive clacking sound.

"Bryce!" I called. My voice was hoarse as the moan of the wind outside.

"Ri? ... Ri!" His hand waved from the crevice and then vanished back inside. The clacking resumed.

Trembling, I shambled toward him. He was banging a rock against the shackle's chain link. Scratches covered his arms, and a deep cut trailed down his forehead. Blood soaked his shirt. With his free arm, he reached for me. His opposite arm remained bound to Baxter, who lay unmoving on the ground.

"You're all right," he said as I collapsed into him.

I wrapped my arms around him. Then almost as immediately, I pulled away and looked at Baxter. In the poor lighting, I couldn't tell if he had any wounds.

"His body will heal," Bryce said. "As for his mind ... if we don't banish the Sickness, it will break him, Ri."

I knelt next to Baxter and brushed his bangs away from his eyes. Even in the dim lighting, blood from self-inflicted scratches glistened on his cheeks and scalp. "I can't cure him." I bit my lip, holding back a sob. "I can't cure him without the book."

CHAPTER 39

We stumbled along the forest path, chins tucked toward our necks to shield our eyes from the rain boring down upon us. The clouds darkened with the promise of approaching nightfall. For the past three days, Bryce, Baxter, and I had been sprinting toward my village in a sleep-deprived, uphill journey without the help of the Fireflies. They hadn't returned since Eisanea's death, and I had a feeling that I would never see them again. Wherever they were, I hoped they were safe.

Trembling, I stumbled forward as my feet sank into the soft wet ground. Mud seeped into the battered soles of my shoes and squished between my toes. My stomach twisted and growled as if it planned to devour itself. Cold saturated me to the bone. I pushed forward, my breath ripping in and out of my throat.

I slipped at the edge of a stream and landed in a soggy patch of moss. Mallory's sword fell from my grasp. I reclaimed it and staggered to my feet, wiping my drenched bangs out of my face. The waterfall where Bryce and I had first met tumbled down the nearby bluff.

"We're almost home." I trudged onward. The village's barricade loomed in the distance, its black posts stabbing toward the murky gray sky. I pumped my legs harder, ignoring the deep ache in my muscles until I reached a small door in the enclosure. It swung open before my hand grasped its latch.

"Ri!" Coren pulled me through the door. "I've been watching for you for days. Everyone thought you were dead."

"I'm fine. Is everyone all right?" I asked, looking toward my home. Faint hearth-light shone through the storm.

"Samuel and Katie are fine." He waved us to follow him further into the village. A few men paced near the barricade with spears resting on their shoulders. At the far north and south end of the barrier, men kept watch atop two towers. We followed Coren toward the village's center.

"The Culling attacked four days ago," Coren explained. "Three men died and a dozen more were injured. But there haven't been any attacks since."

He shoved the door open and we crammed inside. I stumbled to the hearth and collapsed to my knees. Shivering, I set Mallory's sword down and rubbed my hands together, savoring the warmth. Baxter and Bryce sat on a bench alongside me. Their teeth chattered as they warmed their hands by the fire.

Kaylan stumbled out of the hallway wearing simple nightclothes. "You made it home!" He knocked over a basket of herbs in his hurry to greet us. He hugged me so hard I could hardly breathe. When he leaned away, he glanced at my companions and then Mallory's sword. The blade shimmered in the firelight.

He frowned. "Carter? Mallory?"

Lowering my eyes, I shook my head. During the journey home, I thought of Carter often. Perhaps—somehow—he had found his way to the Violet Star. Since the Sickness hadn't struck Baxter after we left the temple, I had no way to communicate with Carter's spirit.

"Oh dear." Kaylan rubbed his short beard. "Katie will be devastated."

My heart sank. How would I ever tell her?

Coren offered us blankets, but I waved mine away. "No, I can't stay. I need to check on Samuel." I stood on legs that begged me to sit back down.

"Wait." Kaylan reached toward me. "What news do you have?"

"Good news. We destroyed the source of the Culling. You'll never believe who was responsible—"

"An evil Nightmare queen," Baxter interrupted. His eyes bored into Bryce and me. Before leaving the temple, we had burned Eisanea's corpse in hopes of preventing her from rising again. As the flames rose and curled toward the ceiling, Bryce said, "We mustn't tell anyone that Eisanea created the Culling. Doing so will only cause distrust, fear, and sadness."

Telling Bryce that his mother and Eisanea were one and the same would likely cause those same feelings in him. Though I had told him and Baxter everything else I had learned on my journey, I decided that this secret would follow me to the grave.

"I believe that with its death, the rest of the beasts will perish too," Baxter continued. "Those we encountered on the journey here were either dead or dying."

I recalled the withered nests we had passed while fleeing the temple. Strands of brown Starlight wrapped around wrinkled, dried-out eggs. Emaciated, unmoving beasts shone through the transparent shells. Once we reached the mountains, the Harbingers we encountered dragged themselves along the ground in a desperate search for sustenance. Ribs showed beneath their ebony flesh. Nightmares sprawled on the forest floor, dying. Their once luminous Starlight had wilted to lifeless strands, each fiber frayed like dead grass under a relentless sun. Closer to home, we crossed paths with only the dead husks of beasts and cocoons alike. Vultures perched on top of them, picking and digging for meat.

"Born of my tears, nourished by my hatred," I repeated Eisanea's words. Everyone stared at me, so I added, "I believe Baxter's right.

The beasts are starving without the wrath of their creator to sustain them."

"Scouts have been tracking the forests daily," Coren added. "But we too have only found the rotting remains of beasts."

We stared at the fire for a moment.

"You three must be hungry." Kaylan pointed toward a closet and ordered Coren to retrieve dry clothes for us. He then strode toward a cabinet, gathered two handfuls of vegetables, and began chopping them at the table.

As they roamed out of earshot, Bryce leaned toward Baxter and me. "What do you think will happen to humanity now that Eisanea's dead?"

"We survive," I said. "One day at a time."

The gods might have been against us, but I planned to live on, with or without a soul.

"Agreed," Baxter said. "And we rebuild what's been destroyed."

Kaylan returned with a platter of acorn bread. We all grabbed a slice.

"I need to check on Samuel," I said, chewing the delicious food. "Why don't you both rest here tonight since Kaylan has extra beds? We can regroup in the morning."

They both nodded. I grabbed Mallory's sword and slipped out the door.

Rain clattered in the puddles with the force of hail. In the darkness, all I had to guide me home was the glowing hearth fire through the window. I swung the door open.

Kai was standing on a stool patching a leak in the thatching. Startled by my entrance, he lost his balance and wobbled before grasping a beam to steady himself.

Samuel leapt from his seat. He raced toward me—a mixture of a hop and a skip due to his limp. "Ri, Ri, you're home!" Despite my soaked, mud-covered clothing, he grappled me in a hug. Tears gathered in the corners of his eyes. Ricky circled us, prancing and barking enthusiastically.

"We did it," I said. "We stopped the Culling."

Kai approached smirking. "It's good to have you home. But could you refrain from the sudden entrances from now on?"

I smiled. "At least you didn't lose your stew this time."

Samuel leaned back to look me over. When he spotted no injuries, he grinned. "Ri, I have tremendous news as well. I haven't had a vision in four days. Four whole days. I mean, I'm still forgetful. I can't tell you what I had for lunch today ... but I remember some things. Faint details ... a woman I loved ... a son ... Ri ... I think I had a son." He frowned. "Perhaps I'm just imagining it."

"No, Samuel. You're not." I shook with excitement. He was cured. He was finally cured. I hugged him once more. Rain hammered the roof, the hearth fire barely gave off enough heat, and outside no light snuck through the clouds. But it was the most beautiful day of my life.

Then Mallory's voice snuck into my head, *Do you really want to make Samuel face his past?*

My stomach knotted. I released Samuel and met his eyes. "Samuel, do you remember a man named Robert Renselar?"

"Hmm." His eyebrows knotted together as he studied the ground. "Must be related to Mallory, I assume. But no, the name doesn't sound familiar."

I sighed with relief.

"Perhaps it will come to me." He patted my shoulder firmly.

"Perhaps." My throat tightened.

Footfalls came from the hallway. "Ri!" Katie raced toward me and embraced me. "Where's Carter? Is he at Kaylan's?"

"He's ..." I covered my mouth. My eyes stung with tears.

She shook her head vehemently. "No. No."

I hugged her. "Katie, I'm so sorry."

She slid from my arms and collapsed to her knees, sobs racking her body as she bent over clutching her middle. Clawing at her elbows, she wailed his name over and over.

***

Strips of sunlight filtered through the shutters. I opened my eyes, squinting from the brightness. I sat on my bed, propped against the wall. Next to me, Katie slept grasping the blanket. Her eyelids were red and swollen. She had wept until she threw up, and then wept more, until she eventually dozed off. Carefully, I slid off the bed and tucked her in before leaving the room.

Ricky greeted me with a lick on the hand when I entered the main area, but no one else was home. I rushed to the window. The village bustled with activity. A group of men were having a discussion in the courtyard. Some women picked up the debris from the storm. Children were racing around them in circles. And in the garden, Bryce and Samuel sat atop two stumps.

Samuel said something and Bryce threw his head back in laughter. I smiled as warmth filled my chest.

Not wanting to interrupt, I slipped outside and headed toward Kaylan's home. I passed a pair of gossiping women along the way who were dunking garments into a wash bucket. They hushed their conversation and stared at me as I walked by. As I strode a few feet away from them, one whispered to her friend, "Killed a beast that stood twenty feet tall, that one."

It appeared that the tale of my journey was already traveling around the village, each storyteller reshaping it with their own imagination.

Two men passed me along the way and waved. I jerked my head and looked behind me. No one was there. I waved back awkwardly. Apparently, Samuel and I were no longer outcasts. I suppose saving the world from soul-eating monsters earned us some respect!

I barged into Kaylan's house without knocking, as I often did. Baxter was stuffing food and a jar of Katie's herbal remedy into a knapsack. He glanced at me as I entered and then immediately went back to work. Kaylan and his sons weren't home.

"What're you doing?" I asked.

"Packing."

"Yes, I see you're packing." I smiled. "Why?"

He kept his eyes trained on the knapsack as he buckled it closed. "I'm joining the scouts to inspect the forest."

"Oh. Then I should go too."

"No." He swung the knapsack over his shoulder and headed toward the door.

"I just defeated the Culling. I'm more than capable of helping."

Still not making eye contact, he placed his hand on the door latch.

"Wait." I darted to the door and wedged myself between it and him. "You've been acting strangely ever since we left the temple. Ever since you kissed—"

"Ri, step away from the door." His eyes hardened.

"No." I spread my arms across the door. "I should go too. If the Sickness strikes you again, you'll need my help."

"The Sickness is gone." The muscle in his jaw flexed as he tightened his grip on the door latch.

"It can't be gone." Softening my tone, I added, "The only way you can be cured is if someone else reads from the book. I doubt Mallory recited its passages while tumbling off that cliff."

"So what will you do? Watch over me like a child for the rest of my days?"

"I'm worried about you." I placed my hand on his. "And I'll do what I must to help you."

He released a breath and broke eye contact. "The day I saw Carter, he told me that Black Valley needed me. I have to return."

"Oh."

"Bryce will take me there in one week—the first day of the waxing crescent."

"But—"

He pulled the door open, forcing me to bump into his chest. My cheeks warmed. The last time we had stood so close was the day he kissed me. My heartbeat quickened. I stepped back, composing myself. He stole the opportunity to slip out the door.

"Baxter, wait," I called after him, but he continued to hasten to the men gathered in the courtyard.

Someone cleared their throat behind me and I spun around. Coren leaned against the wall near the hallway. "You're red as a beet."

"No, I'm not." I folded my arms and stared outside. "I didn't realize you were home."

"I was packing as well." Coren joined me, placing a hand on my shoulder. A knapsack bulged on his back. His lips pressed into a firm line. "You look after Katie and I'll look after yours."

"He's not *mine*. We're just friends." Outside, Baxter shielded his eyes from the sunlight as he looked toward the barricade. "But, yes. Please, look after him."

CHAPTER 40

One week later

The sun peeked through a crack in the clouds as I collected blueberries at the perimeter of my village. Nearby, wood chips flew into the air as two men hacked at the barricade.

A portly woman strode to them and wagged her finger. "It's too soon to tear the fence down. You're going to get us all killed."

One of the men rested his ax on his shoulder. "All that remains of the Culling is the stench of rotting beasts. We're safe now."

The woman huffed off, her hands raised in defeat. She passed two mothers harvesting strawberries in their garden. Their children chased each other in a game of tag.

At the far edge of the village, Bryce and Samuel sat on a bench overlooking the vale. They had spent countless hours together exchanging stories.

I peeked at the barricade's door. Baxter hadn't yet returned, but a scout had spoken of him the previous night. He was safe, and from what I gathered, the Sickness hadn't struck him once. Perhaps he truly was cured.

"I'm going to drive myself mad if I keep watching that door." I turned back to my task, ripping berries from the branches.

My heart was foolish. I couldn't fall for Baxter. He belonged in Black Valley and I belonged in Red Ridge. His uncle wanted Samuel executed. He was a series of walls. As soon as I climbed over one, another one awaited. And of course, there was Bryce.

I inhaled a deep breath. There were more important things to tend to than my heart. Katie, for example. She had spent every day weeping in my room with the shutters drawn. If I hadn't coaxed her into changing her clothes or brushing her hair, she would've remained crumpled on the bed, drenching the pillow with tears.

It was nearly noon. I shook a few more berries off a bush, filling my basket. A twig snapped behind me and I spun around.

"Katie?" The pitch of my voice rose with surprise.

She hastened toward me with determined steps. Her green dress flapped in the breeze, and a neat braid was draped over her shoulder.

"It's good to see you outside," I added.

"I want to visit my brother's grave." She stood straight as an iron post, her bloodshot eyes piercing me.

"Of course." I gestured toward the forest.

She strode onward, lifting the hem of her dress so it wouldn't drag in the mud. Since Carter's true resting place lay far beyond the Dark Woods, Bryce and I had built a memorial in the village's burial ground.

"I hope Carter's spirit made it to the Violet Star," I had said to Bryce when we set the gravestone in place. "If he's trapped in this realm, I would do anything to help him."

"As would I," Bryce said. "But unless the Sickness strikes Baxter again, we'll never know. For now, we must comfort Katie. That's what he would want."

Katie and I followed a short path through the forest. Along the way, she collected a few dozen wild flowers, arranging a sweet-scented bouquet of gold, violet, and red blossoms. I plucked two daisies.

We reached the cemetery. Rocks in various shapes, sizes, and colors lay scattered amongst the trees on an endless rug of spring-green grass. Nearly as green as Carter's eyes. Sunlight filtered through the branches, sparkling on the dew. The slight fragrance of flowers mingled with the crisp scent of spruce. Above, birds chattered in the branches.

I placed a daisy next to Carter's memorial: a white rock with small specks that glinted like ice. Then, I stepped aside so Katie could kneel in front of the marker.

"Do you think he looks upon us now?" Katie asked, keeping her gaze locked on the memorial. She gripped the stone tightly.

"Um ..." I nervously tugged against my throat and lied, "Yes, I'm sure of it. He watches over us from the Violet Star's eternal light."

A butterfly circled the bushel of flowers Katie had brought and then landed on the gravestone.

"Look." I knelt next to her and pointed at the butterfly.

She smiled, but covered her mouth as a sob sneaked out. The butterfly bobbed its yellow wings, content as it meandered along the rock.

I placed my arm around her. "Carter once told me that he wanted you to see all of the beauty in the world." My voice cracked. "He still wants that. He wants you to enjoy every day. He wants you to be happy."

She placed her index finger near the butterfly, and it crawled up to her knuckle. It remained there for a few seconds before taking off, tapping her on the nose and then fluttering into the sky.

"Did you see that?" she asked, laughing through her sobs. "It tapped my nose. Just like Carter used to do! Every time he told me not to worry, he'd tap my nose. You saw it, right?"

I nodded, unable to speak in fear of the tears it would bring. Was it a message from him? No, it was a coincidence. But I had never seen such an uncanny butterfly. Perhaps, somehow, Carter had conned his way into the Violet Star. If anyone could, it would be him.

Katie looked up at me and hope shone in her eyes. "Ri, may I have a few moments?"

"Of course." I stepped away, and once out of earshot I whispered, "Carter, if you're listening ... if you're in trouble, I will help you. Somehow, I will."

Being touched by Death's magic allowed me to see the Fireflies and the sand people. Perhaps if I concentrated hard enough I would be able to see the spirits among us.

The other daisy bobbed in my hand as a light breeze slipped through the forest. While Katie wreathed the flowers around Carter's memorial, I wandered to the far end of the burial grounds. There, a black rock stood, looking as though it plowed through the earth with its sharp angles. A beam of sunlight snuck through the branches and skittered over its surface before vanishing.

I knelt in front of the rock and twiddled with the daisy for a few minutes before placing it down. The bright white petals brushed against the dark stone.

"Is that Mallory's memorial?" Katie asked, startling me.

"It is." I grasped the rough stone and it pushed back against my palm. A slight smile tugged at the corner of my mouth. "Most of the time he was rude, but sometimes ... I don't know ... he was almost like a mentor." I stood. "Come on. Let's head back and I'll make you lunch."

***

A warm evening breeze blew in from the window, carrying the melody of crickets. I sat near the hearth washing dinner bowls in a small bucket. The aroma of vegetable stew still lingered in the room. I handed a dripping bowl to Bryce, and he whisked away the moisture with a towel.

"I think this is the first time we've been alone together in days," he said, smiling softly. The firelight offered a soft glow to his complexion and brought out the freckles on his nose.

"I think you're right." I glanced down the hall where Samuel and Katie had retired to their rooms. Silence. "I think they've dozed off."

He nodded toward the corner of the room. "They're not the only ones."

Ricky slumbered with his paw draped over Miss Meow. She nuzzled her head under his chin, kneading her paws and purring.

"I would've never figured them as soul mates." I smiled.

"Perhaps it's puppy love." Bryce chuckled as he collected the dry bowls and set them on the shelf. "It's a pleasant evening, why don't we go for a stroll?"

I wiped my hands dry on my pants. "That sounds wonderful."

Before slipping out the door, my gaze slid to where Mallory's sword leaned against the wall. Next to it sat a knapsack of supplies I had packed for Baxter. He still had not returned. I sucked down a breath as we stepped into the night.

Bryce took my hand and guided me through Samuel's garden. Hints of hearth smoke and mixed blossoms scented the warm breeze. We stumbled along in the darkness. Bryce stubbed his toe on a protruding stone and cursed.

"Why don't we rest a moment so I can stop embarrassing myself?" He grinned.

We sat down on a small patch of plush grass. Bryce wrapped his arm around me and looked toward the sky. I followed his gaze.

Thousands of stars lit the heavens, clustering together in uneven patches of faint and bold light. In some areas, they glowed bright enough to saturate the sky with smudges of blue. The twinkling carried down to the surrounding brush where lightning bugs blinked in swarms.

"The sky is always more beautiful when the moon goes dark," he said.

I had seen the starry sky countless times before, but I had never slowed down to appreciate its splendor. Perhaps I needed someone to help me pause every so often. He continued to stare up, mesmerized. I rested my head against his. He was the one I belonged with. Surely, he was.

His cheek brushed against mine as it plumped with a smile. "I know this will sound silly, but each month I used to watch the sky, counting down the days before I could return to this island. The moon would wane, and the stars would grow more and more plentiful. I always thought the heavens were promising me something … something to give my days more meaning."

"I don't think that sounds silly at all."

He turned toward me and clasped my hands. His hazel eyes brightened with hope. "Ri, I feel like I fit in here—with you and Samuel. This is where I want to be. I want to settle here and put my days of waterfall travel to rest."

"Oh." I jerked my head. "But won't you miss the excitement?"

"Excitement?" He laughed. "I'd rather have peace. Raise a family. Hold my true love's hand until it wrinkles with age."

"That's very sweet." I looked down at our interlocked hands—and then at the barricade door.

"Is something wrong?" he asked. "You look troubled."

"What? No. I'm not troubled. I mean …" I sucked on my lower lip, feeling my forehead crease with worry lines. How could I tell him that I had feelings for both him and Baxter? I didn't want to hurt him.

"Oh no," Bryce went rigid and placed his palm against the side of his face. "I was worried about this."

"Um … you were?" Had he noticed the way I watched the barricade awaiting Baxter's return?

"Yes, ever since you told me Samuel was my father." He dragged his hand down his face. "You weren't adopted. Samuel's your true father, isn't he?"

"What?" My eyebrows sprung up. "No. Samuel absolutely adopted me."

"Oh." He released an enormous breath. "That's good. It would've ruined my day if I found out you were my half-sister. Then what's wrong?"

"Um ... nothing." I turned my back to the barricade. "Nothing at all." I rested my head against his shoulder. As usual, he carried the crisp, clean scent of the forest. I relaxed, enveloped in his warmth.

We sat quietly. His fingertips traveled from the space between my shoulders to the dip in my lower spine and then back up again. His hand moved slowly, as if he found the curve of my back as fascinating as the stars above. My mind went fuzzy at his touch. I closed my eyes. No more looking at the barricade.

"Ri, I want all these things, but I have to tell you something." He inhaled deeply. "I have to return to Black Valley for a while."

"What?" My stomach went hard.

He cupped my jaw and brought my eyes to meet his. "Only for a while. I need to meet with my apprentices and come up with a plan for moving forward. I still want to help those in the Slag."

"But the first day of the waxing crescent is tomorrow." I gaped at him. "You're leaving tomorrow?"

"I would've told you sooner. I've been mulling over this for days." He looked down and rubbed the back of his neck. "I wasn't sure how to tell you, but I can't abandon the people of the Slag. I have to help them."

Of course he would. He would never turn his back on the people who needed him.

"I understand," I said. "But do you think it's safe for you to return?"

"I think so. I'm sure the Culling is destroyed." He brushed his fingertips across my jaw to my ear until they found a loose strand of hair to fiddle with. "As for the Red Bands ... Baxter promised to drop the charges against me, so I won't be on the Stained Wall anymore. He even said he'd help me set up a place where my apprentices and I can tend to the sick and injured. Once everything is in order, I can return here—for good—and only visit Black Valley now and then."

"I want to help you, but I can't leave Katie and Samuel now."

"I know. And I want you to stay here. Look after them both. I'll be all right." He dug into his pocket and removed a sheet of paper with drawings of plants. "These are the plants I collect. Can you gather as many as possible while I'm gone?"

I recognized most of the roots, stems, and leaves.

My hand trembled. "Of course."

"And if Katie feels up to it, perhaps she can prepare more of her herbal remedy?"

"Yes, I'm sure she'll help." I interlaced my hands with his. He grasped them tightly.

"Don't worry, Ri. With the Culling destroyed and an influential friend at my side, I'll be safer in Black Valley than ever before."

I nodded. "You're right. I'm sure my worry is foolish."

He kissed me as softly as the night breeze that caressed my skin. "You have nothing to worry about."

***

I opened my eyes. Bryce was sprawled on his back, and I on my side resting my head on his arm. The pale sun backlit an endless blanket of gray clouds. Mist hung over the village, blanketing it with dank, still air.

"I fell asleep?" I whispered, tilting my head to look up at Bryce.

He turned, pressing his lips against my forehead. "You did." He grinned. "I must've bored you last night with my ponderings of life and the stars and everything in between."

My cheeks warmed. "I didn't mean to fall asleep! I wasn't bored."

"I'm joking, Ri." Laughing, he propped himself up and flexed his wrist. I had been using his arm as a pillow all night, so he probably had a horrible case of pins and needles.

"I hope you weren't too uncomfortable," I said.

"I slept wonderfully." He gazed at me for a moment and then his mouth pressed into a frown. "I wish I could linger here with you all day, but I promised Baxter that I would meet him at dawn."

"Dawn?" My jaw went slack. "You're leaving this morning?"

He lowered his gaze and said, "It's best we arrive at Black Valley early."

From the village came the sound of chatter and bleating goats. The sun rose higher, brighter, a reminder that our time together was dwindling away. We locked our hands together.

"Would you mind caring for Miss Meow while I'm away?" he asked.

"I wouldn't dare tempt her wrath by prying her away from Ricky."

He smiled, though his gaze remained downcast. "I have a few more things to pack and I'd like to say goodbye to Katie and Samuel. Please tell Baxter I'm on my way? He'll be waiting for me just beyond the barricade."

"Um ..." I clenched my jaw and nodded. Considering Baxter had asked Bryce to meet him at dawn, outside of the village, I doubted he wanted to see me. "I'll go tell him now."

***

I slipped out the gate carrying the knapsack and Mallory's sword. A light drizzle fell from the clouds, rippling the puddles scattered on the ground. Baxter sat on a fallen tree at the edge of the forest.

"Ri?" He sat up straighter.

"I can't believe you planned to leave without saying goodbye." Hurt crept into my voice.

He rested his elbows on his knees and looked down at his clasped hands. "Ri, I'm trying to do what's best for you."

"But you're my friend. Why wouldn't you want to speak with me before leaving?"

He scooted down the trunk to make room and gestured for me to sit. I took the offered seat, leaving a sliver of space between us. His clothing hadn't absorbed the crisp scent of the forest. Instead it smelled of the sleet in Black Valley and the smoke of the fires in Sea Dragon's Point. His mouth arched downward into a frown, creasing a faint scar that crossed through the bristle on his chin.

"I shouldn't have kissed you." He kept his gaze on his hands. "It was a mistake."

"Oh." A mistake? The word hit me like a rock to the gut. I fiddled with the loose threads on my sleeves, my mind scrambling for a nonchalant response. "Um … I mean … you don't need to apologize. I knew you never intended to. The Sickness can make a person do absurd things. Things they normally wouldn't do. I haven't even given it a second thought."

I cringed. I didn't sound composed at all.

"You haven't?" His voice lowered with more than a slight hint of disappointment. Though I kept my gaze down, I heard his coat collar rustle as he turned his head toward me.

I looked back at him. His blue eyes searched mine.

Softening my tone, I said, "Um … well, I have thought about it." Why was I admitting my feelings for him? My mouth continued to betray me. "I do have feelings for you. And Bryce. I haven't told him because I'm all mixed up and you're both friends. I don't want to cause tension between the two of you when I don't even know what I want."

Silence. My breath came quick. It felt like minutes had passed, so I started blabbering again. "I'm not sure why it's easier for me to tell you all of this than to him. You must think I'm silly."

"Ri." He reached to touch my arm, but then stopped. He lowered his hand to his side. "I meant everything I said. I do care for you. But I should've kept those feelings to myself. You would never know a life of peace with me."

"I just defeated the Culling," I blurted. "I don't need to be sheltered."

"I know that." The corner of his mouth lifted for a second before falling back into a solemn straight line. "But I have to return to Black Valley and all of its turmoil. I can't abandon my duties, and I could never expect you to abandon yours." He nodded toward my home, where Samuel and Bryce were likely saying their goodbyes.

I lowered my head. Even though I had cured Samuel, I could never abandon him. He needed me still. Didn't he? And Black Valley needed Baxter. I had to let him go. With heaviness in my heart, I said, "I understand."

He placed his hand on mine and caressed my fingers, teasing of a possibility that could never come to be. "I scoured the forest. I'm confident that the Culling is gone. I wouldn't leave you unless I was sure of it."

"I know you wouldn't."

"And if you ever need me—for anything—just ask. Do you still have the amulet shard?"

I removed the compass from my pocket. The sunlight sparkled on the glass face. "Yes, in here."

"Then we're a mere waterfall apart. Remember that." He patted my hand and glanced toward the village. Just then, Bryce passed through the barricade and headed toward us.

"You remember that too," I said. "If the Sickness returns, I hope you'll tell me."

"I will."

I nudged the knapsack toward him. "I packed some supplies for you. And I baked you some loaves of bread, but I burnt them a little." Quickly, I added, "Don't worry, I scraped off the black bits."

He chuckled.

"Why're you laughing?"

"I just imaged you frantically removing the smoking loaves from the hearth and then sawing through the charred crusts."

A smile tugged at my lips. "Well, if you find them too hard, you can hurl them at anyone who gives you trouble."

"I'll keep that in mind." He stood and slung the knapsack over his shoulder. "Thank you, Ri. For everything."

"Wait, I have something else." I rose to my feet and offered him Mallory's sword. "I thought you might want this, since he was family."

He considered the gift. "Keep it. Mallory and I weren't close, and I know he wouldn't want his father to have it."

I glanced down at the gleaming hilt as Bryce joined us. He nodded a good morning to Baxter and then looked at me expectantly.

"I'm going to head to the waterfall." Baxter pointed a thumb in the proper direction and then cupped my shoulder. "Stay safe."

I swallowed hard. "You too."

He patted my shoulder a few times, as if not wanting to let it go. Then, he strode into the forest. Gone.

Bryce cleared his throat. "Well, I guess this is it."

I embraced him. "Please be careful."

He tangled his fingers in my hair, inhaling its scent. "Don't worry. One month and we'll see each other again." When he pulled away, he met my eyes. "I'll be watching the stars grow plentiful in the sky."

"As will I." I hugged him again, and he pressed his lips to my forehead.

After he left, I slumped down on the fallen tree trunk and stared at the forest for what seemed like forever. I tilted my compass back and forth, imagining the shard clinking inside.

"Perhaps I can offer you better company than your troubled thoughts?" Samuel approached from behind, hobbling up the hill. He sat beside me. "Those two will accomplish great things. I'm sure of it."

Samuel still hadn't recalled his past in Black Valley, as far as I knew anyway.

"I've done something foolish." I peeled a strip of bark from the stump and fiddled with it. "I've fallen for them both."

"Oh." He tilted his head and pondered my words for a few seconds. "Well, it's not foolish. You fought and nearly died alongside each of them. It's no wonder you'd have these feelings. But in time, your heart will tell you whom you truly love. You'll have no doubts. None at all."

Did he once feel so strongly for Sera?

He stood. "I see you decided to keep Mallory's sword."

I shrugged. "Baxter thought I should."

"Ah. Well, I may be an old forgetful man, but I know how to do more than just make tea and tend a garden. I could give you lessons if you'd like to learn how to use it."

I perked up. "You can?"

Smiling, he nodded and offered me his hand.

"I'd like that." I rose to my feet. Arm-in-arm, we strolled back to the village.

EPILOGUE

Oblivion
Ri's soul

I sat on the ground next to Death. Bored, I scooped sand into my palm and watched it slide off my fingertips. The fine powder was white and dry as ground-up bone. Perhaps that's what it was. Nothing blossomed in Oblivion except for clouds of mist. They hovered over the flat, never-ending plain of nothingness.

"He's late," I said.

"Relax, he'll be here." Death closed his eyes and stretched. Placing his hands behind his head, he fell backward and sprawled on the ground as if lounging under the summer sun.

The sun. Summer. I sighed. Would I ever know either again? In this wretched realm, the only source of light came from the constant red flares bursting in the murk above.

I smacked my hands together, cleaning them of sand. "How long do you plan to disguise yourself as Carter?"

He opened one clover-green eye. "As long as I need to. He would never trust a pale, hooded god, now would he?"

"Well, you look silly. He'll discover who you truly are eventually. And he'll realize there's something not right about me too."

"Anyone can see there's something not right about you." He poked one of the many splotches on my arm. They resembled black, rotting flesh and roamed over my body like shadows.

I scooted a couple feet away from him. "It's your fault I'm like this."

"No, it's not," he said matter-of-factly. "Samuel had no business attempting to bring you back to your human. It's his fault you're the way that you are."

"His fault? You split me in half!"

"Your human had died. Your soul should have belonged to me." His lips curled in disgust. "But I had to honor the spell Samuel recited, and your human needed a soul—or at least part of one—to resurrect. I didn't know one half would be pure and the other would be vile."

I glared at the horizon. "I wonder if you're pleased or frightened that the vile half sits with you now."

He sneered. "You can't frighten Death."

The silhouette of a man emerged from the mist.

"Here he comes," I said. "I hope he guts you."

"If he does that, you'll be trapped in Oblivion for eternity, foolish soul." Death rose to his feet. "He will join us. Mallory doesn't discriminate against the wicked, as long as he thinks he can use them to his advantage. And his arrogance will lead him to believe he can."

"Sounds like you two have much in common."

"You truly are a bitter thing." He chuckled. "But let me tell you this: no one outsmarts Death. He will do what I need him to do."

"So you think." I stood and paced, kicking the sand. "He killed your sister. He may kill you too."

"I see intelligence is another trait reserved only for your human."

Mallory whistled a cheerful melody and sauntered toward us as if he owned the place. Arrogant indeed. I smiled. Perhaps Death had met his match.

Our guest paused before us. An old scar stretched from his nostril to his jaw. Another sliced through his brow. Blood covered his sculpted chest and stomach. His form was beautiful despite the amulet weaved into his flesh. In one hand he held Death's book. In the other, the roasted thigh of a Harbinger. He tore into it, savoring meat that would've made a sane person vomit. I smiled, biting my lower lip. Too bad more of his clothing wasn't shredded. After years of being trapped in Oblivion, I could've used something enjoyable to look at.

Death whispered in my ear, "Control yourself. Tainted half-souls aren't his type."

I shrugged. "Most men aren't picky if you grab them by the—"

"Enough," Death ordered. He faced Mallory, spread his arms, and flashed a toothy smile. "May I be the first to welcome you to Oblivion."

Mallory raised an eyebrow at him and then at me. He eyed the black splotches crawling over my body. He wasn't fooled. He knew we were evil. I was sure of it.

With amusement gleaming in his eyes, he smirked. "So who wants to kill Fate?"

Death grinned in a way that made me wonder if he hid fangs beneath his lips. "That sounds delightful."

End of Book One

ACKNOWLEDGMENTS

I'm tremendously grateful to my fellow writers who contributed their time and expertise while reviewing my early drafts: Josh Mendelssohn, Craig Snow, Jordan Phillips, Forest Taylor, and Martin Felando. Without their encouragement and guidance, my story would have never been published.

A huge thank you to the following:

Lisa Crea, who proofed my first three chapters and made them shine.

My editor, Aaron S. Kaiserman, whose level of dedication and thoroughness continues to impress me.

The brilliant illustrator, Lindsay Nery, who created the stunning cover illustration.

Victor Sanchez, a master of typography and layout.

Maricela Sanchez, makeup artist and photographer extraordinaire.

Sam Missingham, who reviewed my marketing plan and provided me with expert advice. She is truly passionate about helping authors succeed.

The extremely talented author, Lee Weatherly, who took the time to critique my novel and offer her insightful view on structure, character development, plot, and so much more.

And of course, my family: my parents, who always enthusiastically awaited the next chapter; my mother-in- law and fellow writer, Theresa Gillmore, who critiqued my drafts; my husband, Jon-Paul, who never tired of me bouncing ideas off him; and to my baby son, Connor, who inspires me to be the best person I can be every day.

ABOUT THE AUTHOR

S.J. Lem is a digital art director gone writer in hopes of expanding her creative aspirations. Whether it's introducing dimensional characters, crafting imaginative worlds, or transporting readers into high-stakes adventures, she strives to deliver an immersive experience.

She lives in Chicago with her husband and son. When not writing, she enjoys pottery, gardening, and volunteering. Connecting with readers and fellow writers is one of her greatest joys.

Get in touch today by visiting sjlem.com.

CPSIA information can be obtained
at www.ICGtesting.com
Printed in the USA
LVOW11*1522030717
540214LV00006B/50/P